THE CASE OF THE BEREAVED BUTLER

by
Cathy Ace

FOUR TAILS PUBLISHING LTD.

PRAISE FOR THE WISE ENQUIRIES AGENCY MYSTERIES

'…a gratifying contemporary series in the traditional British manner with hilarious repercussions (dead bodies notwithstanding). Cozy fans will anticipate learning more about these WISE ladies.'
Library Journal, starred review

'If you haven't read any of Cathy Ace's WISE cozies, I suggest you begin at the beginning and giggle your way through in sequence.'
Ottawa Review of Books

'…a modern-day British whodunit that's as charming as it is entertaining…Good fun, with memorable characters, an imaginative plot, and a satisfying ending.'
Booklist

'Ace spiffs up the standard village cozy with a set of sleuths worth a second look.'
Kirkus Reviews

'…a perfect cozy with a setting and wit reminiscent of Wodehouse's Blandings Castle. But its strongest feature is the heart and sensitivity with which Ace imbues her characters.'
The Jury Box, Ellery Queen Mystery Magazine

'Sharp writing highlights the humor of the characters even while tackling serious topics, making this yet another very enjoyable, fun, and not-always-proper British Mystery.'
Cynthia Chow, Librarian, Hawaii State Public Library in Kings River Life Magazine

'A brilliant addition to Classic Crime Fiction. The ladies (if they'll forgive me calling them that) of the WISE Enquiries Agency will have you pacing the floor awaiting their next entanglement…
A fresh and wonderful concept well executed.'
Alan Bradley, New York Times Bestselling Author of the Flavia de Luce books

Other works by the same author

(Information for all works here: www.cathyace.com)

The WISE Enquiries Agency Mysteries
The Case of the Dotty Dowager
The Case of the Missing Morris Dancer
The Case of the Curious Cook
The Case of the Unsuitable Suitor
The Case of the Disgraced Duke
The Case of the Absent Heirs
The Case of the Cursed Cottage
The Case of the Uninvited Undertaker

The Cait Morgan Mysteries
The Corpse with the Silver Tongue
The Corpse with the Golden Nose
The Corpse with the Emerald Thumb
The Corpse with the Platinum Hair
The Corpse with the Sapphire Eyes
The Corpse with the Diamond Hand
The Corpse with the Garnet Face
The Corpse with the Ruby Lips
The Corpse with the Crystal Skull
The Corpse with the Iron Will
The Corpse with the Granite Heart
The Corpse with the Turquoise Toes
The Corpse with the Opal Fingers

Standalone novels
The Wrong Boy

Short Stories/Novellas
Murder Keeps No Calendar: a collection of 12 short
stories/novellas
Murder Knows No Season: a collection of four novellas
Steve's Story in 'The Whole She-Bang 3'
The Trouble with the Turkey in 'Cooked to Death Vol. 3:
Hell for the Holidays'

PRAISE FOR THE CAIT MORGAN MYSTERIES

'…Ace is, well, an ace when it comes to plot and description.'
The Globe and Mail

'Her writing is stellar. Details, references, allusions, expertly crafted phrasing, and serious subjects punctuated by wit and humour.'
Ottawa Review of Books

'If all of this suggests the school of Agatha Christie, it's no doubt what Cathy Ace intended. She is, as it fortunately happens, more than adept at the Christie thing.'
Toronto Star

'…a mystery involving pirates' treasure, lust, and greed. Cait unravels the locked-tower mystery using her eidetic memory and her powers of deduction, which are worthy of Hercule Poirot.'
The Jury Box, Ellery Queen Mystery Magazine

'…a testament to an author who knows how to tell a story and deliver it with great aplomb.'
Dru's Musings

'Cathy Ace makes plotting a complex mystery look easy. As the threads here intertwine in unexpected ways, readers will be amazed that she manages to pull off a clever solution rather than a true Gordian Knot of confusion.
Cathy Ace's books always owe a debt of homage to Grand Dame Agatha Christie…the blend of "cozy" mystery, tragic family dynamics…
pure catnip for crime fiction aficionados.'
Kristopher Zgorski, BOLO Books

For Mum

12th JULY

CHAPTER ONE

Henry Devereaux Twyst, eighteenth duke of Chellingworth, was terribly worried about his butler. For as long as he could recall, his life had benefited from Edward's utterly reliable ministrations. But now? Henry sighed as he paced the width of Chellingworth Hall's great library for the fifth time. Recently, Edward had failed to properly attend to several of his routine tasks, including making arrangements for necessary repairs to be made to Henry's favorite summer jacket.

The duke tutted aloud as he considered how terribly unlike his butler that was. Edward's attention to detail was legendary, and his ability to perform his duties with alacrity and discretion, under even the most trying of circumstances, was commented upon in many a stately pile – something which made Henry suitably proud.

Rolling on his toes as he stood beside the fireplace worrying about his butler, Henry silently cursed the rain, which had been lashing against the windows since late morning. He shivered as he stared down at the less-than-cozy hearth; two ancient brass coal scuttles filled with pine cones and dried grasses weren't going to keep him warm, for heaven's sake. Surely, if the summer sun was determined to provide no warmth, his staff should come up with some suitable alternative? He shouldn't be expected to die of hypothermia just because July was turning out to be a complete washout, should he?

Henry was just about to pull the bell-rope to summon suitable aid when his darling wife, the duchess Stephanie, appeared in the doorway. She was humming a soothing tune to their infant son, Hugo, who was sleeping in her arms. Henry hot-footed it across the yawning expanse of the chilly, book-lined room to greet his wife with a peck on the cheek, and his son with a beaming smile.

'So peaceful,' he whispered, gazing at his child in wonder.

His wife's eyebrows arched dramatically as she whispered, 'That's not what either of us was saying at two this morning, if you recall, dear.'

She smiled, though Henry could tell she was tired out. 'But you're right, he's so beautiful when he's like this that it's hard to think of him as being anything but perfect. Shush now, let me pop him into his basket and maybe he'll nap for a while yet. We need to talk about Edward.'

His wife carefully placed their son into the padded, densely-woven basket that sat within an intricately carved seventeenth-century wooden crib – something she'd joyously discovered during one of her sorties into the uppermost of Chellingworth Hall's 268 rooms. Henry watched her, then told himself off for nibbling his lip, before she did it for him. He'd been dreading this conversation, and now it was upon him.

Edward: Something Had To Be Done.

Stephanie whispered as she led her husband away from their sleeping infant son. 'He's grieving, of course, but there's more to it than that, I'm sure.'

Henry felt wrong-footed. 'Who's grieving? I thought you wanted to talk about Edward.'

Stephanie's brow furrowed. 'I *am* talking about Edward, Henry. You know very well that his brother died not two weeks ago. He's bound to be grieving.'

Henry racked his brain. 'I wasn't aware that he had a brother, let alone that he had a dead one. Why on earth didn't you tell me? I've been laboring under the clearly mistaken belief that poor Edward is...well...getting a little too long in the tooth to keep on top of things. I think you might have mentioned a death in his family, dear.'

Henry's tummy always tightened when Stephanie tutted, rolled her eyes, and went a bit pink around the gills. It seemed to happen quite a lot.

'I did tell you, Henry. I came up to your painting studio at the folly, with Hugo and a picnic basket, and we all had tea together. You said we'd manage to get along, somehow, with Edward going off for a couple of days. He went to visit his sister-in-law. Remember?'

Henry recalled the tea in question – at least, he remembered some rather good ham sandwiches, and scones with strawberry jam. 'Really? I thought you said his sister was poorly.'

'Edward doesn't have a sister, dear. Just a brother. Well, he did. They hadn't spoken for some time, I understand, but…well, blood is thicker than water, as we all know. Just look at you and Clementine. Your sister's driven you to distraction over the years, but you and she are getting along quite well since she and that lovely Julian of hers returned from their honeymoon.'

Henry was still struggling with the concept that his sister had, after several previous failed engagements, finally tied the knot. He chose to say nothing about the spat they had endured just that morning, when she'd telephoned to say that she and her husband would not, after all, be arriving the next morning. It was clear to Henry that marriage had done nothing to improve his sister's inability to understand that an entire household did not need to be attending to preparing rooms for those who would not be visiting. Trying to shrug away his irritation at his sibling's thoughtlessness, Henry did his best to realign his thinking about his butler's recent shortcomings.

'I recall only too well how dreadfully difficult it was for me to come to terms with the death of my own brother,' he mused quietly. 'Of course, poor Devereaux succumbing to measles took everyone by surprise – not least of all his doctors. None of them, nor we his family, imagined that an adult would die of such a seemingly innocuous illness. And so quickly, too. Was Edward's brother's death a sudden one?'

Henry swallowed hard as his wife did the tutting thing again.

'Yes, and his name was Richard, Henry. Shellfish poisoning. I told you. He'd recently become allergic, it seems. We had a long conversation about cross-contamination in commercial kitchens. You even agreed that we should remove prawn sandwiches from the menu at the Hall's tearoom, to be certain that nothing of the sort could ever happen here. And I know they're crustaceans, not mollusks, but the same thing applies to them. Dangerous.'

Henry honestly had no recollection of any such conversation, but didn't dare admit as much to his wife.

He fussed as he took a seat. 'Ah, yes, right. I remember that now. Though why anyone would even want to eat a sandwich containing prawns is beyond me. But still…do you think Edward's so grief-stricken that he'd be acting so uncharacteristically? When Dev died, I had to return to the nest here, and father laid it on pretty thick about how I would have to step up to eventually take on the Seat; that was a bit of a rough go for me, I have to say. And I do recall that, at the time, I was in a bit of a daze about things. Are you saying that's what's up with Edward?'

'No, dear, I'm saying that grief is natural, even for an estranged sibling, but I think something else is afoot.'

Henry nodded, then did his best to adopt a facial expression that suggested curiosity. 'Something afoot such as…?'

Stephanie stood and paced the same strip of carpet which had recently hosted Henry's own worried perambulations.

Distractedly smoothing the tendrils of hair which had escaped her chignon, the duchess sighed. 'I wish I knew, dear. I wish I knew. Edward's so…contained. A virtue in a butler, to be sure, but when one feels one should be able to help a person, that's not such a useful trait. Have you ever had a conversation with Edward, Henry? A real one, I mean; man to man, not duke to butler.'

Henry could feel his eyes blinking almost uncontrollably as he struggled to imagine why on earth he'd have ever done such a thing.

'Not that I recall, dear.' It was the answer he hoped would fit the bill.

His wife's mumbled response of: 'Pity' sounded more sympathetic than judgmental, allowing Henry to feel a wave of relief. However, her next comment of: 'But I think you should ask him if something's troubling him,' sent Henry's brain spinning. He began to feel warm – for the first time that day.

'I…I'm not at all sure that's an appropriate step, dear. Maybe we should give the matter some more thought? After all, it might just be the way the man's dealing with the loss of his brother. Quite understandable, when one considers the situation.'

Henry hoped his wife would agree.

Or that his son would awaken at that moment to distract her.

Or that one of the shelves housing ancient texts surrounding him, that had stood for hundreds of years, would topple, necessitating an evacuation of the entire wing of Chellingworth Hall.

Instead, Stephanie sighed.

Could she be about to agree with him?

'Maybe you're right, dear. I'm so new to all this. To what extent are the personal lives of the staff here private, and to what extent is their general well-being our business? When should we get involved...and when would we be prying?'

Henry said nothing.

His wife continued, 'I know it's our responsibility to be good and thoughtful employers, but Edward's been here such a long time, and he's much more than just a member of staff; he's seen this family through thick and thin – including the death of your brother, and then your father. He was the first to signal the way in which the staff should act toward me when you and I became engaged to be married. That made my transition from being the PR person who worked in the offices here to becoming the next duchess a great deal easier. I shall always be grateful for that.'

Henry didn't know what to say; he'd never considered the personal life of anyone who worked at Chellingworth Hall, in whatever capacity, to be his business. As witnessed by the fact he'd been unaware of Edward having any siblings. As he considered his response, his mind flitted between the people he saw on a daily basis. Was Cook Davies married? Did Mrs Davies Cleaning have any children? He didn't have a clue.

'I think, um...generally speaking...it's best to not pry,' he said.

'You mean we should wait until Edward himself says something?' Stephanie sounded uncharacteristically uncertain.

Henry dared his most emphatic: 'Absolutely.'

'But your mother thinks...'

Henry stood. Ah, that made more sense – this was all his mother's doing. He snapped. 'Mother meddles, as we both know only too well, dear. Is she the one who's been putting these thoughts into your head?'

No sooner had the words left his lips than Henry regretted uttering them. And if he'd been in any doubt about how poorly they had been received, the expression on his wife's face left no room for question.

'Althea hasn't been putting thoughts into my head, Henry. My concern about Edward is my own, and absolutely genuine. It's clear to anyone who knows him that the man's off his game for some reason. It's just that your mother mentioned it to me after we took tea together yesterday afternoon, when Edward spilled the milk. Twice. We agreed that something was amiss, and she suggested I should broach the subject with you. That's not meddling, that's being concerned about a valued member of staff with a long tenure, and an exemplary record for the highest level of loyalty and service. Something I would have hoped you'd understand.'

Henry sighed and gazed again at his son – who continued to sleep, and the bookshelves – which continued to stand.

'I'll speak to Mother about it, dear. Does that sound like a good idea?'

'Indeed, Henry. Now, let's ask for tea in our rooms, and tell Edward we'll serve ourselves.'

'Yes, dear.'

CHAPTER TWO

'No sign of a break in the clouds,' said Mavis MacDonald miserably as she peered out of the tall windows of the converted, ancient barn which housed the offices of the WISE Enquiries Agency.

'Sorry, Mave, doll, what was that? I weren't listening.' Annie Parker's head popped up over her computer screen allowing her to see her diminutive colleague, who stood clutching a mug as she looked heavenwards.

'I said there's no' even a break in these clouds,' said Mavis testily. 'I know we were all praying for rain last month, but we didnae need quite this much of it when it came.'

Annie grinned. 'I know what you mean, Mave. But, there, if we didn't have the weather to moan about, what would we all do, eh? Then we'd have to find something else to go on about, wouldn't we? Besides, I thought this meeting was going to be all upbeat – we're doing okay, for once, in't we? What with you getting jobs for us right and left from Rhodri Lloyd, the solicitor in Brecon, and Carol getting us on the books of her old company in the City of London to do background checks, we're all busy, all the time – or at least as busy as any of us wants to be, what with everything else we've got going on.'

Mavis hooked her neat, grey bob behind one ear, turned, and smiled. 'Aye, that we are, Annie, that we are. And you've a plate that's overflowing, no question. How's the renovation of the Coach and Horses pub going, by the way? I don't feel as though we've had a chance to catch up recently.'

'You're not wrong there, Mave. My head's on a swivel, and no mistake. I knew it would be a lot to organize, but I also thought that most of the work would fall to Tudor, him being the publican, properly speaking.'

'Aye?'

'But he's still got to keep the Lamb and Flag going, because everyone agreed that Anwen-by-Wye – like any other village, really – can't do without a working pub while we get the other one updated. So, yeah, I'm pleased you've all been so flexible about my hours over the past weeks, because I've had to do a lot more than I thought. And I'm glad that the bulk of our work's been stuff you, Carol, and Chrissy have been able to cope with. But I want to hold my end up too. So, come on, are you asking all of us to be here today because you've got a nice big, juicy case coming up for us?'

Mavis consulted the watch she kept pinned to her chest – a habit she'd retained past her retirement from her nursing years with the army. 'Only fifteen minutes, and you'll find out,' she said, with what Annie judged to be a glint in her eye.

'You're up to something, in't you, Mave?' Annie flashed her most winning smile. 'Us Cockneys have a sixth sense about that sort of thing. Come on, I'll keep schtum…the others won't know you told me. Cross my heart. Spill.'

Mavis shook her head. 'Mebbe you could make a fresh pot of tea for when the others arrive? And a plate of biscuits wouldnae go amiss.'

Annie grinned wickedly as she stuffed her feet into her shoes and made her way to the kettle. 'Alright, I won't push it. But I'm breaking out the Bourbons *and* the Garibaldis, so it had better be good news.' She busied herself filling the kettle. 'Did Car say if she's bringing Bertie? Or will Dave keep him today, do you think?'

Mavis sighed. 'Car*ol* will, indeed, be bringing wee *Albert*, because *David* has a client meeting of his own this afternoon. And please, Annie, do try to refer to people by their given names; you know very well that Carol prefers "Albert" to "Bertie". He's her child, and his name is her choice, not yours.'

Annie scrabbled in the cupboard where the biscuits were stored.

'Alright, Mav*is*, I'll try. But you know it's just my way. *Albert* will grow up knowing I love him, whatever I call him, and Car*ol* and me have been best mates for longer than we care to remember.'

She grinned. 'However much she huffs and puffs about what I call her, we both know she doesn't really mind. Oh…there she is now. Gordon Bennett! What's all that stuff she's got with her? I'll go and give her a hand, she'll be soaked to the skin, otherwise.'

Annie raced out of the door and grabbed what she could from Carol's arms, allowing her friend to grapple with her son. Of course, Gertie ran out to help. Annie still thought of her as a puppy, though she and her littermate, Rosie, who was Tudor's dog, were now over eighteen months old. Annie had named her pup in recognition of her own nickname at school, when she'd been called Gangly Gertie; the glossy black Labrador still didn't seem to be growing into her legs at all, like Annie never had. And now they were both getting wet, too.

Annie did her best to avoid Gertie, but she still managed to drop almost everything she'd been holding. She tried to retrieve it all before Gertie made any of the various items she'd been juggling unfit for purpose. 'Let it go now, Gert. Good girl.'

'Ach, she'll no' learn who's in charge if you're that soft with her,' observed Mavis tartly. 'Look at her – she's training you, not the other way around.'

Gertie sat prettily, wagging her tail. She had a small, striped sock clamped in her jaws.

Carol hauled Albert into the office on her hip. He squirmed to reach down to Gertie, who immediately dropped the sock and tried to lick the toddler's naked feet.

Annie shouted, 'Oi, no Gert!' She was amazed when Gertie sat, and looked up innocently at the three women who surrounded her. 'Good girl,' cooed Annie, impressed by her pup's obedience. She bent to ruffle the fur between Gertie's ears and got a loving lick in return. 'See, Mave,' noted Annie triumphantly, 'she knows who's the boss, really.' Gertie lay down on her paws and returned her attention to the lone sock.

Carol said, 'Grab that off her, will you, Annie?'

Annie thought that her chum sounded stressed.

Carol continued, 'I know it's not really cold today, but I want Albert to have socks on around this place. His shoes will be off him in two minutes, and you never know what's on the floor around here. There could be old staples, paperclips, all sorts of things I don't want him treading on. He's so fast, nowadays, that I can't catch up half the time when he takes off toddling.'

Annie noticed that Mavis didn't help to gather up the mounds of extra clothing, blankets, and cushions that Carol had brought. Nor did she attempt to sort out the toys that Annie suspected Carol hoped would entertain Albert while the women had their meeting. Instead, Mavis gave her attention to the tea-making duties Annie had abandoned, and kept checking her watch, and tutting.

Finally settled, Annie and Carol each grabbed a mug of tea, and began to make inroads into the mounds of biscuits Annie had dumped onto two plates.

'She's late again,' noted Mavis dryly. 'That Christine's been all over the place these last few weeks.'

'I couldn't have managed my recent workload without her help,' said Carol.

Annie threw a wink in her chum's direction in support of their colleague. 'I in't been much use, sorry, doll,' she muttered through a mouthful of Garibaldi. 'I hope this bloke they've found to do the decorating in the flat upstairs at the Coach and Horses turns out to be better than the idiot who's doing the work in the pub itself. He's slower than the Second Coming, he is, as my mother would say. I can literally run rings around him – and I have to do exactly that whenever I go over there, because he always seems to be doing something right in the middle of the floor, so you can't get anywhere without him being in the way.'

Mavis chided, 'It's only been a few weeks, Annie, and the pub is over five hundred years old, so it probably needs skillful, and certainly sympathetic, renovations. Rome wasnae built in a day.'

'It would never have been built at all if bloke who's working on the pub was doing it,' replied Annie sharply. 'Can you believe his name is Quick? Wesley – Wes – Quick.' She couldn't help but grin when she saw the expression of disbelief on Carol's face. 'Yeah, exactly. I don't think he knows there's a word that's the same as his name, nor what it means. We won't be able to open for months, the rate he's going, and that lot up at Chellingworth Hall told Tude they wanted him serving from behind that bar, instead of the Lamb and Flag, before the schools break up for the summer. Which they will do, very soon. No way is that pub going to be ready for customers by then.'

'You said that the kitchen's all sorted, didn't you?' Mavis was nibbling a Bourbon biscuit as though there was only one left in the world, and she had to make it last.

Annie always begrudged accepting that the previous owners of the pub had left anything in good order – them having turned out to be a bunch of crooks – but had to admit that the commercial kitchen had needed no more than a deep cleaning and the confirmation that all the gas and electrical connections were in good, and safe, working order. However, she reckoned that Mavis's almost-praise of them deserved no more than a shrug.

She noted, 'More by luck than judgement,' to emphasize her unspoken antipathy toward the previous publican.

'She's five minutes late,' mumbled Mavis as she brushed an invisible crumb from her lap.

'I'll give Chrissy a ring, see what's what,' offered Annie.

'We shouldnae have to be chasing after her all the time,' grumbled Mavis. 'She's an adult, with responsibilities. She should be better at timekeeping. I don't even know why she's not here. She lives upstairs, for goodness' sake. All she had to do was stay in her apartment and walk down that staircase to be here, on time.'

Annie and Carol shared an eyeroll, then Annie wandered away from the coffee table holding her phone.

She tutted. 'She's not answering, so I'll send a text.' She didn't tell Mavis that the text showed Mavis's name and a clock face, followed by a row of emojis of someone's head exploding.

Annie vamped. 'I expect she's almost here and not picking up because she's driving,' she added, sounding as hopeful as possible. Relief washed over Annie when she heard the familiar scrunching of pea-gravel as Christine's Range Rover pulled up outside. 'That'll be her, now. See? Not so late.'

Annie didn't know why she was working so hard to defend her colleague; the meeting had been in all their diaries for two days, and Mavis was right – Christine, of all of them, had little reason to be late for a meeting held in the office, because she literally lived on the premises. Annie slapped on a welcoming smile as Christine bustled through the door, but felt her face fall when she saw the mess her friend was in. Her long, chestnut hair was wet, and plastered to her pretty face; her no-doubt horrifically expensive linen slacks were stuck to her shapely legs, and her silk blouse was indecently transparent.

'What happened to you, doll? I know it's raining hard, but you look like you've been swimming – with all your clothes on. Are you okay?'

Christine rounded upon Annie with a snarl. 'No, I'm obviously not okay. I got a flat tire, and I couldn't get a stupid signal with my stupid phone out in this stupid countryside, so I had to change it myself. And I know I'm late, so don't go blowing your top, Mavis. And you can all be patient for just a bit longer, because I'm going to put some dry clothes on and do something to my hair before I catch my death…which, frankly, sounds like a grand alternative to a full agency meeting right about now. And, yes, I'll take a mug of tea with me, because I'm not only wet but I'm cold through – which I know is a stupid thing to say in July, but I am. So there.' She grabbed the mug of tea from Annie's hand. 'Now you all witter on about me being unreliable while I sort myself out upstairs.'

Kicking out at an excited Gertie, Christine headed toward the spiral staircase shouting, 'And will you keep that blessed dog under control, Annie? I thought you'd taken her for training. You should ask for your money back on that one.'

Annie felt her blood boil as she stared down at her unscathed, but surprised pup.

'Oi you, Miss Honorable flamin' high and mighty Wilson-Smythe, don't you ever do that anywhere near Gert again. It's not her fault that your Chelsea Tractor can't cope with the roads around here, or that you can't be bothered to look after it properly. She's just a little dog, so you watch it. We might be mates, but if it's her or you, it'll be her. She's excited to see you. And the training went well, if you must know. She's able to sit when she's told, and shakes a paw when you ask. If you ask nicely. And don't be too long up there – we've all got lives, too, you know.'

Christine paused on the staircase, clinging to the iron railing, then turned, looked down at her three colleagues – and Gert and Albert, both of whom were also giving her their attention – and burst into tears. She crumpled into a heap, shuddering, and dripping.

Annie immediately felt her tummy clench, with guilt, and made her way gingerly up the winding steps so she could comfort her colleague. She spoke softly. 'Sorry, Chrissy. I shouldn't have shouted, but Gert's still just a puppy, really, and she knows you usually pet her when she sees you, which is why she gets excited. So...'

'I know...I know...' mumbled Christine. 'I'm sorry. You're right. It's not like me to lash out at anyone – animals included. I'm just so...on edge all the time. I can't seem to find my equilibrium at all. And that tire going felt like the last straw. And the rain. Why do cars only seem to need attention when it's raining? And my stupid, stupid phone. The fact that you can't get a signal in so many parts of the Welsh countryside is really annoying. But...okay, I'll stop now, and I'll just get these clothes off and I'll be right back. And thanks for the tea, Annie. And sorry I was late, everyone. Just give me five minutes.'

Christine hauled herself upright and dripped her way to the top of the stairs, where she disappeared into her bedroom.

Annie pulled a face at her colleagues as she descended toward an expectant-looking Gertie, and a joyfully toddling Albert.

She could see he was about to make contact with a desk; Carol was off the sofa and grabbed him up before he managed to damage himself, while Mavis looked on with an expression that Annie judged to be one of resignation tinged with frustration.

To be expected, she reckoned. The meeting hadn't even got started, and she knew she wasn't the only one feeling the tension in the barn.

Ten minutes later, Albert was on his play-rug, completely absorbed by his collection of stuffed animals, Gertie was beside Annie's feet, twiddling her eyebrows, her head on her paws, and all four women who were equal partners in the WISE Enquiries Agency were sitting around the coffee table with their mugs freshly filled. There were no biscuits left on either plate.

'So there you have it,' said Mavis, looking rather pleased with herself. 'What do you think? An interesting potential case. And one that might even do some good…in a sort of comforting way.'

Annie had many thoughts, but she needed to organize them before she uttered a word – everything would come out wrong if she spoke now, she knew that.

Christine was dragging her fingers through her still wet hair as she gazed at the table, her expression suggesting to Annie that the young woman was hoping it might speak to her.

Carol raised her hand. Mavis nodded.

Carol said, 'I think it's a great opportunity, Mavis, but…well, are we up to it? No…I don't mean that. I know we're up to it, when we're all working at full capacity, but that's the thing, see – we're not, are we? Annie and Tudor have to get the pub sorted; you've got all your responsibilities with Althea's new charity; I've got Albert and David to cope with, and David's really quite busy at the moment, with a highly lucrative contract; and Christine's…umm…'

'You can say it,' mumbled Christine. 'Christine's not pulling her weight, and messes things up anyway when she tries to help.'

Annie saw Carol turn pink as she replied, 'I didn't mean that, Christine. It's just that you've been a bit under the weather over the past month or so, and I know you've been up to London more often than usual to see your family, too. But I've been truly grateful for all the work you've been doing on the background checks, and you haven't messed up – you've just hit roadblocks that I'm better equipped to break through, that's all.'

'I've been drinking too much.' Christine shoved out her chin as she spoke. 'I know it. You all know it. Alexander, my beloved fiancé, certainly knows it. And my family's spotted it too. I've never believed I have a problem with alcohol, but it seems everyone thinks I do. So I'm off the booze for a month, just to prove to everyone that I can live without it. Myself included. Not that I doubt for a moment that I'm capable of it, of course. I started yesterday, which is why I went out today – to get a load of fizzy drinks. Water's boring, and I like to fiddle with a glass. So there – that's where I was. I'm on the wagon for a while. Just to prove a point. Alright?'

The leaden silence that filled the barn was pierced by a loud shriek from Albert, which startled all four women, and even led Gertie to lift her head. The toddler's delight that he'd managed to remove a knitted sweater from his stuffed kangaroo's torso proved a welcome distraction for a moment or two, after which Annie felt able to pat Christine on the knee and say quietly, 'And none of us doubts that you'll do it, either, Chrissy.'

This despite the fact that the previous evening she and Tudor Evans had been talking about just how many large G and Ts Christine had been putting away in the bar at the Lamb and Flag of late.

Christine smiled warmly at Annie and said, 'So I say we should accept the contract, Mavis. If it means some legwork in London, then I'm up for that. I can stay with Mammy and Daddy at their place, rather than at my flat in Battersea; I think they'd enjoy seeing me actively not drinking. But can you tell us a bit more?'

Mavis smiled at all three women. 'As I said earlier, Rhodri's client's name is Walter Gulliver; he's in his late eighties, and a little deaf, but Rhodri says he seems to be cogent when he's on the phone. Rhodri believes it's not his memory that's to blame for there being scant information for us to work with, but the fact that he was so young when it all happened.'

Annie asked, 'Was he only a nipper?'

Mavis nodded. 'Aye, he was that. He was only about four when he and his older brother were evacuated from London to Wales in September 1939.'

'Aw, so little,' said Annie.

Mavis replied, 'Aye, and he believes his older brother – who's passed on – would have had much more knowledge of where they were billeted than Walter himself ever really understood. All that Mr Gulliver recalls is that the siblings were sent to Brecknockshire – which is a name he retained because he found it amusing. Brecknockshire no longer exists. It was absorbed across various local government reorganizations into today's Powys; in other words, this very county. Walter's mother was killed during the London Blitz of 1940, and his father died while serving in 1942. When the war ended, he and his brother were sent to live with his late-mother's cousin, who owned a farm in Lincolnshire. His brother was fatally injured in 1949 when he was – tragically, and ironically – examining what everyone believed to be a replica hand grenade that a demobbed soldier had brought home with him, and took to the local pub one evening. The brother's name was Timothy Andrew Gulliver. And that's about it, I'm afraid. Walter Gulliver – no middle name – wants to track down the family who took him and his brother in as evacuees, and he's asked Rhodri Lloyd to undertake an investigation, which he has offered to pass as a case to us. We'll need to interview Mr Gulliver ourselves, of course. In fact, I suggest that I take that duty.'

'Right up your street, Mave,' agreed Annie. 'You had lots of practice talking to the elderly when you were the matron at the Battersea Barracks for retired service-folk, and you're still at it now, given that you live with Althea.'

Mavis snapped, 'The dowager's only in her early eighties, Annie.'

Annie heard a heavy sigh, then Mavis continued with, 'There can be a great deal of difference between what one might reasonably expect of an octogenarian's cognitive abilities when they're eighty-one and when they're closer to ninety. The eighties can be a tricky decade.'

Annie accepted Mavis's sage observation with a nod. 'So, if Chrissy's off to hunt down the London end of things, you're talking to the old bloke himself, Mave, and I dare say *Carol* will be doing her usual wizard stuff with the databases she crunches through, what about me?'

Annie was puzzled. 'You said we'd all be needed, but I can't see how I could help. What did you have in mind?'

At the sound of her name, Carol looked up from her phone – where she was busily typing – to grin at Annie. Annie winked back.

'Well,' Mavis smiled slowly – which Annie knew was always a sign of danger – 'what I didnae mention was where the Gulliver family lived in London. It's kind of Christine to offer to be a pair of feet on the ground, so to speak, but the fact of the matter is that they lived near the Woolwich Arsenal. Not so far from where your parents first lived when they arrived in London from St Lucia in the 1950s, I believe, Annie.'

Annie was amazed. 'Gordon Bennett, Mave, it's just as well they sent their kids away, in that case; they lived in the part of London that had a massive target on it for the Nazi bombers to aim at. And their mum died in the bombings, you said? Not a surprise, really, if that's where she was, poor thing. But I don't think I can leave Tude to fend for himself just at the moment. So, yeah, I could help out with any local insights, I suppose, but maybe I could do that from here? You alright with that, Mave? I don't suppose the old bloke's in a rush to find the people he lived with, is he? Or has he got some horrible disease and we've only got a week before he pops his clogs?'

'Walter Gulliver has recently been treated for prostate cancer, as it happens,' replied Mavis tartly.

Annie felt her head get hot, and wished she could swallow her words. 'Oh sorry,' she said quietly. 'That's me and my foot-in-mouth thing, innit? As flamin' per.'

Mavis smiled. 'The treatment appears to have been a success, but it was the catalyst which spurred Mr Gulliver to begin this search. He wants to find out all he can about the family who took him in, so he can better understand the years he spent with them.'

Carol finally set her phone aside and asked, 'Do we know why he wants to do this?'

Annie reckoned Carol had asked a sensible question. 'Nice one, Car. So, do we, Mave?'

Mavis shook her head. 'Apparently, Walter Gulliver has never married, and has no children, but he's not intimated to Rhodri his exact intentions. That would be his business, should we succeed.'

Carol nodded slowly.

Annie pounced, 'You've been doing a quick trip through the interwebs there, haven't you, doll? Learned anything useful?'

Carol shrugged. 'If it's the same person, then Mr Walter Gulliver is an extremely interesting client: he was the owner of Gulliver Groceries. Sold the business five years ago for something north of two hundred million pounds. He built Britain's largest chain of grocery shops, allegedly turned down a knighthood – twice – and has been noted as being one of the biggest donors ever to charitable organizations that support literacy and outreach programs for at-risk children. He's always referred to in the press as "exceptional".'

Annie noticed that even Mavis looked surprised by the revelation. 'Mebbe it's no' the same man, just the same name, because I think Rhodri Lloyd might have mentioned those facts when he briefed me.'

'He might not have known,' said Carol.

'Oh come off it, Car. How many Gullivers do we all think are romping around the UK?' Annie couldn't help herself. 'His name would make anyone think of them shops, wouldn't it?'

Carol said, 'When Mavis said it, I thought about the book, *Gulliver's Travels*, not Gulliver Groceries. Maybe Rhodri did the same?'

Even Annie had to agree that was a possibility, and it was further agreed that Mavis should check immediately with Rhodri Lloyd, so they at least knew if the Walter Gulliver who was his client was, in fact, the multi-millionaire.

'In any case,' continued Mavis, 'what Rhodri has told me is that all Mr Gulliver knows is that he lived on a "big farm with all sorts of animals", though he'd have been recalling the place from the perspective of a small child. And that's where I believe you can help, Annie – you, too, Christine. I will do my best to get as much as I can out of Mr Gulliver himself – having spoken to Rhodri first, of course – while Carol attacks all relevant evacuee and wartime databases; you two can begin with some general historic and background research.'

'Sounds like a plan,' agreed Christine.

Annie nodded her agreement.

'I remember my father used to watch that TV series, *The World at War*,' mused Mavis, 'and I even watched some of it with him. But I think we all need to deepen our general understanding of the specifics of the whole evacuation process to be able to help Mr Gulliver as much as we can, so I look forward to hearing about what you can dig up.'

'We studied World War Two for history in school,' piped up Carol cheerily. 'I loved it. Though . . .' She faltered, blushing. 'That came out wrong. To me it was all so far in the past, see? Like the Wars of the Roses, which we also did. But, yes, I look forward to diving in – as an adult, with a different perspective.'

Annie did her best to not smile as her chum tried to cover her embarrassment. She said, 'So you'll say yes, then, Mave, get the contracts sorted, and we can get going on The Case of the Exceptional Evacuee as soon as we can, eh?'

'Nicely named, Annie, if it's him,' observed Mavis, nodding her approval.

CHAPTER THREE

Alexander Bright was acutely aware that he was facing a dangerous situation, and believed he knew how to handle it. However, he was equally concerned that he might have to resort to utilizing some of the skills he'd acquired in his youth to deal with it successfully – which wasn't something he was keen to do. He'd worked hard to remove himself from the circumstances of his upbringing in the sink estates of Brixton, where he'd had to resort to being an unquestioning – and eventually incredibly skilled – transporter of suspect packages across South London. He didn't ever want to go back to that sort of life. Now in his mid-forties, he'd finally reached a point where all the businesses in which he had an interest were legitimate, and most of his acquaintances had no criminal records.

He sat silently within the cocoon of his parked car, looking out at the homes of the rich, famous, and titled, which lined the swish square in the Royal Borough of Kensington and Chelsea. This was where he belonged now; one of those houses was owned by the Viscount Ballinclare, his fiancée's father, and he was expected for drinks. He knew he'd be greeted warmly by Christine Wilson-Smythe's mother, the viscountess, and always felt his spirits rise in her company – she was a generous and cheerful woman. He'd recently become one of only a handful of people invited to use her given name of Deirdre, which he knew was a great honor; she always used her middle name of Fiona in company...one of the things Christine's grandmother had encouraged her daughter to do upon marrying a viscount, insisting that she would be better accepted within English society as a Fiona than as a Deirdre.

Alexander smiled to himself about how he, too, had shed an earlier name as soon as he could; he'd been dubbed 'Issy' by his criminal overlords in his youth because he'd been too scared to do more than hiss when asked his name by a particularly nasty piece of work who was blaming him for a package having gone missing.

He mused about how the backstreet pub where that had happened, and this posh pile were only a few miles apart – even if it felt as though they were on different planets – then acknowledged that he and the viscountess had more in common than she could have imagined.

They'd both spent decades doing their best to bury their true roots and convince the world that all that mattered about them was what could be seen as 'new growth' above the dirt and the muck. To only see the person they had become by dint of their own determination and hard work, rather than the person they had once been.

He'd been – almost – completely open with Christine about his past. They were going to spend the rest of their lives together, so that was a given. However, he knew that his fiancée had significantly edited his tales of an horrific early life when she'd spoken of him to her parents. He also knew what that meant: that not just now, but forever, he could never be anyone in their company other than the 'new' him.

Alexander sighed heavily. He couldn't help but contemplate the clouds on his horizon, which were every bit as pendulous as the ones hanging over London that evening. Christine hadn't been herself recently; a light seemed to have gone out in her. They'd not only been drifting apart, but they'd also been firing salvos of increasingly wounding insults as the distance between them grew.

And now he'd been asked for help by someone to whom he owed a debt of gratitude so great that there was no way he could refuse their request. However, if he did what he'd been asked to do, it could mean that some characters from his past who believed 'Issy' to be dead, might discover that he wasn't. And that wouldn't be good.

Alexander's Aston Martin was flooded with light as a black cab pulled up in front of it. Christine's father leaped out, paid the driver, then headed toward his front door.

He thought it was a little strange that the viscount hadn't even acknowledged the presence of his future son-in-law, clearly illuminated in his car. Alexander's heart was heavy as he left the safety of his vehicle. He caught up with Aiden Wilson-Smythe as the man was scurrying between parked cars.

As cheerily as he could make it sound, Alexander called, 'Let's both get in out of this lovely liquid sunshine, shall we?' Aiden was grappling with a hefty briefcase and a summer-weight mackintosh that he was trying to hold over his head. Alexander offered, 'How about I take that?' He held his hand toward the briefcase.

Aiden hesitated, then passed the bag to Alexander. 'Thanks. But don't go looking inside it – there's a pile of paperwork in there that could get me into terrible trouble if it fell into the wrong hands.'

Alexander forced a chuckle. 'Haven't you lot in the City gone completely digital, yet?' There was something…odd…about Aiden's manner. *Bad day?*

The two men made their way toward the porticoed, glossily black front door, which was opened before they arrived by a slight man in a dark suit who rushed out with a large umbrella.

'Go on back inside, Jerry, you'll be soaked to the skin, so you will,' called Aiden over the tattoo of the rain on the pavement.

The young man thrust the umbrella over the viscount's head, attempted to give Alexander as much cover as possible too, then shuffled behind them until all three were inside the house, and shaking themselves off within the hallway.

Deirdre Wilson-Smythe appeared at the top of the wide staircase which bisected the house – part of a terrace of white-stuccoed dwellings which formed a square around an acre of gated, private, communal gardens.

She called, 'Just look at the pair of you – like a couple of drowned rats, so you are. I knew it was raining, but I didn't know it was that bad. You can come and change straight away, before a single drink is poured, Aiden.'

As he dealt with the dripping umbrella, the young factotum asked, 'Would you care for any assistance, sir?'

'I'll manage under my own steam, thanks, Jerry,' replied Aiden.

'Alright if I pop up to Christine's bathroom to dry off a bit, Deirdre?' Alexander thought it strange that his future mother-in-law hadn't offered.

'I dare say our daughter's bathroom is ready for incoming guests, Jerry?' Deirdre sounded unusually haughty to Alexander's ear.

'Indeed, ma'am.'

'Very well, then, Alexander. We'll meet in the drawing room in fifteen minutes.'

'Excellent, thanks,' said Alexander, glad of one last chance to wrap his head around being the solicitous future son-in-law before having to engage in polite chit-chat.

Both men mounted the stairs, where Deirdre greeted her husband with a hug and a peck on the cheek.

Alexander headed to dry himself off as best he could. As he toweled his head in the bathroom, glad he had no more than a quarter of an inch of hair on it, he recalled with amusement how he'd looked when he was a teen. Back then, his hair had been one of the things he'd hated most about himself; his eyes, which he'd inherited from his mother, were light, and his skin-tone wasn't that dark...though far too dark to make him acceptable to the white gangs on the estate where he'd pretty much raised himself. But his hair had most definitely come from his unknown Black father, so he'd decided to sport dreadlocks, to help him fit in.

Unfortunately, not even that had made him popular with the Black gangs in Brixton, so he'd always been a loner – and a scared one at that, until he'd learned how to blend into his surroundings. He'd rapidly discovered that invisibility was the best form of defense for a weedy kid whose mother was usually too drunk to know or care where he was, and with no male relatives to look out for him.

The money he'd made by employing that invisibility on behalf of anyone who wanted to get a package from one place to another, quickly, and without the authorities or rival gangs being any the wiser, allowed him to gradually better himself: he'd bulked up in gyms, and joined clubs where he'd learned various types of combat techniques.

Eventually, good clothes allowed him to mingle with posher groups, where he was accepted thanks to his elocution lessons, and – when he allowed himself to admit it – the fact that he wasn't a bad-looking bloke.

That was how he'd managed to navigate the murky waters of his early life, until he was able to take his leave of the sad little flat in Brixton and move to a bright and airy apartment in Notting Hill, where he'd reinvented himself under his real name, which no one from his past had ever known, nor cared to find out.

Dabbing his Savile Row-tailored jacket dry, Alexander Bright allowed himself to accept that he'd come a long way: he was a well-respected property developer who'd earned a reputation for providing homes for the working poor who needed a landlord who actually cared about their well-being; he enjoyed being a silent partner in an established antiques business – which allowed him to indulge his passion for old, beautiful, and rare artifacts; and he was now also the owner of an antiques shop in the bucolic Welsh village of Anwen-by-Wye, in partnership with a duke. It was an extraordinary rise, when he thought of it like that. But his trusted friend Geordie needed help from him now, and that could mean…

He couldn't dwell on that, he told himself. He donned his jacket, checked his reflection once more – yes, he was properly attired – and headed downstairs to meet his hosts for what he hoped would be a pleasant hour or so of amiable company.

However, when he entered the drawing room, the expression on Deirdre's face above her Aperol spritz gave him pause, then he noticed that Aiden's general demeanor was suggesting that he was less than happy, too.

'Everything alright?' Alexander thought he might as well ask.

'We've talked about it, now that we know, and have wondered if you've told Christine. We've also wondered when you were going to tell us, or if you ever would,' said Aiden, without making eye contact.

'Tell you what?' Alexander couldn't imagine what they meant…at least, he could imagine any number of things they might mean, but hoped he was wrong about all of them.

'About your teenage son,' said Deirdre acidly.

Of all the accusations the viscount and viscountess might have hurled at him, that hadn't been one Alexander had even imagined.

13th JULY

CHAPTER FOUR

Mavis MacDonald was pouring tea for the Dowager Duchess, Althea Twyst, in the sitting room of the Dower House on the Chellingworth Estate. The day beyond the windows was as dark as the previous one, and the rain even heavier – if that were possible.

'At least the roses on the upholstery glow on a day like this,' noted Althea cheerily.

Mavis glanced at the furnishings and acknowledged McFli, the dowager's aged, but sprightly, Jack Russell, who was sitting in the middle of one of the sofas with his tail wagging furiously. 'Aye, that they do. Which might be just as well, given what you've just been telling me. It all seems dreadfully complicated, dear. Just so that I can have a private word with Edward.'

Althea sat upright as she took a slice of seed cake, her eyes glittering in the light of the table lamp, which was much needed, despite the time of year.

McFli took the sight of the cake being picked up as his cue to move; he adopted a 'ready for incoming crumbs' position at his mistress's feet.

Smiling down at her much-loved companion, Althea replied, 'I have known Edward for almost forty years, and I have never seen him seated, in my company, in all that time. He won't spill his guts if I'm here – it'll all be "Your Grace" this, and "Your Grace" that – so you have to crack him open like an egg, Mavis. I know you can do it.'

Mavis shook her head and half-smiled. 'Despite the unnecessary vividness of your language, Althea, I'm no' convinced that I'll be able to get Edward to admit that there's something bothering him.'

'I bet you'll manage it,' twinkled the dowager.

Mavis had her doubts.

'The man's got a shell like a hundred-year-old tortoise; unless he chooses to tell me what's on his mind – that's possibly leading him to not be as efficient at performing his duties as usual – I don't think I'll be able to "crack him open", as you so colorfully put it.'

'Of course you can, dear. You're a formidable woman. Quite frightening, when you want to be.' Althea smiled, her cheeks dimpling as she did so.

Mavis bridled. 'I've never heard such rubbish. I'm no' a scary person at all. I pride myself on being measured and professional in all my dealings with folk – even those who might well deserve less-than-gentle handling.'

Althea put down her cup, and straightened the magenta scarf she was wearing atop a lime green cashmere cardigan. 'I bet all your nurses were terrified of you when you were a matron,' she giggled, 'and I bet not one of them was ever rude to your face – at least, never more than once. You've really no idea how witheringly you can look at a person, do you?'

Mavis dared what she thought of as a mildly disdainful glance.

'There,' said Althea triumphantly, 'that's just what I mean. My knees have gone to jelly just sitting here.'

Mavis tutted and checked her watch. 'When did you say he was due?'

'Henry telephoned to say that Edward had left the Hall ten minutes ago, so any time now. The poor thing will be soaked through, I'd have thought – which is an even better reason for you insisting that he takes a warming cup of tea…to dry out a bit.'

The chimes at the door of the Dower House rang out.

Althea sat even more upright, reminding Mavis of a meerkat. 'Oh, that'll be him now, I expect. Isn't this exciting, dear?'

Mavis tutted. 'Now, to be clear: Ian Cottesloe will answer the door and will invite Edward to fetch the spurious package that your son has asked him to bring here, into this room. You'll take the parcel, then announce you need to see Cook with it, and I shall be left here alone with Edward, whom I shall invite to take tea with me. Have I got that right?'

Althea gave an exaggerated two thumbs up. 'Yes – that's the plan. Ready?'

Mavis rolled her eyes. 'Aye. Now calm down, or the man will know there's something amiss – he's known *you* for forty years, too, don't forget, so I bet he'll be able to spot when you're up to something.'

The door opened and Ian Cottesloe's head appeared. 'Edward, from the Hall, for you, Your Grace. He has a parcel that has to be handed to you personally, he says. From His Grace.' Mavis heard the incredulity in the young man's voice; obviously he wasn't privy to the dowager's machinations.

'Ask him to bring it in, would you? I've been expecting it. Thank you,' said Althea, dimpling.

'Althea, down,' hissed Mavis. She noticed McFli drop to his belly and lay his head on his paws, staring up at her with concern. 'If only it was as easy with a human being,' she whispered as Edward entered the room.

As Althea had predicted, the weather had taken its toll on the man, though Mavis could tell he'd done his best to ensure he didn't drip his way into the sitting room; he'd obviously removed his outwear – and a hat, she surmised – and he stood there looking dreadfully uncomfortable in stockinged feet, presumably having removed Wellington boots.

'His Grace requested that I convey this parcel directly to Your Grace's own hand,' he said gravely, proffering a six-inch cube wrapped in brown paper, and tied with string. Mavis judged it to have been transported in a plastic bag, because it was quite dry.

Althea leaped from her seat, causing McFli to also pop up, expecting some sort of action – which he got. As she stepped away from the table, in her haste, Althea failed to notice that she'd managed to become attached to the linen cloth, so a teacup and saucer, plus the plate upon which she'd placed her as-yet-untouched slice of cake, fell to the floor, and bounced on the Aubusson rug.

McFli darted toward the cake in an instant, knocking against Althea's leg, which unbalanced her, and she toppled over...

Both she and Edward made a grab for each other, which meant Edward dropped the parcel he'd been holding, in favor of getting a better grip on the dowager.

Mavis was beside Althea by the time both she and the butler were properly upright again, and she was able to make sure that the octogenarian had not suffered any injuries. The tiny woman assured her she hadn't, batting away Mavis's hands, and smoothing down her bottle green tweed skirt, then straightening her cardigan.

Edward was pink in the face. 'I apologize for grabbing Your Grace. I thought…I mean, it seemed to be the best course of action in the moment for me to…' He bent to retrieve the package, which gave off the sound of broken…something. Mavis noted that he became an even deeper shade of red. 'I fear the contents might have…um…'

Althea all but snatched the package from his hand and said brightly, 'Never fear, Edward, I am not damaged in any way, and nor, I am certain, are the contents of this package. But I must take it to Cook, immediately. Please, excuse me.'

Mavis watched as Althea trotted to the door. McFli scampered after her when she tapped her thigh, indicating that he should follow.

The butler looked dazed, thought Mavis, so she pounced. 'Nothing wrong with her,' she announced happily as the door closed, 'but I bet you could do with a cuppa. Here, let me pour.'

She offered a chair – not the one where Althea had been sitting, as she suspected that would, indeed, be too much for the man.

She used a firm tone. 'As a medical professional I'm going to go as far as to instruct you to sit and take tea. It cannae be every day that you have to manhandle a dowager, so let's have two sugars in it, shall we, and you can get over what appears to have been a nasty shock. Come along, sit.'

Edward plopped heavily onto the chair and looked at the cup of tea in front of him as though it might contain ambrosia. 'Thank you.'

He raised the cup to his lips and drank it all – which surprised Mavis greatly, as the tea was fresh and therefore piping hot. She wondered if hurried cups of scalding tea had been a part of the butler's life for all the years he'd been at Chellingworth Hall.

Almost as soon as he replaced the cup on its saucer, Edward bounced up out of the seat. 'That was extremely kind of you, Mrs MacDonald. I'll be going now, thank you.'

'No you won't, Edward, you'll sit back down and have a piece of cake, too. You need the sugar,' snapped Mavis. She threw him the glance Althea had suggested was terrifying.

The butler looked visibly shocked, sat down again, took a piece of cake, and put it onto a plate. Mavis wondered if, maybe, Althea had made a valid point about her ability to get people to bend to her will, and did her best to not smile.

'Eat up, it'll do you good. I dare say you don't have many chances for a relaxing cuppa with that lot up at the Hall, do you? Not if I know Henry, anyway. And, no, don't panic, I don't expect you to respond.'

Edward nibbled the cake uncertainly; Mavis judged that the poor man was feeling quite uncomfortable, and realized she had to do her best to put him at his ease or she'd never get anywhere with her task. However, she knew she didn't have much time, so decided upon a bold opening gambit.

'I understand you've recently lost a brother, Edward. My condolences. I have two boys, and I know how such a loss would impact either one of them. Were you two close?'

Edward put down the cake, cast his eyes around the cheery room, and looked just about as miserable as it was possible for a person to be in such surroundings. His darting glance suggested to Mavis that he was mentally hunting for a suitable response.

Mavis said, 'Edward, I've no' got a title, I'm just a house guest – albeit a permanent one – of a dowager. You and I are both human beings who have lived a life of service, though of differing sorts. I hope we're able to have a conversation as two equals.' She held out her hand with a broad smile. 'Hello, Edward, I'm Mavis.'

Edward cleared his throat and shook Mavis's hand weakly, then half-smiled. 'Unusual territory for me, this. Sitting down taking tea at the Dower House. I'd never imagined…nothing like this has ever happened to me before. I don't quite know how to…'

Mavis's heart went out to the man as he seemed to shrink into the chair. He was more than uncomfortable, he was...lost. She made a snap decision.

'Edward, you're a wonderful butler, but you're more than that, you're a man with a family. And you've lost a member of that family. I won't butter you up and lie to you, that's not fair, so listen up...'

Edward's expression suggested terror.

'The duke, duchess, and dowager hatched the plan to get you here, alone with me, so I could try to find out what's the matter. I don't want you to panic, but they've all noticed that you've not been quite your usual self since you got back from visiting your late-brother's widow.'

Mavis could see horror replace terror on the man's face.

'I said "Don't panic", Edward,' she added quickly. 'No one's cross with you, but they are worried for you, and they want to try to understand how they can help you. If you're grieving for your brother they'd understand and would accommodate your taking some time away from your duties. But the fear is that there's something *more* that's bothering you. This is your chance to talk to me about it, rather than having one of them ask. And I think, if you're honest with yourself, you'd much prefer this option. Am I right?'

Edward nodded eagerly. 'Absolutely. But, even so...' He picked up the cake; Mavis judged he was giving himself a moment to think, so she sat quietly, and awaited his response.

Eating appeared to allow Edward to regain some of his composure. Mavis could almost see him thinking through what he would say. Eventually, having finished the cake, and having wiped non-existent crumbs from his mouth with a napkin, Edward sat back in his chair and looked Mavis in the eye.

'My brother and I hadn't spoken for some years, and I don't know his wife well, but she begged me to visit her after he'd died so, of course, I went. I had nothing against the woman, and, with my brother gone, I had no reason to not do as she'd asked.'

Mavis couldn't help but wonder what had caused such a rift within a family, but held her tongue – she didn't want to give the man a reason to stop speaking, something he'd clearly made a decision to do.

'Upon my arrival at their home in Ealing, I learned the circumstances of my brother's passing. His name was Richard, by the way. Richard had suffered from a terrible bout of food poisoning approximately six months before his death and, thereafter, had displayed the symptoms of an intense allergy to shellfish, not something he'd ever suffered from before. He'd been extremely careful to avoid all mollusks since the problem was diagnosed, of course. However, notwithstanding a great deal of diligence on his part, on the evening he died he did, indeed, experience an allergic reaction. Unfortunately, the device containing epinephrine, which he had been carrying with him at all times since he'd been diagnosed, wasn't in his pocket when the symptoms began. Everyone there guessed what was happening to Richard, but no one could help him without that wretched pen. Help came too late, and he died at the table where he'd been supposed to be celebrating the fact that a lucrative contract had just been awarded to a business in which he was a partner.'

Mavis wanted to ask so many questions, but felt it was better to let the man continue.

Edward's expression grew grim. 'My sister-in-law was devastated by Richard's death. They hadn't even been married for a decade. We talked for many hours, and, while I still cannot say I know her well, Rachel – my late-brother's widow is named Rachel – is utterly convinced that his death wasn't an accident. She believes he was murdered, and that she's in danger too. More than anything else, that has plagued my thoughts every moment since I left her. What if she's right? And I don't know what on earth to do about it.'

Mavis reached out to Edward's hand, which lay on the table, and said, 'Don't you worry, Edward. How about we get a fresh pot of tea, and you let me ask you a few questions?'

Edward blinked, twice. 'Thank you,' he replied quietly. 'I didn't know who to turn to, you see.'

At that moment, Althea burst through the door. 'For goodness' sake, Edward – you're surrounded by private investigators, why on earth didn't you say something sooner?'

'Your Grace!' The man looked horrified.

Mavis tutted loudly as Edward shot up out of his chair, leading to yet another cup and saucer rolling across the rug.

'Sit down, Edward, and that's an order,' said the dowager, wickedly. 'I was listening at the door, of course, and you're in a bit of a pickle. Well, the WISE women will come to your rescue, never fear. Cook's bringing a fresh pot, and we'll all settle down for a conference. I've told Henry you won't be back at the Hall for a few hours, and he'll cope perfectly well without you. So sit, and talk. Pretend I'm a normal person called Althea – when we're just us, you know? – and things will go a lot easier. Right, Mavis?'

Mavis sighed. 'Indeed, Althea.'

Althea winked at the shocked butler. 'You're going to have to be open and honest with this one, you know –' she nodded toward Mavis.

Mavis nodded back.

Althea continued, 'And, when all this is behind us, things can go back to being the way they were, with you "Your Grace"-ing me as much as you like. But please drop that for a while, will you? We'll be here forever, otherwise. Got it?'

Mavis bit her bottom lip to prevent an inappropriate smile as Edward slid awkwardly into his chair and nodded.

'Yes, Your…Althea,' he mumbled.

'More cake, Edward?' Althea pushed the plate toward the butler, and Mavis wasn't sure if the poor man was more likely to laugh, or cry.

CHAPTER FIVE

Annie Parker strode into the bar of the Coach and Horses pub as though she owned the place. She didn't; it had been purchased from the previous owner by Althea Twyst, who had then gifted the ancient pub to the Chellingworth Estate. The Estate owned all the land upon which the village of Anwen-by-Wye was built, and most of the buildings too. Indeed, the Coach and Horses pub had once been owned by the Twysts, until it was 'given as a gift' by the then duke to the publican in charge at the time at the behest of Charles I, who'd been impressed by the publican's support for his cause. At least, that was the story Annie had heard, though she gave the tale little credence, because she'd discovered through her own research that Charles I had never got closer to Anwen-by-Wye than Shrewsbury.

Nevertheless, Annie felt confident in being able to enter with the air of a proprietor, because Tudor Evans had been given the role of manager publican of the place by the Estate, and he and she were due to move into the flat above, as a proper couple, as soon as it was fit for them. And she'd made quite sure that the three men who'd been hired by the Estate to renovate the pub itself, and the flat, had been aware of that from day one.

As usual, she had to circumnavigate a pile of…plaster mix – or was it some sort of cement? – on the floor right in the entrance to the pub itself, and glanced across to where Wes Quick was working…slowly. He'd been hired because there were patches crumbling in the corners where the ancient beams – which Annie knew would always drive her to distraction, because they were so low – entered the equally ancient, plastered stone walls. Annie didn't even bother to ask how Wes was getting on – he'd been working in exactly the same spot when she'd visited the previous day.

As she reached the top of the stairs, she could hear the clanging of pipes coming from the direction of the bathroom, which filled her with hope.

She reckoned the original shower must have been designed for tiny people, because the shower head pointed directly at her chest when she managed to get herself into the miniscule capsule that had been fitted about thirty years earlier.

True, standing at six feet, she was a tall woman, but Tudor was about the same height, and the shower really did need to allow them to at least get their heads wet when they wanted to use it. So the Estate had agreed to a new bathroom being fitted. Luckily, the pub had only been given Listed status after the living quarters, and the guest rooms, had been gutted and rebuilt many times over the centuries, so there was little that couldn't be done to those parts of the building, as long at the external aspect remained unchanged.

In the pub itself – the bar area – that was a different matter, as there were original sixteenth-century beams and all sorts of planning requirements to be accommodated, without any changes being allowed at all; Annie was glad that all that folderol was something the Chellingworth Estates Manager, Bob Fernley, had to deal with.

Annie had her hands full dealing with all the matters that *were* hers to manage, so headed directly to see how Angelo, the man responsible for the bathroom, was getting along – and she was impressed. The shower was now a large rectangle, which would all be tiled, with glass doors to keep the room dry, and she could see that he'd already placed the pipe to which the shower head would be attached up at the seven-foot mark, where she and Tudor agreed they'd be happy with it. Given the ancient nature of the building, the man had done a splendid job managing to fit in all the plumbing required for a modern, properly controllable shower. She could see he only had about an inch to spare above the piping…but at least it was in.

She reached forward to tap Angelo on his back as he knelt, and the man almost jumped out of his skin; he was in his own little world, with ear buds blasting something that had a steady beat which even Annie could hear.

He popped his hand into his pocket, stopped the music playing on his phone, and pulled out an ear plug. Just one. Annie reckoned she was honored to be granted at least that much attention.

'You going to be finished in here in a week, then?' She knew the answer was supposed to be yes, but didn't really think it would be possible.

Angelo nodded cheerily. 'No worries. Though it'll take a while for the glass doors to come; they can't measure for them until all the tiling's finished, see? Then they've got to make them to size, then you can book the installation. So you'll probably have a bit of a splashy room for a while. But that's not me. That's the glass people. Sorry, love.'

Annie felt her eyebrows rise. 'Love? We've been through this, Angelo.'

'Sorry, Miss. I mean Annie. Sorry, Annie. Glass isn't me.'

'And where's Dan today? Did he even turn up this morning? Everything I can see looks exactly the same as it did when I was here yesterday morning. Nothing else has been painted, the handles are still on the kitchen cupboards, and there's still that hole in the living room ceiling.' Annie was cross, and didn't mind letting it show.

Angelo gave his attention to his phone. 'He hasn't texted me, and I haven't seen him. But you know him and me aren't connected at all, so I never need to know where he is, do I?'

Not to be outdone, Annie pulled out her own phone. 'I'd better let Bob Fernley know that he's nowhere to be found. Again. He won't be pleased.'

'No need to get the Estates Manager involved. I'll text Dan now. Tell him you're here,' said Angelo quickly, and he started punching his phone with his thumbs.

Annie wondered how many, and which, emojis Angelo might be using to tell Dan that she was on the premises, and after his blood.

'There. He's five minutes away, he says. Had to get some…nah, can't read that. He must be driving.'

Annie tutted, then added, 'Well don't let me stop you from getting on. Nice job managing to get that pipe up that high, Angelo – much appreciated. I'll be able to wash me barnet and me plates at the same time, now. Cheers.'

Angelo looked baffled, then said, 'Sometimes I almost forget you're a Cockney.' He winked, stuck in his ear bud, hit play on his phone, then got back down onto his knees to attend to the farthest corner of what would become – within a week, apparently – a luxuriously large shower stall.

Annie went off to examine the kitchen: it was still a mess of a shell, with gaps for the soon-to-be-delivered new sink, stove, fridge, and – joy of joys – dishwasher. A few upper cabinets were laying on their backs on the floor, and everything was still dirty and greasy. She couldn't believe that Dan hadn't even cleaned the place yet, and she could see that any effort on his part to scrape off the hideous wallpaper had been half-hearted, at best. If she'd thought Wes working on the pub downstairs was slow, this was making her rethink her already challenged understanding of the word.

She pulled out her phone and began to make a list of what still needed to be done, but soon realized she might as well refer back to her original list, because it seemed as though there wasn't one single job that had been finished. Which made her blood boil.

By the time Dan appeared at the top of the stairs, Annie had reached full incandescence. She was about to let him have several pieces of her mind when he held out a box of muffins and a small bucket of coffee.

He looked at her sheepishly. 'Peace offering? I had to go to get my dog put to sleep. Poor old girl couldn't keep going any longer, and I needed a bit of a sugar fix on my way here from the vet. It's been a horrible start to the day. She was thirteen. The best dog ever. It's like having to cut off your own arm.'

Annie immediately thought of Gertie and felt her mood shift...her heart went out to the man.

'Right then. Sorry to hear that. I understand it must be upsetting. Or, at least, I will do one day – though Gert's not even two yet, so still a puppy really, and bouncing with good health, of course. But there, you don't want to be thinking about healthy puppies today, do you?'

Dan snapped, 'No I don't, thanks very much.'

Anne felt bad. 'Sorry. But now that you are here...'

'I'll make up the time, I promise. I'll stay on a bit tonight. It's still light until late – if it ever gets really light with the way the weather is. Should get all that paper down in the kitchen today, then I can give the place a good old degreasing and prep all the cabinets for painting. You won't know the place by the weekend. I'll have those old floorboards looking like new by Tuesday, when the appliances are being delivered. It's all in hand.'

'And the living room, and bedrooms?' Annie at least asked politely.

'Well, like we agreed, the kitchen was the priority, then the living room, then the main bedroom, then the spare. All scheduled.'

'And it will all be ready on time, right?'

Dan nodded and grinned. 'You'll be in on time, no worries. We can't have you two lovebirds out on the street, can we?' He winked wickedly, and Annie decided she'd give him the benefit of the doubt. For now.

'Right then, I'm just going to measure the windows in the bedroom again, to be sure,' she called as she marched off.

She thought she heard Dan muttering something like, 'For the third time?' under his breath, but chose to ignore him. She shoved open the door – which always stuck – and called out, 'Don't forget to make the adjustments to this door, like we discussed.'

'Right-o,' floated back.

Once inside, she measured the window that overlooked the large, fenced, grassy area and the outbuildings at the back of the pub, as well as the one which looked out toward the village green – which was by far the more attractive view. As she checked her measurements, she spotted Carol and Sharon chatting outside the shop – she reckoned Dave must be looking after Bertie for a bit – then turned to check the rolls of wallpaper she'd chosen for the room, but couldn't see them anywhere. She didn't understand why Dan had to keep moving everything all the time.

She shouted through the open door, 'Where's the bedroom wallpaper gone, Dan?' There was no response, so she returned to the kitchen to find Dan munching a muffin while watching something on his phone, his ear buds in place. She wasn't surprised that he seemed to be more interested in his screen than in her.

Having got his attention she repeated, 'Where have you hidden the bedroom wallpaper, Dan?'

Swallowing a mouthful, Dan replied, 'I haven't seen any wallpaper. In the bedroom, you said?'

'Yes. I dropped it off the day before yesterday. Fourteen rolls. I put them in the corner of the bedroom, and they aren't there now. Come and have a look.'

Dan shrugged and followed her to the bedroom, his muffin still in his hand. He glanced around. 'I didn't doubt that it wasn't here, but I haven't even seen it. Haven't been working in here, see?'

'So where's it gone, then? It can't have just walked off on its own, can it?' Annie could feel herself getting warm, and hoped she wasn't going to have a hot flash and get all sweaty and itchy…she didn't need that now.

Dan shrugged again, which really annoyed Annie.

She snapped, 'Come off it, Dan, you must have seen it. It's blue, with flowers. You helped me pick the right paint to match it, for the trim.'

'I remember the sample, and picking the paint, but I didn't see you coming in here with umpteen rolls.'

'Fourteen rolls. You helped me work out how many you'd need.'

'Again, I remember that, but I haven't seen the actual wallpaper.'

'Well, what about the paint? Where's that, then?' Annie could feel the horribly familiar feeling creeping down from the nape of her neck to the small of her back – yes, she was going to have a full meltdown any minute now.

'You got the paint, too?' Dan sounded surprised.

'Yes, of course I did. We agreed what was needed for the room, and I was laboring under the misapprehension that you were actually going to be here, at the flat, for a full day's work, every day, getting on with what you're paid to do, which is the flamin' decorating. I went and got everything myself to save you time, so you could get more done here.'

Dan stepped backwards. 'Alright, keep your hair on.' He glanced at Annie's closely trimmed hairdo and blanched. He mumbled, 'You know what I mean.'

Annie chose to say nothing.

He gathered himself. 'And I haven't seen any wallpaper or paint for this room, other than the samples and charts we looked at together, so there's no point having a go at me about it. Have you asked Angelo? He's always skulking about in the bathroom banging his head to some racket – maybe he's moved it. Ask him.'

Annie retorted, 'Why would he move it?'

'Why would I?' Dan's reply was equally sharp. 'That's just a make-work project, that is, if you've put it in the room where it's going to be used, isn't it?'

Annie didn't want to agree with his well-made point, but also knew that if she didn't get out of the room she'd start to feel the walls closing in on her and she'd really blow her top. She headed down the stairs, shouting, 'I'll be back, to see how that kitchen's coming along,' and slammed the door to the yard behind her, panting and sweating. She knew she'd done herself no favors by losing her temper with Dan; the poor man had lost his dog, and she'd torn him off a strip -- not fair. But it was too late now, she couldn't take it all back, and she needed to meet with Carol in ten minutes.

She walked out to the green where she waved at her chum and colleague who was making her way toward her home. Annie pointed at Carol's house, which was next door to the pub, then waited for her to arrive at the kitchen door.

'Look at us, both soaked,' said Carol giggling. 'Well, you more than me. Haven't you got an umbrella with you?'

Annie realized she'd left it at the Coach and Horses and stepped into the cozy kitchen rather than dash back for it. 'My skin doesn't leak, and it's not really cold today,' she replied, as Carol flapped her own umbrella on the doorstep to dry it off, then dropped it into the stand that was tucked behind the door.

'I popped over to Sharon's shop to get a couple of custard tarts for us to munch on while we talk about Walter Gulliver,' announced Carol, as she peeled off her mac and wellies. 'He *is* the one who used to own all those shops, it turns out. Did you read Mavis's texts last night?'

'Yeah, I did…and I know that's why we're meeting here at your place today, but…'

'What's happened, Annie? Are you feeling alright? You don't look…right to me. It's been a couple of weeks since all those heavy-duty antibiotics you had to take because of when you ended up with that nasty gash – and I know you had all that business after them, well, because of them, you know…'

Annie snapped, 'Can we not talk about that, please?'

Carol nodded. 'Of course. Totally understand. That sort of thing's always unpleasant. Anyway, what I meant was – all that's behind you now, so what's up?'

'Just a hot flash. A big one. But that's not the problem. Well, it is, and it isn't, if you see what I mean.'

Carol put the kettle on, and dumped the custard tarts onto two plates, 'No I don't, so just tell me, Annie.'

'It's flamin' "Dan, Dan, the Decorating Man" – it's true, it's on his van, I swear. He's managed to lose fourteen rolls of wallpaper and a gallon of paint. I put the whole lot of it into the main bedroom myself. You know that – I told you I'd done it, didn't I?' Carol nodded as she rinsed out the teapot. 'Well, it's all gone. Nowhere to be found. That Dan had me thinking I was losing me marbles, Car, but I did put it there, and it's not there now. So where's it got to? You tell me.'

Carol shrugged and smiled warmly at her chum. 'You know what you need? You need a professional enquiry agent, you do.' She winked.

Annie felt a smile spread across her face. 'The Case of the Disappearing Decorating Supplies, you mean?'

'There you go, we'll get right on it, once we've got a cup of tea inside us, alright?'

CHAPTER SIX

Mavis and Althea were sitting opposite a cowed-looking Edward in the sitting room of the Dower House. Mavis had her pen poised above her notepad.

She began, 'Now that we've agreed we'll look into this situation, Edward, I need information. So, please, speak freely, and tell us everything you know. As I've said, you've no need to worry about paying us to help, we're only too happy to do it for a friend, which is how you must consider yourself at this time. No longer a butler, but a friend, who needs help.'

Edward's expression suggested to Mavis that he was still feeling dreadfully uncomfortable, despite his having already consumed two slices of seed cake at Althea's urging. Then she noticed a change in him: his shoulders unhunched, his chin came up, and he looked her straight in the eye.

He nodded. 'Very well, I shall, though it's not something I'm used to doing. Not just sitting here, like this with you, Your...Althea.' He smiled wanly. 'I mean asking for help at all. My father raised me to be self-sufficient in every way. But he also taught me how critical it is to use the right person for the job, so I'll take your offer of your professional abilities in that spirit. Thank you. So...where do I begin?'

Mavis suppressed a tut. 'What about a bit of background on you and your brother?'

Edward nodded feebly. 'Two boys, eight years apart in age – me the older one, of course – and raised not far from here, in Weobley. My father was in service to a retired colonel there. As you know, Your...Althea...I came to Chellingworth Hall to serve the late duke's needs almost forty years ago; I was honored that he chose to retain me when I was such a young man.'

Althea nodded. 'You came highly recommended, and have never, ever let us down, Edward. Thank you. Do I recall correctly that your brother also went into service?'

Edward replied in what Mavis judged to be a strained tone. 'He did, though neither my father nor I believed he was suited to the role. As was proved to be the case a few years later when an…unfortunate incident…led to Richard having to leave the household where he had been engaged as an under-butler. The butler in charge of his training suggested that Richard should find another line of employment.'

Mavis asked, 'And to what area of endeavor did your brother apply his efforts?'

Edward smiled, which shocked Mavis – she was unsure if she'd ever seen such an expression on his face before that moment. 'The irony is that Richard, together with his business partner – one Jon Dacre, originally from Northamptonshire – set up a company called Buttle My World, to train butlers, and other staff, for families and households who need what they were wont to term "a better class of staff". He said he used everything he'd learned from our father, and added on the opposite of everything the butler who'd trained him had done. The company is extremely successful, I believe. He met Rachel, his wife, when she joined their training staff. She had been a butler working in government posts, around the world, and relocated back to the UK. They were married a little less than ten years ago.'

Mavis dared, 'Now you mentioned that you don't know your sister-in-law well, due to you and your late brother having "lost contact" with each other. Could you maybe tell us more about that?'

Mavis noticed Althea sit forward in her seat, and could see she had a telltale gleam in her eye; she hoped that the dowager's obvious excitement wouldn't stop Edward from being as forthcoming as she needed him to be. She dared a swift glare in Althea's direction, but was studiously ignored as Althea innocently sipped her tea, dimpling.

'We fell out about Rachel, as it happens.' Edward's tone was leaden. 'She's a good bit younger than Richard – still only in her early forties now – and Richard and she had discussed the idea of having children when they became married, as one might expect. Anyway, Richard told me that Rachel had said she was quite keen on the idea, but that he was not.'

'Differences of opinion have been known to happen,' noted Althea.

Edward nodded. 'Indeed. In fact, he was dead set against it, to be blunt – but he told me he wasn't going to make this clear to her until after they married. I thought that was the worst sort of underhand thing to do to a woman, and I told him so. He said it was none of my business, but I…well, I did what I thought best, and spoke to Rachel about what my brother had said. He never spoke to me again. I was removed from the guest list for their wedding. They married, they have no issue, she's devastated by his death…so it seems that her love for him was stronger than her desire for children. But Richard and I had both burned our bridges. Things were said. And that was that.'

Mavis scribbled notes and pondered the matter – yes, that would do it…a relationship-ending situation right there. Had Edward acted correctly? Mavis was pleased that wasn't her decision to make, so pressed on. 'And now tell us what you know about his death – which I realize might be difficult, but that's what we need to focus on for the moment.'

Athea settled back into her seat, and McFli sat up, because she had popped a third piece of seed cake onto her plate; Mavis knew the woman would spoil her lunch, but reminded herself she was an adult, after all.

Edward cleared his throat. 'I got a phone call from Rachel, that's how I found out my brother was dead. There wouldn't be anyone else who would tell me; our parents are long gone, and we were the only children. Not even any cousins.'

'And when was this?' Mavis wanted her notes to be comprehensive.

Edward gave the matter some thought. 'Two weeks ago. That's when he died.'

Even as he said the words, Mavis noticed that the poor man's face grew pale.

Edward cleared his throat. Mavis could tell he was steeling himself.

'She phoned early,' he continued. 'Got me out of bed, in fact. I didn't quite know who was calling at five in the morning. It gives a person a real jolt when someone phones at that time, doesn't it?'

Mavis and Althea agreed with the man.

'She told me he was dead, and how and when it had happened, and right away she asks if I can come down to see her.' He paused, nodded at Mavis's notepad, and added, 'Buttle My World has offices in Earl's Court – an address that Richard and Jon believed said all the right things about their nature of staff offering – and he and Rachel bought their flat in Ealing some years back. Richard had sold his little flat in much the same area before they married, and Rachel had a bit of savings to put into the pot.'

Mavis thanked Edward, 'It's always good to have proper information. Might I ask for your sister-in-law's full name?'

'She took my brother's when they married, so she's Rachel Edwards.'

Mavis couldn't help but grin; she realized she'd never known Edward's family name. 'So you're Edward Edwards?'

Edward smiled. 'Not so unusual for Wales.'

Mavis nodded, and reminded herself of the Donald McDonald she'd known as a child. And the Patrick Fitzpatrick.

Edward continued, 'I spoke to Her Grace, the duchess, about me being able to take a couple of days off, and she kindly agreed.'

Mavis spotted that Althea was pulling tiny bits off her slice of cake and dropping them for McFli to grab; she considered kicking the dowager's ankle beneath the table, but suspected it would do no good. Doing her best to ignore the snuffling and truffling at her feet, Mavis leaned forward and asked, 'And is that when Rachel told you that she believed your brother's death to not, in fact, have been an accident? That is the official line – am I correct?'

Edward nodded eagerly. 'Indeed. This is what Rachel told me – though it took her hours, because she was terribly upset.'

'As one might imagine,' noted Althea.

Edward nodded. 'Indeed. The company had just secured a significant contract to train the butlers for a small chain of luxury hotels in Dubai, Qatar, and Oman; Richard and Jon had both been pursuing the business for some time, it seems.'

'A great achievement,' said Althea, smiling.

'Quite. A dinner was arranged to allow the whole team to celebrate the win together, and Richard himself had booked the venue. It was planned for early in the evening. The people at the company have to work some unsocial hours when they are meeting clients and so forth, you see?'

Mavis nodded. She could imagine.

'About six months ago, Richard suffered a terrible bout of food poisoning: he'd been overseas, in Thailand, when it happened, and Rachel told me he came back weighing about a stone less than when he'd gone out there. I didn't see him, of course, but Richard was always a skinny boy, and a wiry man, so I can't imagine he'd have had a spare stone on him to lose, and Rachel said the episode left him weakened. He gradually regained his energy, but a take-away Chinese meal they had at home one night sent him to the hospital. They diagnosed an allergy to some sort of fish sauce in the dish. Further investigation allowed that to be narrowed down to Richard being severely allergic to mollusks. Not crustaceans, which is an important distinction. His reaction was so severe that, thereafter, he always had one of those pens with him that you use if you're suffering from anaphylaxis…his throat and airways all swelled up, you see and…well, that's what got him, in the end. But – and this was Rachel's main point, you see – his pen thing should have saved him, but it didn't, because no one could find it. When he was…dead, someone found his pen on the floor near his jacket, which he wasn't wearing at the time, because it was a humid evening.'

'An epinephrine pen,' said Mavis, writing rapidly. 'They really are lifesavers, if you can use them, as you say. Now, tell me, do they know yet what it was that he reacted to? Did he choose his own food? Was he being careful about his choices? Was he knowledgeable about his condition?'

Edward nodded. 'I asked much the same questions of Rachel. She told me that Richard fully understood the challenges he faced, undertook detailed and thorough research into his condition.'

'Good for him,' said Mavis. 'Taking responsibility.'

Edward nodded. 'Typical of Richard, to be fair. He made himself as knowledgeable as possible about what he should avoid. She said he always erred on the side of caution: avoided any place that offered mollusks at all, if he could; always explained his allergy to servers and – if possible or necessary – to chefs, too; he would often eat vegetarian or even vegan dishes at restaurants, to avoid any possible issues with cross-contamination; he never ate food at banquets, buffets, or the like, where he couldn't be certain of the ingredients. She said they both learned a great deal more than either of them had ever hoped to know about mollusks, and even about the ways in which mollusks are used in stocks and sauces as ingredients you cannot taste, but which are there for various other culinary reasons.'

'That must have been terribly difficult for your brother,' said Althea quietly. 'I expect I would live on cake if that were to happen to me – they can't possibly use mollusks in cake, can they? Not for any reason.'

Mavis sighed, but didn't think Althea's observation deserved any acknowledgement. 'Did Rachel know anything about what Richard had eaten at the dinner in question? Have there been any insights since?'

Edward grabbed his chin and rubbed it. Hard. 'See, that's the thing. She'd asked Jon Dacre – the other chap in charge of the company, with Richard – what had happened that evening. She wasn't there, herself. Did I tell you that? Sorry. She had a nasty summer cold – still had it when I saw her…so she didn't go. Was supposed to, but they agreed she'd be better off staying at home, not spreading her germs about.'

'Very sensible,' observed Althea.

Edward agreed. 'Jon told her that Richard chose his own meal – a chilled vegetarian soup followed by vegetarian lasagna, apparently…so a "safe" meal…and he said that everything was fine until the desserts were served. That was a raspberry and meringue confection. At the time, that was all Rachel knew.'

'The ingredients were checked with those preparing the food, in the kitchen, I dare say?' Mavis assumed such questions would have been asked.

Edward nodded. 'Jon told Rachel that the chef swore there wasn't anything containing mollusks used in any of the items Richard had eaten, and they happened to not even have any mollusks on the premises for any reason at all that evening – though they had been through the kitchen the previous day, when *linguine con vongole* had been on the menu. Rachel happens to know the chef in question and says she trusts him. It's a good kitchen, she says, which means clean.'

'And there'll have been a post-mortem?' Mavis was finally getting to the nitty gritty.

'No.'

Mavis noted that even Althea looked surprised. 'Really? You mean there won't be one – or there hasn't been one yet?'

'The latter. It seems…it seems there's a bit of a queue on that front. You might have seen the news about that tragic bus accident? Pensioners on a trip to Longleat Park. Dreadful. It happened in the same…um…medical area of responsibility. The post-mortem might be next week. Or even the week after.'

Mavis nodded. She was only too well aware of the pressures on the health system. 'So, failing that, what did the attending medical professionals say when they found him?'

'I understand, via Jon and Rachel, that they confirmed that Richard had all the signs of having died of acute anaphylactic shock. I believe they took samples of the dessert that he'd been eating at the time, the other courses having been cleared away and therefore not available to them. But – again – there's no more news about that.'

'So now we come to it, Edward – why does Rachel think your brother was murdered?' Once again, Mavis was irritated by Althea's twinkling eyes across the table.

Edward sighed. 'She was all over the place when I got to Ealing – terribly distressed, as I mentioned. Hardly stopped crying the whole time I was there – I could even hear her through the walls, all night.'

'How dreadful for her, but quite understandable,' whispered Althea.

Edward nodded solemnly. 'Anyway, she didn't tell me this until breakfast time on the day I was leaving. Cornflakes and an accusation of murder – not the best way to start the day, let me tell you.'

'I should say not.' Althea sounded sympathetic.

Edward sagged, 'Rachel – in a nutshell – reckons that it's all about the company. You see, Jon Dacre and my brother used everything they had to set it up – at least, Richard did. I know for a fact he remortgaged the little flat he owned at the time and used all his credit cards to get the business up and running. They made their money back, of course, and many times beyond, I understand, but I always got the impression that Richard was the one who put most of the effort into it all, while Jon just fronted it. He had the name, you see. The Dacre family goes back a long way, and he's got one of those cut-glass accents, too. Richard was the one with the knowledge of buttling, whereas Jon had the contacts. Richard was the one who trained the recruits, while Jon wined and dined the potential clients. I suppose it worked well enough, but – gradually – Richard began to feel he was getting…well, the fuzzy end of the lollipop, I suppose you could say. Flying off all over the world to work sounds glamorous, but it isn't – it's still work. The farthest Jon had to go was to the private clubs in London, or various households around the UK. Richard did all the international stuff, when it was needed. And then there's the will, you see. Rachel said there was an agreement between the two men that each would write a will leaving their half of the business to the other, in the event of their death. So Jon would have known that, if Richard were to die, he'd end up owning the whole thing. And, like I said, it's a successful business…and getting more so all the time: they have an excellent reputation, and the demand for buttling, and providing services for wealthy households, as well as well-established families, is increasing around the globe.'

Mavis was puzzled. 'So Rachel thinks that your brother's business partner killed him – somehow – in order to inherit Richard's share of the business?'

Edward nodded.

Mavis took a moment, working out how best to make her point.

Eventually she spoke gently, 'I can't help but think that's a bit of a stretch…but you mentioned that Rachel feels that she herself is now in danger, too. Why on earth would she think that's the case?'

'Because my brother never did write a will, which means that everything automatically goes to her. She mentioned this to Jon before I got there, when he visited her to pay his condolences. That's when he told her about the agreement between the two men; he was telling her he'd be keeping her on, you see? Anyway, she told him she knew for a fact that Richard hadn't written a will, because they'd been talking about that very thing quite recently, and Richard admitted he'd never got around to writing one. Rachel said that Jon went quiet when she told him, then he went pink, then he went off in a huff, saying that it was "unfortunate" that Richard hadn't kept his word, and that she should take good care of herself. She took that as a threat. Apparently, she's never been terribly keen on Jon Dacre, and worked for the company in spite of him.'

Althea mused gleefully, 'He probably smashed up some shells and sprinkled them onto your poor brother's food, Edward. He sounds like a horrid little man. I used to know some Dacres – they were no better than they should be, the mother, especially, but she was a dancer, like me, so I suppose one shouldn't be surprised. She didn't snag a duke, like I did, though. Got stuck with a banker, who turned out to be incredibly boring and desperate to have a large family. I saw her ten years after they'd married, and she had six children. No figure left to speak of, of course, and quite a doleful expression. I don't see any reason why they should be the same Dacres, but you mentioning the name made me remember her. I wonder what became of her. Milly Dacre, Milly…something, as was. No, it's gone. She was quite wild, until she wasn't. It sounds as though it's a murder for profit. You should bring your sister-in-law to stay here – or even at the Hall, where you can keep an eye on her, Edward. Tell Henry I said so. No, don't bother, I'll tell him myself. Go and give her a ring now. I'll get Ian to drive to collect her.'

Mavis was quite taken aback, as was Edward – if the expression on his usually expressionless face was anything to go by.

She said, 'That's all well and good, Althea, dear, but I think you might be jumping the gun a wee bit.'

She could tell that Althea was about to interrupt, but didn't give her a chance.

'No – now hear me out. There's nothing in what Edward's told us that goes beyond...well, to be honest, bad feelings, grief, and the suspicions that might arise within a widow's mind at such a time. So let's hold our horses, shall we? I dare say Edward feels that would be a step too far, at this stage, too – don't you, Edward?'

Mavis was surprised by his answer. 'To be honest, no, I don't. You see, Rachel's all on her own. Got no family except me. And I've felt dreadful thinking about her struggling on alone...which is why I've been a bit...distracted. If she were here, where I could be certain she was safe – as you said – I feel I'd be much better able to focus on my duties. If...if it wouldn't be too much trouble.'

'No trouble at all, Edward,' gushed the dowager. 'You can choose a room for her. Pick a nice one, and make sure it's convenient for her and you. You get that sorted, I'll tell my son what's happening. See, Mavis? Sometimes I can be helpful.' Althea beamed, her dimples fairly glowing in the lamplight.

'Aye, you can,' said Mavis, while she wondered how Henry and Stephanie would react to Althea's plan.

14th JULY

CHAPTER SEVEN

Carol Hill stared at her almost empty coffee mug; she reckoned the beans she'd used that morning must have been defective, because she wasn't feeling any perkier than she had been when she'd ground them. Hoping the third mug would be the charm, she poured it out, settled into her seat at the kitchen table, and continued scrolling on her screen. Bunty, her calico cat, leaped onto her lap, leaving her spot beside the Aga unguarded.

'You'll find it less unpleasant today, Bunty,' mused Carol quietly. 'It's not raining, and they said it'll be dry for a while…and, hopefully, not too hot. A few days of weather when I'm not sweaty, or drenched by the rain, would be nice.'

'Couldn't agree more.'

Carol looked up to see her husband standing, tousle-haired, in the doorway. Albert was in his arms, wriggling to escape…and that was the end of Carol's chance for any sort of peaceful moments that day. She smiled and stood, holding out her arms for her son, who grabbed at his mother with delight.

'When are you off?' She knew that David had to go into Brecon to meet a client that morning, but couldn't for the life of her remember at what time.

'No need to rush. I haven't got to be there until ten. Coffee date, don't you know? Some fancy place that probably grinds the wheat to make the flour they use in their over-priced buns. I can't believe how many of those little places are popping up these days. Haven't people got something better to spend their money on?'

'It's the tourists – they don't want the old-fashioned, greasy spoon caffs these days, they want gluten free this and decaf that, topped with dairy free whatever.'

'Millennials, eh?' David chuckled.

The couple laughed at their own generation, knowing neither of them felt any affinity at all for the stereotypes.

'Decaf coffee?' Carol scoffed. 'Waste of effort drinking it…and a waste of perfectly good coffee beans in the first place, if you ask me. Caffeine? Bring it on.'

'Speaking of which,' said her husband with a cheeky wink, 'any chance of some for me? I know you've been up for hours, but this one's been bouncing on me all that time. Not exactly the lie-in I'd hoped for.'

'In the pot,' said Carol, kissing Albert's perfect cheeks and grinning at him with delight. 'He's looking well rested – so that makes one of us. What I wouldn't give for some of his energy.'

David stirred sugar into his coffee. 'Come on, love, you're only in your mid-thirties…and I'm not even worried about the Big Four-O yet…though I have got some good ideas percolating about a party. I thought we might rent a place, somewhere quiet, with lots of bedrooms – invite a few old friends for a weekend.'

Carol laughed. 'That's not until next year…why are you thinking about it now?'

'You know what it's like, trying to get away. The people I'd want to invite have got kids, too, so they'll have to plan ahead. Mainly pre-school, like Albert, but there are a couple with kids older than him, so we'll have to think about school holidays, too. Work around that. And I bet all the good places are booked up yonks in advance, so…you know. Planning. Critical path analysis. Getting our ducks in a row. We're both expert at it for others – we should do it for ourselves, for once. Make a plan. Stick to it.'

Carol sighed. She hadn't been expecting this conversation. 'I didn't know you wanted a big do…so you're right, not something here, in the garden, then. I know May can be a tricky month for the weather – so maybe something where we could have a crowd of us indoors, if needs be? How many people were you thinking of inviting?' She suspected her tone hadn't been as accepting of his idea as she'd meant it to sound, and hoped he hadn't noticed.

David sipped his steaming mug. 'Well, a few of the blokes I used to work with at our old company: Sam, Mike, Sanjit, and Sunny, of course. They're all married with kids, now. But it's Eric and Bernie I was thinking of…they've got kids in school. Bernie's eldest is ten now, if you can believe that. When are there holidays around May? I've got no idea, to be honest with you.'

'I'll look it up. Are they still living in Islington?' David nodded. 'Okay, I'll check their dates, because I think different areas might have slightly different dates.' Carol smiled. 'It's funny to think it won't be long before all that sort of stuff is what rules our lives, eh?'

'Not long enough,' replied David, looking down at his son with a warm smile. 'And there's nursery even before proper school. Have you had any more thoughts about that? You know, about him starting somewhere…like when, and where?'

Carol stood. 'No. He's far too young to be thinking about nursery school, or kindergarten, or whatever they're calling it now. And we're coping alright, aren't we? I know there's the odd occasion when the juggling gets a bit too much for the pair of us, but we cope. And every moment with him is precious. I'm sure it's good for him to be with one of us, for as long as we can manage that.'

She didn't want the conversation to go any further – she never did. 'Now, I'm going to hit the shower while you have him for a bit, then I can take over when you get ready and go out. I'm working here today, and I've got a video meeting with Annie and Christine at ten myself, so we can compare notes for me to pass to Mavis, who's getting stuck into some charity stuff with Althea today…so let's get cracking, eh?'

The pair kissed, and Carol headed upstairs while David did his best to stop Albert from toddling after her.

By the time ten o'clock rolled around, Carol was at her desk in what should have been the dining room in the generously proportioned Georgian house they rented from the Chellingworth Estate.

The lovely house stood overlooking the green at the heart of Anwen-by-Wye, and she adored it. She was as ready for her meeting as possible, and was looking forward to sharing what she'd learned about the agency's new client, Walter Gulliver.

Annie and Christine appeared on her screen at the appointed hour, each sitting at their own desk at the office. Carol was always grateful to be able to work at home; it saved a drive, but – more than that – it saved hauling an ever-growing amount of 'stuff' that had to accompany her son when they left home to go anywhere, it seemed. Albert was on a play-mat in the room she was using, and there was a newly installed gate across the doorway. Since he'd started walking, she and David had installed gates wherever they could; in just a few weeks he'd gone from taking his first tentative steps to being almost uncatchable, which had surprised them both.

With Annie at the top left and Christine at the top right of her screen, Carol made the picture of herself as small as possible. She hated staring at her moon face and unruly curls when she talked, much preferring to watch how her colleagues reacted to what she was saying.

'Who wants to go first?' Annie opened.

'I can, if you like,' offered Carol. Christine agreed. 'I've written up my notes, and I'll add what you two have gathered before I pass everything on to Mavis. It's been confirmed that Walter Gulliver is, in fact, *the* Walter Gulliver, of Gulliver Groceries, and I know we all know of his shops, but the first link I'm sharing is that of the corporate website – the history section. That's where there's a good bit of insight into how Walter began his career and built his empire.'

'Nutshell it for us, will you, doll?'

Carol grinned. 'Is "nutshelling" a thing, Annie?'

'It is now. And you know what I mean.' Annie poked out her tongue.

Carol smiled. 'Okay then – in a nutshell – Walter was living on a farm in Lincolnshire, after the war, and we all know that Lincolnshire is renowned for growing a great deal of the UK's vegetables, right?'

'If you say so, Car.' Annie waggled a hand at the screen.

Carol sighed. 'Okay – according to my research, Lincolnshire produces most of the UK's food, and processes about seventy percent of its fish. It's always been an area full of arable farms since back in Roman times, so – yes – Walter was surrounded by veggies, and he ended up working in a greengrocer's shop…which he took over when the bloke who owned it retired.'

'Makes sense,' noted Annie.

'Eventually he opened another, and another, and the thing grew like topsy. He knew the farmers, he knew the customers – and eventually he knew the potential investors, and ended up with what we all know as Gulliver Groceries. There was one in every high street, and they cornered the middle income, middle price-range food market across the country. He sold up just over five years ago and pocketed about two hundred and forty million, if the various accounts I've found online are correct.'

'You said all this when we found out about him, Car,' whined Annie.

'Nothing wrong with confirming facts,' replied Christine tartly.

Carol was surprised that Christine had commented at all, because she'd wondered if she was even listening, she looked so glassy-eyed.

She said, 'Thanks for that, Christine, and, yes, you're right. As I said, that's the company website. Now for the man himself: born in London, parents were Deborah and William Gulliver. I found a few bits about them – other than official records – in the pre-war local papers, because both parents belonged to a local church choir, which used to go out into the streets to sing. The parents were soloists, it seems. But…moving on…I can't find anything at all in any database I can access remotely about Walter and his brother Timothy being evacuees. That's not to say the records don't exist, however. Some records are only accessible in person, especially if the evacuee is still living, which, of course, he is. However, it's clear from my initial digging that the records kept at the time were "imperfect" to say the least.'

'Not really surprising,' piped up Annie. 'I found out – and I'm absolutely gobsmacked by this – that they shifted one and a half million kids in three days. Three days! From September first to September third 1939 they managed to shunt all that lot around the country. Can you imagine what that must have been like?'

Carol admitted she couldn't.

Annie continued, 'The Imperial War Museum's got some brilliant stuff about it all online that I found.'

Annie paused, 'No, that came out wrong. They were such sad stories, a lot of them. I'm not a mother, but even I think it must have been terrible for them, just waving off their kids at a railway station, or even at the end of their road, like that. The photos? Oh my word – tiny kids with little suitcases and labels with their names on them pinned to their coats, in case they got lost. I mean…could you have done that, Car? Sent Bertie off like that? Some were only the age he is now.'

Carol chuckled wryly. 'I don't even like the idea of him having to go to nursery school in a year or so, let alone packing him off to an unknown location. But, there…I also cannot wrap my head around what mothers – and fathers – must have been feeling at the time. War had been declared, and I dare say they wanted their children to be safe…so off to the countryside with them it was.'

'Do we definitely know that's when he left London? Walter, I mean?' Christine sounded almost interested.

'It's what Mavis was told by Rhodri Lloyd,' replied Carol, 'though, when she interviews Mr Gulliver, we can confirm it – and find out more about what he might have already done to discover where he was sent. She's off to see him in Herefordshire tomorrow, isn't she?' Annie and Christine nodded.

'Anything else, Annie?' Carol hoped there was.

'Yes, one odd thing,' said Annie. 'I discovered in my research that Brecknockshire, where the Gullivers were evacuated to, was on the list of places they sent kids, but Lincolnshire was, as well. I wondered why the Gulliver parents didn't just send their sons directly to the part of the family out there that they eventually ended up going to after the war. You know – in the first place, like. I mean, wouldn't that make more sense? Sending them to family, rather than to strangers.'

Carol typed a note. 'Good point. I'll mention that to Mavis – she can follow it up with the client. Anything else?'

Annie nodded across the office. 'Chrissy was looking into farms and stuff at this end, weren't you, doll?'

Christine looked down at something in front of her. 'Yes. Brecknockshire took in evacuees, and there were many dozens of farms at the time. Large and small. It's going to be difficult.'

Carol was not impressed. 'That's it? "There were loads of farms"? I think we could have guessed that, Christine. Couldn't you find out anything else?'

Christine looked grim. 'I know we could have guessed it, but I spent hours online going down blind alleys and rabbit holes just to confirm that was, in fact, the case. Believe it or not, there aren't any maps from the war years showing who owned what land where, nor if they had any evacuees billeted to them. A terrible oversight on the part of the government of the day, no doubt, but maybe they had a few other things to deal with at the time? I dare say there might be secret maps, somewhere, that show exactly how much food, of what type, they were expecting to get from exactly what acreages in the area. I'm sure that some department or other was all over that, because they needed to make plans to feed the population – but I couldn't find them. You're welcome to look. But, honestly, I don't see how even knowing such a thing would help us work out where this bloke was living as a child. If you want my opinion, what we need to do is find a person – an actual human being – who knew the area at the time, and ask them about it. Someone might recall where certain kids were…or what about the school system of the day? Wouldn't they have records?'

'I checked on that,' said Carol, 'and the problem there is that the schools were run quite differently back then. The authorities that oversaw them have shifted and changed so much that it's almost impossible to track down such records. If you know a child went to a certain school, then you can make headway, but without a school name, there's nowhere to even begin – and it's another question I've listed for Mavis.'

'Haven't got far, have we?' Annie sounded glum.

'It's early days, and we can hope that Mavis can find out some facts that'll help us, right? Let's not get downhearted at the beginning of this, eh?' Carol did her best sweet smile, which wasn't lost on Annie.

'You're right, doll – a long way to go yet.'

CHAPTER EIGHT

It was such a lovely day, after all the rain, that Annie walked back from the office to the village. When she got there, she peered into the front entrance of the Coach and Horses to check that the coast was clear. She'd done a fair amount of report writing before she'd left the office, and had hoped to catch Wes, Angelo, and Dan while they were having their lunch break; she'd spotted that they'd all stop at about noon every day. Wes brought his own sandwiches – home-made; Angelo usually had a box full of leftovers; Dan would run across to the Lamb and Flag where he'd often get a pie and a sausage roll – and sometimes a scotch egg too – from Tudor at the bar. Tudor had confirmed he never had a drink when he stopped in.

She was delighted to find all three men deep in conversation about something scandalous that had happened within the Welsh Rugby Union, which seemed to revolve around an unfathomable rule about something or other, from what she overheard.

Cheerily shouting, 'Just got to measure the windows in the spare bedroom,' she mounted the stairs as fast as she could, then darted into every room. Definitely no paint or wallpaper, anywhere, but the kitchen did seem to be making progress: the walls were clean and ready for patching and painting, and the cupboards were all back where they should be, their old hardware finally removed. She felt a wave of relief wash over her, then headed into the bathroom.

Oh yes, that tile choice for the floor had been the right one, and for the base of the shower, too. But she'd seen them deliver the toilet that morning, and now it wasn't anywhere to be seen. Hoping it just hadn't made its way upstairs yet, Annie descended to the bar.

'Looking lovely up there, isn't it?' Dan sounded chipper.

'Oi – not too bad down here, either, right?' Wes puffed out his chest.

Annie glanced at the wall above the massive hearth; it certainly looked a great deal better than it had – the surface was smooth and ready to be whitewashed, she reckoned.

'Yes, it's coming along a treat down here, thank you, Wes. And Dan – I can see you've really got a lot done, thanks for that too. And that tiling in the bathroom looks smashing, Angelo. Ta. Is the toilet they delivered this morning still down here, somewhere? I couldn't see it upstairs.'

Angelo wiped his lips with the back of his hand. 'I haven't seen it. I thought it hadn't come yet. They haven't left it out the back, have they?'

Annie shrugged. 'I was looking out of my front window this morning – across the green – and I saw a bloke carry our toilet through the front door. Your van was here, Dan – you must have seen or heard something.'

Dan looked confused. 'Yeah, I was in early – wanted to get going, you know? – but I didn't hear anyone come in, and no one came to tell me about a toilet. What time did you see them?'

'About half seven.' Annie had looked at the bedside clock at the time because she'd been afraid she'd overslept: seeing someone carrying a toilet into the pub had thrown her, and there'd been Joan Pike pushing her mother around the green in her wheelchair, too. Joan didn't usually do that until later in the day…which was why Annie had panicked, and checked the clock.

She stared daggers at Wes, who shrugged. 'I got here at eight, as usual. Don't look at me. I haven't seen any toilets about the place, and I think I'd have noticed one just sitting in a corner. I came in the back way, and it wasn't there, then.'

Annie crossed the bar and pulled open the door to the yard at the back of the pub. There wasn't a toilet lurking anywhere. 'So where the devil is it?' She knew she was talking to herself, but didn't care.

'Maybe you should phone whoever was supposed to deliver it?' Angelo was trying to get the lid back onto his plastic lunchbox. 'Maybe they couldn't get Dan to hear them if they shouted out, so took it away again. Wouldn't they have wanted someone to sign for it?'

Annie nodded. 'Yes, good thinking, Angelo, I bet they would have done. I'll phone them when I get their paperwork out of the pile back at the Lamb. Keep up the good work then – right-o, I'm off.'

As she crossed the green toward the Lamb and Flag, Annie knew in her heart that the toilet had been delivered and that someone had swiped it. But who would want to steal a toilet? It wasn't something you could take to another pub in another village to flog, was it? Maybe wallpaper and paint, but not a toilet, surely?

Tudor was behind the bar looking a bit flustered when she arrived.

'Small G and T, please, Tude. Heavy on the T.' She didn't usually have a drink at lunchtime, but felt she wanted one now. 'And I'll have a pie, if you've got one. Just a pie – don't bother with any chips, I'll have it on its own. Ta.' She leaned across the bar and pecked him on the cheek he was offering.

'I needed that,' he said, smiling. 'But what's got you ordering a drink at this time of day? That Dan still not making enough progress at the Coach?'

Annie took the glass from the bar and sipped. 'Lovely, Tude, ta. No – he's got a lot done, to be fair. But the toilet's gone.'

Tudor hesitated as he was heading for the kitchen. 'What do you mean, "the toilet's gone"? The toilet you said they'd delivered this morning? The new one?'

Annie nodded. 'Yeah, the old one went in the skip. The new one? Nowhere to be found. That's fourteen rolls of wallpaper, a gallon of paint, *and* a toilet, now. All gone.'

'Let me warm up that pie you want, and I'll be back,' said Tudor, disappearing from sight.

Annie stared at her drink, wishing the bubbles that burst on its surface could fizz away her irritation.

When Tudor returned from the kitchen, he wiped his hands and said, 'Just a few minutes. Now look – what do you want to do about this? It's not right, and it's obviously causing you concern. I had no idea there'd be all this sort of thing to have to keep an eye on. I mean, you'd think that people would do the job they've been paid to do, wouldn't you? Delivery people deliver stuff, don't they?'

Annie sighed. 'I'll take this drink and that pie upstairs, and I'll dig out the phone number for the toilet people.'

She chuckled. 'You know what I mean. Just to make sure they didn't take it away with them, after all. If they didn't…well, I don't know what to do. Have a bit of a think, I suppose. But, don't panic, Tude, the kitchen's ready to go and the pub is coming along, despite how I've been going on and on about Wes being slow. The bathroom's looking good – except for the big hole in the tiles where there's supposed to be a toilet, of course. And the kitchen and the living room should be done, if only Dan can maintain the effort he's obviously put in since I saw him last. So – we'll get there. At least, I'll be doing my best to make sure we get in on time. But I have got a few more bits to do for the agency, and maybe we can take Gert and Rosie out for a walk when Aled gets here? He's doing three till eleven today, right?'

Tudor nodded. 'He is – and us popping out about half three should be good. It'll be as dead as a doornail in here then, so we can properly relax, knowing he'll be here if someone decides to pop in. These past couple of days the rain's been a nightmare. Maybe now that it's forecast to be good for a few days people will venture out again. We could do with the business, Annie…though I know that's not really my problem any longer. We've just got to nurse this place along until we move to the bigger place – then it'll be all hands to the pumps, no doubt.'

A pinging noise from the kitchen distracted him. 'That'll be your pie. Shall I bring it up for you? I don't like the idea of you going up those stairs with both hands full…you know what you're like.' He winked.

'Oi, you – if you're going to make fun of me, then pick something other than my clumsiness, will you? You know I'm still not right after my recent encounter in a graveyard…so let's be having less of that. And, yeah – you're right, I shouldn't risk it. One thing I won't miss about this place is them stairs – tiny they are…not designed for people with proper-sized plates, like mine.'

'I've heard you refer to your feet as flippers yourself, on many an occasion, so I'm not touching that one with a bargepole,' said Tudor. 'Go on, I'll be up in a minute.'

When Annie reached the top of the stairs and opened the door, Gertie and Rosie jumped up at her, their tails wagging.

She managed to get past them to put down her drink, then bent to pet them both, and snuggled her face into Gertie's velvety ears, which lifted her spirits immediately.

By the time she was settled at the table with her pie and her drink, both dogs had positioned themselves at her feet. The table had become a dumping ground for the mass of paperwork and files that were connected to the renovations at the Coach and Horses, so Annie looked at the steam coming from the pie, thought better of biting into it for a while, and started rummaging, until she found what she was looking for.

When she got through to the bathroom supplies shop, she held on until she could speak to someone in authority.

'To whom am I speaking, please?' She'd learned that tone from Althea – it always worked.

'My name's Jones, the store manager. You wanted to speak to me. How can I help?'

'You delivered a toilet to the Coach and Horses pub in Anwen-by-Wye this morning.'

'We did? Let me check my records. I hope there's no problem. Yes, here we are – am I speaking to Annie Parker?'

'You are.'

'Right. Yes. The model you ordered was delivered this morning. As I said, I hope there's no problem. It was in good condition when you signed for it.'

Annie hesitated. 'When I what?'

'I'm looking at the sheet here. Signature's just a squiggle, but it's there. Time was seven forty-three this morning.'

'That's not what happened, Mr Jones. I wasn't even at the Coach and Horses at that time. Are you able to speak to the person who delivered the toilet?'

There was a pause then: 'Hang on.' Annie heard a muffled shout. 'He's here right now. Let me ask him.' More muffled chatter. 'Yes, he says you signed for it, having inspected it.'

Annie sighed. 'Can he describe me?'

'Pardon?'

'Ask the delivery driver to describe me to you, please.'

Muffled words.

'He says you're about five foot two, in your thirties, with blonde hair, and you both talked in Welsh.'

Annie shook her head. 'Mr Jones, I'm six feet tall, and a real living, breathing Cockney who doesn't speak Welsh at all. Oh, and I'm Black. I think we have a problem, because whoever signed for that toilet, she wasn't Annie Parker.'

All she heard was: 'Oh heck…is there any chance you could pop in?'

'I'll be there as soon as I can get a lift.' Annie hung up. She didn't think that a pie would have the power to make her feel better, and wished she'd asked Tudor for a large gin, not a diluted one.

CHAPTER NINE

Alexander ended the call with his fiancée and looked across his office toward where Bill Coggins usually sat. Bill's chair was unoccupied, because he'd gone out that afternoon to do a valuation of a collection of 1960s and '70s designer clothing that might come through the auction house, if the woman who was thinking of selling it decided they'd do a good job for her. Both Bill and he knew the company didn't have a reputation for that sort of thing, but they both accepted that they had to move with the times and, these days, there was money to be made in all sorts of goods from the middle of the twentieth century, even if they both preferred dealing with items that were centuries older.

At that moment, with Christine's snippy farewell still making his heart ache, he wished his colleague was there. Bill and his wife, Nat, had become quite good pals with Alexander and Christine, and he'd have been tempted to ask Bill if he'd mind Alexander inviting Nat out for a coffee. Alexander didn't have anyone to talk to about how much Christine seemed to have changed since they'd become engaged, and he trusted Nat's opinion. But…he just didn't feel comfortable phoning Nat without running it past Bill first. Then he told himself that was stupid, because it was the twenty-first century. Then he picked up his phone…then hesitated. No, he'd wait.

While his phone was in his hand it warbled with the tune he'd programmed to let him know it was Geordie calling – the 'Flight of the Valkyries'. He accepted the call, straightened his shoulders, and braced himself; these days he didn't dare guess what Geordie might be calling about.

'Geordie. How are you?'

The man's voice was heavy. 'Not good. Can't find him anywhere. Gone to ground. Sorry. I've done my best, honest. Looks like I'll be needing that favor, after all.'

Alexander tried to sound upbeat when he replied, 'No worries. You and me? We're a team, Geordie. You've had my back all these years – and I'm happy to try to repay what I owe you. We should meet. Where are you?'

'At the construction site in Thornton Heath.'

Alexander felt his shoulders hunch; the redevelopment of a row of six flats above six shops had turned into a nightmare – and all because he'd been distracted enough when he'd completed their purchase to not notice a clause stipulating that the existing tenants of both the flats and the shops retained more than the usual rights of non-owners. And one of them was playing hardball. She'd run the launderette in the corner unit for more than twenty years and thought of it as her domain – without which the local community would grind to a halt. Alexander knew she had a point, and had gone so far as to offer to rent a local community center so that the informal drop-in sessions that had taken place at the launderette for mums and kids could continue. But, no, not even that was enough to shift her. So they were working around her. Not ideal.

Knowing he really did need to see what was happening there, Alexander replied, 'Okay, I'll come to you. I'm at the antiques warehouse in Chelsea Harbor, I'll get there as soon as I can. An hour, if I'm lucky. See you then. And, Geordie, try not to worry. Your brother's a resilient type – he's survived okay up to now, and I'm sure we'll manage to track him down this time, too. Hang in there, mate. See you soon.'

'Cheers. See you.'

Alexander checked around, making sure he'd gathered up everything he needed into his pockets. His gaze lingered on the photo he kept on his desk of him and Christine. They'd been so happy just a few months ago – none of the sniping and pointed barbs that seemed to pepper their every conversation nowadays.

He set the alarms, locked up, and slid into his Aston. He never lost the delight of being able to do that.

However, once he was on the road, his mind wandered back to Christine. At least he was relieved that it had been clear from their conversation earlier that her parents had said nothing to her about what had turned out to be an incredibly difficult evening he'd spent with them.

He'd managed to get over the shock he'd felt when Aiden had told him what had happened. It seemed that the viscount had received a couple of emails which claimed that the sender knew all about Alexander having fathered an illegitimate son, and threatening to make the information known in such a way that it would harm the viscount's reputation – unless he paid up. How much paying up the viscount would be required to do, the emailer hadn't said.

When Alexander had read the emails themselves, what had really made an impression upon him was the amount of vitriolic language they contained. He wondered why anyone might say such vicious things about him.

Thus, what had been planned as a chatty hour over drinks with his future in-laws, had turned into a long evening of him trying to convince them that the sender of the emails was spewing a particularly vindictive form of fiction – solely designed to fleece them. By the time he'd left the Wilson-Smythes, Alexander had been pretty sure he'd convinced them that all the claims were false. He hoped they'd truly understood that he wasn't the sort who would treat a woman so poorly that she'd choose to have their child secretly, without telling a soul, rather than have him involved in the child's life. The emailer, who styled themself 'TISTRU', was a complete liar; he'd emphasized that many times. Yes, he'd left trusting – hoping – that they'd believed him. But they'd been shaken, that much was clear.

The trouble was, Alexander knew he was hiding so much about his past from them that he was concerned that when he *was* telling the truth, they could sense the other lies behind his words. And he couldn't have that. He wouldn't allow these threats to further endanger his relationship with Christine. They were facing enough problems as it was.

As he pulled into the building site where his Marion Rental Properties logo was emblazoned, Alexander felt the familiar mixture of pride and sadness. He was proud of what he was doing by sticking to a business model that advanced the opportunities available to the working poor. But he was always sad that he'd never really got to know his mother, in whose memory he'd named his company.

He could see Geordie, some way off, standing beside a pile of bricks. His friend, and sometime right hand, had already sweated through his T-shirt, and had caught a good bit of sun on his shaven head and around his thick neck. Alexander's heart went out to the man; for all that he looked as though he'd just stepped out of a boxing ring, Geordie – while he could more than take care of himself if a bit of fisticuffs was called for – had a gentle soul, and a moral compass that meant he always thought carefully before he threw a punch, and often felt badly about having done so. Alexander understood him well; they'd been friends and colleagues for years, and he relied upon Geordie's ability to manage multiple job sites, as well as provide reliable insights into potential suppliers. His knowledge of the ever-so-slightly dodgy world of construction was worth its weight in gold, as was his support of Alexander in other, less obvious ways.

The two men nodded their greetings to each other, then toured the site, with Geordie pointing out progress, and problems. Alexander took it all in; the fact they weren't talking about what they both wanted to discuss was palpable, but they continued on their rounds, both gesticulating as they walked. Alexander was satisfied that anyone seeing them would imagine nothing more than a routine visit, which was what he wanted. What they both wanted. When they reached the last building in the row, they stopped.

'She's in there, like nothing's happening,' said Geordie, jerking a thumb toward the launderette. 'Little Miss Flamin' Bigheart. I don't get it – why can't she see that what we're doing will make things better…for her and the rest of the community? She won't even talk to me now.'

Alexander nodded thoughtfully. He could tell that Geordie wasn't happy about the situation, and nor was he.

Peering through the window he could see Winnie Singh bustling between the massive machines, most of which were in operation. She navigated her way around four pushchairs while carrying a loaded plastic basket with seeming ease; at five feet tall, and about as meaty as a pencil, the tiny woman writhed her way between toddling children and their chatting mothers with a smile on her face, and sweat on her brow – which couldn't be helped by the fact she was wearing a brown velour tracksuit that was almost adhered to her tiny body. Alexander admired her tremendously, but knew he had to get her to leave the shop so that the place could be gutted: it needed essential structural repairs to allow it to survive another fifty years. However, she'd countered all his arguments with a steely, 'But it's fine, no problems here,' which he had to acknowledge there weren't, but he feared there soon would be.

Unable to face yet another run-in with Winnie, Alexander said, 'Let's leave her for today, and find a spot where we can talk. I need you to fill me in on your brother.'

'I can get everyone out of the site office, if there's anyone in there. It's like an oven, but it's private.'

Alexander nodded, and they shut themselves into what Geordie had accurately described as an oven – and they couldn't even open the window or door, because they needed absolute privacy.

Alexander started. 'So you've checked all the usual places, and no sign, eh?'

Geordie's shoulders sagged. 'Yeah. Not a peep. He's not been at his flat for about a week, judging by the stuff in the fridge and in the kitchen sink. His ex-wife hasn't heard from him – something for which she's grateful – and I phoned the company he works for, and they say he's *persona non grata*.'

'Do we know why?'

Geordie nodded. 'Yeah. He let down a client they'd been buttering up for a while, so dumped Sean when the client dumped them.'

'That'll do it,' said Alexander.

'You're not kidding. He's done that a lot – let people down.'

'Companies won't stand for it, especially these days.'

Geordie nodded. 'They acknowledged he's good at what he does, but he's in his late thirties now, and there's a lot of young guns coming up in the programming world, they said, so he shouldn't be hard to replace. He didn't have a desk at their offices to clear out, even, because he's been working from his home for the past three months or so, which I didn't know. If I had, I'd have been all over it; I thought he was still having to make himself presentable to turn up there every day. If I'd known he wasn't, I'd have known that was a danger sign. Honestly, I thought that last stint in rehab had got him sorted. But holed up in his own place all the time? Not good for him. I still can't fathom how he's able to do what he does and be using that stuff at the same time. I know they called him a "functioning addict" when they took him in last time, but how that happens is beyond me. I've seen him at his lowest points, I know – but to get his brain to do what it does when he's back on that stuff? No idea how that works. It shouldn't.'

'It happens,' said Alexander thoughtfully. 'Though the line between being able to function and being completely out of it must be razor thin. You've checked the hospitals, I suppose?' Geordie nodded. Alexander hesitated. 'And he's not…'

'Not on a slab, unidentified, as far as I can find out,' said Geordie heavily. 'Though I can't help but worry that he's dead somewhere and hasn't been found yet. Like I said, he could be anywhere.'

Alexander wanted to grab Geordie and hug him, but knew that wouldn't go down well.

Instead, he replied stoically, 'Not really *anywhere*. He's got his stamping ground, as we both know. Since he came to live in London, he's settled into his patch. We've found his dealers before now, and they've all been in and around Brixton. I know the place is much more gentrified than it was when I grew up there, but I'm only too familiar with the back streets, which haven't changed much.'

'Yeah. You and I both know how hard we have to work to make sure our work sites aren't overrun with people looking for somewhere to spend the night.'

Alexander agreed.

Geordie looked lost. 'With the way the developers have done their best to turn Brixton into the Land of Milk and Honey – there aren't a lot places people can crash for much more than a few hours around there. But…if he's managed to find himself a secluded spot to get himself off his head, and no one's been there for a while…well, you know what I mean.'

Alexander did. And he knew he had to help. His path toward paying back his debt – incurred when he'd transported all those suspicious packages – was one he walked with determination, and guilt. But then, he told himself, no one had ever suggested that the road to redemption would be an easy one to follow.

He sighed, and said, 'We need to get out there, Geordie. Boots on the ground. You and me, thinking like an addict, finding the dark corners and looking in all of them for your brother. We've got to hunt him down. And we can do that. It'll be difficult, and unpleasant, and – maybe – even dangerous. But we can both take care of ourselves in a pinch, right, mate?'

Geordie forced a wan smile. 'Too right.'

'So let's make a start today. I've got some stuff in my car that I think we need – a change of clothes and footwear to start with. Those work boots of yours will be fine, but these –' he stuck out his handmade Italian leather shoe – 'these won't cut it. Nor will my motor. I've rented a banger we can use. We'll pick it up on the way.'

Geordie managed a chuckle. 'Being engaged to a private detective's rubbing off on you, pet. We're going undercover, right? I can do that. For Sean.'

'Yeah, *pet*, for Sean,' said Alexander, rising. As he plodded to his car, he thought of everything Geordie had done for his brother over the years. Addiction was a terrible blight on everyone who loved a person, not just the addict themselves.

As that thought lingered, he wondered how Christine was getting on with being off the booze – it had been a few days so far, and she'd told him earlier on that she wasn't feeling any better for it. He hoped that didn't mean she'd be reaching for a bottle any time soon…even if it was a fancy vintage, with a hefty price tag attached.

As he opened his car's boot – it was big enough for his needs, though he'd never had to test the theory that you could fit two sets of golf clubs in there – his phone pinged. He took a moment to check the text. It was from Aiden: he'd received another email threatening to expose the story that his soon-to-be son-in-law had mistreated a woman, impregnated her, and fled, leaving her to raise the child to his teen years alone, this time with a photograph of the supposedly 'secret son'. Alexander opened the photo, which Aiden had forwarded. He had to admit that it showed a boy who bore a striking resemblance to his younger self.

Another text pinged in.

TISTRU WANTS FIFTY GRAND IN USED NOTES, OR HE'S GOING TO THE TABLOIDS WITH IT. HE'S GIVEN ME THREE DAYS TO GET IT. WE NEED TO TALK. AGAIN.

It bothered Alexander that the text was all in capitals, but he managed to push his frustration from his mind, and handed a heavy bag to Geordie. 'Let's change in the site office, then get going,' he said, more gruffly than he'd meant.

Geordie peered inside the bag. 'You reckon we're going to need all this?'

Alexander closed the boot. 'I know the place has been tarted up almost beyond recognition, Geordie, but we're going into the parts of Brixton that don't have a single yummy mummy or spandex-clad middle-aged cyclist to their name, so we'd best be prepared for the worst…while we hope for the best.'

Geordie nodded sullenly. 'Belt and braces it is, then. Sean, eh?'

Alexander nodded. 'Yeah, Sean.'

15th JULY

CHAPTER TEN

Mavis was impressed by Walter Gulliver's home. She'd half expected the retired multi-millionaire retail magnate to have chosen to live in some sort of ghastly modern monstrosity, so was delighted by the proportions of the large, but not overwhelming, Edwardian mock-Tudor home. Even more appealing was the way it nestled within a well-tended garden and was located at the end of what she assumed was a private road, rather than merely a country lane.

To have settled in Herefordshire, following what she knew had been a couple of decades of his working life spent in London, Mavis imagined the man might well have felt himself to be drawn to the area where he'd spent his youth. She was less than twenty-five miles from Chellingworth Hall, though across the border and now in England, so he was living quite close to what would have been, once upon a time, Brecknockshire.

After she'd parked her Morris Traveller as much in the shade of a large tree as possible, Mavis took a moment to check her appearance in her rear-view mirror before she made her way to the front door. The man who answered was most certainly not Walter Gulliver: in his thirties, he towered over her, sported a spiked, white-blond shock of hair, a pair of khaki shorts and a white T-shirt, with fat-soled white tennis shoes on what Mavis suspected was the largest pair of feet she'd ever seen.

'You're expected, Mrs MacDonald.' Spoken with a smile and what Mavis detected as an Irish lilt, the young man beckoned her inside. 'Mr Gulliver is in his study. Would you care for a cold drink? Mr Gulliver will be taking lemon barley water, but I dare say we'll have whatever might take your fancy.'

'I'll have the same as my client, thank you. Shall I follow you?'

'Please.'

The young, unnamed man led Mavis along a surprisingly stark corridor and opened the door to a room that lacked any adornment whatsoever. Mavis was surprised, because the exterior of the building had suggested someone who liked texture in a home, but the interior had no personality.

As the tall, skinny man ducked to enter the room ahead of her, Mavis noted that her client, Walter Gulliver, didn't raise his head. Instead, he remained bent over a large book that sat open upon a massive, dark, walnut desk. The top of his head, which was about all that Mavis could see, was bald and covered with dark spots, with a horseshoe of white hair surrounding it. When he looked up, his face appeared to have sunk in on itself; Mavis guessed he'd lost all his teeth and wasn't wearing dentures. This wasn't what she'd expected of such a wealthy man.

She was even more taken aback when the man stood, because he hardly changed height at all. Approaching the desk, she reckoned he had to be even shorter than Althea, and she was barely reaching the five-foot mark these days.

'Welcome, Mrs MacDonald,' said the tiny man in what was a surprising, though pleasant enough, falsetto. 'You've met the indispensable Collins, and I'm sure he'll bring whatever it is you've asked for momentarily. Thank you, Collins. Forgive me, Mrs MacDonald, these days, I find I prefer the rigors of a hardbacked chair to anything else. Will you sit across from me, here at the desk?'

Mavis was pleased that the meeting would be conducted in a more businesslike manner than if they'd repaired to the armchairs dotted about the large room.

She nodded, took the seat offered, and observed, 'You've a fine garden, Mr Gulliver. Is that a passion of yours?'

'A passion, but not a skill. For a man who urged the country to eat their veggies, I lack a green thumb, and have been known to make even vases of flowers wilt.' He chuckled heartily, producing a sound that put Mavis in mind of Carol's wee bairn, Albert. It made her smile.

'Luckily, we're all good at different things. My congratulations to your gardeners. Now, shall we begin?'

Walter Gulliver's expression shifted. 'I like a woman who doesn't go in for idle chit-chat. Thank you, Mrs MacDonald, I believe we'll get along swimmingly for what I have in mind.'

'It's Mavis, please.'

'And Walter, in that case. So where shall I begin?'

A smile flitted across Mavis's face as she realized this was the second time in just a short while that a man had asked her the same question. 'Where you feel you'd like to – or would you prefer me to ask questions?'

Walter ran his liver-spotted hand across his liver-spotted head. 'You go first, then.'

Mavis nodded, and began to work through the list of questions she'd compiled. She rapidly established that Walter had made as many investigations into his situation as an evacuee as he could, and had not been able to find a record pertaining to his name at all, anywhere.

'In that case, we'll no' duplicate what you've already done, Walter. Maybe your answers to a few more questions could give us another, more fruitful, direction for our enquiries.'

'Ask away.'

They each sipped the chilled barley water that Collins had deftly, and discreetly, placed on a side table, and which Walter had served to them both.

'Tell me what you recall of your time on this farm in Brecknockshire, Walter. Can you describe it to me? Did it have any particularly memorable features, for example?'

Walter closed his eyes and spoke quietly. 'It was on a hillside, and it was cold in the winter, and hot in the summer. My brother and I slept in a room above the hayloft – a dilapidated old wooden barn. It had never been painted, and was heavily weathered.'

He paused then added wistfully. 'It had a very particular...odor.'

He grinned, and Mavis joined him.

Pressing on, the man added, 'The farmhouse itself was quite small, stone-built, though it accommodated the family of four. There was Mr and Mrs Davies, their son David who was my brother's age, and they had a little girl.'

Walter Gulliver paused, and smiled sadly. 'They always called her their *"Blodyn Bach"*, which means Little Flower. I think her name was Blodwen, but I can't be sure of that, because they never used it, and, in all honesty, I can't even tell you why I think that. Maybe because *Blodyn Bach* sounds a bit like Blodwen? I don't know. I was still just a child, you see, so things are…muddled. Which is a part of my general frustration about this period of my life. All four of them spoke both Welsh and English. My brother Tim and I only spoke English, of course, so I remember being confused when I arrived there, because they'd jabber away in Welsh when they didn't want us to understand them. At least, that's what I thought at the time. Upon more mature consideration, I realize it might just have been because that was their first, and natural, tongue.'

'As a Scotswoman now living in Wales, I can agree with you that it's a confusing language, but I'm surprised you didn't pick it up when you were there. You were so young that you might have been able to quite easily.'

Walter gave a childlike chuckle. 'You're an insightful woman, Mavis. And you're right; as the years passed, I became more than able to follow their "private" conversations. I never let on, of course. And their chats – though almost whispered – were rarely that interesting. Indeed, they seemed to communicate about nothing more than farm business, household matters, and – occasionally – their children. Mrs Davies was taken ill at one point, and both she and the girl disappeared. I have no idea where they went, because it wasn't mentioned, but I know the little girl never came back – not even when her mother did. At least, she hadn't returned by the time Tim and I left.'

'So, an unremarkable farm, with an unremarkable family – named Davies, which won't help a great deal, I suspect. Rhodri Lloyd told me you said there was a variety of animals on the farm. So it wasn't a particular type of farm?'

'If my brother were still alive, he'd have been much better at this, because I was still not ten years old when I left.'

'But I'm sure you remember some things about it,' pressed Mavis.

'To my eyes, it wasn't solely a sheep farm, nor a dairy farm. That's all I can say. There were sheep, and pigs, as well as cows that had to be milked, horses they used for some of the equipment, and there were a great number of chickens. And rabbits. Lots of rabbits, which I was allowed to feed from my earliest days there. At that time, of course, I had no concept of what the war might have required of a farmer. However, I have an impression that anything that could be raised, that would provide food, was there. There were a great number of vegetables grown as well, year-round, and I believe that's where I developed my love of seeing things grow. Unfortunately, I became extremely upset when I saw the first animals being killed for meat, and that horror remained with me. I have been a vegetarian for my entire life. It's done me no harm.'

When he grinned with what she judged to be satisfaction, Mavis could see quite clearly that the man did, indeed, have teeth, but they were tiny, making her think, yet again, of a small child.

'And school? Did you attend school?'

Walter looked across the desk coyly. 'No. Mr and Mrs Davies said we didn't have to go to school, and none of we three boys ever contradicted them. She taught me to read, and I know she did some rudimentary lessons with her Little Flower, and with Tim and David. When I did finally get sent off to school in Lincolnshire, I realized immediately that I had missed out on a great deal in some ways, but not so much in others.'

Mavis leaned in. 'How so?'

Walter smiled. 'You see, I'd learned at the farm by *doing*. For example, I knew more about the night sky, and the weather, and the seasons, than most. I understood an enormous amount about plants and animals, as well as the basic requirements of construction and engineering, because we were put to work fixing walls, woodwork, and engines, as soon as we were able. I could count, and do mental arithmetic, and the farmhouse had a lot of books, so – as soon as I could read – I devoured them. I loved the way they took me to places that weren't a farm on a hill, and to times when there was no war.'

Mavis nodded her understanding.

He continued, 'When I finally encountered teachers, they said I was bright, and I took every advantage of the lessons they offered, too. But, by the time I was sixteen I'd had enough of being cooped up in a classroom, and took myself off to do other things. I dare say you've read all about me on my old company's website; I wrote the piece myself, so it's accurate. From barrow boy to multi-millionaire in six, easy decades, one might say.'

Mavis was enjoying Walter's self-deprecating way of talking, but pressed on. 'What about the son of the family, David Davies? Is there more you can tell me about him? Do you think he would have stayed on at the family farm, for example? Was that what would have been expected of him?'

'I'd say absolutely yes, but, again, I have no real sense of him as anything other than a big boy who spent much more time with my brother than me. My brother had to tolerate me, because of our shared blood; David had no such reason to be bound to me. I recall he found me rather irritating; it was he who always poo-pooed the idea of my being allowed to spend any real time with him and Tim, when we weren't all attending to our tasks around the farm.'

'It sounds as though you two Gulliver boys were treated as free labor by the Davieses. Did they work you hard?'

A look passed briefly across Walter's face that Mavis read as sadness.

He replied quietly, 'Not overly hard, though I was given ample opportunity to learn the meaning of responsibility, duty, punctuality, and manners. Not bad lessons to learn, but I dare say I felt as though they could have taught them to me more kindly.'

Mavis decided to move on. 'Are you in possession of any photographs taken at the time? Any mementos you kept?'

Walter smiled. 'No mementos, no. Tim and I left without even what we'd brought, which was little enough. They clothed us as we grew, of course – in my case, largely in hand-me-downs from their son, but we had nothing else from them to keep. I am not aware that the household owned a camera, unlike today's world where folks seem to be snapping away at all sorts of things every other moment.'

Mavis couldn't help but share a smile with him at this comment.

'However, I do have two photographs that might be of use to you. Here is one taken on the day my brother and I were sent to Wales. The only reason I have it now is because my mother had the foresight – as it turns out – to send this to the part of her family who resided in Lincolnshire, otherwise it might have been lost when she herself perished in the Blitz.'

'Why did you no' go to them in the first place? My colleagues have established that the area in Lincolnshire where they lived – and where you were eventually sent – was also accepting evacuees at the time.'

Walter smiled sadly. 'It's something I've wondered about myself, but, of course, I was never able to ask my parents, and the question didn't arise in my own mind until I began my research, and found out the same thing you did. By then there was no one left to ask. So – along with too much else in my life – it's something I have to accept I shall never understand. But, at least there is this.'

He handed Mavis a large black and white photograph. It was blurry, and showed two boys, holding hands. The taller of the two carried a small suitcase and wore a belted coat, with a cap. He was clearly wearing shorts beneath the coat. One of his knee-length socks drooped at his ankle. The smaller boy – which had to be Walter – was almost ball-shaped, he was so short and round. He, too, was wearing the sort of coat that Mavis thought would not have looked out of place on a man in his forties, and also wore a cap. But he had no suitcase – instead, a teddy bear dangled from his hand. Both boys were scowling at the camera, and each had a large label pinned to their coat's lapel. Someone had written on the original photograph – presumably one of the Gulliver parents – TIMOTHY AND WALTER GULLIVER, SEPTEMBER 2nd 1939.

'I was a round little fellow, wasn't I?' Walter spoke thoughtfully, not looking at the photograph. 'As far as I can recall, that's a good likeness of Tim at the time.'

Mavis smiled. 'Aye, you were a bonnie lad. And your brother's no less appealing. You said you had two photographs to give me?'

'Yes, this one might also help. This one was taken of us not long after we arrived in Lincolnshire in 1945.'

He held out another picture – obviously a copy, not an original. 'There are others from the years we spent there, because that family did have a camera, but this one would show me and Tim looking most like we did when we were in Wales, it having been taken not long after we left there. Quite a change, eh?' His eyes were flinty as he finally surrendered the second photograph.

Mavis studied it carefully. Less blurry than the first, it showed two boys who appeared to have been forced to stand beside each other. Both were a great deal thinner than they had been six years earlier. Tim had sprouted significantly, and was proudly wearing long tweed trousers, a shirt and tie, and a jacket. He looked like a young-old man, not a fifteen-year-old boy. Walter had grown a little and he had slimmed down a great deal, too. He was still in short trousers, and his expression was still as somber at it had been in the photograph taken of him years earlier, as was his brother's.

She looked up at the man sitting opposite her. 'You two are no' smiling, I can see. Not in either photo. I can understand why that might be the case in the earlier one – you were being taken away from your home and your mother, after all. But in this second one – the one taken after you'd moved to Lincolnshire – you both still look a wee bit miserable. Were you no' happy there?'

Walter sighed. 'It was…the start of a new life, for me. I missed the place in Wales I'd come to think of as "home". As for Tim? Maybe that's just how the lens caught him at that moment, or maybe he, too, missed Wales. I can't say, I'm afraid. It's always been an enduring sadness for me that I didn't really know my brother. We didn't have the chance to communicate – or else we didn't take the chances we had. Poor Tim. It was a real tragedy that he never got to fulfil his potential. I think he had great things within him because what I do recall of him is the ability he possessed to fix any engine with almost no supplies – a skill which Mr Davies allowed him to develop on the farm in Wales. And he understood how to make pretty much any vehicle go faster than it was supposed to.'

'I was told it was a grenade that got him. It that true?'

Walter rubbed his head. 'Yes. It happened in 1949, so Tim would have been nineteen. He wasn't living at the family farm in Lincolnshire any longer – he'd got himself a job at a garage on the outskirts of Lincoln itself, and was living in rooms there, above the premises. He was in the local pub one night when a demobbed soldier brought into the place what he swore afterwards he believed to be a fake hand grenade. They all started mucking about with it. It went off in Tim's face. Didn't stand a chance. His was the only death, though the soldier who'd brought the thing lost an arm, the landlord lost an eye, and the pub was damaged, of course.'

'I don't suppose your brother kept a diary or anything like that when you were in Wales, did he? Or might he have kept any mementos from that time?'

Walter shook his head. 'Nothing. All of which explains why I'm stumped. I turned to Rhodri Lloyd because he's got himself a reputation for being good at tracking people down…which I now understand is based upon your company's abilities. So I really do hope you can help. I desperately want to find out where I'm "from" you see, Mavis. Yes, I know I'm originally from Woolwich, but I have no memories of the place at all. And by the time I got to Lincolnshire, I was already formed in so many ways – in all the important ways, in any case. So I was made on that farm – and I know nothing about it, nor the people who played a role in helping to make me into the person I became. As you can see, I am old. I am running out of time. No, I hope I'm not going to die in the foreseeable future, and my health is pretty good, considering, but I've left it too long. I was there, alone, in a hospital room – I have no remaining family, you see – and I realized that there was a great big hole in my life, and I need to fill it. I hope you understand, Mavis. And I hope you can help.'

'We'll certainly do our best, Walter.'

CHAPTER ELEVEN

With Mavis away in Herefordshire interviewing Walter Gulliver, it had been agreed that Carol would meet with Rachel Edwards when she arrived at Chellingworth Hall. Carol enjoyed going to the Hall, though she hadn't expected the interview to be taking place in the family's private sitting room, with a full silver service morning tea having been set out, nor for the duchess, and the dowager, to be in attendance. She reckoned Althea had something to do with all the planning, so took her chance to have a quiet word before Edward's sister-in-law joined them.

'Mavis didn't tell me it was going to be like this,' she hissed. 'Did she agree to this? I thought it was just going to be me and Rachel having a chat. If what Edward told Mavis about Rachel's state of mind is right, won't we terrify the poor woman even more? This is all a bit full-on, isn't it?'

Carol still grappled with the fact that she was able to talk to a duchess and a dowager as though they were old chums, but did it anyway. At least she didn't snap at Althea the way Mavis did sometimes.

Stephanie replied, 'Althea invited me, and I thought we should all have tea, to make things less formal.'

'And I seconded that idea,' added Althea, sitting primly on her seat, wearing what Carol thought was a sort of silk sack. It was tied around her neck, and gathered above her ankles, and her arms poked out of slit sleeves. The dowager also appeared to be wearing a cardigan underneath the sack, because her arms were sheathed in lemon fine-knit wool, which rather clashed with the vibrant orange sack-thing.

'She's settled in, I know,' continued Althea airily. 'Edward told us she arrived late last night, but I want her to know she's welcome. Shush, now, here she comes, let's not frighten the horses. Oh dear, come back, McFli...I'm sorry Rachel, he seems to like you. How are you with dogs?'

Carol was surprised when she saw Rachel Edwards in the flesh; knowing Edward as she did, she'd conjured a picture of his late-brother's wife as being someone she could imagine by his side, she supposed, but Rachel Edwards was like something out of a fashion magazine. She was dressed in what was undoubtedly a sensible navy trouser suit, with a white shirt, and wore flat, comfy-looking brogues…but the sheen of her simply cut hair, the assurance with which she entered the room, and the elegance of the way her hands moved, marked her out as a woman who would turn heads. And that was before you even considered her face, which was striking, despite the lack of a scrap of make-up. She had creamy, blemish-free skin, and cheekbones Carol would have killed for. Twice.

'Please, join us,' said Stephanie, rising. 'You're most welcome, Rachel. I am Stephanie and this is my husband's mother, Althea. Let's do away with titles while you're our guest, if that suits you. And this is Carol Hill, who's one of the women who run the WISE Enquiries Agency. It is they who will be providing their professional services concerning your…situation.'

Carol was impressed by Stephanie's gracious welcome of the woman who took a seat and nodded at the three of them – and McFli to whom she spoke first. 'Thanks for the welcome, McFli, and my gratitude to you, Your Graces. I shall do my best use your given names while we're in private company, thank you. And thank you, Carol – and your colleagues – for taking my concerns seriously. Edward has spoken highly of your abilities.'

'Of course, we're dreadfully sorry about the death of your husband, Rachel,' said Stephanie. 'We've seen only too clearly the impact his passing has had upon Edward, so I can only imagine how difficult it's been for you. I know we need to address some topics that are going to be less than pleasant for you, so I thought tea?'

'And I thought cake,' added Althea. 'Cake helps with everything, don't you think, Rachel?'

The tilt of Althea's head and the gleam in her eye made Carol wonder if the dowager was posing some sort of challenge for the woman, but she couldn't work out why Althea would do such a thing.

'Tea and cake have eased many a difficult moment throughout history, so I dare say they will prove useful today, thank you,' replied Rachel, smiling. 'And Edward has told me great things about Cook Davies's seed cake; I understand it's an ancient recipe, so am honored to have the opportunity to sample a piece…or two.' She winked wickedly at Althea, who giggled.

Carol noticed that the dowager's dimples were already making an appearance, and she hoped the rest of the so-called interview would progress smoothly. She didn't want it to drag on forever, because she'd left Albert with Joan Pike an hour earlier for what she'd promised would be 'just a while'; David had had to go into Brecon…yet again.

Once everyone had their choice of tea, and cake, and the small talk died down for a moment – and Althea stopped hogging the conversation – Carol dared to begin. 'Our team is eager to help, Rachel, and you already know that Edward has given us as much detail as he can about everything that's happened, so I wonder if you feel up to answering a few questions?'

Rachel turned to give her full attention to Carol, which Carol found a bit overwhelming. Rachel's eyes were of the deepest brown, and Carol felt them burrowing into her confidence. 'Of course, Carol, that's why I'm here. Well, that, and because I'm so upset.'

Carol didn't think that Rachel looked at all upset, and noticed that her chocolaty eyes weren't swollen, or even rimmed with pink. Yes, she'd only had Mavis's account of what Edward had told her to go on, but she'd really expected to be facing a woman dissolving with grief, whereas Rachel appeared to be completely in control of her emotions. Carol told the niggling feeling she had, that Rachel should be more upset…more distraught…if her husband's death was such a loss to her, to go away. People grieved differently, she knew that.

However, Carol also knew how she'd feel if David had died suddenly and she believed it had been a suspicious death. Yet here was Rachel looking well-turned-out, and being able to chat about recipes.

Was that…normal? Or highly suspicious?

'Thanks, I'll try to be brief,' said Carol, determined to press on despite her misgivings.

She cleared her mind, and focused. 'Edward seemed to think that you're not convinced that your husband's death was an accident. Can you explain, in your own words, why you feel that to be the case?'

Carol was taken aback when Althea jumped in. 'It was the pen thingy and the fish thingy, wasn't it, dear?'

Carol wanted to say so much, but satisfied herself with explaining, 'I was rather hoping that Rachel could tell us herself, Althea. Thanks.' She hoped the dowager would stop talking long enough to let Rachel get a word in – and to allow Carol to try to make an informed assessment of the widow's state of mind.

'Althea's sort of hit the nail on the head, to be honest,' replied Rachel evenly. 'Richard was never without his epinephrine pen, and I understand that it had fallen out of his jacket pocket – which was on a chair where he wasn't able to get to it. But even that was unlike him; to my knowledge he always kept it in the pocket of his trousers. And as for "the fish thing"? Both Richard and I had put a great deal of effort into researching what foodstuffs he should avoid. There is no way that a dessert should have contained anything to which he would have reacted. And his reaction would have been fast – almost immediate, in fact – so it wouldn't have been because of something he'd consumed in an earlier course. It had to be the dessert.'

'I cannot imagine having fish as a dessert,' mused Althea loudly. 'Sounds disgusting. Fish are all well and good on a Friday, or even as an entertaining participant in a dance, but in a dessert? I don't think so.'

Rachel grinned. 'Oh, I love the Fish-Slapping Dance, Althea. One of my favorite Monty Python bits. So short, but such an impact. The way Michael Palin goes over into the canal? Just wonderful.'

Althea beamed, and Carol wondered if her dimples might split. 'Thank you, dear. One of my favorites, too. John Cleese manages to keep a straight face so well, don't you think?'

Rachel nodded, and nibbled her cake, Stephanie sighed and sipped her tea, and Carol began to understand why Mavis spoke so sharply to Althea, on occasion.

She realized she had to take control of the situation, or else she'd be there all day. What on earth was Rachel thinking, encouraging Althea like that? Didn't she want to focus on her husband's death? Carol was still trying to come to terms with why – and how – Rachel was able to appear so detached from the devastating grief a woman must feel when her husband dies.

'So, other than your husband's rescue medication being unusually out of reach, and the chance that he was reacting to something in his dessert – is there anything else, Rachel?'

'I think that's quite a lot. And there's Jon Dacre, his partner, himself, of course. I believe he killed Richard because he wants to take over the company. But now he's found out that he won't, so I think he might be after me next. Edward has suggested that I sell my share of the business to Jon, or even to someone else. Of course, I couldn't possibly sell to another party, because then I'd be putting a target on their back, wouldn't I? And as for selling to Jon? Well, first of all, I don't think he's got a bean, and secondly, that would be like letting him get what he wanted, wouldn't it? Which I shall not do. And, finally, I don't want to sell. I like training butlers; I'm rather good at it, and we have a wonderful team at Buttle My World, so that's just not the way I want to go. So, yes, I think Jon killed my husband, and I think that's why. Of course, until they open up Richard's body, and analyze what he ate, we're not going to know much more, are we? However, I do believe Jon wants me out of the way too, so I'm grateful to be here, safely out of reach of the murderous man.'

Carol realized that she, Althea, and Stephanie – and even McFli – were all staring at Rachel by the time she'd finished her little speech. In the case of Althea and McFli, they were staring open-mouthed, and Carol had to rub her nose to try to hide a totally inappropriate smirk when the dowager and her dog snapped their jaws shut at the exact same moment as each other.

Althea said, 'I say, you've given all of this a lot of thought, haven't you, Rachel? I cannot imagine I could be as clear-headed about such matters if my husband had just dropped dead at a dinner party.'

Carol held her breath – how would Rachel react?

Althea continued, 'It was bad enough when my darling Chelly ailed for some time then finally succumbed. But at least one had the comfort of knowing he was released from his pain. Yours just went out for dinner. It has to have a completely different impact. And yet, you're able to look the way you do, and speak as you are doing. Quite extraordinary.'

If Annie had said such a thing aloud, Carol would have been tempted to kick her under the tea table, but she didn't think she dared kick a dowager, even if she was allowed to talk to her 'as though she were a real person', as Althea always liked to put it. However, Carol was quite glad that Althea had verbalized what she, herself, was feeling, and wondered how Rachel would respond.

'I have no choice but to be level-headed about it all, Althea,' replied Rachel calmly. 'Richard is dead. Nothing will bring him back. All the plans we'd made for our future are now nothing more than pipedreams. We'll never do those things, or visit those places together, because there is no longer an "us". The least I can do for him, and for myself, is to find out why he died. In the meantime, I have to keep myself out of what I truly believe to be harm's way. I absolutely understand that you might think it unlikely that one partner in a business would kill another just to gain control of said business, but I believe Jon has it in him to do just that.'

'Why?' Carol asked the question reflexively, without really knowing she was about to do it.

'Why what?' Rachel looked puzzled.

Carol elaborated. 'Why do you think Jon Dacre has it in him to have killed your husband? Or anyone, for that matter? Murder isn't something most people would consider a viable business option, after all. What's he done in the past that makes you believe him capable of this now?'

Rachel sat back in her seat. Her eyes narrowed. 'It's not one big thing, it's a myriad little things. He's always ready to cut corners, and his dismissive attitude toward anything that's not his own opinion is well known.'

I know a few people like that, thought Carol.

Rachel sat forward, her eyes narrowing. 'He's arrogant to the point of being a bully, and he never, ever listens to another person's point of view, however well-argued it might be. He will bray over a joke that's nowhere close to being funny if it's cracked by a client, or a potential one. However, he would whine on about how Richard has...*had*...no sense of humor, or couldn't take a joke – which was how Jon would attempt to explain away any of his acerbic little barbs when they went a bit too far and produced a reaction he didn't care for. He's an oily character who oversteps the mark time and time again, seemingly without consequence. I don't doubt for a moment that, if he decided to, he would go through with murder just because he'd think he'd never get caught. I don't think he knows that the word "comeuppance" even exists – and I want to see the look on his face when we prove what he did, and make sure he pays the price.'

Once again, Carol noted the wide eyes around the tea table, and said, 'Thank you. That helps. But...is there anything more specific?'

'One of the jabs he used to like to make toward Richard was that he was a "waste of skin". Richard was the one who did all the real work. Jon has ridden on Richard's abilities for years. Yes, he's good at greasing all the right palms – largely because he's so greasy himself. But, recently, he's been questioning Richard's methods in front of other members of staff. Other than myself, I mean – he hasn't held back in front of me for years. So – specifically – he's been undermining Richard in front of other trainers, and I think that's a sure sign that he no longer valued Richard's importance to the business.'

Carol nodded. 'Thank you. I appreciate your candor. Of course, as professionals we'd have to consider if anyone other than Jon might have had a reason to want to kill your husband.'

Carol was thinking, *Like you, for example*, but didn't utter the words.

She continued, 'Certainly your opinion of Jon Dacre as being a potential killer is important, but it does make me think that it would be useful if we could find a way to meet with the man himself – just so we could have a more...objective...take on him.'

Althea sat a little more upright and put down her tea. Carol steeled herself: she could already spot the danger signs.

The dowager said brightly, 'You'll need someone for an undercover caper, then, Carol, so that the chap doesn't know we're investigating him. I could do that. I could be a potential client, and get him to slime all over me.'

Carol and Stephanie exchanged a panicked glance.

'I don't think that would be appropriate, Althea, dear,' said Stephanie, also relinquishing her cup and saucer, 'nor does Carol, I'm sure.'

Carol replied quickly, 'I certainly agree with you, Stephanie. Althea, it's not something you should be helping with, thanks. But I think Christine would fit the bill nicely. The daughter of a viscount? A trained private investigator, who's good at reading people, too? She could do it. And I know she'd be only too happy to help. She's been popping back and forth to London over the past few weeks, and said she'd be willing to do so again. So that's settled then.' Carol reckoned she had to bring the meeting to a close. 'I'll speak to Christine, and we'll get her in there as soon as possible. Now, if you don't all mind, I'd better get away so I can collect my son from a kind neighbor who's looking after him for a little while. Lovely to meet you, Rachel. I suggest we chat on the phone a bit later, so we can come up with exactly the sort of services Christine should say she's seeking, just to make sure that Jon Dacre takes the meeting himself. If I could have your number, please?'

As Carol drove back to the village, she made a mental note to research how long it would really be before an allergic reaction to mollusks would take effect. Had Rachel said it would be immediate so that her alibi of not being at the dinner party would hold water?

She wondered if she'd just been introduced to a cool-as-a-cucumber husband-killer, but realized that – before she could possibly voice her concerns about Rachel to her colleagues – she'd have to work out if the woman could have killed her husband without having been with him at the time when he died.

CHAPTER TWELVE

Annie Parker stomped up the stairs to the flat above the bar at the Lamb and Flag, huffing and puffing. The massive bag she was lugging was full, and heavy, and the stairs could be treacherous – as she knew only too well. By the time she reached the top, Tudor had rushed to help her, as had Rosie and Gertie – though their frantic scrabbling was less helpful than Tudor's strong arms.

'What on earth is in this thing?' Tudor looked surprised when he felt the weight of the bag.

'Half a dozen cameras, and all the gubbins they need to go with them. It's mainly the batteries that weigh a ton,' replied Annie, greeting the little yellow and black Labs as their tails wagged furiously…and as they sniffed hopefully at each of her hands. With no treats forthcoming, they resigned themselves to happy licks, then trotted toward their beds in the corner near the unlit fireplace.

'And what are they for?' Tudor placed the bag carefully on the floor. 'Got a job on that I know nothing about?'

'They're for us. You and I will be installing them at the Coach and Horses later this evening, when everyone's left for the day.' Annie sat at the dining table and caught her breath.

'Is this to do with that toilet going missing?' Tudor moved to the fridge, returning with a bowl of salad leaves. 'I kept this cold until you arrived because it's so warm up here I thought it all might wilt. I'll dress it now, if you're ready to eat.'

'What's with it?'

'Cold roast chicken breast, alright?'

'Yeah, I could eat a horse. And the jockey. I missed lunch. Had to watch that lot across the green eating theirs, then get back to the office. And it's not just a toilet that's gone, but that wallpaper, and the paint, and now some plaster, too. So, yeah – the cameras are for us…well, you know, for the Estate, really – and us.'

Tudor grabbed a jam jar from the counter and started shaking it. 'I've done the balsamic vinegar dressing you like. You can add your own hot sauce on your plate. I'm not touching it tonight, ta.'

'Bad tummy?'

'Not doing well with the heat that's come back after all that rain. And the blinkin' humidity. And the stress. I think it's best if I eat plain food for a bit. But I know you can't live without your hot sauce, so just see to yourself, tonight. And…what plaster?'

Annie shook her head. 'It seems that Wes uses a specific plaster on those walls over there. Has to be the right ingredients to be allowed by the Listing people, he says. Anyway, like I told you, he's nearly finished that part of his work, but he had one bag left which he said would be just enough for the last little bit, and it's gone. He got in this morning, used up what was left in the bag he had on the go, went to get the new one, but couldn't find it. Swears blind he knew exactly where it was – tucked behind the bar itself, he said. But it's gone. All four of us searched the whole place. And he's got to order it specially. Won't get another bag for two days, so that's another hold-up. He said he can get on with other things in the meantime, but that's not the point. Somebody is walking off with our supplies, and I won't have it, Tude.'

Tudor attended to their plates at the counter, then presented Annie with her dinner.

'Oh, that looks lovely, Tude. Smashing presentation. Ta.' Annie reached for the large bottle of hot sauce which lived on the kitchen table. Her mother made sure she never ran out, by sending her boxes full of the stuff – a favorite family brand that it was much easier to get in London than out in the wilds of the Powys countryside.

'That looks like a lot, even for you,' commented Tudor as Annie splashed the sauce over the entire contents of her plate.

'I fancy a bit more zing tonight, Tude. Got to make sure I'm full of energy for when we go out on our secret mission later on, right? And nothing's better at keeping me going than this stuff. I don't know why I don't have it on my cereal in the mornings to be honest, and it might even work better than coffee.'

Tudor chuckled, which Annie enjoyed, because it made his lovely face light up. They chatted as they ate, Tudor moaning about the fact that his 'To Do' list kept getting longer, not shorter, and that – once they'd moved into the Coach and Horses – he was never going to move again, ever, in his life.

Annie pointed out that such a claim was unrealistic. 'Come on, Tude, we're only going to be able to live there while you're running the pub, and you won't want to be doing that into your dotage. Look at me, I've lived in seven different places since I left the family nest, and I'm still standing. Well, just. Most of the time. Mind you, I thought I'd got rid of everything I didn't need when I moved from London to Anwen-by -Wye, but I've managed to accumulate all sorts of rubbish during the past eighteen months. I know my cottage is tiny, but I keep finding stuff I've shoved into corners, and under furniture. I can't believe some of the things I've got that'll have to go. I mean, I know the flat over at the Coach is a lot bigger than this one, but it's going to be the two of us, with all we've both got, having to fit in there. Which brings me to wardrobes…'

Tudor grinned. 'Of course it does…we seem to talk about wardrobes every day, if I'm not mistaken.'

Annie gave him a playful thump. 'I'm allowed. And it's going to be a problem: that big bedroom isn't as big as you think, when you allow for four wardrobes in there. And don't say we won't need four, because we will. You've got two here, and I've got two at my place, and they're all full. I just cannot see what I can get rid of that I haven't already chucked. For me it's the shoes that's a problem: if I didn't have such big feet all my shoes would be smaller, but I do, so they're all huge. I've been looking online for alternative storage solutions for shoes, and I found these cube things. I'll show you later. I thought we could have them at the top of the stairs. You know…where there's that useless space when you reach the landing.'

Annie watched Tudor as he chewed his last piece of chicken, looking thoughtful; she liked the way he always saved a piece of meat for his last mouthful – she'd done the same thing her whole life.

Eventually he replied, 'See, I was thinking of hooks there – somewhere to grab a coat on the way downstairs, and saving carrying it through the place when you come in. And there's all the dog stuff we have to accommodate – leads and such like.'

Annie sighed. 'Yeah, you're right, I'd forgotten about that idea. Maybe some cubes underneath the coats? Just a row or two on the floor, not right up the wall, then?'

'I'll have a look at what you mean by cubes, then maybe we could measure up when we're there this evening. When did you plan on us going, by the way?'

Annie pushed away her empty plate and looked at her watch. 'Well, it's a sunny day, so it should be light enough for a couple of hours yet. The electricity's off in the place, of course, so we'll need some natural light. The blokes working there in the day have their battery powered this and that, and that's why I brought all the batteries for the cameras. They last for days. So…maybe in half an hour, when our dinner's gone down? I don't know how long it's going to take us. Carol's so good with all this stuff, but she's tied up with a few things at the moment. And Chrissy? Well, you know what she's been like lately.'

Tudor nodded. 'She hasn't been into the pub for a few days. She alright now?'

Annie nodded absently. 'On the wagon for a bit. Not a bad thing, I reckon. She's been tucking it away this past few weeks. Looking like a wet weekend every time I see her.'

'You're not wrong. Like we were saying the other day, she's been going through the large G and Ts down in the pub like there's no tomorrow. Taking a lot of taxis, too, which is good, of course. I know she's young, and I dare say both you and I used to drink a lot more than we do now when we were her age, but it can't be good for a person, really, can it? Not that I'd have thought that when I was that age, of course.'

Annie chuckled. 'You and me both.'

Tudor grinned. 'Some of those rugby club dos were legendary, I can tell you. I recall we used to manage a gallon of bitter each, no problem.'

He shook his head. 'Different times, eh? I couldn't manage more than a few pints now – and all my years behind a bar have taught me how destructive it can be to not listen to your body when it comes to alcohol. Not that I'm against drinking – that wouldn't be a good thing for a publican, would it? But there's drinking in moderation, with the odd bit of over-indulgence thrown in, and then there's hitting it hard, all the time. I hope she feels better for packing it in for a bit – though I'd be happy to be selling her pints of squash, if it meant more customers, to be honest.'

Annie mused, 'Maybe we should think about "mocktails", or at least a wider offering of non-alcoholic drinks, for the Coach, Tude. They do say a lot of young people are getting more "sober curious" these days. Though, since most of us spend the vast majority of our lives completely sober, I'm not sure what there is to be curious about.'

'All over it, Annie. Got to think of the drivers, too. I mean, other than the locals, anyone using the place will have driven to the village, won't they? They won't be coming in on the bus, given the service around here. Did you hear that they've cut another two buses, by the way?'

Annie nodded. 'I did. As someone who can't drive…yet…it should bother me more, I suppose. I'm glad so many people around here are able to offer me a lift when I really need one. But, come on, let's get our act together – we need to get going. We'll drag these two pups around the green so they can do their business, then they should be alright up here on their own while we go to install my sneaky hidden cameras. I hope they show us what the devil's going on over at the Coach, because I think I know who's doing it, but I need proof.'

A couple of hours later, Annie and Tudor were satisfied that they'd managed to cover the front and back doors to the pub, the staircase, and most of the flat upstairs, with the cameras, and Annie announced she was happy with the quality of the feed from each of them to her tablet.

As the couple stood in the middle of what would – one day soon, she hoped – be their sitting room, Annie took it all in.

She whispered, 'It's going to be lovely, when it's finished, Tude.' She added, 'Quiet, innit? Why is that? We're still overlooking the green, but it seems calmer here than at the Lamb.'

Tudor walked to the front window. 'I think it's because this place is set much farther back from the road than the Lamb. The beer garden in the front and up the side acts as more of a buffer. Not that there's much going on out there at this time of the evening. Come and look at the sky, Annie – it's a fabulous sunset tonight.'

Holding hands as they watched the sky blaze, Annie jumped at a creaking sound behind her. Spinning around, she whispered, 'What's that?'

Tudor shrugged. 'Just an ancient building cooling off at the end of a warm day, I expect. We don't notice it at the Lamb, because we've got used to it. We'll have to get used to the sounds of this place, too.'

Another creaking sound led Annie to grab Tudor's hand more tightly. 'That's one heck of a lot of "cooling", Tude. It sounds like the beams are going to snap. That can't be right, can it?'

She noticed that Tudor's reply sounded less confident, when he said, 'Probably nothing. And don't forget that the whole place is empty – things will echo less when all our furniture's in here, and we've got a few rugs down, that sort of thing.'

Annie listened intently in the darkening room, then hissed, 'That's a door, that is, Tude…a door creaking on old hinges. There's someone downstairs, in the pub. Come on, let's find out who it is.' She dropped his hand and tiptoed to the top of the stairs. As she began to descend, she realized she couldn't move without making every stair creak. Then a door slammed. 'There's definitely someone down there. Come on.'

She gave up any attempt to be quiet and pounded down the stairs into the pub itself, with Tudor following as fast as he could, calling, 'Hang on a minute, Annie…'

The pub was empty, and much darker than the flat had been – the small, ancient, leaded windows were letting in less of the last light of the dying day.

Annie stood stock still, then heard the banging again. She darted around the end of the bar toward the back door, which led to the yard behind the pub. The door was swinging on its hinges, but she couldn't see anyone in the yard, nor any vehicles.

'No one here, now – but there was someone, Tude. This door was locked earlier on, when we were working down here. We both know that, because we tried it, didn't we?'

Tudor nodded. 'We did. It was. That's…weird. And a bit unsettling. Anything on those cameras of yours?'

Annie tutted loudly. 'I tested them all, but I haven't started the system yet. I'll do that right now. I hope we haven't missed our chance to see what's what.'

16th JULY

CHAPTER THIRTEEN

The Honorable Christine Wilson-Smythe sat upright in the elegant chair in the reception area of Buttle My World in Earl's Court, with her handbag on her knees. She'd chosen a good one, and had decided upon a cream silk two-piece that suited the weather and her role for the day – that of a young woman of excellent breeding who was on the lookout for some temporary help at her titled family's London home.

She'd pressed the urgency of her requirement when she'd made the appointment to ensure she'd be able to see the proprietor himself. That was how his personal assistant had styled him when Christine had spoken to her the previous afternoon. She'd thrown a few things into an overnight bag and had arrived at her parents' home around ten, just in time to have a bit of a natter with her father, then collapse into her bed. She'd felt ridiculously tired after her drive from Wales, and – even as she sat waiting for her target, Jon Dacre, to appear – she still felt less than well-rested, despite a good, solid eight hours' of sleep.

Annoyed at her body's continuing shortcomings – despite not having touched a drop of alcohol for days – she realized the receptionist must have misinterpreted her loud sigh as a sign of impatience.

The young, almost alarmingly slim, woman glanced at the clock on the wall and said, 'Mr Dacre will be along shortly. He's never late for a client meeting. It's still only two minutes to ten.' She smiled brightly, then returned her attention to the screen in front of her.

Christine couldn't be bothered to respond with anything more than a half-smile, and did her best to focus on the task at hand; she was there to gain an insight into the character of a man believed to be capable of murder by a grieving widow and – as she now understood to be the case from Carol – a bereaved butler, too. Edward had been won over by his sister-in-law's certainty in the matter, it seemed.

A moment later, a door opened and another young woman – much the same type as the receptionist – entered, holding out her hand. 'You must be Miss Wilson-Smythe. I'm Mr Dacre's personal assistant, Lila Stevenson. We spoke yesterday. Mr Dacre is ready to see you now. Please follow me. Might I bring you some refreshment?' 'Tea, please. Lapsang Souchong with lemon, thank you.' Christine had decided to be a 'quirky client', so thought it best to start as she meant to go on.

The young woman wasn't even slightly fazed as she opened the door to a palatial office, and withdrew, announcing, 'Miss Wilson-Smythe, Jon.' She backed away so that Christine could enter, smiling slyly as she did so.

Christine noted that Lila had uttered her boss's name with a level of suggested intimacy that she felt inappropriate, and telling.

Jon Dacre stood beside a slightly-too-shiny desk of gargantuan proportions, in a room that screamed 'interior designer'. Yes, the unprepossessing 1960s exterior of the building had turned out to be a true promise of the interior Christine had seen so far, but this room? Well, someone with a large budget, and a penchant for fluid lines, modern sculpture – and so-called 'pops of color' – had been let loose on the place. In fact, as she glanced around, Christine reckoned that if a color existed, there was a 'pop' of it in Jon Dacre's office. It was almost dizzying, because her eyes didn't know where to settle within the stark white shell.

Eventually she managed to give her attention to the man himself: he was just as unpleasantly shiny as his desk, and was walking across the office toward her, beaming. No, Christine immediately adjusted her thinking; the man was slithering, snake-like across a rug covered with multi-colored wavy lines that were making her eyes go funny.

Immediately she noticed the rug, she reckoned the designer of the room had to have been someone who would never need to consider the interplay between thick rugs and kitten heels.

'Ah, Miss Wilson-Smythe, a pleasure to meet you. I hope your dear father is in fine health. Your mother, and your brother's family too, of course. And yourself, though that I can see to be the case.'

Christine wished she had a sick bag with her…almost literally. Within the time it took the man to reach her, she'd considered the idea of bursting his bubble immediately; she'd mentioned her appointment to her father when she'd arrived the night before, and he'd confirmed he had no knowledge of the company, nor of Jon Dacre, so she knew for a fact that Dacre's insinuation that he knew her family was bogus.

Of course, she also couldn't help but recall her father's rather odd energy the previous night at the same time, but she'd been so tired she hadn't chosen to ask him what was up. Something most certainly was – he'd been like a cat on a hot tin roof, almost hopping about when they'd been chatting. She pushed aside thoughts of her father, and decided to keep her powder dry, so replied, 'The family's all in rude health, thank you, Mr Dacre.'

Waving toward two curvaceous, lemon-hued armchairs arranged beside a blood-red coffee table that was shaped like a teardrop, Jon Dacre said, 'Please, it's Jon.'

'Thank you, Jon,' Christine replied. She didn't make the return offer of a first-name basis for their conversation.

As she did her best to settle herself, she was glad she'd worn trousers, and couldn't for the life of her work out how older potential clients might manage to sit at all, let alone comfortably, in the bucket-style chairs. Maybe Jon only offered them to his more spritely clientele?

'I understood from Lila that your needs are urgent – she mentioned a death in the family of the butler in question?'

Christine nodded – it was an elastic version of the truth. 'He'll be gone back to the Old Country for a while. Irish, you know, like our family.'

She'd decided to allow her natural, though frequently masked, Irish lilt full rein for the meeting, the way her father did when facing a particularly obstreperous client; what worked for him might work for her, too.

Jon nodded, his expression immediately grave. 'My condolences to all those concerned.' He paused for a millisecond, then beamed. 'So, how can we help?'

'I'm at my wits' end, so I am,' gushed Christine.

Jon replied smoothly, 'We are more than adequate to meet your needs for a temporary replacement for any buttling requirements your family might possess, or, indeed, any number of ways of delivering a range of services you might require.'

'It's just my parents at the London house, most of the time,' replied Christine politely, 'and they have the usual requirements. A single butler would do, I'm sure. Though they'd need to be a good fit, in terms of personality. I wouldn't have come here if I didn't think your general training was up to snuff, of course. However, my parents are very particular people, so that's why I've come in person.' She prayed that her parents never found out about how she might end up portraying them.

Jon nodded vaguely. 'I'm sure we'll have someone who'll be ideal, Miss Wilson-Smythe.' He started scrolling on the pad he had clasped on his lap. 'To be clear, the rest of the household consists of…?'

'A driver-cum-handyman-gardener, and his wife, who cooks and cleans. They both live in. This post would also require that. It's a four-storey building, so stairs are a given, of course.'

'Personal valet duties for the viscount and viscountess?'

'Indeed. And the budgies.'

Jon Dacre's head shot up. 'Pardon?'

'Mammy loves her budgies, so she does. Has…oh, more than a dozen. They have their own room, of course. Caged at one end so Mammy can sit in there with them. The post requires their well-being to be attended to. As well as the dogs.'

Christine's recollection of what Annie had told her about Iris Lewis's budgies had flitted into her mind, and it had come out of her mouth before she could stop it.

'I see,' replied Dacre, doing his best to not look flummoxed. 'And how many, and what size of dogs are we talking about?'

Christine enjoyed the way he'd chosen to gloss over the issue of the budgies.

'It varies,' she replied airily. 'Mammy and Daddy foster dogs. Sometimes it's no more than three or four, sometimes as many as a dozen. All sorts, of course.'

'Of course,' managed Dacre evenly. 'And they'd all need to be walked by your butler?'

'Twice daily,' replied Christine with an indulgent smile. 'Dogs are not allowed in our square's private gardens.'

'I see, so someone good with animals.' He smiled, ingratiatingly.

'Yes. The monkey isn't much trouble. Daddy mainly looks after him himself, though he has been known to roam.'

This time she had him: Jon Dacre's eyebrows shot up. 'The viscount has a pet monkey? In the house?'

'Yes. It's just a little one. An Emperor tamarin.' Christine dug into her recollection of a documentary she'd recently seen about the creatures. 'He's called Jerry, and has a lovely droopy white mustache thing. Has the entire attic to himself. Daddy was given him as a well-intentioned, but rather impractical, gift about fifteen years ago. Poor old Jerry's getting on a bit now, and he can become a bit fractious. Daddy does his best to make sure he has enough to keep him happy in terms of exercise, and entertainment, but he needs a bit of personal interaction on a daily basis, so the butler steps in when Daddy's too busy. And the replacement you have in mind for us will tend to his feeding and cleaning requirements, too. So, yes, personal valet services for the whole family – human, furred, and feathered.'

Christine beamed as though her requests were the most normal thing in the world, then added, 'Which is why I'd like to meet your potential candidates, or at least have a face-to-face interaction with them on screen. It's important that they understand what all my family members will need of them.'

Scrolling madly, Jon Dacre replied, 'I have one or two names rising to the top of the list, some excellent references when it comes to interaction with household pets like cats, dogs, and even rabbits, guinea pigs and hamsters, but nothing specifically about budgerigars.'

He paused for a long moment, then added – almost tragically, 'Nor tamarins, I'm afraid.' He looked up. 'I could make a few calls, if that would suit?'

Christine shifted...to the extent that she could within the snug confines of the chair.

She had to push him. 'I had rather hoped to be able to move forward now, Jon. Our butler will be leaving today, you see, and – now that you better understand our requirements – I'm sure you can see we need to get someone in to take over his duties right away. Of course, humans can manage for a while without constant attention, but animals cannot be reasoned with.'

Jon's darting eyes suggested to Christine that he was struggling. 'And there's no possibility of being able to bring in one person to deal with the animals, and another for more…human requirements?'

'The man we have now manages admirably and, as I said, most of the chores are dealt with by others. My parents' buttling needs are just the everyday ones…not really enough to fully employ a person.'

The man's nostrils flared as he gave the matter some thought. 'I have two candidates who come to mind. I have them cued up on the pad here. Maybe I could allow you a few moments to peruse their CVs while I check…some other records. If I may, I'll leave you here with that, and the tea Lila brought in. I shall return momentarily.'

Christine acceded to the man's request with a nod, and he all but flew out of the room, finally allowing her to smile. *What a great craic!* The man's face had been a picture…especially when she'd mentioned the monkey. She made a mental note to swear Jon Dacre to secrecy before she left – because she didn't want the world and his wife to think her parents were as mad as two boxes of hair, and she suspected that 'weird habits of the famous and titled' would be a favorite topic of discussion for the man who'd just oozed his way out of his really over-the-top office.

Christine could understand why Rachel Edwards disliked the man; he was an eminently dislikeable type. But a killer? She'd have to dig further to get a better feel for that.

She took almost no time to read through the CVs of a man and a woman, each in their thirties, to whom Jon had directed her attention. The man seemed most suited to the job in question – if only the job existed. With a background in the military, and a passion for every sort of animal, so he said, he seemed to fit the bill.

As did the woman, to be fair, whose background as a kindergarten teacher would have well-prepared her – Christine assumed – for a job where entertaining monkeys, dogs, and budgerigars was required. Then she leaped up and raced to Jon's desk – tripping twice on the blessed rug. His laptop was open, but asleep. She wiped a knuckle across the pad to wake it up but got a screensaver, showing a group of people all waving at the camera. Christine pulled her phone from her pocket and snapped, then used her knuckle to move the arrow to the diary icon and pressed – she reckoned the thing would be password protected, but didn't see the harm in trying anyway.

To her amusement, the screen opened…to a completely empty diary. Then she saw the fat, leather-bound book to her right, with the word DIARY stamped in gold on its cover, tutted at herself – what was wrong with her? – and opened it. She didn't know what she hoped to find, exactly, but flicked to the page for the day when Richard Edwards had died. The event in question was noted but nothing else that day.

She flicked back a few weeks and spotted a capitalized note that simply said: OYSTERS! RICHARD…LOL! It struck a nerve, so she took a photo. She continued to flick back through earlier dates, but to no avail. She found those three little words suggestive – though, if someone were planning something underhand, would they really make such a note in their diary?

When Jon re-entered the room, Christine was showing an interest in the potted rubber plant beside his desk.

'Is this real?'

He stared at her, then the plant, then his desk diary, and replied coolly, 'It is. Please, feel free to touch it.'

Christine squashed the leaf between her fingers. 'Gosh, so it is. And there was me thinking it was a good fake. It's so pristine. It almost looks as though it's been polished.'

Jon waved her to her seat again as he answered, 'It has been. Lila takes care of it. There's some special stuff one can use to buff this type of leaf to a shine. And she takes care of the watering, and so forth.'

'Is that mother of pearl on top of the potting compost? The iridescence is quite beautiful.'

Jon glanced casually toward the pot as he, too, took a seat. 'I believe so. Lila said it was a good idea because there are so many colors in this room, and the mother of pearl contains them all. Now, about your requirements…'

Jon sadly acknowledged that he didn't appear to have access to anyone else, who was available immediately, who might be better suited than the two candidates he'd highlighted. It amused Christine that he managed to do so in a way that implied he had any number of other people on his books for whom managing a household overrun by an entire menagerie would be well within their realm of experience, but that they were currently employed elsewhere.

'Is it possible for me to meet with these two candidates here, today?' Christine didn't have to try to look eager, she was.

'May I?' Jon reached for the tablet and scrolled again. 'Mr Burrows lives in Cleethorpes, so it's unlikely he could get here today, but we could see if it would be possible for you two to chat online. And as for Ms Knox? She's in London, but over in Streatham. She might be available – but maybe not until this afternoon. I'll phone her.'

'I have to be in central London this afternoon. Maybe I could meet her there, somewhere? That might be more convenient for both of us. In a public place, of course. Meeting for a coffee would be lovely. I'd suggest a venue. And, yes, an online interview with your Mr Burrows would suit. Before I leave the premises? I assume you have private rooms here.'

'Indeed. Please, allow me a few moments to make the arrangements. Would you care for fresh tea? I'll have to take my leave of you, I'm afraid – a luncheon engagement.'

'But of course, Jon, I can't expect to keep you all to myself, now can I?'

She went as far as fluttering her eyelashes just a little. He all but leered back at her.

'No thank you to the tea, Jon,' she said firmly, 'but if you had a hot chocolate, with some whipped cream, and a sprinkling of cinnamon sugar on top, that would hit the spot admirably.' Christine smiled innocently as the man's eyebrows popped up again.

'I'll have a word with Lila on my way out. I'm sure she'll be able to organize whatever you want. I'll send her in with it, but it might take a few moments.'

Looking as though he'd been shot out of a cannon, Dacre left the room, and Christine leaped from her chair; she hoped it would take the lovely Lila a good while to rustle up a beverage that would meet Christine's exacting requirements. She crossed the annoying rug – catching both her heels again, twice – and rounded Dacre's desk.

By the time Lila appeared with a mug of something that looked a bit like an ice cream float, and a rigid smile, Christine was back in the uncomfortable chair flicking distractedly through a copy of a magazine offering country homes for sale – if you had a spare few million pounds. She also had a fresh appreciation for the idea that maybe Rachel Edwards had a point about Jon Dacre: oily, and with a potted plant that used broken oyster shells as a mulch – some of which was now in her pocket. And that note in his diary? That might be damning evidence of his murderous intent...because she couldn't begin to imagine what else it might mean.

CHAPTER FOURTEEN

Although she didn't know it, at the about the same time that Christine was having a bizarre video conversation about the dietary requirements of an Emperor tamarin with a neat-looking, if surprised, man in the north of England, her fiancé's good friend Geordie was holding a weedy youth up against a wall in South London, his arm across his throat, ensuring said youth gave his full attention to Alexander Bright.

'You know you know him, and I know you know him, so tell me where you saw him last.' Alexander didn't need to raise his voice. In fact, he knew he was much more likely to achieve the desired effect if he whispered. Which he did…into the man's disgustingly filthy ear.

The youth was shaking. 'I 'aven't seen 'im for months. Not since you was around 'ere last time. Nowhere near him, I've been, like you said. He might be getting stuff from someone else, but not from me. Honest. Cross me 'eart. I 'aven't sold him a single baggie for months. And I won't, neither.'

Alexander nodded, and his friend and confidant allowed the young man to sink to the ground.

He looked down at the sorry sight; the bloke was probably only in his mid-twenties – maybe about the same age as Christine? – but he had the appearance of a man fading into nothing…his face lined, cheeks hollow, gaps in his teeth, his eyes yellowing. Alexander reckoned he was using too much of his own merchandise.

Alexander hissed, 'Okay, Joss, let's say I believe that you haven't been selling to Sean again…but have you *seen* him?'

Weary, wary eyes looked up. Joss held out his hand. 'Any chance of a few quid for a cuppa and a sandwich?'

Geordie reached down and grabbed the man's soiled jacket. 'You've got the front to ask that? You won't spend anything we give you on food. We all know where it'll go.'

Alexander pulled a tenner out of his pocket. 'So, have you seen him?'

Joss grabbed the note. 'Couple of streets back there's an old church hall. Not used now. Got a tree growing out of the roof. Big metal fence. Saw him over that way about…um' – he counted his fingers – 'nine, ten days ago?'

'You asking, or telling?' Alexander bent down.

'Telling. About then. It was a Thursday, I know that. After dark. Late. Maybe closer to the morning? Dunno, to be honest. It was a hot night, before the weather broke and all that rain came. Weird, really – he had a big, puffy, yellow jacket on, and it weren't cold.'

Alexander and Geordie exchanged a glance.

'I know the jacket he means,' said Geordie quietly. 'Sounds like Sean.'

'Here's a sandwich, Joss,' said Alexander, fishing out one of three packages he'd stuffed into his pockets before the pair had set off on their Sean hunt. 'I hope chicken's alright for you.'

Joss grabbed the sandwich, leaped to his feet and grinned as he turned to go. He called, 'Yeah. I managed to put my vegetarian phase behind me when I rediscovered the joys of bacon,' and he was gone, disappearing from the alleyway onto the street beyond.

'I can imagine what Sean was doing around here in the early hours,' said Geordie heavily. 'Fancy checking out the place he mentioned? Might be good to do it in daylight, even if the place appeals to a different sort after dark.'

Alexander agreed, and the men headed back to the main drag through Brixton, and turned in the direction Joss had indicated. They finally had a lead.

The streets were busy, thronged with people going about their daily lives, largely unaware that there was a parallel universe existing around them, which was how Alexander always thought of it.

It was impossible for Alexander to miss the fact that the area was now home to many people who had so much more money than those who'd lived there decades earlier, when Brixton had been his home. He studied how the well-dressed young professionals talked on their phones as they bustled past invisible street kids whose backpacks contained everything they owned.

He noted the way that pushchairs that costs hundreds of pounds were steered carefully around gaggles of ethnically diverse young men and women who lounged against the walls of shops, eyeing the backsides of the young mothers once they'd passed with a mixture of envy and loathing.

'Cleaned parts of this place up a bit, haven't they?' Geordie's observation was for Alexander's ears alone.

'The bits out here, that are easily seen, have been shined up alright,' replied Alexander. As they turned into a residential road, he added, 'This area used to be full of squats; I bet you can't buy a studio flat in one of these converted Victorian houses for less than a couple of hundred grand now. But then there's that.'

He pointed to an elderly man – at least, he appeared to be elderly – asleep in the front garden of a terraced, red-brick house, where the landscaping and decorative objects in and around the entryway suggested it was a family home. He reckoned the owners would have paid well over a million for it. A brand-new BMW was parked outside.

'I bet they'll be in for a shock when they open their front door.' He kicked a used needle into the gutter with the toe of his boot. 'Sleeping it off, I suppose.'

Geordie nodded silently, then whispered, 'I hope Sean's not come to that.'

'We both do, mate. But, listen…whatever state we find him in, we'll do our best to sort it, between us. Right?' He grabbed Geordie's arm. 'We'll find him, I promise.'

Geordie shoved out his chin. 'Is that the place that nasty little dealer meant? There can't be too many buildings of that sort around here, I suppose.'

'Let's walk past it first, give it the once over. You make out you're taking a call, and I'll look as though I'm bored, got it? There's a couple of lookouts over there, and another behind that tree on the corner, which might mean we're walking right into someone's territory.'

Geordie nodded, pulled his phone out of his pocket and said loudly, 'Gotta take this – I'll walk and talk.'

The men ambled, with Geordie making a good job of carrying on half a fake conversation – which seemed to come with jokes on the part of whomever he was speaking to – while Alexander kept his head down, but his eyes, and ears, alert. Two youths swooshed past on bicycles and honked an air horn at them, making them both jump – which amused the kid they were approaching who was leaning on a tree.

As they passed, the boy stuck out a hoodie-clad arm. 'Got any spare change?'

Alexander didn't even pause. 'Gave it all to an old bloke sitting on a bit of cardboard outside the Tube station.'

As they continued, the youth called, 'He'll only spend it on *beer*. I'd have made better use of it.' He laughed manically and ran off along the road toward the two other youths who were holding their ground at the next corner.

When the two men reached the three youths, Geordie surprised Alexander by holding up a photograph of Sean and asking, 'Have any of you lot seen this bloke?'

Alexander felt his body become rigid; they hadn't agreed on a direct approach like this.

'Who's askin'?' The tallest of the trio spoke.

'His brother. I'm worried about him. He's been seen around here. I'm trying to find him.' Geordie's tone wasn't aggressive; Alexander judged he was allowing himself to sound as tired and desperate as he felt.

'You talk like him,' said the middle-sized one.

'Shut up,' snapped the tall one. 'We 'aven't seen 'im. Now bog off. These streets is dangerous for blokes like you.'

Geordie asked, 'What do you mean, blokes like us?'

The trio giggled. 'Old and past it,' said the one who'd been by the tree, 'who give their money to even older blokes who'll waste it on cans of beer, that's who.'

Alexander put up his hands in a sign of submission, and tried to make himself small.

'Alright, men, you can see my mate's worried about his brother. If any of you had a brother who'd gone missing, you'd try to find him, wouldn't you? Help him if he needed it? It's only natural, right? And we thought you might have seen him around, that's all. No harm in asking, is there?'

His life on the streets had taught him to ask questions where the likely answer took the respondent from seeing you as a threat, to thinking you were at least a human being. He hoped he still had the knack.

'I've got six brothers, and I wish every one of them would leg it,' said the tallest of the three, which drew laughs from his mates.

'Well, we're grateful for your time, aren't we?' Alexander gave Geordie a stare that he hoped conveyed that they should make a swift exit.

'Yeah. Cheers.'

The men walked on, the youths stayed where they were.

A voice called after them, 'Be careful who you ask about him.' They didn't turn to see who'd spoken.

Alexander hissed, 'Don't turn, don't look anywhere, just keep your head down and keep walking, then make a sharp right around the corner when we get to the end of the block. We need to get back onto the main road, where we can blend into the crowds. As soon as we turn the corner, and are mingling, take your jacket off, and put this cap on.' He shoved a baseball cap into Geordie's hand. 'Then we head back toward the Tube station. If we get separated, I'll see you on the platform.'

Geordie hissed back, 'Sorry, mate, I had to ask – they looked like runners for dealers, and I thought Sean might have been buying from them.'

'It's not a problem, just do what I said.'

The two men changed their appearance as they jostled through the throngs, and managed to stay together until they reached the entrance to the Underground station. Alexander was happy that they hadn't been followed.

'Now, don't get your hopes up, Geordie, but I saw a flash of a puffy yellow jacket heading toward the railway bridge along there. Don't run, but let's go, quickly. Follow me, and stay close.'

Geordie grabbed Alexander's arm, then released it. 'Right, let's go.' Alexander used all his height to peer over heads, and managed to catch another glimpse of the distinctive jacket. They walked beneath the first bridge, then the second, gaining on the figure.

'It's him. That's his walk,' said Geordie excitedly. 'He's alright – walking around just fine. Just wait till I get him…' He increased his pace, and the two men rounded the corner behind the yellow-jacketed figure as it turned into Brixton Station Road, where cafés and shops were housed beneath the arches of the railway line that ran overhead. The figure disappeared into a coffee shop, and Alexander grabbed Geordie roughly as he made to follow.

'Give it a minute, mate, let's see what he's up to. He doesn't know we're here, so let's get close, and observe. Out with the phones, and let's break apart – but no confronting him, right?'

Geordie agreed – grudgingly, it was clear – and they did as Alexander had suggested, both appearing to be wandering aimlessly as they chatted on their phones, immersed in non-existent conversations.

Within a few moments, the yellow jacket exited the café. Alexander could see that it really was Sean, and could also see that Geordie was no more than a couple of feet from him. But Sean didn't spot his brother, because he was having an animated conversation with an older man who'd left the coffee shop with him.

Alexander felt his stomach lurch as he recognized one of his employers from thirty years earlier. Those decades had been kind to Alexander, but not to Big Tony. The last time Alexander had seen the man, he'd been standing at a bar not half a mile from where they were at that moment, giving an order for someone who'd reported his activities to the police to be 'dealt with'. Now Big Tony was emaciated, and using an electric wheelchair. However, Alexander could see he still had that air about him that would tell anyone who chose to look him in the eye that he shouldn't be messed with.

Alexander covered his face with his phone and hand, then managed to catch Geordie's eye. He shook his head, wandering away from Sean and Big Tony, indicating that Geordie should follow.

When the two men met, he could tell that his friend was at the end of his tether. 'I'm glad Sean looks alright, but...but why didn't you want me to talk to him? All I want him to know is that I'm here for him.'

Alexander gazed into his friend's eyes, hoping he'd understand. 'That bloke he was with? His name's Big Tony. He might not look like much to you, seeing him for the first time today, but he used to rule a part of this area, and not by dint of his charm and winning personality. If Sean's connected with him, then he might be involved in something other than getting his hands on a personal supply of drugs. We need to tread carefully, Geordie. I know he's your brother, but Big Tony is nothing but trouble. Deadly trouble. And I know where he used to do business, and...and I might be able to find out what's going on. If you can be a bit more patient.'

Geordie looked worried sick. 'You're the most faithful friend a man could have, pet. Thanks.'

Alexander chuckled. 'You're welcome, pet.'

CHAPTER FIFTEEN

Christine felt positively queasy as she sat in the waiting room in Harley Street; she blamed the tooth-deadening sweetness of the small bucket of hot chocolate that Lila at Buttle My World had topped with what must have been half a can of whipped cream. Of course, Christine had drunk the entire thing as she'd talked to the potential butler in Cleethorpes, who had eventually declared himself unsuitable for the task in question because of his aversion to 'flocks of birds'. She wondered how the man managed to live a normal life – but knew very well he'd been lying; the idea of an aviary, a varying number of dogs, and a tamarin, had been too much for him.

But she'd learned a few valuable things during their conversation. Firstly, that the man had been recruited by Richard Edwards, and trained by Rachel, and he gushed when he spoke of them. Secondly, that he'd not yet once been placed by Jon Dacre. Thirdly, when he spoke of Jon, Christine sensed more than reserve. She'd pressed and cajoled him, until the man had admitted that Jon's manner with him was always brusque. She reckoned he'd been polite.

Christine looked at her watch. Again. She'd made the appointment to see her doctor as soon as she'd made the plan to come to London, but she had less than an hour until she was due to meet the other potential butler – Twyla Knox – at a café just off Oxford Street. She'd chosen it because it was only about five minutes from where she was currently sitting, but the doctor was running late – an emergency appointment, the receptionist had said.

Finally, Christine was admitted, and she was greeted warmly by Dr Warren, who'd been her family's general physician since she'd been a teen. With pleasantries exchanged, Christine listed her symptoms, and expressed her concerns about her general feeling of torpor.

Dr Warren did everything she'd expected him to do – examining her body by pressing here and there, peering everywhere else, and taking notes when he returned to his desk.

He also drew blood, then asked her to produce a urine sample.

'I want to run a few tests on these, but that will take some time. Would you be able to return in two hours? I'll see you then, and we can have a chat about any findings.'

Christine grinned. 'I'm a lucky gal to have access to super-speedy Harley Street testing, aren't I, Dr Warren?'

The doctor winked one of his kindly eyes. 'Indeed you are, my dear. Two hours then?'

'Two hours.'

Christine headed away from the doctor's office, which was housed in one of the almost identical buildings for which the street was world-famous, toward the café. She needn't have worried; she was in plenty of time for her meeting, and was able to find a corner table, and have a plate of pasta on it before Twyla Knox arrived.

Christine explained that she'd missed lunch, and made it clear to the server that Twyla was her guest. She allowed the young woman – a jumble of acute angles with a scrubbed face and a halo of dark curls – to tell her all about herself as she inhaled her pasta. She listened with increasing alarm as the chatty Twyla recounted various interactions she'd had with previous clients. Christine was horrified to think that someone who'd been hired by the people in question with an expectation of discretion would be so loose lipped, then realized that it might be to her advantage. She decided to not bother with all the rubbish about animals, and get straight to what she really wanted to know, which was how the dynamics worked within Buttle My World, and what the young woman thought of Jon Dacre. She knew this approach was risky, but she thought it a chance worth taking.

Christine said, 'I met with Mr Dacre earlier today, and I have to say I wasn't impressed. I'd expected someone of more substance to be running a company with such an excellent reputation. Is he a good trainer?'

Twyla addressed the corner of the table. 'That's not Mr Dacre's area of responsibility. Mr and Mrs Edwards trained me up.'

'Were they good trainers?'

'They were strict, but fair, and I believe I received comprehensive training from them both. I…I've never spent time alone with Mr Dacre. Indeed, other than when I attended my training courses, I've never visited the offices in Earl's Court.'

Christine pounced. 'Because…?'

Twyla responded in what Christine could tell was a guarded manner, for the first time in the past hour. 'No particular reason.'

Christine pressed. 'Lila Stevenson seems efficient. Very…present for Jon, I would think.'

Twyla Knox snorted coffee. She wiped her face, and the table, then said, 'I'm terribly sorry.'

'No problem. Is she that attached to him, then?' Christine winked, and hoped Twyla wouldn't be able to resist a chance to gossip a bit more.

The young woman studied her coffee for a moment then said, 'When I was at the office for my training, Lila made a point of chatting to me and the one other young, female trainee, about how close she and Jon were. I know for a fact she didn't bother sharing such insights with any of the male trainees. She was warning us off – not that I had the slightest interest in the man. Not my type at all. Though I gathered from the receptionist that Lila and Jon have been at it for a couple of years now. In fact, Lila was once the receptionist, but she got promoted, and then they took on Apple.'

Christine was confused. 'Apple?'

Twyla grinned. 'I know, stupid name, isn't it? She's the one at reception. Says Lila barely talks to her, except to go on about how wonderful Jon is to her, or how horrid he's being to her. Up and down, apparently. They're going through a bit of a strange patch at the moment it seems. Did you know that Mr Edwards, the man who trained me, died recently?'

Christine shook her head and looked suitably scandalized. 'No. Was he old? Was it an accident?'

Twyla leaned in, obviously in her element – as was Christine, though she was doing her best to not show it.

The young woman dropped her voice. 'Not old at all, well, not really. Died at a dinner they were all having. Apple was there. We text a bit. She told me all about it. Anyway – in the days before poor Mr Edwards died, Lila was lording it over Apple something rotten, apparently, then, when he was dead, she wouldn't let Mr Dacre out of her sight. Apple said she went all weird when they found out that Mrs Edwards was going to take over running the company with Mr Dacre after her husband died. Lila and Mr Dacre had a huge row in his office, Apple said. She didn't know what about, but Mr Dacre was shouting about not having enough money to be able to get married, according to Apple. Since then – and he only died a few weeks ago – Lila's been all over Mr Dacre again. Apple reckons they've made up.'

Christine pressed. 'Do you think marriage is on the cards for Lila and Jon?'

Twyla pushed away her empty cup, looked around, then whispered, 'Apple said Lila's been talking about rings. And not the sort you get in the high street – the sort you have to make an appointment to go to try on. She's even told Apple that Mr Dacre will be able to afford to spoil her rotten, soon. They were all out celebrating the company winning a big new contract when Mr Edwards died, and even Apple got a bit of a bonus, so maybe that's what Lila meant.'

Either that, or Jon reckons he'll get his hands on the other fifty percent of the business, soon, thought Christine. She was glad that Rachel was safely installed at Chellingworth Hall.

Checking her watch, Christine knew she had to make a move, and decided to deliver a bit of a life lesson to Twyla.

'Thanks for meeting me, Twyla, but I don't think you'll be suitable for my family's needs.'

Twyla looked crestfallen, and also stood. 'But we've been getting on like a house on fire, haven't we?'

Christine sighed. 'Gossip is caustic, Twyla, and no one – and I mean that quite literally – wants a member of their personal staff blabbing about their private life, to anyone.'

Twyla looked quite taken aback.

Christine added, 'You said that Mr and Mrs Edwards trained you well. I can only imagine that the first thing they told you was that any butler needs to be utterly discreet. Maybe they should have gone one step further and defined that word for you, because you don't seem to have a clue what it means. Thank you, and goodbye.'

Twyla grabbed her bag, and stomped huffily out of the café. Christine felt awful for having pumped her…but knew she'd been right to warn the woman about her inability to keep her mouth shut.

She paid the bill, then headed back to Dr Warren's office, wondering what sort of texts might fly between Twyla and Apple that afternoon, then she phoned Carol to pass on all the news she'd gathered, Carol being the one who was accumulating all the incoming information on The Case of the Bereaved Butler, then passing it out around the team.

'Got to go now, Carol. Got a thing I have to do for a bit, then I'll text later. By the way – anything more on The Case of the Exceptional Evacuee? Anything you need me to do while I'm in London?'

Christine's heart always swelled when she heard Carol laugh. 'Not at the moment, but I bet you there'll be something, on one of our cases, by tomorrow. Mavis has sent me her report of her interview with Walter Gulliver, and I'll send that out as soon as I've added what I've found out. This evening, I should think, because I'm picking up Annie to go to talk to a bloke who's about ninety but, apparently, has a sharp mind, and a great knowledge of local farms and so forth. He provided a fair bit of the information for the local history display they installed at the Market Hall when they did it up, so it'll be after I'm back from that.'

'That's just fine, Carol – like I said, I'm not short of things to get on with here.'

'So what's this now then? A family thing? Not slipping off the old wagon to have a fancy cocktail in one of those swish places you're always going on about, are you?'

Christine sighed. 'No, I'm not. It's nothing important. Talk later, Carol. Hugs to Albert.'

Christine popped her phone into her pocket as she entered the hallway of her doctor's office.

The receptionist smiled, then ushered Christine to Dr Warren's door. 'You're early, but he's got no one with him, and he told me to send you in as soon as you arrived.'

Christine thanked her, and entered the inner sanctum feeling better than she had done in some time. That pasta had really picked her up. Maybe she wasn't eating enough carbs?

Dr Warren rose as Christine took a seat across his desk. 'And how are you feeling at the moment? You look…well, I have to say you have rather better color than you did a couple of hours ago.'

Christine laughed. 'You know, it's the same with the dentist, isn't it? You make an appointment, and the toothache goes away. Well, I feel like a bit of a fraud, now, doctor, because I've just eaten a much heartier meal than I usually do during the day and have to say I feel much better for it. I think I've been worrying about nothing – maybe I simply need to adjust my diet.'

Dr Warren tapped his desk with the end of what Christine noted was a rather lovely fountain pen. 'You said earlier that you admit you don't consume a balanced diet, that regular meals seem to pass you by.'

Christine nodded. 'I did, because they do. Like today – I missed lunch completely, and if it hadn't been for the fact that I'd arranged to meet someone in a café that offered proper meals as well as snacks, I might not have eaten until dinner time. I know it's not good for me, so if that's what it is, I'll make myself do better. Maybe that, and staying off the drink for a while, will help.'

Dr Warren smiled. 'I agree. You'll need a much more regular meal pattern, you'll need to attend to your nutritional intake as well, and you won't be drinking for about – oh, let me see – probably another seven months or so, at least.'

Christine winked. 'I was thinking of more like a few weeks to be honest, doctor.'

Dr Warren shook his head. 'You've really no idea, have you? Your symptoms left me in little doubt, but I thought it worth investigating thoroughly. You're pregnant, Christine.'

Christine felt as though she'd been kicked in the head.

She could feel her heart thumping. Could hear it, too.

The doctor kept talking, 'You're probably about eight weeks along. Your blood test results showed a slight iron deficiency, which we can address, and you really will have to plan to eat wisely, and, yes, stay away from alcohol.'

Christine began feel hot…to hear white noise…to be aware of the surface of the wooden chair arms she was gripping…then she realized she was being stared at by her doctor.

'Christine? Are you with me? I can see the news has come as a bit of a shock.' Dr Warren rose, pulled a bottle of water from a mini fridge, poured it into a glass, and placed it in front of her. 'Sip that,' he suggested gently.

Christine noticed that she was sweating, so sipped the cool water with gratitude. Her mind was awhirl, her hands shaking. Could this really be happening? To her? She and Alexander had been so careful. Always. What had happened?

She managed, 'But…but I'm on the pill.'

Dr Warren smiled sympathetically. 'Not one hundred percent effective. But maybe you'd been poorly a couple of months ago? Any bouts of sickness? Prior to the morning sickness setting in, that is.'

Christine stared. 'I've been having morning sickness? I thought it was the drink…' Her heart plummeted. 'I've been drinking like a fish, so I have. Dear God, doctor, what if I've harmed it? I didn't know…had no idea. Oh no, what have I done? I'm not ready to be a mother…I can't even look after myself. I still act like a child, half the time. Everyone says so. Oh doctor, what shall I do?'

She watched as the physician sat back in his chair and steepled his fingers. 'Well, the first advice I shall give you is to not panic; a great number of women who become pregnant unexpectedly have been living a normal life, which would probably include drinking alcohol, and by far the vast majority of their babies are born with no ill effects. So, please, don't worry about that. You cannot undo the past.'

Christine mumbled, 'If only.'

The doctor continued calmly, 'Stress in the mother can be just as harmful for a developing fetus, you know. Let's try to keep a sense of perspective, shall we, as we move forward.'

Christine might have bitten his head off, but he gave an avuncular smile, and she nodded, dumbly.

He continued, 'That said, it's good that you chose to stop drinking several days ago, so we'll look on the bright side…at least you're not a smoker. As for your general health? There's absolutely nothing wrong with you that a balanced diet, and maybe the odd supplement, cannot address. So there – you have a head start: you're young and healthy, and have access to, if I may say so, excellent medical attention. I can, of course, refer you to a suitable obstetrician.'

Christine felt her head nod an acknowledgement, though she wasn't aware she'd made it do so.

'Thus, you're well set for the physical aspects of your pregnancy. As for your emotional, and mental, readiness for it? Well, that's something we can discuss. But I wouldn't advise that this is the right moment for that conversation. I think you need a little time to let this sink in. When you're ready, we can talk. However, just so you know, in order for *every* option to be available to you, you still have a couple of months or more to think things through. And maybe talk them through with the father. I read the announcement of your engagement; am I to understand that a wedding is being planned for the near future?'

Christine felt trapped. A baby. Alexander. Her parents. A wedding? A baby. She managed to stand and said, 'Thank you, Dr Warren. I'll tell those I wish to know about this, when I wish them to know it. You understand?'

The doctor also stood. 'But of course.'

Christine thanked the receptionist as she left, and felt her feet take her down the shallow steps, across the pavement, and to the curb. The gratitude with which she climbed into a black cab a few moments later was matched only by the keenness of her desire to get to her own flat in Battersea as soon as she could. She couldn't face her parents. She needed to be alone.

One thought kept rolling around in her head, *How could I have been so stupid?*

CHAPTER SIXTEEN

Annie was ruing the moment she'd agreed to accompany Carol to see an old farmer who lived – as far as she could tell – almost literally in the middle of nowhere. 'So how did you say you found out about this bloke?'

'Your Tudor mentioned him, because I'd been asking around to try to find someone who knew a lot about the area back in the war years.'

Annie shrugged – as best she could, given the position of the seat belt. 'And how did Tude know about him? And why didn't he tell me?'

Carol didn't take her eyes off the road, for which Annie was grateful. 'I don't know why he didn't tell you. Maybe you didn't ask the same questions I did? I know you two have been focused on all the packing and planning to get yourselves into the new pub. As for how Tudor knew him? Well, he said he knows of him, rather than knowing him personally. Mr Howells was one of the people who contributed to the words and pictures used to describe the area's history when they made that new display for the Market Hall in the village.'

Annie stared out at the rolling, sheep-dotted hills and valleys. 'All that rain we had greened everything up lovely, didn't it? Is it much farther?'

'I hope not. And the first thing I'll be doing when we get there is asking to use the loo. I hope it's not…you know…well, I hope it's a decent one, not something in an outhouse that's not got a proper seat, or anything like that.'

'Gordon Bennett, Car, we're not going to some horrible little hermit hovel, are we?'

'We'll soon find out. This is where we turn off. Oh dear, it's a bit steep.'

As Carol coaxed her vehicle up a rutted track that appeared to lead nowhere, Annie grabbed the side of her seat, and the handle on the door. 'Mind out, Car – my rear's still recovering from that nasty tumble I took.'

Carol replied distractedly, 'I bet this was like a waterfall a few days back – I can't imagine how you'd come and go up here when the weather's like that.'

Finally spying a single-storey stone cottage and some outbuildings, Annie felt relieved that she wouldn't have to endure the bumpy ride for much longer. At least, not until they left. 'After all that jostling about, I might end up fighting you for the bathroom – whatever it's like,' she said with a chuckle.

They pulled to a halt in a small yard, which was almost totally surrounded by buildings constructed from the local stone, all in various states of looking as though they were gradually returning to becoming piles of rocks.

'It's a bit run-down,' said Carol sounding wary.

'It's disintegrating,' replied Annie. 'We'd better get on with this, or there'll be none of it left. What's his name?'

'Hywel Howells.'

Annie shook her head as she unfolded herself out of the car. 'I've said it before, and I dare say I'll be saying it umpteen times more – the way the Welsh use names, you really would think they didn't have enough to go around.'

Carol smiled as she, too, emerged from the car, and smoothed down her long, stripey, cotton dress. 'I know…but it's tradition. My money's on him being the eldest son of the family, or maybe the only one. We'll see. Annie, the back of your blouse is all caught up.'

Annie waggled her hand behind her back and pulled at the edge of her blouse. 'Typical – it must have ridden up when I sat down. It probably looks like a crinkle-cut chip now. Ah well, there's nothing I can do about it. I like this blouse – it matches my shorts a treat.'

'Your mother's amazing at that…matching colors; I know you said she posted you that blouse after she'd seen the shorts on you in a photo.'

Annie nodded. 'Eustelle's got a good eye, always has. Reckons it comes from years of pairing things up when she worked at the launderette. Right – will you take the lead?'

Carol nodded and the couple strode toward the front door of the building that looked most like a home. Carol knocked, and Annie saw a bit of green paint flake off. She didn't mention it. Carol knocked again, and a bigger flake dropped to the floor.

Carol turned to her chum. 'Did you notice that? See? It's left a hole.' She looked horrified.

Annie shrugged. 'Maybe you shouldn't knock again…the whole door might collapse.'

'*Shwmai.*' A female voice called across the yard, and both women swung around.

Annie listened as Carol and the woman spoke in Welsh, guessing that Carol was explaining why they were there. Annie at least understood it when Carol introduced them by name – Annie smiled and waved when she heard her own – and she picked out the words *teleffon* and Howells. The woman headed off, her mobile phone at her ear.

'Mr Howells' granddaughter-in-law says he's up in the top field. She's phoning him to say we're here. He'll be down in a few minutes.'

Annie's heart sank. 'We're going to be hanging around this place all day.'

Carol snapped, 'Look, I don't want this taking longer than it has to, either – I want to get back to Albert and David, but we might have to nurse him along a bit, to make sure we get what we need from him.'

Annie felt a bit put out. 'If he's going to talk Welsh, like that woman, what was the point of me even coming? I'll be useless. There's no way you can translate everything so that I don't feel left out.'

'She also speaks English, and he does too. But I speak Welsh, and we're in Wales, so I suppose the two of us just found it easier to do the preliminaries in the language we grew up using.' Carol tutted. 'It's not about excluding the English, Annie, it's about just allowing the Welsh to be Welsh. But, yes, we'll do what we can in English, but don't forget that he's old. His brain and memory might not work as well in a second language, which is why I'm the one heading this one up, not Mavis – remember?'

Annie knew they'd all agreed that Carol should lead The Case of the Exceptional Evacuee because Mavis would be coordinating The Case of the Bereaved Butler, and in any case – as Carol had just pointed out – there was a chance that her Welsh language abilities might be required, given that they were hunting down a family of Welsh-speaking farmers.

'I think we'd stand a better chance of drawing him out if we were inside his home – he might even have some old photos, or need to refer to stuff he has there,' said Annie thoughtfully, not wanting to belabor the Welsh thing.

Carol smiled. 'Good idea – can that be him?'

Knowing that the man they were due to meet was well into his eighties, Annie had expected to see a wizened creature, all but ready to pop his clogs. The man walking toward her was short, but upright, spry, and wiry. He was sporting a canary baseball cap, its peak shielding his eyes from the sun, and a red-and-blue checked, short-sleeved shirt which allowed his vein-roped, skinny arms to poke out. His short, bowed legs were encased in faded jeans, and he was wearing vivid blue wellies. Not at all what she'd had in mind. As he approached, an exuberant black and white collie darted from an outbuilding and trotted beside him.

Greeting the dog first, with a gentle touch and a soft word or two, Hywel Howells offered his hand as he said, 'Carol?' Carol nodded and took his hand. 'So you must be Annie.' Annie shook his hand. 'You're Tudor Evans's partner, right?'

'That's me,' she replied, smiling.

'Good man, Tudor,' he said. 'He's always kept a good pub, I hear, and is a wonderful addition to the community.'

Annie liked his rich and tuneful voice…and what he was saying. 'He is,' she agreed.

'I'll make us a pot of tea, and we can have a chat. Eirlys – that's who you met – says I can talk the hind legs off a donkey, so you've been warned. But I'll do my best to stick to the point.'

Annie and Carol exchanged a worried glance as they followed Hywel into what turned out to be a cozy cottage, full of mod cons, and not at all the sort of run-down place the state of the front door had suggested.

'The facilities are through there,' said Hywel, waving an arm. 'I dare say you'd both like to use them – most people do when they've driven all the way up that track.' He chuckled as Carol wasted no time, and Annie cursed herself for not being quicker off the mark.

By the time they were all sitting at the well-loved kitchen table, with mugs of tea and a plate of homemade biscuits, Annie felt ready to take on the world.

Carol gave Hywel all the facts – scant though they were – about the farm and the family they were trying to locate. He sipped his scalding tea as he listened, and Annie grabbed the chance to take in her surroundings. The place was clean and neat, there was no shortage of family photographs dotted on every surface, and doilies and vases of flowers suggested a woman's touch. Carol had said that Hywel was a widower, so Annie suspected that other female members of the family were responsible for the appearance of the cottage, and the décor.

She tuned back in when Carol kicked her ankle and said sharply, 'That's right, isn't it, Annie? We'll be extremely grateful for any help Hywel can give us.'

'Absolutely,' said Annie as fast as she could, then she added, 'this cottage is lovely, Hywel. It's so clean, and beautifully done up. So many happy faces smiling at you from the family photos all the time, and those doilies must be handmade.'

'All my dear late wife's work, those doilies. And the antimacassars. Loved to crochet, she did, but it got a bit much for her eyes in the end, especially with the tiny hooks she used. Now my daughter looks after it all for me. Says I'm hopeless. Of course, I know very well that I could do it all for myself, but it means she spends time here with me, and I'm always able to talk her into stopping her dusting to share a pot of tea.' He winked. 'It's nice when folks drop in. She makes these for me, too.' He pushed the plate of biscuits toward the two women. Annie dared a third.

He added, 'David Davies, you say? Well, there's enough of them around these parts. I can think of two farms with men by that name, but one of them is definitely too young to be your David Davies – though he could be your one's son, of course. I can give you the names of those farms before you leave so you can phone them. Of course, it might be that the son didn't stay connected with the farm. A lot of sons don't want to follow in their father's footsteps, like mine didn't. It's my daughter and her husband, and their son and his wife, who look after this place now – and they do a good job. Don't live here, of course. They have a house and a barn on the other side of the hill, with a smallholding. And that's the other thing, see? Lots of what would have been farms back then don't exist any longer. They might have been bought up to make a bigger place that was more economical to run, or they've been broken up into smallholdings, that are easier to cope with. And the farm houses themselves? They'd be mainly all stone-built around here, if they had any age about them...no, hang on now, one of the Davieses I mentioned isn't stone, it's pebble dash, so that one's out, I suppose. What I can also tell you is that, during the war, it wasn't unusual for farmers to branch out into crops and animals they'd never dealt with before. It's all well and good having a load of sheep, but sometimes people made the decision to focus on growing and raising what they wanted to eat, and a variety of things they could trade, rather than have to try to sell one type of crop or animal. It's not ideal up here for cattle or pigs, but there's nothing to say you couldn't keep a few of anything, as long as you set aside the right bit of land for it...so that doesn't help to narrow things down.'

For all that she was feeling a bit of a sugar rush, Annie felt dejected; she'd suspected that finding the right farm would be – and she smiled when she thought it – like looking for a needle in a haystack, but this wasn't getting them anywhere.

'And you said there was a Blodwen Davies?' Hywel leaned forward.

Carol nodded, 'Possibly a Blodwen Davies.'

Annie saw a shift in the man's demeanor.

'Now just a minute,' he said brightly. 'I was in school with a Blodwen Davies. If you give me a sec, I might remember where it was that she lived – though I have to be honest and tell you I might never have known. I remember Blodwen because she was a pretty girl. We were all taught in one big room back then, so I can't be sure of her age.'

He frowned, and Annie felt she could almost see him peering back through the decades.

'She was small, so I suppose I imagined she was younger, but she acted older. Mainly played by herself…no, there was another girl she was always with. Fast friends, they were. Don't remember her friend's name. Blodwen was good at reading…oh yes, that's right…Mrs Thomas used to have her reading aloud in front of the class quite often. Nice speaking voice. Had a dress with pink flowers on it, I remember.'

Annie hoped this was leading somewhere.

'No idea what happened to her.' His eyes narrowed. 'She was still there when I finished school, but I was out of there as quick as I could be – needed on the farm, see? No – wait, now…I heard about her years later. Married a butcher, she did. Name of…now I know that's in there somewhere. I recall it was exceptionally suitable for his trade. Let me have a top up of tea, and it might come to me.'

Annie and Carol had let Hywel chatter on without interrupting, both realizing it was probably best to allow him to wade through his memories in his own way, but Annie wanted to steer him in the right direction. 'He wasn't Mr Bones the Butcher was he? Like on the Happy Families playing cards.' She added a cheeky grin.

Hywel lit up, and Annie hoped she'd hit the nail on the head.

Then his face fell. 'No…but something like that.' He sipped his tea, and Annie could see his lips moving, as though he were mouthing different names, to see if they felt right. 'Got it! Peaswell. Of course.'

Annie felt her brow furrow. 'How's "Peaswell" got anything to do with being a butcher?'

Carol glared at her.

'We always used to get dried peas in a box from the butcher's shop in the winter, to go with our faggots. Peas. Butcher. Peaswell. See?'

He looked pleased with himself. 'She'd be Blodwen Peaswell now – if she's still alive, of course. But that's an unusual name to be going on with, isn't it?' He looked delighted, and both Annie and Carol slapped smiles on their faces.

'Anything else?' Carol asked.

Hywel attended to his dog, who was seeking attention. 'Good girl, Eirlys,' he whispered.

Annie couldn't stop herself. 'Your dog's named after your grandson's wife?'

Hywel looked puzzled. 'No, that would be *twp*, wouldn't it? If I went out into the yard and shouted "Eirlys", they'd both come running. This is Eirlys. My grandson's wife is Kate. You met her.'

Annie looked at Carol, whose eyes were telling Annie not to pursue the matter, so she didn't.

'Now let me write down the name of that farm, for you – the one with a David Davies on it and a stone house, and then I'll be back up to the top field. It's a nice spot up there. Used to be my wife's favorite part of the farm that did. I feel closer to her when I'm there, see?'

Having taken their leave, and with a few biscuits for each of them wrapped in greaseproof paper, Carol concentrated on getting them back to the road in one piece, while Annie hung onto whatever she could.

Finally on a well-made surface, Annie relaxed her grip, shook out her bloodless fingers and said, 'So a Blodwen Peaswell and a farm with a David Davies. Do you think he really knew what he was talking about? He mixed up his dog and a member of his family – he might have this all wrong, too.'

Carol sighed, and looked at the road ahead. 'It's a phone call to the farm, and a little bit of digging for me to track down a butcher – and he was kind enough to try to help, so I'll give him the benefit of the doubt.'

Annie nodded. 'Glad of the company as much as anything, wasn't he?'

They paused to turn at a T junction. As vehicles passed in front of them, Annie spotted one she recognized.

'That's Dan our decorator. What's he doing all the way out here at this time of day? He should be painting our flat. Carol, follow that van.'

Carol giggled, then turned to face her friend. Annie made sure that her expression made it perfectly clear she was serious. 'Come on, Car, pull out, or we'll lose him. My money's on he's up to something.'

CHAPTER SEVENTEEN

'Put your foot down, Car – he's getting away from us.' Annie was squirming in the passenger seat, annoying Carol.

'Stop wriggling about. I can't drive over the vehicle in front of us, Annie, and there's nowhere to overtake, so keep your hair on.'

'Oi, no cracks about my hair. You know it's the bane of my life. Well, that and me feet…and me back. Anyway, I'm making sure I don't lose sight of him. Look, he's turning off. Where's he going? Turn here, Car.'

Carol did her best to maintain her cool. 'I will. I'm already indicating. And he's going to Builth Wells, or heading that way, at least. That's where the road goes. No, hang on, he's turning off up that lane.' She pulled to the side of the road.

Annie squealed, 'Follow him!'

Carol unbuckled her seat belt. 'If we drive up there, he's bound to see us. Let's leave the car here and follow on foot.'

'He could go along there for miles. I don't mind a bit of sneaky observation, but I don't fancy traipsing through the countryside for who knows how far. It's hot, and humid, and there'll be things all over the place that want to bite and sting me.'

Carol said, 'You sound like a small child. Do you want to know what he's up to, or not?'

'Yes.'

Carol knew she'd won. 'Well, in that case, get out of the car and let's go.'

Annie grumbled like a teenager as they trudged along a muddy lane with tall hedges on both sides. Carol slammed an arm across Annie's chest as they rounded a bend – the height of the hedges had obscured their view of a house that was just feet away.

Annie pushed herself forward and peeped through the branches. 'That's his van,' she hissed.

Carol nodded – trying to communicate with a glance that she knew that, because she'd been the one following it.

She mouthed, 'I know' silently, though she was shouting inside her head. She elbowed Annie out of the way, pulled apart a few branches, then grabbed her phone from her bag and started snapping.

Annie pawed at Carol's arm, and pressed up against her back, trying to look over Carol's head. Carol's arm got scratched and she glared at her chum, who backed off a little.

'What's he carrying?' Annie hissed right into Carol's ear.

Carol showed her the screen of her phone and enlarged the shot. 'Tiles? Boxes of tiles, I think.'

Annie leaned away from Carol. 'If he's nicked our bathroom tiles, I'll have him. Cost an arm and a leg, they did…but, hang on, they can't be ours…Angelo's used up all of ours. Here let me see.'

Carol stepped back so Annie could take her spot beside the hedge. Taller than Carol by a head, Annie pulled apart some higher branches, and Carol watched as her chum grabbed her own phone, and began to snap. Annie whispered, 'He's shutting up the van…if he comes back this way, he'll see us.'

Carol considered the possibility of the pair of them making it back to her car in the time it would take Dan to turn his van around; Annie with her long legs and spare frame might have been able to manage it, but she knew she didn't stand a chance…she'd never been built for speed.

She grabbed Annie's arm. 'Come on, there was a gate we passed, let's get that far and get over or through it. We can wait until he's passed, then we can walk back to the car.'

As they scampered along the lane, Carol hoped the gate would open. When they got to it, she even said a little prayer, because she knew there was no way she'd be able to get over it. Annie in shorts? Yes. Her in a long frock? No, no matter how stretchy it was.

Luckily, between them, the pair managed to wrench the gate open. They'd just got through it, and ducked behind the hedge, when the grubby white van emblazoned with a cartoonish painter, and the annoyingly catchy slogan, bounced along the lane past them.

'That was close,' said Carol turning to her chum, who was sitting in a puddle, with both shoes covered in what Carol hoped was mud.

'I slipped.' Annie sighed. 'No harm done. Except that my bum's soaked through.'

Carol did her best to not laugh as she held out a helping hand, but she couldn't manage it. 'Glad you're not hurt,' she said as she grinned at her friend.

'It's your car I'm going to have to sit in all the way back to the village,' said Annie, wiping off the drips and scraping her shoes on tufts of grass.

'I've got some spare blankets I keep in the back for Albert, and I'll open up a few of his nappies on the seat for you to sit on – they absorb a lot more than you'd think.'

'Lovely,' said Annie, sounding disgusted. 'I suppose at least we now know that Dan's stealing from people other than me and Tude…well, he's stealing from the Chellingworth Estate, really, because they're the ones paying for all the renovations, and the supplies. Those tiles definitely weren't from the Coach and Horses, though; all ours were in white boxes, those boxes were brown.'

'I wonder who lives in that house. Do you know Dan's address? I mean, it looked as though he was delivering them, rather than "taking them home".'

Annie replied, 'Nah, it was Bob Fernley who gave him the contract. I could ask him.'

Carol wondered aloud, 'Have you told Bob about the thefts yet?'

Annie shook her head. 'I've borrowed some of the cameras we keep at the office for surveillance jobs, and me and Tude put them up around the Coach last night. I wanted proof before I said anything. And, even with what we've seen today, that's still not actual evidence that he's been walking off with stuff from the pub, is it?'

Carol knew she had a point. 'I understand. Well, watch the recordings from the cameras and see what you see, then, I suppose.'

She hoped there'd be something useful.

She continued, 'And check with Bob Fernley about where Dan lives – it would be useful to know, in any case. I'll let you do that, because I want to get on with following up what we got from Hywel Howells, and writing up our report, alright?'

They'd reached the car. Carol added, 'Right-o then…let's get those nappies out and get you home. You're a pitiful sight, so I'll drop you at the back door of the Lamb, and hopefully, you can get up to the flat without anyone seeing you.'

'No, Car – drop me at my cottage, will you? Tude's worried enough about me getting hurt as it is, without him seeing this mess. I'll clean myself up, then walk across the green. The tablet monitoring the cameras we set up in the Coach is at the Lamb, so I can look at it over there, while I'm having my dinner. And promise me one thing, Car?'

Carol couldn't help but smile. 'What? Don't tell anyone you've been sitting on nappies in my car this afternoon?'

'Got it in one, doll. Ta. Don't think I'd ever live that one down.'

17th JULY

CHAPTER EIGHTEEN

It was three in the morning, and Christine Wilson-Smythe hadn't slept a wink. She'd paced, flung herself into and out of bed, and she'd cried until she thought she had no more tears left in her. And all the time her hands kept creeping toward her belly, where she was still finding it hard to believe lay a conglomeration of cells that would, one day, become a child.

She couldn't be pregnant. Couldn't have a baby. She wasn't ready to be a mother. She was only in her twenties and had her whole life ahead of her. Having a baby would rob her of her independence. She'd seen it with Stephanie, and she'd seen it with Carol; they were each tied to their child, having to put its needs ahead of their own every moment of every day. They'd both wanted children – in Carol's case, Christine knew it had been an almost overwhelming desire. In fact, Carol had been so desperate to bear a child that she'd walked away from her high-flying career in the City so she'd be less stressed, and therefore possibly more likely to become pregnant.

Christine felt a moment's guilt when she thought of all the women out there, all the couples out there, trying so hard to become parents, whereas it was the last thing she wanted. Standing at the window of her flat in Battersea, managing to catch a slight night breeze on her glistening skin, she wondered how she'd ever cope if she always had to put another human being's needs ahead of hers…then felt guilty about that too, because she knew that everyone who'd ever told her she was selfish was right. But was that the worst thing to be? To live a life where one felt fulfilled, because one could choose what to do when one wanted to do it. Within reason, of course, because everyone had responsibilities of some sort.

Padding through her flat to the kitchen, she ran the water until it was cool, and drank a couple of glasses. At least she now knew why she'd been feeling so...not herself. The sickness, the tiredness, the mood swings...it all made sense. Why on earth hadn't it occurred to her that she might be pregnant? Especially when she'd missed one of her, albeit irregular, periods. Looking back, she was pretty sure she could pinpoint when it had happened. It was a natural process, of course, but that tummy bug must have led to her birth control pills becoming ineffective. So she was, as Dr Warren had said, probably about eight weeks gone.

Even knowing the point on the calendar when it had started, so she could better work out when she'd give birth, didn't help. It just made her think of all the things she'd done in her life so far, and what she'd be stuck with having to do, and not do, for the next seven months – and forever, beyond that.

Forever was a long time.

Seven months was a long time.

This single night was a long time.

Dr Warren had done his best to put her mind at ease about how the way she'd been drinking during the past several weeks might not really affect the embryo – but he didn't know exactly how much she'd been knocking back. Frankly, she wasn't even *really* sure about that herself. However, that one not-so-small detail aside, she knew she stood a good chance of having a healthy baby.

But...

She sat on the edge of her bed twisting a sheet as she grappled with the Other Thing...

What about Alexander?

How would he react?

The topic of having children had come up on several occasions, but she'd always cut the conversation short because it was one she wasn't ready to have.

Good grief...if she wasn't even ready to talk about starting a family, what did that mean?

That she was far from ready to do it.

But…if she told him she was pregnant, and he really wanted her to have the baby, to be a father, then they'd fight about it, and that would be the end of them.

There'd be no coming back from that.

So she couldn't possibly tell him until she'd come to terms with it herself. Until she'd made a decision that was right for her.

And she was a long way from that.

Indeed, depending on what she decided, she might never tell him. She wasn't the only one who hadn't worked out what all her symptoms had meant, after all.

And…what about her family?

Her mother would support her whatever she decided, Christine was pretty sure of that.

Her father? He'd probably go along with her mother.

Her brother? Did she really care? Well, yes, because he was a good man and she actually liked him as a person. He'd probably be on her side. Besides, even if he wasn't, she wouldn't have to listen to him carping on about it because they hardly ever saw each other as it was.

And she'd be out of it all, in any case, in Anwen-by-Wye.

Or…would she?

The question hit Christine like a train: could the agency cope with two of its members having to consider childcare as well as investigating cases?

Carol and David were a brilliant team, but even they had to rely upon others to help them juggle their work and Albert's needs on occasion. If she went ahead with this…and if Alexander wasn't on board – or even if he was, but still working out of both London and Anwen-by-Wye – how on earth would she manage? It was…and would be…so complicated.

She had the funds to be able to engage a nanny, of course…but was that what she'd want for her child? To be in the care of a stranger?

If so, why on earth have the child in the first place? That wasn't a family dynamic Christine wanted…she didn't think.

Or…maybe it was the only realistic way forward.

After yet another trip to the loo – all that water had to go somewhere! – she sat beside the open window again, watching the traffic. She noticed that there wasn't much of it about, and looked at her watch.

She'd not slept all night, and it would be dawn soon. She felt ragged, which wasn't surprising. And her mind was still awhirl.

Standing in front of the mirror, she saw a young woman who was at a crossroads in her life, without the faintest idea about which path to take…though the road to which she felt her feet naturally drawn was the one that had 'FREEDOM' on its signpost.

She crawled into bed and hugged herself – glad to be alone, but knowing that she really wasn't.

CHAPTER NINETEEN

Dawn was breaking, and Alexander Bright had been up for an hour. He felt completely wired, and not even an extra vigorous workout had helped him to rid himself of the tension he felt in every part of his body. He was vibrating, as though he were about to explode. He'd texted Christine the previous evening, but she'd replied that she was tied up with a case. And he'd been too exhausted, and worried about what he was facing with Geordie, and Aiden, to push. Then he'd hit the coffee and he'd hit the phones, contacting people who knew people, who knew people – hoping he could gather the information he was seeking without anyone other than a few trusted souls knowing it was him doing the asking.

When Geordie ambled out of the spare room, he looked fresh and ready to go. Alexander realized that working so late and only getting a few hours' sleep was not the best way to act before you'd agreed to an early start. It also occurred to him that had he been ten years younger, he'd have been feeling fine after what he'd just done. Back then it had been nothing for him to socialize all night, maybe accompany a young woman home, then be back at work as the sun came up. Now? Now he really needed more than three hours' sleep.

'Any coffee?' Geordie asked sleepily. He looked around. 'Never mind.'

He headed for the pot he'd spotted on the countertop. 'And any word?' He poured himself a mug.

Alexander did his best to clear his head. 'Some. It's as I thought. Big Tony hasn't shifted his center of operations: he used to work out of the upstairs rooms in his mother's house. Her being downstairs gave him useful cover. She's long gone now, so he has the run of the place, and is still there. I know where it is. Seems we didn't need to go skulking around Brixton trying to find out if anyone had seen Sean – word is he's been in and out of Big Tony's place a fair bit this past month or so. But no one's sure why.'

Geordie balanced on a sleek chrome stool. 'I can't see Sean dealing. He's kept his life together pretty well, and the last time you helped me get him into that rehab place I believed him when he said he wanted to get clean, and to stay that way. He's so clever in other ways. Had the whole world at his feet, given what he can do with computers.'

Alexander felt his heart go out to his friend. 'I know that's how we think, mate, but for addicts, they can't see that they've got the world at their feet; all they can see is the rocky bottom of a deep pit. I reckon he did believe he wanted to stay clean, Geordie…but addiction's a terrible thing. All it takes is being in the wrong company, and there it is – on offer – and you're back thinking you can manage it, that you are the boss of it, rather than the drug being the boss of you. And, like you say, he did manage it well for so long, that maybe he thought he could get back to that so-called "balanced" point again. But…yeah, if he's not dealing, then I can't think why he'd be in and out of Big Tony's place. I've asked people to find out if Big Tony's into anything other than drugs and moneylending these days, but nothing on that front yet.'

Geordie stared into his mug. 'Now that we know where we can get hold of Sean, maybe we could just go and pick him up, and dump him back into rehab? Somewhere…secure? You know – another intervention.'

Alexander considered his response carefully. 'The last time was a mess, if you recall. He made such a racket when we hauled him out of his flat that we nearly got picked up by the boys in blue ourselves. There's only so many times you can "intervene" before it starts to look a lot like kidnapping.'

Geordie nodded, looking despondent.

'Besides,' added Alexander, 'if he is up to something with Big Tony, then he might also be under his protection, and we do not want to mess with any of that lot. Tony MacNamara might be old, and relying on a wheelchair to get himself about these days, but he rarely raised a hand himself in any case – not once he could afford to hire others to do his dirty work.'

Alexander pictured the younger version of Big Tony in his mind's eye. 'I reckon that's another thing that won't have changed about him. Kept a stranglehold on his turf, when all the gangs wanted it, by making sure everyone knew there'd be a price to pay if they moved against him. And an unpleasant one at that. No, if Sean's being looked out for by Big Tony, for some reason, I don't think that scooping him up is on the cards, unless we have a watertight plan. Sorry.'

'What about we find him, and I talk to him, then? He's my brother. I've got to try *something*. It's good that we know he's not lying half dead in a doorway somewhere, but he's not at his job anymore, and he's left his flat. He's got to be staying somewhere, and he's got to be making money somehow. I need to know all about that. I mean, what's he up to? What's made him walk out on his life, yet he's still able to come and go from some ageing thug's headquarters in South London? I have to try, Alexander. He's my blood.'

Alexander didn't understand Geordie's point about a blood bond, because he'd always been an utterly solitary being. But the bond he felt with the man he was looking at meant he didn't need to: he'd do it for him, for his friend, Geordie. He was getting past the point of believing that Sean could be saved from himself, but Alexander hoped he might still be able to save Geordie from being dragged down by his own brother, which was exactly what was happening. Though Geordie couldn't see it.

Alexander sighed. 'I say we head back to Brixton Tube station, and hope we spot Sean. We know he doesn't drive, so that's our best bet, because all the buses go past the station, too. Then we'll do what we can to get you a chance to talk to him. Alright? We'll take the hired car, because it might come in handy – as a place for a quiet chat, if nothing else. But that means we'll have to park it somewhere, and there's nowhere we can do that, that I know of these days, until half eight. There's a place we can park for four hours after that – which should give us enough time.'

Geordie chuckled. 'The chances of Sean doing anything before half eight in the morning would be slim to nil, I'd say, so that'll be alright. So, if we can't get going now, why did you suggest such an early start?'

'Because I didn't know that this was what we'd be doing this morning. But, I tell you what, now that we've got the time – I'll take the chance to drive you around the area for a bit. You don't know it like I do, and you might find it instructive.'

The pair headed down to get into the cheap rented car that had replaced Alexander's sleek vehicle in the underground car park. Their trip out to Brixton from Alexander's flat overlooking the Thames was unremarkable, and they spent an hour or so sitting in traffic that moved slowly enough for Alexander to give a running commentary about the entire Brixton area. As he did so, he allowed himself to reassess his knowledge about lanes that had once allowed access to certain areas, but were now blocked, and the streets that were gentrified, as opposed to those which had still escaped the attention of developers.

'I'm surprised we haven't done up more of these sorts of places,' observed Geordie as they drove. 'Right up your alley they are – not the best of areas, but not far from them, with lots of housing stock that could be made fit for families needing a leg up. I know we've done a few out here, but why not more?'

Alexander was aware of how much he'd told Geordie about his previous incarnation, and how much he'd kept secret. He couldn't tell Geordie that the reason his company wasn't more active in the 'real' Brixton was because it would be too dangerous for him. It might allow some people to put two and two together and possibly realize that the well-thought-of developer Alexander Bright bore a resemblance to an almost mythical, but presumed dead, transporter from decades ago, named Issy.

He lied. Too easily. 'I missed the boat, Geordie. The prices shot up, and you know I run a business, not a charity. It's best I concentrate on the bits of South London where the blokes with deep pockets, who use business models that mean they'll sell at sky-high prices when they're finished, aren't interested. That's how I can keep doing it…by nibbling away at the edges to develop rental properties where I can charge what people can afford.'

'Look – there's Sean!' Alexander felt the car shudder as Geordie's bulk swung around in the passenger seat.

Within seconds, the big man was already unbuckling his seat belt and opening the door, even though they were still moving. Alexander tried to pull his friend back in, but he was gone.

Frustrated because he was beside a bus lane, with no chance to pull over or get off the main road, he continued driving, watching the scene unfold in his rear-view mirror. It wasn't good. Geordie was chasing his yellow-jacketed brother toward a side street, then out of his sight.

Alexander managed a left turn at the next set of lights, then drove around the back streets to get to where he could cross the main road, to go in the general direction that Sean and Geordie had been heading.

It didn't take him long to find them – but he was more than dismayed by what he saw. The pair were on the pavement, on a fairly decent street, with Geordie sitting astride his brother, who was swinging upward with flailing arms, with little effect. Alexander pulled into a space that was clearly marked as being for residents' use only, jumped out of the car, and leapt across the pavement to stand over the pair.

'How's the brotherly chat going, Geordie?'

'I should have known you'd be involved in this, somehow.' Sean's voice came out as an angry, high-pitched whine as he stopped bothering to wriggle.

Geordie remained where he was, pinning his brother to the ground. 'He declined an invitation for coffee,' he said, sounding grim.

'Look at you,' spat Sean, 'can't do anything without your boss telling you to, can you, dear brother? Well, just you wait – the mighty will be fallen soon…turfed out of all those nice clubs he belongs to, while all he does is stand you a pint in some scabby pub. Mr Fancy Dancy Bright is going to be dumped by all his high society chummies before you know it. It's true, you know, all true – he will. Oh yes indeed. Then I bet you'll let me get on with my life, the way I want to live it.'

Alexander felt a pricking at the back of his neck. 'What do you mean, Sean?'

'You'll know soon enough,' sneered Sean. 'Now get off me, bruv. I'm late for a meeting with some people who actually want me to make the most of myself. Not like you.'

Geordie looked down at his sibling. 'You using again, Sean? I'm only trying to help.'

Sean wriggled, with no effect. 'Help? When have you and him ever helped me? Got me locked up and dried out a couple of times, yeah, but that's not really "helping me", is it? That's just making you two feel good about yourselves. Nowhere to be seen when I get out.'

Alexander saw Geordie flinch. 'That's not true, Sean – I've been there for you every time. I managed to keep that job of yours open for you the first time, and found you a new one the second time. I kept paying your rent when you were in rehab, and Alexander even paid for the rehab itself. That's not nothing, Sean. Look at yourself – you've walked away from a good life. And for what?'

Sean laughed manically. 'Oh…so much more than you could ever imagine, bruv.'

'I know you got all the brains in the family, Sean – you're so good with those computers. But this illness of yours is controlling you. Please…let me help.'

Alexander watched as Sean's eyes darted, trying to spot some way out of his situation. 'Strong in the arm, thick in the head – that's you, bruv. Let him give all the orders, pay all the bills, and you'll let yourself be his beefy sidekick. Me? I've found myself someone who can put my skills to good use…and I've got a nice little payday coming my way. Now let me up. There's net curtains twitching all over – the Bluebottles'll be along any minute now. This street's a nice one – they'll bother turning up.'

Alexander knew Sean was right. 'Let him be, Geordie. He's got a point. Remember what I said about an intervention being seen differently by some? Time to go.'

As Geordie rose, Sean scrambled to his feet, laughing cruelly. 'An intervention? Listen to you, you sanctimonious…whatever. Enjoy it while you can, Alexander. And I'll enjoy it when it's all taken away from you. Toodle-pip.'

As Sean ran off, Alexander and Geordie got into the car, and headed toward the main road.

Alexander didn't say anything: he didn't have any words that could comfort his friend. Also, he was busy wondering what Sean had meant by his taunts.

Had Alexander's old boss, Big Tony, worked out that he'd once been Issy? If he had, would he have told Sean? And what might that mean for Alexander? His businesses? And the life he had planned with Christine?

Or…was Sean referring to something else entirely?

Alexander couldn't help but wonder if Geordie's brother was somehow connected with the threats coming from someone calling themselves TISTRU. It struck him that Sean's words were not only vicious, but pointedly personal, like the emails Aiden had received. Could Sean be TISTRU? Alexander hoped not, because he knew he'd have to answer any such direct attack upon himself and his hoped-for happiness with a response that would put a stop to any possible future danger.

CHAPTER TWENTY

Annie sat at the kitchen table in the flat above the Lamb and Flag and watched as Carol bounced Albert on her knee at the dining table in her house just across the village green.

She divided her attention when another box popped up on her laptop screen and Mavis appeared with Althea close beside her, peering into the camera. Mavis's microphone wasn't on, but Annie could tell the women were bickering.

'Stop fiddling, dear' were the first words Annie heard from Mavis, quickly followed by 'I wasn't fiddling, I could see the microphone wasn't on' from Althea.

'It's on now,' said Annie and waved. 'Chrissy said she'd be on in five minutes a few minutes ago. It's not like you to be late to one of these meetings, Mave.'

Mavis tutted. 'Some of us –' her expression told Annie that she meant Althea – 'insisted on a fresh pot before we started. But we're here now and…ah there she is. Good morning, Christine. Oh, are you alright?'

Annie took in the sight that was Christine Wilson-Smythe: lank hair, bags beneath her eyes, and she'd obviously been crying. Annie suspected a run-in with Alexander. She was worried about her friend and colleague; for all that she was young, and beautiful, and titled, and wealthy, Christine hadn't seemed truly happy for a long time. 'What's up, doll – have you and a hedge had a bit of an argument?'

Christine didn't even smile. 'Had a bad night. Let's not dwell on it, alright?'

At least Annie didn't hear the sharpness in Christine's tone that had been all too evident of late.

Annie decided to be upbeat. 'Good report you sent in Chrissy – great progress on the Bereaved Butler case.'

Christine mumbled, 'Thanks.'

Annie pushed on. 'That Jon-Boy sounds a bit slimy, and that note in his diary? OYSTERS – RICHARD LOL? Could be evidence he was planning to do away with poor old Edward's brother, after all. What do we all think?'

Aware she'd taken the lead – when that was usually Mavis's role – Annie looked at the part of the screen where Mavis and Althea's faces filled the feed from the Dower House to see a surprised Mavis, and a dimpling Althea.

'Aye, a good start,' agreed Mavis, 'and thank you for taking the time to meet with two of the members of the Buttle My World staff, Christine. We learned a lot, but it's no' enough, is it? I've spoken with Stephanie this morning, who reports that Rachel Edwards has settled into her temporary life at Chellingworth quite nicely – and that Edward is back on form, which she made clear was a great relief for Henry.'

'My son's delighted, of course,' interjected Althea, 'but he really wants everything sorted out properly because then Edward will be happier…and we all want that, don't we?'

Annie watched with amusement as Mavis rolled her eyes toward the camera and said, 'Aye, we all do, dear,' before continuing. 'So, what do we propose as a next step?'

Once again, Althea's head popped into the frame and she said, 'You're still in London, aren't you, Christine?'

Christine nodded. 'Battersea.'

Annie couldn't help herself. 'I thought you were staying with your parents.'

Christine sighed heavily. 'I was, but I just fancied my own space for a while. Mammy and Daddy can be a bit overwhelming at times, especially Mammy. So, yes, I'm still in London, Althea, what can I do for you?'

Althea stuck out her chin. 'It's just that Rachel didn't do a particularly good job when she packed to come to stay at Chellingworth, it seems. Put in a pile of work clothes, but nothing she can really relax in. Could you pop to her place to pick up a few more things for her, do you think?'

Mavis turned. 'We're no' a fetching and carrying service, Althea.'

Annie admired Althea's ability to look utterly innocent, and sound utterly wounded, simultaneously.

The dowager pouted as she said, 'The poor woman's just become a widow, believes her husband was murdered, and that she might be next. We've gone so far as to offer to investigate her husband's death, and Henry and Stephanie have welcomed her into their home, for safety's sake. Don't you think we should make just a bit more of an effort?'

Mavis tutted but, before she could speak, Annie observed, 'How's Chrissy going to get into Rachel's place? It's not like she took a key for it with her to London, is it? Is there a spare somewhere?'

Althea dimpled. 'That's the wonderful thing – she doesn't even need a key. Rachel's front door has one of those combination lock things. The code is...hang on...' Annie allowed herself to share a grin with Carol as Althea screwed up her little face, closed her eyes, then shouted, 'Seven, six, nine, three,' with delight. 'That's it. Trombones and BBC Radio Wales. Seventy-six and ninety-three.' She beamed.

Mavis visibly shuddered as Althea shouted close to her ear, then asked curtly, 'And when, pray, did you dig up this particular nugget of information, dear?'

'When you went gallivanting off to see that Gulliver chap, leaving me behind to entertain myself. I had tea with Rachel and Edward, and we had a lovely chat. She's quite a woman, you know. Buttled for some incredibly important people over the years, she has. One of them was someone I once knew, slightly. Lovely chap. Horrid wife, unfortunately. Never knew how to keep her mouth shut. Just wittered on for hours and hours about nothing of the slightest interest to anyone but herself. And such a meddler, too.'

Mavis held up her hand. 'Thank you, Althea. Dare I say it takes one to know one?' She turned to face the camera. 'So, moving on – is there any chance you might be able to get to Rachel's home to collect some additional belongings for her, Christine?'

Althea waggled a piece of paper above Mavis's head. 'Their place is out near Ealing Common, and she gave me a list,' she called.

It looked to Annie as though Mavis was physically pushing the dowager away from the camera.

'Send me the address and a photo of the list,' replied Christine with a smile – *at last*, thought Annie. 'I'll go out there later this morning. I can bring it with me when I drive back tomorrow. I'd like just one more night here in London, and I don't think I'm up to the drive today in any case. Ealing and back I can manage – if that's alright with everyone.'

'If you're feeling up to it,' replied Mavis. 'You're looking a bit peaky, if you don't mind me saying.'

'I do,' snapped Christine, surprising Annie. 'Let's get on, alright? What about the Exceptional Evacuee case? Carol, Annie…any more progress?'

Once again, Annie noticed that Mavis looked a little put out that someone else had chosen to move the meeting along – or maybe she was miffed that Christine had bitten her head off? Either way, Annie reckoned it was best if she kept her gob shut and let Carol do the talking – she was the one leading the case after all. She looked at Carol on the screen, realized that wasn't achieving anything, so said, 'Car, over to you, doll.'

Carol looked up from where Annie guessed Albert was playing. 'Nothing much more since I sent the report last night. I rang the farm suggested by Hywel Howells, but got no answer. Left a message. No return call, yet. I'll try again when we've finished here. Then I'll get going with a deep dive online trying to find a Blodwen Peaswell, or a Peaswell family, at least. More when I have it.'

'That's an unusual name,' piped up a now-invisible Althea. 'There was a butcher by that name over on the outskirts of Brecon some years back.'

Mavis turned away from the camera and said in a muffled voice, 'Why did you no' tell me that?'

Althea appeared, looking put out. 'Why would I? It's the first time I've heard the name in about a hundred years.'

Mavis began with a huffy retort, 'But it was in the notes…'

Mavis paused and tutted. 'Ach, sorry, dear, I sometimes forget you don't actually work with us, so you don't have to do all the reading we do, just so we make sure none of us misses anything. So, tell us about these Peaswells. Speak up.'

Althea crossed her arms and squared her little shoulders. 'That's all I know. It's an odd name, and there was a butcher with that name. And no, I don't remember exactly where, or exactly when. But a long time ago. That's it. Is it important? Have I helped?' Even through the camera Annie could see her eyes glinting.

'It's a great help, thank you, Althea,' said Carol. 'It'll narrow down my search and save time, I'm sure. I'm grateful for that. Now – what about Dan the decorator, Annie? Are you going to talk about him, or shall I do it?'

Annie was caught off guard by Carol's mention of Dan. 'I wasn't really planning on talking about it at all,' she said quietly.

'What's this?' Mavis appeared to be on full alert, and even Althea's head bobbed up again, which was exactly what Annie hadn't wanted. She and Tudor had agreed they'd try to make as little trouble for the Chellingworth Estate as possible, because Althea, and Henry and Stephanie, had already been so generous to them by giving Tudor stewardship of the soon-to-be-renovated larger pub.

However, Annie felt she had no choice but to explain everything that had been going on at the Coach and Horses, though she didn't do it happily. By the time Annie had given a full account of the whole situation, she could see that Carol was bouncing Albert on her knee, and that Christine was looking...well, ten times worse than she had, and on the verge of tears. She concluded with: 'So I'll tell Bob Fernley after this meeting, and ask him for Dan's address.'

Seeing that Christine was staring bleakly into her camera – *at her? At Carol and Albert?* – she added, 'Chrissy...now don't go telling me off, and don't say there's nothing wrong. You look like you've seen a ghost. Come on – we're your friends – what's up?'

Christine managed, 'Nothing, really...it's nothing...' before she dissolved into a teary, sobbing heap.

Although they weren't all in the same room as each other, Annie could almost feel the silence as the four women allowed Christine the time she needed to have a good cry, then blow her nose, and gather her wits. The odd yap from McFli, and a few gurgles from Albert notwithstanding, the silence continued until Christine spoke.

Her voice was thickened by tears, her eyes bloodshot. 'Look, I can't talk about it. Not yet. Don't worry, there's nothing wrong with me, or anyone here in London. It's not something I want to discuss, that's all. But I don't want you to worry about me.'

'I think it's a bit late for that, doll,' said Annie. She hoped her tone let Chrissy know she meant well.

Christine managed a weak smile. 'Yes, I know. Sorry about that, too. But…I just can't. I'll get that stuff from the Edwards home and bring it to Chellingworth with me tomorrow. Right, I've got to go.'

Annie stiffened when Christine's screen went blank. 'Gordon Bennett – she's a right mess.' It was out of Annie's mouth before she could stop it.

Mavis sniffed, then added, 'I don't hold with talking about friends or colleagues behind their backs as a rule, but maybe we should have a chat about Christine, at some point. The girl's not been herself for some time, and this outburst might mean she needs help she's no' willing to ask for.'

Althea chimed in. 'It's terribly difficult to ask for a hand, or even for advice, when one is used to fending for oneself. I know she's affianced to Alexander now, but that's a recent development, and she's always been headstrong and almost alarmingly independent. Maybe I should have a word with her mother. I know her a little.'

Carol looked away from her son and into the camera long enough for Annie to see the anxiety in her eyes.

'Hold your horses there, Althea,' said Annie. 'Yeah, Chrissy's in a bit of a state, but I don't think we should go telling her mum. For all we know, that's the person she's got a problem with. Not that me and Eustelle ever fall out, but I do know that mothers and daughters can really have a go at each other sometimes. You have done with your mum, haven't you, Car?'

Carol glared at the screen. Annie wasn't playing tit for tat, but Carol's expression suggested that was what she thought. She replied, 'Me and Mum don't always see eye to eye, that's true…but I also think Annie makes a fair point, Althea. It's not our place to involve Christine's family at this stage. She's a grown up, after all. She should be allowed to tell them, and us, about whatever it is that's got her so down in her own time. But I do think we should be open to her needing to share anything, with any of us, when she gets back tomorrow. And to all agree to keep any confidences she might ask us to, as individuals.'

Everyone nodded their agreement.

Mavis said, 'So, to be clear: Carol's getting on with research into Blodwen Peaswell for the Evacuee case; Annie's following up with Bob Fernley on The Case of the…have you named the case yet, Annie?'

Annie said quietly, 'The Case of the Disappearing Decorating Supplies – or maybe The Case of the Dodgy Decorator, haven't decided yet.'

'Very well,' said Mavis, 'we'll let you finalize that, as you always do. Meanwhile, Christine will help out Rachel with a delivery of fresh clothing, while Carol and I continue with our coordinated online research into Jon Dacre and Buttle My World. Unfortunately, other than having established that the man appears to be as odious as Rachel led us to believe – and knowing that he made some rather suggestive notes in a desk diary – I don't think we have much more to go on. Though maybe we could ask Rachel to talk to his personal assistant to find out if she knows of any good reason why the man might have put together the idea of oysters and laughing at Richard. Yes, I'll ask her to do that this morning.'

'I'm having tea with her and Edward soon,' said Althea brightly. 'You should join us.'

'Good idea,' replied Mavis. 'Let us know if you need any help with the matter at the Coach and Horses, Annie. You've no reason to handle that on your own. We're a team, after all.'

Annie smiled her thanks, and the screen went blank.

Sighing, she booted up the system to watch the recordings made by the cameras at the Coach and Horses earlier that morning. All she'd learned about Dan from the previous day's recordings was that he did actually do some work, but in short bursts, with a lot of talking on his phone in between times. And that he'd left the site early, which she'd already known, because she and Carol had seen him. Nothing at all had happened at the pub after dark, so she was pinning her hopes on whatever Dan might have been doing for the past few hours to provide some evidence of his pilfering.

CHAPTER TWENTY-ONE

Carol settled Albert with a few of his favorite toys so that she could get some work done – her first task being to phone the farm where there had, back some few decades, been a David Davies. Delighted when a female voice answered after the third ring, Carol explained why she was calling – without being too specific.

'We've been here thirty years,' said the voice. 'We're Thomas. I think my dad bought it from a Davies, but I'll have to ask him, and he's out in the fields at the moment. We don't have a reliable signal around here, so there's no way I can reach him until he comes in for his lunch. I'll ask him then.'

Carol dared, 'Your mother wouldn't know?'

'We lost her about fifteen years back.'

Carol could have kicked herself. 'I'm so sorry for your loss.'

'Ta. You never get over it. I'll ring you back when I've spoken to Dad. So…David Davies, and a couple of evacuees called Gulliver. Like *Travels*, right?'

'Yes, like *Gulliver's Travels*. Thanks. I appreciate it.' She disconnected, and then encouraged Albert to walk with her into the sitting room, where she knew David was ready to take over, so she could work on her laptop.

'No snacks, and lots of cuddles, got it,' he said, as he took charge of their son. 'It's nice I can be here today – and I'm glad I get to work here without having to go to as many meetings as I have done recently. That's the end of it now, for a while, in any case. The new job starts tomorrow, so I'll do a bit of preparatory reading while I'm with him. You alright in there on your own?'

Carol laughed. 'Yes, I'll be fine. If I can just get some pounding done, I might get somewhere. We'll meet for an early lunch – just a snack, alright? Then an early meal later on.'

David grinned. 'It's a date – kitchen table at eleven thirty. I'll be the bloke with bags under his eyes and a stuffed animal in his pocket.'

'And I'll be the woman with the stain on the front of her dress,' chuckled Carol, wiping at a bit of strawberry jam that Albert had – somehow – managed to smear on her at breakfast time, which she'd only just spotted. 'I sat in a meeting like this, and no one mentioned it. Maybe they're all used to seeing me covered in food, I don't know. Later, *cariad*.' She waved at Albert, then shut the door.

Carol loved doing online research, and – once she'd settled herself – her fingers flew. She scanned screen after screen, and article after article, typing notes into a separate document as she went along, saving links beside facts, and referencing her findings. By the time the alarm went off to tell her she had ten minutes before she needed to break for lunch, she was feeling quite upbeat about her findings.

'You're looking pleased with yourself,' said her husband as she entered the kitchen. 'Cheese on toast alright?'

'Add a bit of mustard and call it Welsh Rarebit and it'll be lovely,' she said cheekily. 'Or I'll just have it the way you've made it and add my own, on the plate.'

'Option two for the lady in blue – with the red stain – it is,' said David, placing a plate in front of her with a flourish.

He began to feed Albert, who seemed quite content to be in his highchair at the table, with Bunty keeping a watchful eye from the floor directly beneath him. Carol munched and watched as they played.

She'd managed to eat half her lunch when her phone rang in her pocket. She recognized the number and said, 'Got to take this, back in a tick.'

She answered the call, and shut the door as she stood in the hallway. 'Thanks for phoning back, is that Mr Thomas?'

'No, it's me again, his daughter,' snapped the voice.

Carol thought the woman's manner seemed a bit off, whereas she'd been friendly earlier in the day. 'Oh yes, hello again.'

'Yes, Dad did buy the place from a Davies, and it was a David Davies. He bought the farm thirty-one years ago. Doesn't know why he sold. And that's it. Except to say that Dad wasn't too happy about things, as it all turned out.'

Carol was puzzled. 'Oh, I'm sorry to hear that.'

'Yeah, well, it was because the buildings weren't as good as he'd thought, and the land wasn't up to much in quite a lot of parts. And there wasn't even as much of it as there should have been. Not an honorable person, Dad said. Sorry we couldn't help more. Good luck with it.'

Carol spluttered, 'Did you ask about evacuees?'

'They never talked about anything but the land and the price, sorry.'

Carol felt deflated. 'Well, thanks for asking. Bye.'

She re-entered the kitchen to see David mopping up a spill on the floor. 'He just can't hold his drink, this one,' he joked. 'Bad news for you, by the looks of it.'

Carol smiled. 'Not got anything useful from the farm we had as a lead, but I think I might have found something about the butcher I'm trying to track down. At least, I've found the start of a trail: George and Blodwen Peaswell owned a butcher's shop until about forty years ago, when it closed down due to the death of Mr Peaswell. The funeral was a big affair because he was a deacon at a local church. They had a daughter. So that's something. But where do I go from there? I'll have to give it some thought.'

David suggested, 'The church itself? Might they have records?'

'Gone. Demolished, ten years ago.'

'The daughter?'

'Likely to have married, so I'll follow that lead, but that's…time-consuming.'

'What about other butchers? Do they all know each other, do you think?'

Carol grinned. 'Excellent idea. I'll find some other well-established butcher's shops – not that there's a load of them left – and ask if they knew the family.'

'You'd have got to that without me,' said David rubbing his wife's hand.

Carol grabbed his fingers. 'I know – but that's what teamwork's all about…oh, hang on, my phone's going again.'

She looked at the call display. 'It's Christine, I have to take this – in the other room. I might be a while.'

She answered as she left her son and husband to their own devices. 'Christine? What can I do for you?'

Carol didn't want to assume that Christine had phoned to confide in her about any personal matters, so stuck to her more professional tone.

'Have I caught you at a bad time, Carol? Are you doing something with David, or Albert? I can phone back later, after I've been out to Ealing.' Christine sounded more perky than she had done at the meeting, which Carol took to be a good sign.

'You're fine, just let me sit down so I can chat in comfort. Right. So…you say what you want, and I'll listen.'

'First off, sorry I was such an idiot during our meeting. I'm much better now. Just needed to have a word with myself. And there's nothing wrong, really. I'm just a bit…down. Got a few decisions to make in life.' Carol waited quietly until her chum added, 'About me and Alexander, you know?'

Carol didn't 'know', though she had a few ideas. But she realized that wasn't what her friend wanted to hear. 'Tell me what you mean, exactly.'

Christine sighed. 'Do you really think we can make a go of it, Carol? You've known me for years, and you've got to know Alexander quite well since we've been together, I think. I know there's the age difference, and the difference in backgrounds…but I do love him, Carol. Do you…do you think he loves me? Loves me…enough?'

Carol knew she was wading into treacherous waters; telling friends what you thought of their partners could lead to unforeseen consequences, as she'd discovered when an old mate had broken up with a boyfriend who was well and truly lambasted by all her girlfriends…only to have them get back together. None of the girlfriends were invited to the wedding.

Carol chose her words carefully. 'You're right about the differences, but he does seem devoted to you, Christine. That said, you two haven't been as lovely-dovey in the past little while.'

She heard Christine chuckle.

Carol added, 'Now, I'll be honest and say I don't know why that is. I can't say more than that really.'

Carol dared, 'Well, except…is there something fundamental you two have disagreed about? Something that might become a bigger problem the longer you're together? Or…you know…have you been falling out about things like wedding details – stuff that, ultimately, doesn't really matter, and will pass?'

Carol heard Christine draw in a big breath.

Her friend replied thoughtfully. 'The wedding thing? Yes, that got bad, fast. That's why I said I didn't want us to even talk about it, or plan it, for a while. But that wasn't really Alexander's fault, that was about Mammy and Daddy wanting to take things over. But you're right about us not getting along. And I think a lot of that's been down to me, if I'm honest. I've been a bit…cranky. I wasn't sure why, but I've wrapped my head around that now. So the thing about us not being lovely-dovey – which is funny, but correct – might well be a thing of the past. If…if I can get my moods sorted out, when I'm with him. And, no, there hasn't been a problem at a fundamental level. I'm just…oh Carol, he's gorgeous of course, and he's got that Bad Boy thing about him…but he's become a bit boring, of late. I know he's in Anwen more often because he's opened that shop with Henry in the village, but even when he's with me in Wales he's busy, so I don't really see that much more of him. It's the boring thing that bothers me most though, I suppose, because even when we do see each other we don't do anything. But, see, that might be good, really. Do you ever think David's boring?'

Carol weighed her response. 'He's always been pretty level-headed, Christine. When he worked for me, after I left the company, and now. He hasn't really changed. I don't think he's boring, but that's my judgement, not yours. I love the fact that he wants to be with me and Albert – or even just with Albert, like he is at this moment. He's steady, and loving, and hardworking, and funny, and always ready to put me and Albert first…which I don't consider boring, but I dare say some might think it is. Does that help?'

There was no answer, but Carol thought she heard Christine sob.

Carol wondered if she should be more proactive.

She spoke hesitantly. 'Has something happened, Christine? Has he asked you to move in with him – here? Or in London? To postpone the wedding? Or to set a date? Nothing bad's happened, has it? I can't believe I'm saying this, but he's not…acted aggressively toward you, has he?'

Christine gushed, 'No, good grief – he'd never do that. Not in his character. And no, it's not about the wedding, or even living together. It's…it's nothing specific. I just keep thinking that he's changed a lot since I met him. To start with, I think I wanted him to. It was a bit like a challenge: could I tame a wild animal? And it looks like I have. And I'm not sure that's what I wanted to happen, except that, maybe it is really a good thing, after all. But…what if he changes back again? He's well set up now, Carol, and his businesses are doing nicely. We all know he's got some pretty shady contacts from his past – we've even put that to good use to help in a few of our cases. But…what if he starts to miss that part of his life? What if I and…what if I'm not enough for him?'

Carol couldn't help but laugh. 'Oh Christine – you'd be enough for anyone. You're gorgeous, and clever, and you really take life by the throat and shake as much out of it as you can. Now you know I also think you're sometimes a bit too gung-ho for your own good, but I dare say that's because you're young enough to think you're immortal. And you don't have the responsibilities that I do. Not that I ever was much of a "wild child", but having Albert has slowed me down even more. Mind you, I'm not complaining, because – as you know only too well – having a child was important to me. And David, too, of course.'

'Yes. You both really wanted him, didn't you?'

'We did. Which is as it should be. You can't start a family without knowing what you're letting yourself in for – though I think it's impossible to really understand, to be honest. I never knew I'd feel like this about anyone other than David. Albert's our life. In a good way.' Carol paused, then added, 'Oh listen to me going on and on – this is supposed to be about you.'

Christine had a catch in her voice when she replied, 'No – this is really helpful. Thanks. Now let's stop chatting and get on with business, eh? If I get away now, I might hit the lunchtime traffic on the way to Ealing, but I'd get back here before the rush hour kicks in.'

'That's it?' Carol was puzzled. She didn't think she had any greater insight into what had been bothering Christine than before they'd started talking.

'It is, Carol. I admire you and David more than I can say – you were both cut out to be parents. I just wish more people who weren't ever designed for your sort of life could realize it before they jump into it with both feet, then regret it. It's not good for them, and it can't be good for their offspring. So, yes – thanks for that. You know what? I might do a little light shopping on the way back from my visit to Rachel's place; I've had my eye on a nice top, and today might be the day I give in. It all depends on how I feel – because I can please myself.'

Carol grinned, delighted to hear Christine sounding more like her usual self. 'Of course you can, and I know how much you value that freedom. You're nothing if not a free spirit, Christine.'

'You're right – I'd be nothing if I weren't a free spirit. I'll let you see whatever it is I buy when I get back tomorrow. Maybe a little fashion show? Thanks, Carol, you're a good friend. I knew you'd be the right person to talk to. I value your opinion.'

'My opinion about what? I haven't really said anything.' Carol knew she'd tried hard not to.

'No, but I've answered a question I've been asking of myself, anyway. See you tomorrow. Bye.'

Carol disconnected, feeling puzzled. She wasn't sure what had just happened, but was glad it appeared that she'd helped a friend.

She stuck her head into the kitchen. 'If it's alright with you two, I'll get back to my desk now.'

David had Albert on his chest and was burping him. 'I don't know when we'll have to stop doing this, but I love it,' he said, looking a little ashamed.

'I do too, it's lovely to have him so close, and him wanting it. Ah well – let's make the most of it, eh? The "Terrible Twos" are on the horizon, and we might be glad of these memories. See you later – I'm off to track down a butcher.'

And track down a butcher she did. Half an hour later Carol was punching the air with a feeling of achievement that never got old: she'd just spoken to a man in Brecon who didn't just remember George and Blodwen Peaswell, but was still in touch with their daughter, and had her phone number, too. She was looking forward to her next call.

CHAPTER TWENTY-TWO

When Mavis and Althea had arrived at Chellingworth Hall for morning tea, Mavis hadn't expected it to become such a large gathering. Yet here she was, at almost the usual time when she and Althea took lunch, still sitting with Henry and Stephanie – and Hugo, of course – to one side of her, with Edward – who'd eventually been persuaded to take a seat – and Rachel to her other side. Althea was sitting opposite her, where she was out of the reach of Mavis, which had proved to be a Very Bad Thing on at least three occasions, so far.

'Why don't you phone this Lila person in Jon Dacre's office now, dear?' Althea was smiling sweetly and addressing Rachel. 'You could go into another room to do it – you don't want all of us staring at you, do you? No time like the present.'

Everyone's eyes turned to Rachel – except for Hugo, who was fast asleep.

Rachel nodded. 'If you think that will help. But…my main concern is this: how on earth would I know that Jon had scrawled "OYSTERS – RICHARD LOL" in his personal desk diary? I haven't been in his office for ages. In fact, as I might have mentioned a few times, I avoid spending any time alone with the man. So how would I know?'

Mavis watched the faces around the tea table: Henry looked completely vacant; Stephanie's brow was furrowed; Edward was nibbling his lip; and Althea was almost bouncing on her chair.

Mavis wasn't surprised when Althea's hand shot up into the air and she said, 'I know…I know. You must say that someone's told you. But not Christine, of course. You can't blow her cover – we might need it again. There must be other people you know who go into this Jon's office all the time. It could be one of them. But not Christine.'

Mavis sighed. 'Does anyone come to mind, Rachel?'

Rachel was the one to nibble her lip this time. 'Well, a few people pop in and out of there, I suppose.'

Everyone waited, as Rachel obviously gave the matter some more thought. 'People do go in there, especially when he's out for part of the day. He keeps a lot of reference books in a funny-shaped cupboard in his office. We use them when we need to check something like an arcane table setting, or to find the answer to a highly specific question. Some of the books are quite old. In fact – oh yes, I was in there getting one just a week or so before Richard died. I needed to double check on whether there were any special requirements for a hybrid buffet/plated service layout for a kiddush luncheon for a bar mitzvah. I didn't riffle through his diary at the time, of course, but…oh, what the heck, I don't mind if Lila thinks I'm a snoop. She's only there because she's Jon's on-again-off-again girlfriend in any case. I'll tell her I looked in his diary because I was trying to see when he might be free for something or other, and the odd note I saw back then has got me thinking now. What about that, Mavis? You're the professional; would that work, do you think?'

Mavis enjoyed the spotlight for no more than a moment before she replied, 'If you act naturally, I think it could. It's a good story; its success will lie in its delivery. But don't overthink it – that way it'll all come out as though you've rehearsed it.'

Rachel nodded, then stood. 'Right, I'll give it a go. For all that she's not the brightest lightbulb in the box, Lila's usually pleasant enough, and…well, alright then, more gullible than most. Has to be to put up with Jon, I dare say. I'll make the call outside.'

Stephanie offered, 'Why not go next door, into our small private sitting room? The noise coming up from the members of the public milling about down in the Great Hall might make things on your end sound rather peculiar, otherwise.'

Rachel nodded, and took her leave.

With his sister-in-law no longer a member of the group, Mavis could tell that Edward's discomfort at being seated in the company of his employers was growing. She decided to engage him directly, so he at least felt there was a reason for his continued presence.

She asked, 'How do you think Rachel's holding up, Edward? To my eyes, she's been very much in control of her emotions since she arrived. Do you think she's…well, do you think she's coping rather *too* well?' Mavis had found it curious that the woman had been so seemingly detached, and yet driven.

'I believe you're correct in your assessment that she appears to be in control of her emotions, but I don't think I could say that's a bad thing. That being said, I am, of course, most grateful to you all for allowing her to stay. I know she feels safe here.'

Mavis had noticed that Edward had appeared to come up with a solution to the knotty problem of Althea, and then Henry and Stephanie, insisting that he used their names, rather than their correct form of address, while such unusual circumstances were prevailing – he'd stopped referring to anyone as anything at all. She wondered at the mental gymnastics the poor man must be performing to make it all work, without failing to follow his employers' direct instructions, nor actually using their names, which he clearly couldn't bear to do.

Althea chipped in. 'Any news about the devious decorator, Dan, Mavis? Have you heard about that, Henry? One of the chaps Bob Fernley retained to do the renovations at the Coach and Horses pub is pinching all sorts. He even swiped a lavatory.'

Henry looked nonplussed. 'Somebody's stolen a lavatory? Good grief, how would one even go about such a thing? I'd rather imagined they were firmly affixed to the floor.'

Althea giggled. 'Not a used one, Henry. A new one. The one that was supposed to be installed in the bathroom for Annie and Tudor. And he took the wallpaper.'

'Off the walls?' Henry looked shocked.

Mavis noticed that Stephanie – quite unnecessarily, she thought – gave her attention to her sleeping baby, while Althea muttered, 'Don't be silly. New wallpaper. Still in rolls. What use would wallpaper off the walls be, dear?'

'There's no news about it at all, that I've heard,' said Mavis evenly, hoping Althea would drop the subject. She didn't.

'That's money out of our pockets, Henry,' she continued, 'and it's bound to delay them opening up the pub. Or I suppose they might be able to open the pub, but not move in. Which would lead to an awful lot of to-ing and fro-ing, wouldn't it? You should talk to Bob about the budget. I've seen on those home makeover shows on TV that they can do a whole house in a week, if they throw enough people at the job. We should do one of those things – so they can get it all sorted out in time.'

Henry bridled. 'No, Mother. We've had television people crawling all over this place in the past, and I don't think it would be fair to impose such discombobulation upon others.'

'I don't think your mother means that the renovation should be televised, Henry,' said Stephanie returning her attention to her husband. Mavis saw a twinkle in the duchess's eye as she spoke. 'Things like that take rather a long time to arrange. I suspect Althea means that we should consider allowing the purse strings for the job to loosen a little, so that more people could be called upon to achieve the desired outcome more quickly.'

'Exactly what I said.'

Mavis only caught Althea's mumbled comment in passing, because Rachel Edwards appeared at the door in a state of great excitement.

'I think we might have him!' All heads turned in Rachel's direction, including Hugo's…whose eyes popped open. He instantly began to bawl.

Rachel closed the door quietly, and apologized profusely for having woken the baby. Stephanie picked him up to try to soothe him, and Henry stood, fussing about, and being shushed by his wife, even as she was shushing her son.

Mavis was on pins, desperate to know what Rachel's exclamation had meant, but she owed it to her hosts to wait until their son had quietened down, which took quite a few moments.

'I'll take him to our rooms,' said Stephanie, eventually.

Edward shot to his feet. 'I shall accompany you, if you wish.' He moved to open the door.

Stephanie shook her head as she passed him. 'Please remain with the group – I'm sure you want to know about any progress. Henry can tell me all about it when he joins me. Right, Henry?'

'But of course, dear. I'll be along shortly.' The duke retook his seat, while Edward continued to hover beside the door.

Althea said, 'Rachel, Edward, please sit. And tell us all about it, Rachel. What have you dug up that can sink the blighter?'

Althea stubbornly refused to meet Mavis's eye as she waved the two members of the Edwards family to their previous seats, then sat bolt upright, staring at Rachel.

Rachel began. 'It's not exactly evidence, I know that, but I think it's hope. Lila understood why I would ask about that diary entry – and I think she believed me when I said how I'd come to see it. In any case, the oysters? Jon had announced to Lila one morning – out of the blue, she said – that he was going to treat her to an oyster dinner at his place. I won't repeat everything she said, but, suffice to say, she was delighted to hear that she was invited to dine with him, to enjoy a delicacy that's purported to possess qualities related to virility. She confirmed that the dinner took place, and that's all you need to know about that.'

Rachel paused and Mavis noticed that she rearranged her shoulders before she added, 'That's all I needed to know, too – but I got a lot more detail, that I'll never be able to forget, or unimagine, unfortunately.'

'Fascinating,' said Mavis.

'Is it? Why so?' Henry was on full alert. Mavis suspected he was paying special attention so that he could do as his wife had asked, and deliver her a full account of any developments.

Althea dimpled. 'Oh yes, go on, Mavis…do your thing when you think of something brilliant.'

Mavis tutted quietly. 'I'll have to do some research, to see if it's feasible – but I'm wondering if a person might boil, or somehow grind up, oyster shells, then spray or pour a liquid onto someone's food. That could certainly explain how a dessert proved fatal for a man with an allergy to mollusks.'

'I say, that all sounds rather complicated,' observed Henry.

Althea clapped. 'See? It's brilliant.' McFli stood to attention at the dowager's feet and licked her leg. She looked down and added, 'Yes, you too, McFli. Good boy.' The dog settled his head onto his paws again, satisfied – Mavis assumed – that his status within the pack had been confirmed.

Rachel leaned forward, her eyes ablaze. 'You're right, Mavis – that could be it. I hadn't thought it through that way, I just knew it all felt…wrong, somehow. Now – how can we prove it?'

Mavis felt she'd been put on the spot. 'I think the first thing we have to do is find out if it's even a possibility. I'll speak to Carol, and we might be able to track down someone who could tell us if that's the case. Then…if my theory holds water…we'd have to try to find out if Jon Dacre is, in fact, in possession of a small bottle, or maybe an atomizer filled with ground up oyster shells. Though it would have been an easy thing to dispose of, of course. And any sensible person would do so, with rapidity, I'd think.'

'I'd have dumped it down a drain on the way out of the crime scene,' announced Althea.

Henry spoke thoughtfully, 'He could have emptied out the potentially damning contents and refilled the container with something innocuous.'

Mavis noticed that Althea's face showed complete amazement as she stared at her son, to whom she said, 'Nice one, Henry.'

Mavis mused, 'Aye, any such container might now have been put to innocent use, as was so cleverly suggested –' she nodded her gratitude toward the duke – 'in which case it might still be found, and might still be forensically useful. Or – equally possibly – it's been disposed of.'

'He chucked it. My money's on that,' said Althea firmly. 'Anyone with two brain cells gets rid of a murder weapon, don't they? Oh – sorry, Rachel, that was terribly insensitive of me, dear.'

Rachel said, 'Thank you. But it's how we have to think, isn't it? Like someone who's awful enough to do the deed.'

The pause that followed seemed to suck all the air out of the room.

Eventually, Rachel sighed. 'Jon knows the value of a pound, I'll give him that much – especially when it's out of his own pocket.'

She looked thoughtful, then added, 'Maybe he wouldn't have wanted to waste whatever he'd spent on implementing my husband's murder. In which case, there's a possibility of proof.'

Mavis nodded. 'I'll take my leave now, to follow up on my theory. I'll phone you to report my findings, Rachel, and to agree our next steps. It might take a little time, but you'll be safe here, whatever the truth of this is.'

Althea beamed. 'Yes, you will, dear, we'll all make sure of that, won't we, Henry?'

Henry spluttered a fairly convincing, 'But of course,' then added – with less certainty, 'no one actually knows that you're here, do they, Rachel?'

Rachel shook her head. 'No, I haven't told anyone. With…with Richard gone, who would I tell?'

The anguish in the widow's tone made Mavis's heart ache, and she noticed how Edward's gaze lingered on his sister-in-law's face. 'You're my brother's wife, and as close to a part of him as I have left. I'll make it my duty to ensure your safety.'

CHAPTER TWENTY-THREE

After the team's online meeting, Annie had watched the recordings of the activity at the Coach and Horses that morning, and hadn't been at all surprised to discover that Dan had turned up about an hour later than he should have done, and finally set to work after eating what had appeared to be a crusty roll with a fried egg inside it. He'd managed to make a right old mess with it.

She needed to finish the paperwork for the expenses she'd incurred when she'd been laid up after being injured during a recent case. Carol had been banging on about wanting the details so she could get everything off to the insurance company.

With that pain in the backside dealt with – Annie laughed when she thought of that because it had, literally, been a pain in the backside…or at least *near* her backside – she steeled herself to get on with what she'd promised herself she'd do that morning: she had to clear out her wardrobes. She'd made the decision to follow the advice of every decluttering website she could find online: sort things into three piles labelled 'KEEP', 'DISCARD', and 'CHARITABLE DONATIONS'.

To date, she'd got as far as making the signs.

However, she reckoned it would be easy enough once she got going. An hour later, her spare bedroom looked as though the contents of two clothes shops had been dropped from a great height. By a helicopter. That was crashing.

Annie realized that what all those websites had failed to mention – probably on purpose – was that you couldn't possibly make any decisions at all until you knew exactly what you owned. Hence needing to have everything out in the open, all at once.

Amazed to discover she owned six pairs of jeans, Annie couldn't decide which to keep without trying them all on. She labored through the sweaty process, only to discover that four pairs didn't even fit any longer.

And it wasn't because they were too small – result!

Staring at herself in the mirror, Annie had to admit she'd changed shape over the past eighteen months. In London, there'd been a bus stop almost outside her front door, a lift up to her flat, and she always used the escalators in the Tube stations. It wasn't as though she'd been afraid to walk in London. It had been her home for her entire life. She'd lived and breathed London, and had walked every street and lane she'd needed to with confidence. It was just that she'd never really needed to walk that far.

Since her arrival in Anwen-by-Wye she'd walked…and walked…and walked. She still couldn't drive, the buses were almost non-existent and – allowing for lifts she grabbed when she could – she had to live her entire life walking from her cottage to the office, to the shop, to the pub. And then there was Gertie to be walked at least twice every day, and all those extra strolls with Tudor. She couldn't quite believe it, but her thighs and backside had shrunk…it was like a miracle, and she hadn't even noticed.

Four pairs of jeans were baggy on her – four! And they were all clean, so it wasn't as though she'd stretched them out. Annie was delighted, and she immediately started her first pile by folding the baggy jeans and placing them neatly on the chair in the corner of the spare bedroom with the 'CHARITABLE DONATIONS' sign propped on top of them. Then she decided she couldn't do anything but try on all her clothes and give them a proper reassessment in the mirror. It was a hot day outside, and the window in the small eaves' bedroom was tiny, so as she pulled things on, twirled, and pulled them off again, she became more and more sweaty, and less and less enthusiastic about the entire undertaking.

Gertie had wisely chosen to drape herself across the landing outside the bedroom door, and paid no attention to Annie's cries of delight and dismay until a woolen jumper – which had acquired several really annoying moth holes since Annie had tucked it into a drawer when the weather had warmed up – dropped onto her head. Annie had forgotten Gertie was there, and thought that the landing was the best place for anything that wasn't even good enough to give to a charity shop.

Gertie let out a pitiful whine, then stood and tried to shake off the offending garment, but it was stuck to her collar. She took off down the stairs with it trailing after her.

Annie knew that an energetic dog, with a large jumper attached, could do a lot of damage in a short time in a small cottage stuffed with furniture, so she ran down the stairs in her undies, calling, 'Gert...come on, girl, let me help you.'

Gertie had already made it to the kitchen and was out of the back door, chasing the jumper in circles in the small yard where Annie stored her rubbish. Annie watched in horror as Gertie knocked over one of the bins. It was the little one, with all the food scraps inside it, and the contents ended up splattered across the flagstones, and attached to the jumper itself, as well as her pup.

Annie assessed the situation. Tudor and she had 'enjoyed' long conversations about how she had to take better care of herself. Even the counsellor, who she'd been seeing since she'd found the body of someone whose life she'd felt she should have been able to save, had said the same thing: Annie needed to stop, and think, before she acted...before taking what might turn out to be a dangerous course of action.

And there she was, barefoot, almost naked, with goodness knew what slimy, sticky, and possibly sharp, things all over the floor, so she... didn't step outside. Instead, she stood in the doorway speaking softly to Gertie, until the dog calmed down and trotted over to her. They went into the kitchen together, where Annie shoved her feet into her wellies, pulled on some rubber gloves, and then an oversized apron her mother had sent her when she'd first moved into the cottage – believing her daughter was about to be magically transformed into some sort of domestic goddess, no doubt. Once she was protected, Annie disentangled Gertie from the offending piece of knitwear, and placed it into the bin that was still upright. She wiped down her writhing pup – who took what she obviously believed to be a jolly good cuddle in her stride – then she swept up the yard and dumped everything back into the little bin, which she replaced in its original spot.

She turned and looked at what she'd achieved, her rubber-gloved hands on her apron-encased hips. She felt proud of herself.

'And that, Annie Parker,' she said aloud, to the wall, 'is what you can do when you think before you act. Tude would be proud.'

She strode into the kitchen, slipped on a bit of apple that Gertie had squished and carried in beneath a paw, and was halfway to the ground before she managed to break her fall by grabbing the frame of the door. As she righted herself, with no more than a nasty scrape on one forearm, she whispered, 'You never saw that, Gert – right?'

Gertie offered licks and grunts.

Dressed in a rather more decorous outfit of a lilac top with matching shorts, Annie and Gertie enjoyed their lunch of a ham sandwich – half the crusts being ripped off by Annie and dropped to Gertie as she ate – while Annie caught up with the recordings from the rest of the morning at the Coach. She'd shut the door of the spare bedroom, deciding she'd be pushing her luck if she tried to do any more modelling.

Annie didn't hold out much hope for any boggling insights from the pub, and pressed the fast-forward button, which at least made it look as though Dan, Dan the Decorating Man was painting the room the way they always showed it happening on the TV; she even hummed the Benny Hill theme tune as she watched. It was actually quite entertaining. She watched as Wes and Angelo joined Dan for what was obviously due to be a lunch break, then the three went downstairs into the pub and left Dan alone with…Annie paused the recording of the pub area, and went back a bit, then forward again, at the proper speed.

The recording told her that she was watching what had happened at about five past twelve. She looked at her watch; good grief, that was an hour and a half earlier – where had the time gone?

No wonder she'd been peckish. As she knew was their habit, all three men had gathered with their lunches around noon, then Angelo and Wes had gone through the back door of the pub – presumably to sit outside in the shade to eat.

It looked to Annie as though Dan had waved them off, and then she saw a man enter from the front door. A stranger – to her, at least.

He was wearing a light-colored baseball cap, a checked shirt, and jeans by the look of it – Annie was guessing, because the recordings weren't in color. She couldn't tell the man's age...and she couldn't imagine why there'd be a connection, but she couldn't help but be reminded of Hywel Howells.

After no more than a couple of minutes, what appeared to be a chat between two men who knew each other became a shoving match. Then the man with the hat punched Dan in the face. Annie watched as Dan reeled backwards. This made her even more sure the man couldn't be the octogenarian she and Carol had met on his farm.

She sat closer to the screen, knowing there was no sound recording, but hoping to spot...something...to be able to identify the man who had now grabbed Dan by the arm, and was dragging him toward the front door. Neither Angelo nor Wes had returned to the pub to find out what all the fuss was about...so maybe it had happened quietly, or maybe they'd closed the big old wooden door after them when they'd left?

That was it. Nothing else happened until Angelo and Wes ambled back into the pub at just gone half twelve. Angelo walked to the front door of the pub, returning almost immediately, then they both carried on with their work. Annie pressed the fast-forward button again, but there was no sign of Dan...and then she caught up to the live feed.

She went to the front door of her cottage and looked diagonally across the green at the corner where the Coach and Horses stood: no sign of Dan's van. She looked down at Gertie and apologized, 'I can't take you with me to a building site, Gert, but let's get you over to Tude's for a bit. I've got to check on something.' She grabbed her phone and her bag, put Gertie's lead on her, and all but dragged the poor creature – with one short break – right across the middle of the green to the Lamb and Flag.

Barreling through the front door, Annie marched up to Tudor who was sweeping up some sort of mess behind the bar and thrust Gertie's lead into his hand. He looked up with surprise.

'Sorry, Tude love, urgent work thing...concerning matters at the Coach. I'll be back when I can, and I've got my phone. Bye.'

She heard Tudor call, 'Take care,' as she raced out again.

When she arrived at the Coach, she saw that Wes was up a ladder so didn't want to disturb him. She pounded up the stairs calling, 'Angelo?'

'Bathroom – of course,' came the reply.

Annie stood in the doorway. 'Who was that who came to see Dan at lunch time?'

Angelo got up slowly and straightened out his back; Annie thought she could hear it cracking. He looked puzzled. 'I didn't know anyone had come to see him at all. All I know is he was gone when Wes and me came back in after eating out the back. Him gone, van gone, not a word to either of us. He's not the most reliable bloke I've ever shared a site with, Annie.'

'You're not kidding,' snapped Annie, unprepared to say more. 'Left any of his stuff around, has he?'

'That's all his lot over there. He doesn't usually leave that behind, so I don't know what he's playing at. It even looks like he's left his house keys. How's he going to get into his house without them, that's what I'd like to know.'

Annie pounced on the large bunch of keys sitting on top of a canvas bag. The zip was open, and she peered inside. Was that a pile of cash in there?

'Angleo, come over and watch me have a look in here, will you?'

Angleo ambled across, wiping his hands. 'That's his bag – personal. I'm not sure you should go poking about in…oh my giddy aunt…is all that money? Real money?'

Annie had pulled out a large envelope literally stuffed with twenty-pound notes. 'Yeah, it looks real to me…and I saw something earlier on that's made me a bit worried about Dan's safety, which is the only reason I've had a look in here. Okay, here's what I'm going to do: I'm taking this with me – look, I've zipped it up, safe. He's got my number – if he comes back looking for it, tell him to phone me. I'm taking these keys too. Tell him I've got them.'

Angelo looked both puzzled, and uncomfortable. 'Have you tried phoning him?'

Annie could have kicked herself. 'You're right, I haven't but I'll do that from next door.'

Now Angelo looked merely puzzled. 'Why are you going next door?'

'Carol and David Hill live there. She's a private investigator like me, and we need to do some investigating…privately.'

'You're a…private investigator? I thought you were going to be living here and running this pub.'

Annie paused at the top of the stairs. 'A woman can be more than one thing at a time, Angelo. In fact, that's one of our strengths.' And, on that note, she left.

CHAPTER TWENTY-FOUR

Christine had felt a weight lift from her shoulders after her chat with Carol. There was no way she was ready to have a baby...to be a mother. Although Carol hadn't said as much, Christine had realized that not only did *she* know she wasn't ready to be a parent, but anyone who knew her even slightly would understand that to be the case, too. So the decision about continuing with her pregnancy wasn't an issue any more. She wouldn't tell Alexander, she'd just phone Dr Warren and make an appointment to see him to make a plan to...get things back to normal.

Thus, she'd begun her drive from Battersea to Ealing in relatively good spirits, but there'd been a nasty smash on the Great West Road, so she found herself sitting in all but stationary traffic as older vehicles threatened to overheat, and many drivers of more modern ones did just that. She was thankful for the cocoon of comfort that was her Range Rover, and indulged in singing loudly to songs about youth and love and freedom and acting a little wildly as she inched along. With annoyance eventually dampening her good spirits, she realized that, if she got held up for much longer, she'd run the risk of hitting the rush hour traffic on the way back home. *As though that could be worse than this,* she thought.

Finally arriving at the Edwards' address, she was pleased to see that they lived – well, Rachel lived – in an Edwardian home. The flat was on the ground floor of a house on a long, hook-like street close to the Ealing Common Tube station, where all the properties were almost identical. She could see why Richard and Rachel Edwards had chosen the place: all they had to do was jump onto the District Line and they'd be delivered to Earl's Court, and their office base, quite easily.

She used the code to open the front door and entered a short hallway. To her right was the main bedroom, the door open. She peeped in. It was a bit of a mess – clothes strewn across the bed. Men's clothes.

Rachel had sent word that her clothes were kept in the second bedroom, which she used as both an office and a dressing room. *Why would Rachel have thrown her late husband's clothes around? A symptom of her grief?*

The hall jogged to the right, but Christine saw the open-plan sitting room and kitchen to her left, and the garden beyond. Rather than heading directly to get the clothes Rachel had asked for, Christine ventured into the sitting room, more to have a look out at the garden than anything else; it looked large and verdant, which surprised her.

She paused at the kitchen counter. There was a blackboard on the side of the fridge, and on it was scrawled: *Chellingworth Hall – Pick-up driver will phone.*

As she approached the French doors that almost filled the end of a boxy extension which stuck out into the garden itself, two things occurred to her simultaneously: the French doors were not shut, and she'd heard a sound behind her.

Christine froze.

Rachel hadn't mentioned any pets…so what was that noise? There it was again. And why were the French doors not shut and locked?

Pivoting on her toes, she crept back to the hall, her ears, eyes, and nose on full alert…there was an odor, something sweet. She didn't think she'd registered it when she'd arrived, or maybe she'd believed it to be one of those air freshening devices, but it was strongest near the hallway door that led to what had to be the second bedroom, or the bathroom. She held her breath.

Someone was inside the room, and they were opening cupboard doors.

Didn't they hear me arrive?

Christine knew she'd not bothered to open and close the front door quietly when she'd entered – why would she? – but now she wondered if whatever noise she'd made had simply gone unnoticed by whomever was rummaging around in what had to be a bedroom, because there couldn't possibly be that many drawers and cupboards in a small bathroom.

Having established where the noise was coming from, Christine knew she had to make a snap decision: get out now…or confront the person doing the searching. It wasn't difficult. She flung open the door and shouted, 'Oi – what are you doing?'

Facing her was a young man in blue shorts and a blue blouson jacket. The expression on his face told Christine he'd believed himself to be alone in the flat and his first move further informed her that he had no intention of staying there. He dropped whatever he was holding, and ran straight at her, but Christine grabbed both sides of the door frame to block his path.

'You've got no business being here,' she screamed. 'Who are you?'

The teen – at least, he was spotty and youthful…and, yes, he stank of cologne – bounced off Christine with a loud, 'Oomph'. He looked surprised that his run at her hadn't achieved more, then retreated to the far end of the room – which wasn't that far, because it was quite a small room. Eyeing the single window, Christine reckoned he was trying to work out if he could make his exit that way. They both appeared to reach the same conclusion at the same time: unless he was going to be able to break the glass in a sturdy, modern, double-glazed unit, the door was his only way out.

'I said, who are you? And what are you doing here?'

Opportunist thief? Something else? He's been trying to find something in here…and maybe in the main bedroom, which would explain the clothes in there being strewn about.

'That's my business,' he replied with a swagger.

Christine could tell he was going to make another break for freedom, and she didn't think she'd be able to stop him with her body again, so – as he ran at her, bellowing – she stood to one side, and he hit the wall beyond the door with what she accepted as a satisfying cry of surprise and pain.

She grabbed at his jacket, and they struggled for what felt like minutes, but might only have been seconds. Determined she wouldn't let go of him, the youth managed to – somehow – wriggle out of his jacket, leaving Christine holding it, but nothing else.

He flung himself toward the front door, which was now just steps away, and managed to wrench it open. Then he tripped over the threshold, and sprawled onto his face in the little front garden.

Christine was on him, his jacket still entangled around her arm, her cross-body bag waving about as she windmilled her arms onto his back.

'Help!' She screamed as loudly as she could. *Please let someone hear me!*

With more strength than Christine could overcome, the young man forced her off, got himself up onto his feet, and made a break for the gate.

Christine managed to grab the sleeve of his T-shirt as he grappled with the latch then, as she held on, he twisted her around and pushed her, hard.

She staggered backwards across the narrow pavement, bounced off a car parked at the curb, lost her balance, and came down with a crack onto the edge of the garden wall. She felt her head hit, then a searing pain, then…nothing.

CHAPTER TWENTY-FIVE

Alexander Bright wondered why Christine hadn't replied to his texts, then reasoned she was probably still fuming because of the last row they'd had on the phone. At least, that was what he hoped...because, if her parents had told her about the claims that he had a secret son, and that they were being blackmailed by someone calling themselves TISTRU, then he was in even more dire trouble than he was facing with Geordie and Sean.

'Something the matter?' Geordie was pacing the length of Alexander's apartment, not seeing the majesty of the view, nor anything but the clock on the wall.

'Christine's not answering my texts.'

'Lovers' tiff, pet?' Geordie managed a wry smile.

Alexander shook his head but said, 'You could say.' No one needed to know about the blackmail, not even Geordie.

Alexander suddenly felt old. Compartmentalizing his life had been something he'd always done; at first, it had been out of necessity, then it was out of choice. But the burden of not being able to be an entirely whole person with anyone was starting to weigh him down. He had hoped – with all his heart – that Christine would be the person with whom he could be completely open and honest. He'd got almost all the way there, but then she'd started to pull away from him. Was he really unlovable, as his mother had never tired of telling him? Had he scared Christine off? He'd tried so hard to straighten out his life. Was it all for nothing? And now here he was talking to people he'd rather not, to find out what a dangerous thug of a man had been getting up to for the past few decades – a man who he hoped still believed him to be dead.

He felt he was at a crossroads, and his feet were naturally drawing him toward the path with the signpost that said 'EASY STREET', which meant stopping his hard work to remain totally legitimate, and falling back into at least some of his old ways.

'I've texted him a million times. Why doesn't he answer me, Alexander? I'm his brother.'

Alexander stopped thinking about himself and gave his attention to his friend. He needed to focus on the matter in hand, not try to make life-changing decisions on the hoof.

He said, 'Try to relax, Geordie, you might need all your energy if Sean does accept your offer to meet on neutral turf…without me being there.'

Geordie dumped himself onto one of Alexander's leather sofas, which made a loud noise. Both men looked at each other, then burst into raucous laughter…which they found hard to stop.

Eventually, pink-faced, Geordie said, 'If we can both laugh that hard at a fart sound, there can't be much wrong with the world, right, pet?'

Alexander wiped his eyes. 'You're not wrong, pet.' His phone warbled, and he grabbed it. 'Yes – what news?'

He waved Geordie back into his seat as he tried to listen in. 'Hang on a minute. Right, go ahead – you're on speakerphone, and it's safe for you to speak openly, Reggie. What have you got?'

The disembodied voice of Reggie sounded tinny, and yet hypnotic. 'I've done the best I can, mate. Word is, like you said, Big Tony MacNamara has stuck it out at the family home since the old days. In a wheelchair because he's got bad feet from diabetes. He still stuffs himself with cakes and pies, and manages to remain like a stick, but there you are, that's the word. Been in it a couple of years. Hasn't slowed him down. Generally still only into two things: drugs, and moneylending. Two cash businesses which we all know both feed off the needs of the vulnerable. Uses the cash he makes from each to fund the other. But he's upped the game, it seems – by which I mean bigger loans, to a different type of borrower: seems he's even "investing" in businesses where they don't mind how dirty the money is.'

'Like?' Alexander snapped.

'Car washing, minicabs, the usual. Anything where cash is king and there's an upfront need for money…then he bleeds them.'

Geordie said, 'You'd think the ride-sharing thing would mean people don't want minicabs anymore, wouldn't you?'

Alexander replied, 'Not for people whose lives revolve around cash. If you've got money you can use via your phone, you've got money that can be traced. Anyone who gets paid in cash, or doesn't want the taxman knowing what they're up to, will still be using minicabs.'

'Exactly,' said Reggie. 'Thing is – everyone agrees there's something changing, but no one can agree about what he's up to.'

'What's the word, Reggie?'

'General consensus is it could be something to do with online scams – though what type…well, that's where the rumors are running rife. Front runners are: messaging people saying you're a relative in trouble and you need money; offering stuff that doesn't exist for sale online so you have to show up in a car park with a pocket full of cash – then guess what happens. And something that I, personally, don't think he's got the ability to do – having a whole load of what appear to be real websites where you sign up for something that looks like a great deal on a membership of an actual real thing – you know, like a gym, or a spa. Something that reels in the middle classes, not the cash-in-hand mob – then taking their money electronically, and disappearing the website before anyone can trace where their dosh has gone.'

Geordie and Alexander locked eyes and said, 'Sean,' as a chorus.

'What did you two say?'

'We reckon we know of a way Big Tony might have extended his business empire to fleece a group with credit cards and bank accounts, Reggie. Thanks. Anything else?'

Reggie's tone was bleak. 'He's still got the reputation of making sure a bloke he thinks has wronged him, or who owes him, gets a good beating as warning number one, with things getting worse from there on. Word is, he's never really got over the death of his kid brother, and takes it out on the world around him. Did you hear about that?'

Alexander muttered, 'Something.'

Geordie asked, 'What about his brother?'

Reggie said, 'They fished him out of the sea about thirty years back.'

'That's awful,' said Geordie. 'Was it an accident?'

'The thinking is that it wasn't.' Reggie sounded somber.

Geordie said, 'Oh dear,' as he pulled a face at Alexander.

Reggie continued, 'Seems the kid brother and a mate of his – who worked for Big Tony back then, a bloke called Issy – went out for a bit of a jolly in someone's boat down near Hastings. The kid brother ends up dead. His body took days to wash up. They never found the other one, though they found a good deal of his blood on the boat. Also presumed dead. They reckoned no one could have lived if they'd lost that much blood. Big Tony always believed someone had got to the two of them. Killed his kid brother, and his kid brother's mate – who just happened to be one of his prized employees – to get to him. Some say he's never stopped looking for whoever did it.'

'Like I said, I heard,' said Alexander.

He felt every punch of the fight he and Mickey MacNamara had slogged out on that tiny boat. Heard the crack as Mickey had fallen hard onto a metal fitting. Felt the sting of the tears he'd cried as he'd chucked his mate's body over the side, then the sting of the knife he'd used to cover the boat with his own blood. And all because of a girl in a seaside pub who'd given Issy one too many fluttering glances, when Mickey had his eye on her. He'd told Mickey it was stupid to start throwing punches on a boat that size. But Mickey had been drunk...so drunk...and wouldn't take telling.

Alexander snapped back to reality when he heard, 'Anything else, Alexander?' Reggie sounded willing to help.

'That's enough, cheers, mate. I owe you one,' replied Alexander, looking at Geordie, who nodded.

Reggie concluded, 'You're welcome. You know what a difference it made when you got my sister into that flat down in Streatham Vale, away from that drunken lump who'd fathered her two kids. A lifesaver that was. She's like a different person, now. And you don't owe me one at all – I still owe you several. Bye.'

Alexander perched on a stool at the kitchen counter. 'So do we reckon Big Tony's used his ability to supply Sean with good quality drugs in return for your brother's enviable computing skills to run this fraudulent website thing?'

Geordie nodded. 'Sounds like that would be right up Sean's street. I bet he's got no idea that he's caught up with such a dangerous man.'

Alexander chuckled darkly. 'Yeah, Big Tony can be quite the charmer, when he wants to be. That house where he is now, that used to be his mum's? You could go in there and eat your food off the floor – which is saying something when you think about the flotsam that used to wash up in the place. Always dressed well, was polite in company. And you could almost hear him purring when people called him "Mr MacNamara". What a leech. We've got to get Sean away from him, Geordie. Look, I've got an idea – but it'll take both of us to make it work, and a fair bit of luck, too. And it could get…a bit dodgy.'

Geordie sighed. 'He's my brother. I'll do anything it takes. Tell me your idea.'

'Hold that thought,' said Alexander as his phone rang. 'I have to take this, sorry, mate.' Alexander accepted the call from Aiden Wilson-Smythe. 'Alexander here. Any more news?'

Geordie half stood, but Alexander shook his head and waved him down, then stepped out onto his balcony and shut the door behind him.

Aiden spoke fast. 'I got another email from TISTRU, with another photo attached. I'm sending it now. He's reminding me of his deadline. Can you see it? That's you, isn't it? Is that the mother of the child you're with?'

Alexander looked into what looked like his own face on the screen of his phone. Yes, that was definitely him – about fifteen years back when he'd been getting his property company going. The young woman with him? He had no idea of her name, but they appeared to be at some sort of party. Were they together? Or had they just been in close proximity to each other when the photo was taken? He had no idea. She looked vaguely familiar, that was all.

He replied, 'Aiden, look, as agreed, I'll rustle up the cash. Ask TISTRU where he wants us to deliver it. Just string him along. I'll sort it. Keep in touch with me, and don't say anything to Christine.'

He didn't dare ask…did he? 'Have you seen her by the way? Is she okay?' He didn't add that she wasn't replying to his texts.

'I haven't seen her today, and I won't tell her – we don't want her upset by all this. You can tell her about it when it's behind us.'

Aiden paused and sighed, heavily. 'If it ever is, of course. If this TISTRU person doesn't think he's onto a good thing and decides to bleed us dry. We need to talk about that aspect, Alexander.'

'We do. But not now. So, she's okay, then?'

'Went over to her Battersea flat on her own last night, and I think she's going back to Chellingworth tomorrow. Seemed…well, a bit off when I saw her, but her mother spoke to her a couple of hours ago when she was sitting in traffic somewhere, and Deirdre said she sounded quite upbeat, which makes a change, I must say.'

'Look, I will sort this, but I've got something else on my plate that needs my immediate attention, Aiden. But we'll talk soon. And let me know what this character says, okay?'

'Will do.'

The men disconnected and Alexander re-entered the flat.

'Problems?'

Alexander was focused on the photo on his phone. He was expanding it and moving the picture around the screen. He held out the phone. 'Is that the side of your head in this photo, Geordie?'

Geordie took the phone and stared, then smiled. 'Yeah, that's me. Remember those sideburns I had? No idea what I was thinking. That looks like the time we had a big get-together down at that riverside pub in Hammersmith. Remember? We'd just finished that job on that big, detached house down there. One of your first.' He handed the phone back.

'Who's the woman? Remember her? Was I with her?'

Geordie laughed. 'You're kidding? That's Gary's wife. Remember him? Massive bloke.'

Alexander nodded. He did.

'You and her? Never. He'd have flattened you, and she was so smitten with him she'd never give anyone else a second glance. Had three kids by then, they did. Ended up with six, I understand. In Sunderland now – or somewhere like it. Lost track of them a bit.'

Alexander was wracking his brain. 'Who'd have taken this photo, then, Geordie?'

Geordie shrugged. 'I dunno. Could have been Gary himself, I suppose. Of his wife, with his boss, you know? Or any of the dozens of other people who were there that day. To be honest...well, it was a good party, until it wasn't. Sean was starting to show signs of going off the rails even back then, and you and me invited him along whenever we could, remember? He had several too many that day, and I ended up having to go with him to the local A and E. Alcohol poisoning it was, that time.'

Alexander put down his phone and buried his head in his hands. *What had Sean said when he'd shouted that Alexander would soon be losing all his 'chummies'? That it was 'true — all true'? Sean. TISTRU. Of course, Sean.*

Obviously unaware of what was swirling in Alexander's thoughts, Geordie continued, 'So what's this plan you've got to save my brother, then?'

CHAPTER TWENTY-SIX

Annie knocked loudly at Carol's kitchen door, didn't wait for an answer, and marched in. She managed to catch Bunty who looked as though she was about to make a break for freedom through the open door, which she closed quickly. 'Car – I need your help.' There was no answer. 'Car?' Annie strode into the hall. 'Car?'

Carol's head appeared at the top of the stairs. 'Shush, Annie – what do you want? I'm up here changing Albert, with David. You know – five minutes of family time?'

Annie charged up the stairs. 'Dan's disappeared – he's been grabbed, I know it. You've got to help me.'

Annie smiled at David who was standing in the doorway to Albert's room with a tiny T-shirt in his hands. She locked eyes with him, and tried to judge his mood.

'I'll hold the fort here,' he said, then added, 'Nice to see you, Annie. See you when I see you, Carol.' He shut the door.

Carol glared, and shooed Annie down the stairs into the kitchen. She closed the door.

'I love you, you know that, Annie, but you have to learn to respect that there are times when I choose to put my family first.' Carol looked upset, which surprised Annie.

Taking a seat at the kitchen table, Annie allowed herself to calm down, then said, 'Sorry, Car. You're right, I have to learn to think before I act. And I am trying to do that, honest, but...'

Carol joined her friend at the table and sighed. 'Go on – what?' She looked at her watch.

Annie snapped, 'What, got somewhere to be?'

Carol snapped back, 'As a matter of fact I do. I've made an appointment to meet Blodwen Peaswell's daughter in Brecon in an hour. I was – literally – taking five minutes to be with my son and husband before I left. So make it quick.'

Annie felt wounded, and allowed it to show. 'I'll come with you.'

'No, you won't. Why would you do that? Aren't you busy enough? What's all this about Dan disappearing, for example?'

Annie organized her thoughts, and ran through what had happened as rapidly as she could. She held up the bunch of keys and the canvas bag full of cash. 'These keys can't all be for just him. Look, a lot of them have got tags on them. For example, this one. Wasn't that place we followed him to outside Builth Wells called Rose Cottage?'

Carol took the keys and examined them. 'Yes, it was. There was the sign with the arrow at the end of the lane. And that's what this key says. Hmm…you're right, it's odd. Especially given there are six other keys with names on them. One of them says "COACH" – do you think he's got one for every job he works on?' Carol glanced at her watch. 'Oh, look at the time – I've got to go, Annie.'

'I thought we could visit the cottage again.' Annie did her best sweet smile.

'Okay then – but go to the loo right this minute…you know what you're like. I'll see you in the car.'

As Annie buckled herself into the passenger seat, she decided to focus on something other than Dan, Dan the flamin' Decorating Man.

'Good job finding the Peaswell woman, how'd you manage that, then?'

Carol smiled at her friend's appreciation, then gushed about how wonderful it was that the team was always able to find a way to get things done, no matter how stumped they might be at the beginning.

Annie congratulated her chum again, then tuned out a bit as Carol went on and on about having tracked down some bloke who taught at the university in Swansea to find out about the likelihood of being able to poison someone with an atomized solution of oyster shells…which was a possibility, it seemed, as long as the shells had been ground to dust.

Carol had also discovered that could be achieved by using a hammer to break them up, then a pestle and mortar to grind them to a powder. Annie didn't bother asking how Carol had discovered that; she suspected that quite a bit of time watching videos online had played a part.

'Heard from Chrissy at all?' Carol had drawn breath following her detailed explanation, so Annie took her chance to change the subject.

Carol hesitated, then said, 'I spoke to her earlier. She sounded alright. Reporting in before she went to visit Rachel's flat in Ealing Common.'

'Ealing Common is basically on the way here. So, what I don't get is why she would go all the way back into London if she's already halfway to Anwen.'

'It's not halfway – it's a long way from being halfway,' Carol clarified, then added, 'we're nearly there, if this GPS is right. Now you can actually help – look out for this road.' She pointed at the screen.

Affronted that her chum didn't think she'd been of any use thus far, Annie kept her eyes peeled then shouted, 'Next left, there,' making Carol flinch.

Finally parked in the driveway of the house where Carol had informed Annie a woman by the name of Trudy Williams lived, they got out, and Carol rang the doorbell.

Ten minutes later, with a pot of tea in front of them, Carol and Annie listened as the small, neat Trudy Williams spoke fondly of her late parents who had, apparently, been keen on documenting the history of the family. The two detectives shared a smile, and Annie could tell they stood a good chance of making some progress when Trudy opened a cupboard to reveal about three dozen photo albums.

Trudy announced, 'After Dad died, Mam decided to make this her mission in life. You'll see that the spines of the albums tell you what's inside. I think these might be the ones that could help.'

She placed two albums on the kitchen table. One spine said 'HILLTOP YEARS – BLODWEN DAVIES', the other said 'SCHOOL – BLODWEN DAVIES'.

'Mam made notes in them too, you see?' Trudy opened the heavy cover of the first volume and peeled back translucent paper. Photographic prints made of thick card were affixed to the page with little corner attachments, their colors in the brown and cream range, rather than black and white. Beneath each one was a three- or four-line description of what was depicted.

'Most helpful,' said Carol on behalf of the pair, as she turned the pages past the baby photos.

'That's her big brother, David,' said Trudy at one point. 'Oh yes, that's in the notes, of course.'

Annie felt her hopes rise that this was the right Blodwen Davies…the one with a brother and a family that had taken in two evacuees from London. 'He didn't keep the farm on?'

'Sold it once their father died. Mam had left by then. My uncle and his wife moved to a place just outside Aberystwyth, where he had a smallholding. There till he died. Mam never understood why he left this area. He said he wanted to be by the sea. Quite different to around here.'

They reached the end of the album without any photos showing two additional male children at the family farm, and it was obvious that Blodwen was in her late teens when the album stopped – long past the time when the Gulliver boys would have been in Wales, anyway.

Trudy looked at their glum faces and said, 'Maybe you'll have better luck with the other one. You take a look, and I'll freshen the pot.'

Annie rolled her eyes wearily at Carol, who fixed a determined smile on her face and swapped the albums. The second one was slimmer, and largely featured head-and-shoulders shots of Blodwen throughout her time at school, with class photos also arranged in date order. Both women easily identified Hywel Howells; he really hadn't changed that much – older, of course, but he'd always, obviously, had a vibrancy about him.

Between the formal portraits were a few snaps of what were probably school outings, and Annie noticed that Blodwen always appeared to be holding hands with another girl. The girl with her looked much more coy than Blodwen, and Annie had the strangest feeling that she'd seen her before…somewhere.

She checked back to earlier photos. Nothing before 1941 showing this girl, but after that she was everywhere. Annie took control of the page-turning and went to the back of the volume. There was Blodwen Davies in a floral dress, and she was standing beside…

'Look, Car. It's Iris. Iris Lewis. My next-door neighbor. That's her, isn't it?'

Carol peered at the photo. 'It certainly could be. What does the note underneath it say?'

Annie read aloud, '"Me and my Little Flower off to a dance at the church hall. This was the night I met George".'

'Little Flower! Iris!' Annie and Carol chorused.

Trudy almost dropped the pot, but managed to get it safely onto the table. 'Oh yes, Mam's "Little Flower". I asked her about her loads of times, but she never told me who she was, just that they'd lost touch as soon as Mam met Dad and they started courting. She never said, but I think it was one of those friendships that was extremely close, but couldn't survive Mam being interested in a boyfriend. Dad was her first ever boyfriend, see – you'd have seen from the photos that she was a right old tomboy until then. There's people I was in school with that I don't mix with anymore – and they only live down the road. I think Mam said this one went off to college. A rarity around here in those days, I'd have thought. Especially for a woman. I wonder what became of her.'

'If I'm right,' said Annie, 'she qualified as a teacher, pursued a long and fulfilling career in education, and now lives in Anwen-by-Wye…where she's able to indulge her penchant for budgies.'

'Budgies, you say? Well, they had that in common too, then – mad about her budgie, was Mam. We had them all the time I was growing up. One after the other, not loads at once. They can live a long time, you know. I was the one who ended up looking after her last one when she'd gone. Thought the blessed thing would never die – and they're a real commitment. Then it literally fell off its perch one night. I can't say I was sorry. I've still got the cage, in the garage. Huge thing it is. About three feet tall.'

Annie was keen to get going. 'Can we take snaps of these photos, Trudy? I'd like to show them to the person we think is in them.'

'No skin off my nose. I like to keep the albums, because they meant so much to Mam. Mind you, I dare say my kids will just throw them on a bonfire when I'm gone. Won't mean much to them, will they?'

Annie and Carol felt compelled to have at least one cup each from the fresh pot, then both accepted the offer to use the bathroom. They finally headed out to the car, with their mobile phones now containing photos of Blodwen Davies and the young woman they believed to be Iris Lewis.

As they reversed out of the driveway, Annie said, 'Can we go to Rose Cottage now, please?'

Carol nodded. 'Yes, that's where we're heading. Well, that was a turn-up, wasn't it? Thanks to Hywel Howells – who, as we know, managed to mix up the name of his dog with a family member – and a bit of a misdirection to Blodwen Davies, we got there. In the end. I think. He's muddled up that Blodwen Davies with Iris. Who turns out to be Anwen's very own Iris Lewis...the "Little Flower" from Walter's youth. What a bit of luck.'

Annie smiled. 'Not luck, Car. We wouldn't have found that out because we wouldn't have been looking at Trudy's photo albums unless you'd put in the work. Like my mother always says, it's amazing how much luckier you can get, the harder you work.'

'Thanks, Annie. And I know you're right. But, hang on a sec...do you happen to *know* if Iris Lewis was a Davies before she married?'

Annie replied, 'No, but it wouldn't surprise me if she had been – almost every other person around here is either a Davies or a Jones, or once was a Davies or a Jones, or knows umpteen of them, and is related to half of those. It's weird – how do you keep track?'

Carol chuckled. 'Of what?'

'What do you think?'

'I don't know.'

Annie sighed loudly. 'How do you know if you're related? I mean, there you are, down the disco one Saturday night, and you've had a few, and this handsome bloke asks you to dance, and then before you know what's happening, you're smooching to the last record of the night, and you're thinking, "Hmm, he's a Davies and my mother was a Davies, too". You'd have to stop to go through your whole family tree before you...you know.'

Carol vibrated with giggles. 'I don't know what sort of discos you used to go to, Annie, but it sounds to me as though it would be a good idea to find out more than that much about each other before any...hanky-panky. And, yes, people do work out if they're related early on – it's quite important. And it's an extremely good reason for there always being at least one person in a family who's going to put in the work to keep track of these sorts of things.'

'You're not kidding,' said Annie thoughtfully. She changed topic. 'You know what? I think that Dan's been taken off the premises by someone he's ripped off, or stolen from, like me. They've spotted that something's gone, like I did, and they've worked out it could only have been him, so they rocked up to the Coach and hauled him off.'

'How did they get there?'

Annie didn't understand. 'Pardon?'

'There hasn't been anything parked in front of the pub all day that I'm aware of, and I live right next door to the place. There wasn't an unusual car out there when we left, was there?' Annie had to agree. 'So how did this mystery man in the hat get to Anwen-by-Wye to have it out with Dan? If he'd come in his own car, then took Dan off in Dan's van – as you're suggesting he did – then where's his car gone?'

Annie grinned. 'He wasn't alone – someone else drove, then he made Dan drive him away in Dan's own van.'

Carol replied calmly, 'There was a yellow car...small, an older hatchback. Passed my window slowly. Once. Maybe someone arriving at the pub...parked at the side? Could have left the village by going around the green. Or he did drive himself, parked for the few minutes you saw him – which I admit might well be something I missed – then he left, and Dan left independently?'

Annie sighed. 'Yeah, you're right, Car – we can't be sure, can we?'

'Nor can we be sure he's gone to this Rose Cottage again.'

Annie wouldn't give up. 'But it's the only name on a key that means anything to us. They're all cryptic, unless you know what they mean in the first place. COACH could mean anything, unless you know it means the Coach and Horses pub in Anwen-by-Wye, for example. It's our only lead. We should follow it.'

Carol sighed. 'Alright then, we'll park where we did the last time,'

'No, Car. What's the point of us lumbering all the way up and down that lane when we're going inside the house anyway?'

Carol's eyes flicked toward Annie for an instant. 'We're doing no such thing. That's breaking and entering. Mavis would skin us alive.'

'It's not breaking if you've got a key.'

'To pinch your favorite saying for once – Gordon Bennett, Annie...that's not a distinction we should be making. We aim to uphold the law, not break it.'

Annie sulked. 'You've not been backwards in coming forwards when it comes to a bit of digging around online in places you shouldn't really go.'

Carol bristled. 'We've said we won't talk about that. And, in any case, it's different. This is someone's home, Annie. And we don't know whose. Look we're almost there, but I'm going to keep on driving unless you promise we'll just give the place the once over – from outside. We'll walk up the lane, in case we need to do the peeping through the hedge thing again. And this time, be careful where you're putting your feet. You went through four nappies the last time.' Carol burst out laughing, and Annie joined in.

Finally alongside Rose Cottage, and peering through the hedge again, the women exchanged a look of relief that there was no vehicle parked in the lane, so they ventured closer. The house wasn't at all cottagey in the way that Annie's home was: it looked like a 1930s building – a perfect cube, pebble-dashed, with a steeply raked roof. What appeared to be the original front door had a sunburst of leaded glass in an oval pane at its top.

Annie grabbed at Carol's hand and whispered, 'Front door's open.'

Carol nodded. 'The homeowner might be in – thinks it's quite safe to leave their door open all the way out here.'

Annie headed up the path, and felt Carol tug at her sleeve. Her friend hissed, 'Stop it – you shouldn't.'

Annie reached the front door and decided to go for it. 'Yoo-hoo...anyone home?'

When she turned, she could see that Carol had slapped her hand onto her face and was shaking her head in disbelief. Annie knew she'd taken a chance, but she didn't think her actions warranted such a damning response.

She turned toward the house again, stepped forward and knocked loudly on the door, 'Anyone in?' The door swung open, inviting her in. She paused for only a second or two as she heard Carol groaning, then crossed the threshold. 'Oi – anyone at home? Hello-o!'

She looked over her shoulder at Carol and announced triumphantly, 'The place is deserted – anyone here would have answered by now, wouldn't they?'

At that moment, a cat scampered past Annie, giving her quite a turn. It had shot out of the rear of the house. As she watched it go, and saw where it had been, she pointed to the tiled hallway floor. 'Look – blood.'

Carol appeared to be more concerned about that cat. 'That could be an indoor cat, and now it's out. That's not good,' she said.

Annie snapped, 'Forget the flamin' cat. Look, Car...it's tracked blood all along the hall on its paws. *That's* what's not good. It came from back there.'

Carol was at Annie's shoulder. 'I'm right here, Annie. We'll do this together. We don't want you seeing something that might – you know, trigger you.'

'What on earth are you talking about, Car? I'm fine, but I think there might be someone here who's not.'

'But if we go back there to see...what's what...there might be something that could take you back to the last time you found a dead body. And your counsellor said you were doing really well.'

Annie paused for a moment. 'Thanks, Car, you're a real mate. You're right, she said I was doing well, and I am...though I can't deny that my tummy's doing somersaults at the moment, if you know what I mean. But we're here, and there's blood, and someone might need us. So what are we going to do? Phone the police? An ambulance? And just wait? We have to do this. We must investigate. It's actually what we do for a living. I can't not do that. We might save a life.'

Carol nibbled her lips, then nodded. 'I'll go first,' she said.

Annie allowed her to pass her in the narrow hall. Carol pushed open the door ahead of them, which was already ajar.

The kitchen was in disarray: pots, pans, and broken china were strewn about the place. And there was a bloody knife on the floor...and blood. But no body. No one at all, though mounds of discarded, bloodied kitchen roll lay in heaps on the counter.

Carol and Annie made short work of dashing into and out of every room downstairs, with Carol leading the way. Then they ventured upstairs, and did the same thing. The house was completely undisturbed everywhere but the kitchen.

As they left the third of the three bedrooms, Annie felt herself getting sweaty. A wave of nausea ran through her entire body. *The relief of not finding a corpse?*

She didn't want to make a big thing of it, or worry Carol, so said simply, 'Back in a tick,' and darted into the bathroom. She wasn't terribly sick, and she felt better after a few moments.

Carol was waiting for her at the top of the stairs. 'I've phoned Constable Llinos Trevelyan. Explained everything. She's at the end of her shift, but said she'd come anyway – once she's cleared it at HQ.'

Annie smiled weakly. 'Nice having a local police officer on speed-dial, innit?'

Carol grinned, and agreed.

Annie added, 'And when she gets here, we can tell her that's my toilet in the bathroom.'

Carol managed a chuckle. 'That's why you were so long? You were examining the toilet?'

Annie nodded. She sort of had been.

'And how can you be sure it's yours, Annie? They all look so much alike. It might just be similar, or even the same model. Yes, you can tell this house has been freshly decorated, and that – other than the kitchen and one bedroom – most of it hasn't even really been lived in since it's been done up, but I think you're stretching it a bit.'

Annie started down the stairs. 'I'd agree with you, Car, except for one thing.'

'Go on then, what?'

'The wallpaper in that main bedroom is what I picked out for ours, and the trim's the matching paint. Dan's nicked the lot from us and put it all in here. And I think that might be his blood in the kitchen, too.'

Carol made a face. 'Because?'

'Because as well as the knife on the kitchen floor there was a weird black, plastic round thing. It was covered in blood, too. And that's what Dan's been using to score the wallpaper he's been removing up in our flat. It even had his stupid logo thing on it, on a sticky label. It…it's likely to be his blood, isn't it?'

Carol joined Annie at the front door. 'Well, whoever's blood it is, they aren't here now. When Llinos arrives – or maybe even while she's on the way – she can set the wheels in motion to officially check all the hospitals for anyone coming in with knife wounds. I think it's high time we let the police handle this one, Annie.'

Annie still felt a bit wobbly. 'This is me not disagreeing, Car.'

18th JULY

CHAPTER TWENTY-SEVEN

When Christine opened her eyes, the first thing she was aware of was that, wherever she was, it was dim…almost dark. The second thing she noticed was the beeping noise. The third? That her head was pounding.

'Thank the Lord, she's awake.'

Christine panicked. 'Mammy? Is that you? Where am I?' She tried to lift her head, but it weighed at least three tons.

'Stay still, my darling. Yes, I'm here, and your daddy's just gone to get a cup of coffee. He'll be back any minute. I'm going to press the button to let them know you've woken. Just lay still, and don't worry – you're going to be alright.'

Christine tried to remember what had happened. Rachel's house. The young man with the blue jacket. Bouncing off the car. 'What time is it? Is there any water?'

Christine saw her mother's face directly above her. 'Don't worry about the time, just lay there, still. Here's a cup with a straw. Have a suck on that. But don't suck too hard.'

Christine did the best she could, but it was more difficult than she'd imagined. She knew that sitting up would be impossible, so she allowed her mother to help her drink, then wipe off what she'd dribbled.

'Thanks, Mammy. Do you know what happened? How did I get here? And where's here? If you don't tell me, I'll only worry.'

Deirdre Wilson-Smythe sighed. 'You're at Ealing Hospital. Someone found you on the street out in the Ealing Common area and they phoned for an ambulance. They brought you here. Lucky you were so close. You were brought in at about four yesterday afternoon. You've been…sleeping off and on since then. You've got a broken eye socket, and a concussion. But they say you won't lose your eye.'

Christine couldn't turn her head to see her mother, but she could hear her sobbing as she spoke. 'Oh my darling, when they phoned us we thought we were going to lose you. We got here as fast as we could.'

'Did you say four o'clock yesterday? You mean it's tomorrow?'

'Yes. But you're fine. Like I said, they've done what they can for the moment, but they'll need to keep an eye on you for a while. Oh dear…sorry, I didn't mean to say that. You know what I mean. Observation. Your daddy wants to move you to a private clinic that's closer to home, so we'll talk about that later. They'll need to keep checking on you as the swelling goes down, you see. Just so they can be sure you don't need surgery. But they said your eye was reacting to light just fine. Though things might be blurry for a while. Orbital fracture, but not a bad one. No little bits of bone shattered in there, or anything like that. You'll be fine.'

Christine was struggling to take it all in when her father appeared. 'She would wake when I wasn't here, wouldn't she? Gone for two minutes, so I was. How are you, my darling girl? Did you buzz for the nurse, Deirdre, like they said?'

'I did that.'

'So where are they? There were three of them all standing about looking at that massive board they've got at the end of the corridor when I came past. I'll go and get one of them now.'

'They're probably busy,' said Christine as he left the room.

'Everyone's been busy,' said her mother.

'Has Alexander been here?' Christine had to ask.

'We don't think he knows yet. Your father hasn't been getting any replies to his phone calls or texts, and I know all your lot are trying to get hold of him too.'

'My lot?' It suddenly occurred to Christine that no one in Anwen knew what had happened. 'You've got to let me phone them, Mammy. There was a man at Rachel's house, and he got away. He was the one who pushed me. There was a note on the fridge – he might have seen it. He'll know where Rachel is. I don't think he was a thief.' As she spoke, she realized that none of what she was saying would make sense to her mother.

'Don't worry, dear. It's all taken care of.'

Christine clenched her fists with frustration. 'No, it's not, Mammy. Please, just let me make one phone call to Carol?'

'No work for you, young lady,' snapped her father as he re-entered the room. 'Someone will be here in a minute. Apparently, they can tell from the monitors that your vitals are all good, but the doctor wants the chance to talk to you about how you feel, now that you're more *compos mentis*. You've been rambling.'

'Can't you get hold of Alexander?' Christine felt panicked.

'I wish I could.' Her father sounded utterly frustrated, though not angry, which she thought odd.

'Doesn't anyone know where he is? Is he alright?' As she thought of her fiancé, Christine suddenly remembered that she was pregnant. The knowledge hit her with as much of a wallop as it had when Dr Warren had first told her. She didn't dare say anything – but, in that instant, she knew that the most important thing was to find out if everything was alright. Suddenly her aching head was awhirl. You usually had to tell them if you thought you could be pregnant before you were X-rayed, didn't you? Had they X-rayed her and not known? What might that do to the embryo?

But she wasn't keeping it, was she? She'd decided that.

So, did it matter?

Christine closed her eyes.

Damn it.

Yes, it did.

She sighed. She might not be ready to be a mother, but she realized – with a mixture of horror and desperation – that the thought that she might not be about to become one after all had made the prospect more…real. More…what she wanted. In about seven months' time, if that were still possible.

'Don't cry, my darling,' said her mother unexpectedly. 'It can't be good for your eye, and they said that sneezing will be bad for you – so try to not get all blocked up.'

Christine hadn't been aware she was crying, but it made sense. 'Oh Mammy, what's to become of me?'

It was at that point that she heard someone enter the room, and there followed a blur of medical interactions that left her feeling more certain about what to expect as a result of her injuries. Her parents hovered the whole time, and she struggled with the idea of asking them if they'd leave so that she could ask the doctor about her pregnancy in private, but felt that wasn't fair to them.

The doctor rushed off, beeping as she went, and Christine was grateful she at least had some real insights into the damage to her eye socket which could, apparently, have been a great deal worse. All the signs were good that she'd make a full recovery without needing any surgery – and that had come straight from a doctor. A nurse came along a few minutes later and adjusted Christine's bed so that she was half sitting up, which was helpful, because it meant she could see what was going on around her – through one eye.

When Christine had managed to assure her parents that she was comfortable, wasn't thirsty, or hungry, or over-tired, or likely to be able to relax unless they told her why she didn't need to speak urgently to her colleagues, her mother settled down and spoke quietly.

'You weren't totally unconscious when that couple found you. In fact, you spoke to them until the ambulance got there. Told them that the blue jacket you were holding belonged to the man who had attacked you. You wouldn't let go of it. Got quite stroppy about it, so they said. When your father and I arrived at the A and E, you gave it to him, which you might recall. He passed it to the police, in case it could help them.'

'Good. Thanks.'

Her mother continued, 'But it wasn't until later that I found one of those plastic wallets that holds business cards on the floor underneath the bed they had you in, out in the area with all the emergency cubicles. The police had gone by then, so your father and I agreed the best thing we could do – since we couldn't get hold of Alexander – was to phone Carol. Which we did, last evening.'

'Oh, that's grand. Thanks.' Christine felt relieved.

Her mother leaned in. 'Carol, and all of them, have been brilliant.'

'They always are,' said Christine with feeling.

'They all send their love, of course, but we agreed they were better off staying in Wales and handling things from that end, rather than any of them coming here. That's right, isn't it? You didn't want any of them here in the hospital with you? I know you and Carol are good chums, but...'

Christine saved her mother. 'Best they stay there, yes. What was in the wallet?'

Her mother looked surprised. 'Business cards. For a private investigations agency based in Hounslow, of all places. Though you lot are all at Chellingworth, so I suppose Hounslow isn't all that unusual. Carol took over, and she's been sending texts all the time. I'm not sure she can have slept at all.'

'And?'

'Now don't you go worrying that poor little injured head of yours, my darling girl. Just let me hold your hand, and everything will be fine.'

Christine knew her mother meant well, but wanted to fling herself out of bed and get on with something that involved more than flopping about with a sore head.

'She'll never rest until she knows.' Christine's father spoke gently, then chuckled. 'My daughter's too much like her father, aren't you, my girl?'

'Yes, Daddy. Please tell me, then I'll rest, I promise.'

'I'll do better than that,' said her father. 'I'll dial. Use my phone. Let Carol tell you herself. It's only one of your eyes that doesn't work, so just use your ears, and keep your head where it is.'

Christine spoke as soon as she could hear the line was open. 'Carol, it's me Christine. I'm fine. Eye's going to be okay. Let's not dwell on that – I have to know what's going on. Is Rachel okay? That chap in her house probably saw a note on her fridge that said Chellingworth Hall – he might be on his way there by now – or even there already.'

She spoke fast, not wanting Carol to interrupt before she'd passed on the vital information.

Carol replied excitedly. 'Oh Christine, it's lovely to hear your voice. Don't worry, we're all over it. I know about the bloke who thumped you, and the police do, too.'

Christine was truly relieved.

Carol continued, 'So listen up: the bloke works for a firm of private investigators who say they were hired to find Rachel Edwards. They've said they didn't know why their client wanted to find her, and have not – so far – named their client. At least, if they've told the police, the police haven't told us. Which is neither here nor there. Rachel won't be leaving the Hall until the police have interviewed her. They're involved, now, because of the attack on you. Mavis has been on the phone with them, back and forth, for quite some time last evening, and this morning.'

'Thank her for me, will you Carol?'

'Don't worry, we're all here for you. Mavis tells me Rachel's hoping they'll take her concerns about her husband's cause of death more seriously because of this new development, so there's that, I suppose. In the meantime, they've picked up the bloke who hit you, like I said, and he's claiming it was an accident. The police didn't tell me about that part – but it's all over social media. They hauled him out of a pub in Hounslow last night, and that's what he was screaming – that it was an accident – when they did it. At least a dozen people filmed it all. So, please, don't worry about it. Rachel is safe. The police are involved, and we can take care of everything at this end of things.'

Christine closed her one good eye. She could rest easy. 'Thanks, Carol.'

'Silly sausage, it's what we do. For our clients, and for each other. Now, do you want me to pop down to London to see you there? David can cope with Albert – we've already talked about it.'

'Please don't. I've got Mammy and Daddy here. That's…enough.'

'Umm…I'm still trying to get hold of Alexander. You haven't got any secret numbers for him, have you? You know – a phone only you two use, or something like that?'

Christine wanted to laugh, but didn't dare. 'No, we just use our normal phones to talk to each other. But…thanks, Carol. Yes, if you could keep trying, that would be grand. It would be…good to see him. I look a right state, I bet, but I wouldn't care. I'd like to see him…to feel his hand in mine.'

'Good to see your fiancé when you're stuck in a hospital bed with some horrible injuries? Yes, I should think it would be. There must be a reason he's not answering anyone's calls or texts.' Carol paused, as though she was expecting a reply, then added quickly, 'No bad reason – just a reason. You know.'

Christine wasn't so sure; it was incredibly rare for Alexander to be out of touch with the world for so long. If people had been trying to get hold of him since the previous afternoon, with no luck, she couldn't imagine what that might mean. Didn't want to.

Carol added forcefully, 'He'll have let his battery die, or something like that. Please don't worry about him, Christine, focus on yourself. Get the rest you need to be able to heal. We're on top of everything here, I promise.'

'Anything on The Case of the Exceptional Evacuee? And what about Annie's decorating supplies? What's going on there?' Christine didn't want to be stuck in the bubble of her hospital room without knowing what was going on in Wales.

Carol sighed. 'We think we've tracked down the daughter of the family who took in the Gulliver brothers. And it looks as though she's Iris Lewis, Annie's next-door neighbor, if you can believe it. And Dan the decorator is in hospital in Brecon. Annie and I are off there to see him shortly.'

'Why's he in hospital?' Christine felt immediate sympathy for the man.

'Umm…long story, but he got a nasty gash from a knife. We'll find out more later – and I promise we'll let you know. But, like I said, don't worry about Rachel. Mavis is overseeing that situation and Edward has sort of set himself up as Rachel's personal guard.'

Christine suddenly felt as though she'd been run over by a bus, and could even sense her one good eye closing. 'Okey dokey. Talk soon,' was all she could manage. Her father took the phone from her hand, and she knew she was slurring when she said, 'All good. Fancy a nap, now.'

CHAPTER TWENTY-EIGHT

Alexander was beginning to doubt himself, and his plan. He was aching all over, reeling from a lack of sleep, and stressed. He knew he looked, and smelled, disgusting. As did Geordie. The two of them were dressed in clothes they'd bought off two men they'd happened upon in a back alley in Brixton, and they'd now been huddled in the doorway of a disused, crumbling old house close to Big Tony's place since about five the previous afternoon. They weren't directly opposite the home where the man's operations were based, but it was as close as they could get without their presence being too obvious.

In the hours following his enlightening conversation with Reggie the previous day, Alexander had put all his energy into working out how he could bring down Big Tony once and for all, thereby – hopefully – releasing Geordie's brother Sean from any possible future connection with the man and his online scams, or illegal drug supply. However, in order for any such plan to be judged a success from their point of view, Alexander and Geordie had to not get personally involved, *and* had to be able to scoop up Sean before he could get nabbed in any potential raid on the premises by the police. But it was now late morning, and they hadn't seen hide nor hair of Sean. Nor of the police. Hence Alexander's sinking feeling.

His absolutely essential, and totally pukka, connections with the local planning gurus meant Alexander had been able to foster equally pukka connections with the local constabulary, and, while he certainly didn't want them to know that he was the source of the anonymous tip about Big Tony MacNamara's latest 'business endeavors', he'd used that inside knowledge to get the information directly to someone high enough up the food chain that they could – and would want to – get things done…fast.

Along with every petty crook and drug dealer in southwest London, the police were only too well aware of Big Tony's criminal undertakings and had been for years.

However, because no one was ever prepared to testify against him, they had failed to get Anthony John MacNamara convicted of anything other than petty crimes. Thus, Alexander had dropped the juicy, and hopefully irresistible, tip into the lap of an officer with quite a lot of braid on his uniform who, nevertheless, was still chasing promotion. The headline of the tip? That Big Tony was now funneling money through real bank accounts, representing a much better chance of the police being able to join the dots, and make a strong case for the Crown prosecutors to pursue.

The 'anonymous tipster' had also been kind enough to mention that – just in case they weren't aware of it – Big Tony's operational base functioned as a home overnight, and as a business during the day, and suggested that any raid should take place during 'office hours', thereby giving the police the chance to grab as many people who worked for Big Tony as possible. Posing as someone with insider knowledge and good reasons to want Big Tony to be targeted, Alexander had gone so far as to suggest that the more people who were questioned, the more likely it was that the police might be able to find someone prepared to inform on Big Tony's 'cash businesses' too, especially if they thought he'd be out of the picture for a while. In fact, he'd painted Big Tony as a man who was facing the end of his capability to be a powerful threat to those who worked for him.

Even as he'd heard himself say it – through the voice distorting app on his disposable phone – Alexander hadn't been sure the police would buy that particular nugget; he assumed they'd have their own informants on the street who'd be telling them that Big Tony was as formidable as ever. However, he wagered that, if the bloke he'd given the tip to was truly the sort of man Alexander believed him to be, he'd use that suggestion to push for action sooner, rather than later.

Alexander had done one more thing to make the need for a raid appear pressing: he'd said that Big Tony was about to shift the online fraud operation to bigger premises.

He'd forcefully made the point that if they wanted to catch him with incriminating evidence on *their* patch – they'd better act before that happened.

He'd told them the move would be taking place at noon the next day. Today. He'd reckoned that would give the officer time to make his case for a raid, and get a team in place.

He'd sent the tip just a couple of hours after he'd talked to Reggie. Shortly thereafter, he and Geordie were in Brixton, dressed in their stinking clothes, and with their hopes high that, somewhere in the local nick, plans were being made to nab Big Tony.

Not wanting Sean to be there when whatever happened, happened, Alexander and Geordie had done all they could to be on the spot when Sean left, or arrived at, Big Tony's house. Geordie had, grudgingly, agreed that they would use the force necessary to take his brother – but he'd only done so on the basis that he would be the one applying the force. They'd found a good spot in a back street for Alexander's rented banger, which meant they had the means to get Sean away from the area as quickly as possible, after they'd grabbed him. Alexander had already made arrangements with a rehabilitation facility near Brighton that they'd both agreed had enough security in place for Sean to be safe from anyone connected with Big Tony, and to not be able to do a runner.

'Weird not having a phone, isn't it?' Geordie had mentioned several times how 'disconnected from the world' he'd felt since they'd hunkered down; neither of them had anything on their person that could identify them.

'Not the worst thing in the world. Hopefully no one's broken into the car and nicked them, or any of the other stuff we left there.'

Geordie smiled. 'I hope not. I don't know anyone's number these days – they're all on my phone. It would take me years to build that list again.'

Alexander nodded. 'Take it all for granted, don't we? Hey, has Sean got one of those puffy jackets in green, as well as a yellow one?'

'Green's not his color,' replied Geordie, then he chuckled.

He looked to Alexander as though he was thinking back over the years when he added, 'Always hated green, did Sean, since he was little. Said there was enough green in the world with grass and trees. Didn't care for either of them, really. Why, what have you seen?'

'Walking down Brixton Hill. Blue cap, jeans, green puffy jacket. Is that Sean?'

Geordie peered from beneath a tatty hoodie. 'Looks a bit like him, though Sean wasn't limping the last time we saw him. He swaggers. Always has, since he could walk. Our mother said it made him look drunk. He thought it made him look cool. That bloke's got no swagger. But that one there? *That's* Sean.'

A figure in a yellow puffy jacket, now positively identified as Sean by his brother, ran up behind the figure in the green one and jumped on its back, seemingly playfully. The figure wearing the green jacket turned and swung, windmilling its arms. Sean backed off, his arms raised in mock surrender, then the figure in the green jacket limped as fast as it could down the hill.

'This is it, Geordie. You ready, mate?'

'As I'll ever be, pet.'

They shared a grim smile, then hauled themselves from their filthy corner, and started to stagger up the hill toward Sean. They were acting drunk, their faces covered, pushing and shoving each other as they went. They split apart as they reached Sean. Alexander grabbed him from one side, Geordie grabbed him from the other. Both men held onto an arm each.

Geordie slapped a hand over his brother's mouth as he said, 'Sean – listen to me. We're taking you off the street to help you out. Again. I know you don't want to go, but it's for your own good. If you struggle, I will hurt you. I won't want to, but I will.'

Alexander knew that Geordie could take care of himself in a fight – he'd seen him do it.

He also knew that having him in your corner was always worthwhile and could often stop a fight before it began, because he had a look about him that spoke of a man unafraid of violence.

But Geordie had never sounded as terrifyingly threatening as he did at that moment. Alexander knew it came from a place of desperation for his brother's well-being, but hearing it surprised him.

However, he was even more surprised when he heard what came out of Sean's mouth.

Sean all but collapsed in their arms. His eyes filled with tears. 'Thanks, bruv. Thanks for caring. Take me away, please? I…I don't want to go back there. They're not good people.'

It was clear to Alexander that Geordie was as shocked as he was, because both men must have loosened their grip on the slithery jacket just enough for Sean to wriggle free, kick his brother in the shin and scream, 'Suckers!' as he laughed hysterically, and began to run up the hill, away from them, and from Big Tony's house.

Alexander headed after him, but Geordie grabbed him back. 'Leave him. He doesn't deserve saving.'

Alexander turned. 'Just one more chance? Come on…I haven't sat in these stinking clothes for hours on end to *not* grab him. He's not as fast or as healthy as he thinks he is. We'll get him. Come on.'

With that, Alexander took off at speed, pushing himself as hard as he could. He eventually managed to grab at Sean with a flying rugby-like tackle and brought him to the ground. He zip-tied his hands before they could do any harm, then slapped a strip of duct tape over his mouth – he'd had it in his pocket all night, but it still had enough stick left in it to do the job.

When Geordie got there, the two men grabbed an arm each and marched a kicking and wordlessly bellowing Sean to the car, hoping no one would notice what they were doing, or at least choose to not do anything about it.

'Sit in the back with him, Geordie. I'll drive. Here's your phone. I'll just get the GPS working on mine, then we'll go.'

When Alexander turned on his phone it all but exploded with notifications of missed calls and texts. In the back, Geordie and Sean struggled with each other, until Geordie tightened the seat belt around his brother so much that he was clamped to the seat.

Alexander didn't need to read more than a few texts. He scrolled through to the recent ones. His stomach churned. Christine was in trouble. She'd been in trouble since yesterday afternoon. She'd needed him, and he hadn't been there for her. He felt immediately drained. Empty.

He looked around at Geordie and Sean, looked at his phone again. His heart was thumping…and that wasn't because he'd just run up a hill.

He made a decision. 'I'll drive us down to Brixton and jump on the Tube. You'll have to take him down to Brighton on your own. Sorry, mate. Christine's in the hospital. Ealing.'

'Whatever you say,' replied Geordie. Alexander could see in the rear-view mirror that he was close to tears, shaking his head as he stared at his brother's puce face, and bulging, venomous eyes.

Alexander pulled onto the main road and headed down toward Brixton. At the next set of lights, he was waved through by a uniformed police officer who was stopping traffic going up the hill by setting up a diversion sign. He hoped it was to allow for tactical vehicles for an impending raid…

CHAPTER TWENTY-NINE

Carol and Annie hadn't chatted to each other much in the car on the way to the hospital in Brecon, where they hoped to see Dan. Instead, Annie had been thinking about her talk with Iris Lewis first thing that morning, and Carol had been on the phone speaking to her mother.

Annie had only been able to hear Carol's part of the conversation, but it had been enough.

When Carol finally – with a fair amount of exasperation – ended the call and pulled out her earbuds, Annie said, 'Do I gather your parents have sold their farm?'

Carol responded in Welsh – Annie assumed she was swearing – and then she most definitely did swear in English.

'So...you're not happy about it, eh?'

Carol slapped the steering wheel. 'They'd said they were considering it, but Dad was dead set against taking the land out of proper agricultural use, and I never thought they'd find a buyer who wanted to keep it going as a farm. Not in this day and age. Anyway, they've only gone and sold it to some couple from Cheltenham who think that the world needs more ancient breed sheep and unpasteurized cheese. Apparently, they're going to set up a weaving cooperative, too.'

'Maybe they watched too many episodes of *The Good Life*? I hope your parents made them pay a fortune for it.'

Carol sighed. 'More than Mam and Dad ever thought they'd get for it, that's true enough.'

'And that *is* what they need for their future, innit? Money to live on, now they're a bit too old to be running a sheep farm.'

Carol deflated a bit. 'I know. But...still.'

'Car, you're here with Dave and Bertie. It's all ahead of you. They deserve a rest. You've said that yourself. Well, this means they can do that.'

'They signed the papers two weeks ago, Annie. Didn't want to tell me. Then they choose to do it when I'm driving.'

'That must hurt, Car. Sorry, doll. But buck up – you'll see more of them now. They can come and stay with you. Help out when you need a couple of pairs of grandparenting hands.'

Annie noticed that Carol seemed to stiffen up. 'Yes. There's that, I suppose. Anyway – we're nearly there and you haven't brought me up to date with what happened with Iris this morning. Does she remember Walter Gulliver? Will she meet him?'

Annie gripped the dashboard as Carol navigated the aisles between rows of cars in the hospital car park, hunting for a seemingly non-existent parking space. 'Yes, she did remember him. Said he was a nice boy. Quiet, but nice. Said she'd be glad to have him over for tea, but didn't fancy travelling to his place. I passed the news to Mavis, and she said she'd talk to Gulliver. Iris seemed pleased she'd have the chance to talk about times past. I want to be in on that conversation…I like Iris. Besides…let's be honest, Car, we don't know exactly why this Gulliver bloke *really* wants to track down the people who looked after him during the war, do we? I know Mavis is good at judging people – in fact, I think "judgmental" could be her middle name – but I believe one of us should be there when he and Iris meet. He might…well, he might be less than kind to her. That PI agency from Hounslow sent someone to Rachel's flat to try to track her down – and we're all pretty sure that wasn't for a "good" reason. That company might not have known why their client really wanted them to find Rachel, like we don't really know what's in Gulliver's mind.'

Carol had to agree with that.

When they'd finally parked, Annie wriggled out of the narrow space available to open her door, then the pair headed to find Dan, Dan, the Decorating Man…whose name turned out to be Dan Douglas, as Constable Llinos Trevelyan had informed them in her official capacity, when she'd located him in hospital.

Standing outside the goldfish-bowl-like room that housed four patients, Annie said, 'I thought you lot would have him handcuffed to his bed.' She was disappointed that he wasn't.

Llinos screwed up her face beneath her hat, which Annie knew she hated.

The police officer chuckled. 'Not for a few bits of wallpaper and a toilet, no Annie, no handcuffs. Nor for that bag of cash – which might be his by rights. He's not been questioned about it all yet, you see. Mind you, he's got a few tubes coming out of him, so that'll keep him where he is for a while. Blood loss was quite bad, as it turned out. They were surprised he'd managed to drive himself here. His van looks like there's been a massacre in the front seat. And be quick. I've come early, so I can see you two with him; there's a sergeant coming in half an hour so we can take Dan's official statement. You're on the clock.'

Annie wrinkled her nose. 'Right then, let's have at him – I want to know what's been going on, and why.'

As Carol and Annie entered the room, and Llinos continued to peer through the massive window, Dan Douglas let out a loud groan and called, 'Nurse…I need more painkillers. And I'm not up to visitors – make them go away.'

Annie sat on the single chair beside his bed. 'Not gonna happen, Dan. I am sitting here until you tell me all about it, and that one there –' she jabbed a thumb in Llinos's direction – 'is going to wait outside. You and her, and her boss, can talk it through officially later on. This is just you and me – and Carol's my witness.'

Carol said, 'I'm recording this – alright with you, Dan? That way you'll have evidence if Annie crosses the line – makes any threats, that sort of thing.'

A look of real concern crossed Dan's face. 'Yeah, you record it. And you make sure you're polite.' He tried to cross his arms, but tubes got in the way.

Annie said, 'I know what you stole from the Coach, and I saw it all in place at Rose Cottage, so there's no question you nicked it. I want to know why all the stuff that was supposed to be in my flat is in someone else's house.'

Dan's eyes slid from Annie to Carol and back again, then his face took on a pained expression, and his chin started to pucker. Annie wondered if he was going to cry, but he held back the tears.

Dan's voice cracked as he said, 'I'm sorry…so sorry. I was just trying to help. Honest.' He tried to compose himself, but failed.

His chin puckered. 'You had so much, and that lot at Chellingworth have even more. And it's my brother, see? He's been away in the army, and he's being invalided out. Friendly fire, they said, at a training exercise. Terrible mess he's in. He can get about alright, but he's gone a bit in the head. PSTD, they said.'

'PTSD,' said Carol. Annie glared at her.

'That's it. Can't stand noise, now. His wife managed to find that cottage, and bought it, but it was in a right old state, and they won't let him come home until he's got somewhere nice to live. She'll be there to look after him, and it's in the middle of nowhere so he won't be bothered. But doing it up was costing more than she had...so I've been...um...taking a few bits and pieces from various jobs I've been on, over the months. It all adds up. Not always her taste, but, you know, beggars can't be choosers, can they?'

Annie was amazed at the man's bravado. 'You sayin' your sister-in-law don't like the wallpaper I picked for my bedroom, that's now on the walls in hers? You can rip it all off again, if that's the case.'

Dan smiled weakly.

Annie pressed, 'So who did this to you? Who was that bloke you had a run-in with at the Coach?'

Dan looked surprised. 'Who I...what?'

'Cap, checked shirt, jeans. You and him had a pushing match in the bar at the Coach, when Angelo and Wes were off having their lunch. You lost. Then scarpered. Who was that?'

'How do you know about that?' Dan seemed flummoxed.

'Doesn't matter how I know, I just do. So...?'

Dan swallowed. 'A...another client. He'd worked out that I'd...taken something. Found out where I was and...came to ask for it back. I told him I couldn't do that. He wasn't best pleased.'

'Is he the one who did this to you? What did you nick off him? A gold-plated bath? This is serious, Dan – they reckon you could have died of blood loss from that wound of yours. And I dare say he's still out there, somewhere...just waiting until you're alone again.'

Dan didn't say a word, but shrank into his pillow.

Annie made eyes at Carol, then looked out into the corridor where a woman she'd never seen before was talking to Llinos, who nodded her head. The woman came into the room and looked down at Dan, her face chalky, her breath coming in gasps. She was almost in tears.

'I just heard. Are you alright? Oh, Danny my– hang on, who are you two? You're not nurses. Or doctors.'

She glared at Annie, who was convinced the woman had just been about to call Dan 'my love'. *Wife? A girlfriend?*

'We're just making sure Dan's alright,' said Annie to prevent Dan from answering. 'We're trying to find out what happened – who might have done this to him.'

The woman became rigid. 'He'll live. So leave him alone. Go away. You're bothering him, I can tell.'

Annie and Carol exchanged a glance. Carol handed Annie her phone, to continue with the recording, and left the room.

Dan and the unnamed woman watched her go. 'No point you staying, love,' said Dan to the woman, his chin out, trying to look brave and unconcerned – as far as was possible.

The woman lay a hand on his shoulder. 'There, there, Dan – don't say anything. Who is this one really? Not police, is she? Plain clothes?'

'Client,' said Dan quietly.

The woman looked puzzled.

'And you are?' Annie had to know.

'Dan's sister-in-law. Trish. What's it to you?' She pushed a curl of suspiciously yellow-blonde hair off her cheek.

Annie could see that Carol had Llinos checking something in her notes; she was shaking her head. She gestured to Carol to some back in.

'So what's the word, Car? Has our Dan here been telling a few porkies?'

'Sounds that way,' said Carol, nodding.

'Go on then,' urged Annie. 'Let's have it.'

Carol said, 'Dan's got a brother, yes. Name of Joseph Douglas. But Joseph hasn't been in the army. He's just out of prison.'

Annie asked, 'Oh dear – what did he do?'

Carol looked grim. 'Incarcerated because he knifed someone in a pub in Rhyl. Nasty business. Constable Trevelyan informs me that Joseph was released the day before yesterday. Registered address is Rose Cottage. Wife Patricia. She works nights for a cleaning company. Just told Constable Trevelyan she heard about Dan from a mutual friend.'

'So you're the one who doesn't like my wallpaper, eh, Trish? Too tasteful for you, is it?' Annie wanted to goad the woman.

'What's she on about, Dan?'

'Nothing.'

Annie pressed, 'I hope you think of me every time you sit on that toilet – I spent ages choosing it, you know, and when they had to send a replacement they didn't have another one the same as the one I'd ordered, so now I get a Plain Jane model, while you get the one with the nice bits around the base that I'd set my heart on.'

Trish stared at Annie, then said to Dan, 'Is she on something?'

Dan grabbed Trish's hand. 'Don't. I'll explain later.'

Trish pulled her hand away. 'You'll explain now.'

'I'll explain,' snapped Annie. 'He stole it all – all the supplies to do up your house.'

Trish's pale face flushed pink. She glared at Annie, then turned her head to look at Dan. 'You said you were picking everything out especially for me, that it would all be a surprise for me when I moved in proper. Kept telling me to hang on in that horrible little flat I've been stuck in until it was all done.' She slapped Dan, who was all but defenseless. 'You said…you said so many things.'

Annie pounced. 'Really? You didn't think it was odd that you had to go to a pub where he was working to pick up a toilet. A toilet that you signed for.'

Trish was crying. 'He said it was the best place to get it delivered. Said it was a good deal.'

'Yeah,' said Annie. 'Nicked is the best deal going, if you don't mind breaking the law. Listen, Car, I think you should tell Constable Trevelyan that she'd better get the word out that Joseph Douglas has been up to his old tricks again.'

Annie gave Trish a good look up and down. 'I think his lovely wife's been doing more than helping Dan here pick out bedroom curtains. Isn't that right, Dan? Oh, and – by the way – we've caught that whole incident at the Coach on camera; I'm sure it'll be enough for an identification of your brother to be made. Did you drive your husband to the Coach and Horses pub in Anwen-by-Wye yesterday in a yellow car, Trish, by any chance? Did he come out of there telling you that him and his brother had been happy to see each other? What did he do then? Drop you off somewhere? Do you know that Dan nearly died of his injuries?'

Trish Douglas looked close to collapse. Annie offered her the chair, and she sank into it, shrinking as she did so. She didn't even look up when she said, 'You two Douglases? You're as bad as each other. Every other word out of your mouth is a lie, Dan, and your brother's got a temper on him that I really haven't missed.' She finally looked up, and stared at Dan, tears running down her face. 'If he's done this to you, because he's found out about us, think what he could do to me.'

Annie watched as Dan nodded, looking shaken. 'You're right. Tell them where he is, Trish. I'll tell them what he did. Get that policewoman in, will you?'

Annie called to Llinos, 'You'd better caution him, Constable Trevelyan, before you let him tell you anything. He might be giving you information about his brother to help your lot to apprehend him, but he's got a few things to answer for, too.'

Eventually, Annie and Carol left. Llinos had asked for a car to be sent to a pub on the outskirts of Brecon to collect Joseph Douglas – and to go prepared for him to not respond well. She was busy taking the details of the fight between the brothers at Rose Cottage that had resulted in Dan being sliced, after which Joseph had taken off in Trish's car – leaving his brother to bleed to death, for all he knew. They'd also received word that Llinos's sergeant would arrive at the hospital to take over from her in a few moments.

In the car park, Carol hugged Annie. 'You did a great job.'

'Nah, it weren't just me.' She hugged Carol back.

The pair pulled apart, and Annie winked. 'I could tell right off the bat what was going on between them two. Plain as the nose on your face, it was. It was Llinos having all the background info, and you knowing what needed to be done in the moment, too, that helped. No, it weren't all me, Car. And I bet Dan never even had a dog. Forget The Case of the Disappearing Decorating Supplies, this one's going in the books as The Case of the Decidedly Dodgy Decorator.'

Carol shrugged. 'Fair enough. Your choice. But what's that about a dog?'

'A sob story he spun for me one morning when he turned up late, that I bought at the time. Come on, let's get back to…where? Office? Village? The Hall?'

'You phone Mavis while I drive – ask her how things are going, and if they need us – or if we've done enough for today.'

'As always, the perfect division of labor.'

CHAPTER THIRTY

Henry had attended to his ducal duties all morning and was about to join his wife and son in their private dining room for luncheon. It irritated Henry that their *actual* dining room was off limits for lunch when Chellingworth Hall was open to the public, but he'd been told – in no uncertain terms – that the laying of an impressively large table, with all the appropriate settings and centerpieces, was popular with visitors. Which meant that the *actual* table in the *actual* dining room was set every morning, and cleared every evening. Edward had informed him that the public could not be allowed to view anything but scrupulously clean tableware, so that was the system.

As thoughtful as ever, Stephanie had suggested they reduced the turnover to every other day – thereby alleviating what she felt to be an unnecessary burden on the kitchen staff, who were required to wash and dry all eighteen place settings. Her initiative had been well received. However, she had backed down after a member of the public had pointed out that there was a large spider in one of the fine, nineteenth-century crystal glasses on the table, and that had been that.

As Henry clumped his way along a back corridor, winding his way along the route which the public was not allowed to use, he reminded himself how critical their presence was to the financial well-being of the Hall, the Estate, and even the village of Anwen-by-Wye. The weight of his responsibilities to his Seat felt heavier with each step.

His spirits rose only when he saw his wife and son's smiling faces when he entered the small dining room, then they slipped a little when he spied his mother and Mavis MacDonald entering through another door…and noticed that the table was laid for eight. Who on earth would be joining them? He'd been looking forward to a pleasant tête-à-tête with his wife; now, it appeared, some sort of gathering was about to take place…and no one had said a dickie bird to him about it. He was beginning to wonder when he'd last felt he was the master of his own home. He sighed, but tried to hide it.

Doing his best to appear pleased at the prospect, Henry managed, 'Mother, Mavis, what an unexpected pleasure. Are we to have even more guests for luncheon, Stephanie, dear?'

The duchess was doing something to Hugo's hair – of which, Henry thought, he'd begun to sprout rather an alarming quantity, of late. He had no idea if that was normal, but was rather surprised to see how white-blonde it was; he'd always had brown hair, until it had started to become more grey – and rather more distinguished-looking, he thought – and Stephanie's was the color of a lovely brown horse named Fandancer…or Fandango…or some such, that his mother had once doted upon. But Hugo? His hair had no color at all, which concerned Henry somewhat. And such curls, too. He hoped the boy would grow out of it, because that sort of hair might make his life at school quite difficult.

Stephanie finally gave her attention to her husband. 'Rachel will join us, of course, and we're hoping we'll be able to convince Edward to sit beside her. Carol and Annie are due to arrive shortly. With Christine recovering from her injuries in hospital, we thought it a good idea if the rest of the WISE women gathered here, so we could all compare notes regarding progress in The Case of the Bereaved Butler.'

'The…what?' Henry had become used to various tales of different types of investigations taking place around him, but this?

His mother settled herself at the table with a snappish, 'Edward. Our butler. He's bereaved. His brother. For heaven's sake, Henry, you know exactly what Stephanie is referring to.'

Henry sighed and took his seat. 'Shall we wait for everyone, or begin?'

Stephanie did that tutting thing. 'Of course we'll wait, Henry.'

Not the proper dining room. Now a delay. Henry wasn't the master in his own home. A home that came with the weight of the world attached to it.

Rachel Edwards' arrival was followed by pleasantries. Edward had insisted that he would only attend the luncheon in his proper role, news which Henry was rather relieved to receive.

In his role as butler, he appeared briefly to announce that Carol and Annie had arrived, which led to everyone bobbing up and down at the table, and a great deal of kerfuffle being required before they were all, finally, able to begin their melon salad.

Henry's didn't last long. He was famished.

As Henry waited with as much patience as he could muster for the next course to arrive, he did his best to make suitable noises, at appropriate moments, as the women surrounding him discussed Christine's lucky escape in Ealing, the exact nature of her injuries – which made him rather pleased the next course hadn't yet arrived – and her likely path to recuperation and recovery. The next topic, which accompanied the welcome arrival of smoked trout with a leafy salad, pickled beetroot, and boiled new potatoes, was the news that the private investigator who'd been apprehended in Hounslow – Henry had heard of the place, but wasn't quite sure where it was, exactly – would be charged, but that his boss was still refusing to name his client.

Mavis said, 'Cooperating with the police is something all private investigators should have as one of their priorities. We most certainly want to respect our clients' privacy, but this is a situation where he should speak up.'

Rachel said quietly, 'Do you think Jon Dacre hired them to find me? I feel so terribly guilty about poor Christine. I feel it's all my fault.'

Henry had noticed that his butler's sister-in-law had been rather quiet throughout the discussions about Christine, and her comment finally illuminated why that was the case. It hadn't occurred to him that she might feel that way, but he thought, on balance, it made sense: Christine had only gone to Rachel's flat to get some bits and bobs the woman had forgotten to pack when she'd hightailed it up to Chellingworth, after all.

'I'm sure she'll forgive you,' was his considered response.

The duchess tutted, and his mother snapped, 'Don't listen to my son, Rachel. Christine being attacked was in no way your fault. It's entirely the fault of the reckless young man who did it.'

Henry sucked in a breath; why had he said anything at all?

He thought he should at least respond with a: 'But of course,' which he did, then he decided it was best to give his attention to his smoked trout, and just listen.

As the conversation wandered from topic to topic, Henry found it all to be quite dizzying. His ears pricked up when he heard the Chellingworth Estate being mentioned, and discovered that Annie and Carol had successfully apprehended a tradesman who'd been stealing decorating supplies purchased by the Estate for use at the Coach and Horses pub, who had then managed to get himself stabbed by his brother, with whose wife he'd been having an affair, while said brother was in prison. It all sounded terribly sordid.

It also transpired that the violent brother was now in police custody, and that the non-violent, but nevertheless criminal, brother – and the adulterous wife – were 'squealing' on him. Henry found some of Annie's terminology to be quite interesting, but it worried him that his mother tended toward that sort of language more and more, too.

Carol took over for a while, and seemed to be talking about butchers and evacuees, which he couldn't quite put together, unless it was something to do with meat rationing during and after the war. No, she was now talking about the chap who'd owned all those grocery shops, and had sold them for a huge amount of money a few years ago. How was he connected to Iris Lewis? Henry decided to pay more attention, and he'd finished his main course, in any case.

'Walter Gulliver is being driven to Anwen-by-Wye this afternoon,' said Carol.

Mavis added, 'It'll be wonderful for him and Iris to see each other again, I should think.'

Annie chipped in, 'She was all a-flutter when I told her about him. Her budgies were too – they really seem to pick up on her moods, don't they?'

Henry had never understood the appeal of keeping anything in a cage. Indeed, he felt tremendous sympathy for any creature who had to live that way; gilded or not, a cage was still a little jail cell.

His rumination upon his own lifestyle was rudely interrupted when his mother said, 'Henry? What do you think about it?'

Henry's tummy tightened. What had he missed?

'Pardon?' It was all he could manage. Best not to guess what was expected of him.

'The blighter who killed Edward's brother, of course. How can we get evidence that him knowing that poor Richard had an allergy and that he'd made a note about oysters means that he really did it?'

Henry felt compelled to respond, but could only manage: 'Search the premises?' It was something that seemed like an action-oriented reply, which was clearly what his mother was after…she always was.

'Excellent idea, Henry. I agree with my son. A search needs to be made of Jon Dacie's home.' Henry was delighted that he appeared to have said something useful.

However, his spirits fell when Mavis replied rather acidly, 'But we've no ability to do that. That's the job of the police.'

Henry couldn't disagree, but felt sufficiently emboldened to offer: 'Have they refused to do it, or have they not asked him if they may? If the man knows he's being investigated, surely he'd want to clear his name?' He paused, then felt that the expressions of his guests suggested he should add, 'If he's innocent, of course.'

Rachel said, 'When I spoke to the police about my concerns again, and even when I explained what we'd discovered thus far, they still didn't seem to be terribly interested in following up. They still appear to believe that Richard's death was a tragic accident, though how that squares with a firm of private investigators being retained to track me down, I don't know.'

'Couldn't you at least search his office?' Henry spoke out of desperation.

The duchess replied calmly, 'Home, or office, Mavis's observation is correct, dear. One cannot – as a private citizen – just go tramping about in people's houses or flats or places of work without the proper authorization. Unless one pays a fee at the door, as we ask our day-guests to do, of course.'

Henry perked up when he saw a large trifle being deposited on the sideboard. Just the ticket!

As he readied his palate for the explosion of flavors it was about to experience, he said absently, 'I rather thought this all revolved around the fact that Edward's brother died intestate, and that, as such, his half of the business has passed to Rachel, rather than the Dacre person. Doesn't that mean that you own half of the business premises too, Rachel? Can you not agree to a full search of the Buttle My World offices?'

He tucked into the bowl of trifle which had been placed in front of him with the delight he'd felt since he was a small child: trifle was the best possible dessert, because it had a bit of everything in it, and – as an adult – there was also the zing of that hint of sherry, too.

Henry was astonished at what happened next. Rachel shot up from her seat, shouting, 'But of course! What a fool I've been. Come on – who'll come to London with me? Mavis? Carol? Annie? We can turn the place upside down – it's half mine.'

Henry was delighted when Mavis suggested that Rachel should finish her luncheon before anybody went anywhere, but it was rapidly agreed that Mavis would accompany Rachel on a sortie to Earl's Court, and that the pair would depart later that afternoon.

As soon as she'd polished off her tiny portion of trifle, everyone agreed that Rachel should leave, accompanied by Edward, to pull together a few things for an overnight trip. Henry contemplated a second helping of trifle, as plans were made for Mavis to head back to the Dower House so that she, too, could prepare an overnight bag.

A few moments later, while enjoying his indulgent, though small, additional spot of dessert, Henry was as taken aback as his guests to hear a right old rumpus outside the small dining room.

There was a terrible noise as something heavy fell, or was thrown, against the door itself, then…nothing.

CHAPTER THIRTY-ONE

Upon hearing the calamitous noise, all eyes turned toward Henry, who felt compelled to leave his last spoonful of trifle in the bowl, and go to the door to discern its cause. He'd rather expected Edward to arrive to inform him about what on earth was going on, but, upon pulling open the door, he could see why that hadn't happened: Edward was on the floor sporting a bloodied nose, and a slim, greasy-looking chap, wearing a horribly shiny suit and a garish tie, fell into the dining room, his back having been up against the door itself.

The man, whom Henry had never seen before – *a visiting member of the public, perhaps?* – appeared dazed; his clothing was in disarray, and his lip was bleeding.

Much to Henry's chagrin, the unknown man immediately began to shout, 'Call the police! I've been assaulted! I want to report an attack!'

A woman appeared in the hallway next – *which was supposed to be private!* – and began to wail too. 'Oh my poor, dear, Jon – what's that big man done to you?'

Henry was rapidly surrounded by four women and his infant son, whose expression told him he was about to burst into tears, as well as being faced by two wailing adults, and a bloody-nosed butler. It was quite overwhelming.

'I say!'

'Don't say anything, Henry,' said Rachel Edwards firmly. 'Hello Jon. Hello Lila. What brings you to Chellingworth Hall this fine day? Could it be that the private eyes you hired told you where I was hiding from you? And you've come here to kill me, too? I know what you did to my husband, Jon Dacre. It's probably just as well that his brother got to you first, because I'd have done more than split your lip.'

The man squealed, 'Brother? Who? What?'

Rachel shouted, 'You killed my Richard. Stole his life from him, and my future from me.'

The man looked horrified.

Rachel screamed, 'You ground up those oyster shells and squirted them onto his dessert. See? We know what you did, and it's only a matter of time before we prove it. And as for trying to kill me as well – just so you can get your grubby little hands on the rest of the company – well now you've been caught at that too. Call the police? You'll bet we'll call the police. This lot have got them on speed-dial – and not just the ones who come when you phone nine-nine-nine, actual people with actual names, and personal numbers. So there. What have you got to say to that then, Jon Bloody Dacre?'

Though the – until then – seemingly unflappable Rachel still appeared fit to burst, Henry wanted to draw breath for her by the time she'd finished her utterly understandable tirade. He still didn't feel much the wiser about the whole thing involving oyster shells, though the idea of them being added to a dessert didn't appeal to him at all.

The man he now knew to be Jon Dacre – Edward's late-brother's business partner and now, he assumed, Rachel's – pushed himself up off the floor and onto his elbows.

For a man being accused of murder, Henry thought he looked more affronted than guilty, an impression which was borne out when the man said huffily, 'I haven't the slightest idea what you're talking about, Rachel, and – yes – I insist the police be summoned. And if someone here knows them by name, then let's get hold of one who's got a bit of clout in these Godforsaken parts.' He turned to the rail-thin woman who was crying and dabbing her face. 'I told you we shouldn't have come,' was all he said, and she became even less in control of her sobbing.

His trifle had become a sweet, but distant, memory for Henry by the time the entire group had all made their way back inside the dining room. Rachel fussed over Edward's nose, the Lila person fussed over the Jon person, and Mavis flitted between the two pairs offering nursing advice. Meanwhile, his wife announced that she didn't want their son to be subjected to whatever might happen next, and promptly took him off to their bedroom.

Then Henry's level of anxiety rose even further – which he hadn't thought possible. And all because of his mother.

For some unfathomable reason, she was fiddling with her mobile phone. He was grateful when Mavis noticed too; if anyone could control his mother, it was Mavis.

'Who are you phoning, dear?' Mavis was direct, if nothing else.

'Someone who can help,' replied his mother tartly, then she shouted into her phone, 'Yes, Chief Inspector, it is I speaking. No, this is nothing to do with the bus trip, though all the plans are in hand. Tudor's really good at that sort of thing.'

'Why are you phoning Carwen James about a bus trip at this moment? What bus trip? Is it really that important?' Mavis sounded puzzled, which Henry took as a good sign, because he was, too.

His mother covered the phone. 'I'm not phoning him about the bus trip – which is a little surprise I'm planning for next month. Let me be, Mavis.'

Henry noticed Mavis roll her eyes as his mother continued shouting, 'We have an emergency at Chellingworth Hall. Please come as quickly as you can.'

Mavis muttered, 'He'll no' be able to do that, Althea. He's no' that sort of policeman.'

Althea poked out her tongue. 'Yes, only you can help. Of course it's urgent, or I wouldn't be phoning you on this special number you gave me. Yes. Please. Half an hour? I suppose so. Yes, of course you are. Maybe one other officer with you? Or two, maybe. We have a murderer here, you see, and we can only confine him for so long.'

Henry could hardly breathe.

Jon Dacre screamed, 'Who are you talking about? Not me, I hope. I'm the one who's been attacked. I'm the victim here.'

Henry watched as his mother continued loudly, 'Yes, that's him. He's here with his "moll", I suppose you'd call her. No, no one's been murdered here, now – they were killed weeks ago, but he was planning a second killing today. It's all to do with Christine being attacked in Ealing.'

She paused, listened, then snapped, 'Yes, I know it's not your case.'

Another pause. 'But the man responsible is here, now.'

She shouted, 'Yes, the killer. Here. Now. So I suggest you come and do something about it. As soon as you can. And please do not use those siren things, they'd only alarm the public, and come to the rear of the Hall – it'll be less obvious. Thank you.' She disconnected.

An unnatural hush fell over the room.

It was Lila who broke the silence. 'Who on earth are you all, and who were you talking to?'

Henry noticed his mother's dimples kick in as she replied to the young woman, 'Althea, Dowager Duchess of Chellingworth. My son, Henry, the duke. My companion and dear friend, Mavis MacDonald, and her two colleagues at the WISE Enquiries Agency, Annie Parker, and Carol Hill. They're private investigators, you know,' she said, staring pointedly at Jon. 'The man whose nose you bloodied is Edward, our esteemed and valued family butler, who is also the brother of the man you murdered, Richard Edwards. And Chief Inspector Carwen James is on his way here now, with fellow officers who will take you into custody.'

'Gracious,' said Lila quietly.

Henry helped his mother into a seat as she responded with an airy, 'It's "Your Graces", actually.'

Henry could see that Lila had stopped crying, and was now staring at each person in the room in turn. The poor thing seemed to be diminishing as he watched her, and there hadn't been that much of her to start with.

Rachel hissed, 'You picked a bad one, Lila. Jon only ever looks out for himself. If he's got you mixed up in this in any way, you should take your chance to talk to the police when they get here. Has he asked you to hide anything in the office for him? Or even in your home? A small container of something – probably liquid. I wouldn't put it past him to do something to implicate you.'

Jon squealed, 'Implicate her in what? I haven't done anything wrong. Tell them, Lila – I wouldn't hurt a fly.'

As far as Henry could tell, Lila had no intention of doing any such thing. She glared at the man, pursing her lips. Little red spots appeared on her unhealthily hollow cheeks.

Even Henry noticed the man blush as he stammered, 'Well…I know I've hurt you…but I didn't mean to do that…I just don't feel the same way you do about us…and I am doing my best to let you down gently, which isn't easy when you're stuck in a car with a person for hours on end. I don't mean *that* sort of thing…I mean what they're accusing me of. Tell them. Please?'

To Henry's eyes, Lila looked…trapped. She appeared to be trying to get as far away from Jon as possible…out of the room if she could. Henry could understand why – the chap was obviously capable of violence. Murder, even.

His heart sank when she started to sob again; he never knew what to do when a woman cried, so he stepped forward and offered her a clean handkerchief. It seemed appropriate.

'Thanks, Your Grace,' she mumbled. Henry was relieved when she turned toward Rachel and asked, 'Is there somewhere I can…you know…gather myself a bit? All of this has come as a great shock.'

Rachel nodded, and escorted the blubbing woman out of the room. He was glad to see her go. His mother was waggling an arm at Edward, to try to get him to take a seat, though he was declining her offer. Henry also spotted that Annie and Carol had stepped back from all the action, and that Carol was doing something that looked like texting on her phone. He couldn't imagine what was so urgent, or important, that it took precedence over ensuring that a killer didn't leave the room and go on some sort of rampage throughout the place. However, he admitted to himself that Jon Dacre didn't look as though he intended to leave. In fact, it looked as though the glaring match that was going on between him and Edward, and then him and Rachel, when she returned from delivering the weeping Lila to…wherever, was fixing him to his seat with greater efficiency than any rope could do.

Henry checked his pocket watch: still twenty minutes before Carwen James and his officers were likely to arrive – what on earth would they do until then?

Henry was at least grateful that Annie and Carol seemed ready to rejoin the main group.

They'd been whispering together after Carol had stopped doing whatever it was with her phone that she'd found so vital – he could tell that something was about to happen.

He steeled himself.

Carol began politely, 'Since we're all having to wait for the police, I wondered if you'd like us to tell you what we believe you've done, Jon.'

'I'd be delighted if you'd fill me in, because I haven't the foggiest,' replied the man. 'Though, I'd like to take the opportunity to say to you, Edward, that I sympathize with you for the loss of your brother. He was an excellent colleague. We didn't always see eye to eye about things, but we've worked well as a team for a good amount of time. I shall miss him greatly, though not, of course, in the way that you and Rachel will.'

His little speech surprised Henry; he sounded a bit unctuous, but generally sincere.

Carol didn't appear to have been put off her stride at all, though, and Henry settled himself on a chair to listen; maybe if Carol explained things they'd make sense to him – Carol was good at that.

'You and Richard, Edward's brother, had a business relationship wherein you believed he'd written a will leaving you his half of the business in the event of his death, is that correct?'

Jon wriggled a bit on his seat. 'Yes…we both agreed to the same set-up, when we established the business. But…'

Carol held up her hand. 'Is it also true that you only discovered that Richard had not, in fact, written such a will after his death?'

'Well, yes, but…'

'So it would be true to say that you really did have an expectation that Richard's death would result in you inheriting his half of the business?'

Jon scratched his chin, then winced as he made contact with his cut lip. 'I suppose so. But…'

Henry could see what Carol was doing; it was rather like one of those courtroom dramas that Stephanie sometimes liked to watch on television.

Carol was asking leading questions, to build a case against Jon, and she was pacing the floor in front of him as she did so, which Henry could tell was making the man uncomfortable.

Annie jumped in. 'Rachel has told us about how you and Richard disagreed about the direction the business should take, and we've heard you're short of cash. So, what was it? Did you need the extra money, or was it control you were after?'

All eyes turned to Jon, who spluttered, 'Richard had by far the better business brain, while I did all the entertaining. It had worked extremely well for the company, so why would I have wanted to change it? Yes, we were talking through the options for future growth, and we didn't agree. That's not the end of the world…'

Henry was as startled as Jon when Annie swooped down to the man's ear and hissed, 'But it was the end of the world for Richard, wasn't it? The end of his life.'

'We have a photograph of a note you made in your diary, Jon,' said Carol. Henry didn't know what she was showing Jon on the screen of her phone, but she asked pointedly, 'This is your handwriting, in your desk diary, correct?'

The man babbled, 'That looks like my diary, yes.'

'And did you make this note?'

Jon looked again. 'Yes.'

Henry noticed that a significant look passed between Annie and Carol. He had no idea what it meant, but he knew it was something important. He was surprisingly keen to know what.

Annie asked, 'So would you care to explain it, please? It says "OYSTERS! RICHARD…LOL!" as you can see. That's a bit odd, wouldn't you say?'

Even Henry could tell that Jon was nervous.

The man babbled, 'Well…out of context, I suppose it might appear so. But, well, I went to Lila's one evening for dinner, where she stuffed me full of the blessed things. I'm not too keen on oysters, if I'm honest, I think they're terribly overrated.'

'Hear, hear.' Henry had spoken without thinking, and immediately realized he'd done something inappropriate.

Jon nodded, then continued, 'Anyway, far from the night of passion I think she'd hoped for – Lila's a bit too keen for her own good, you see – I ended up with a bit of a dicky tummy. Headed for my own home, and my own bathroom, as soon as I could. I wrote that note to remind myself to tell Richard about it. Knowing he was allergic to the things, I thought he'd enjoy a bit of a laugh at my expense.'

Carol pressed, 'And what about the fact that you use crushed oyster shells in a pot plant in your office? Why would you choose to do that?'

Henry couldn't imagine what Carol meant.

'I didn't,' spluttered Jon. 'Well, there are shells on top of the soil in the pot, yes. But they're mother of pearl which is…oh yes, I see, that comes from oysters, doesn't it? Ah – I'd never connected…well that was Lila's choice. Said it was something she'd seen in one of those home décor magazines.'

Annie asked, 'Did you hire a firm of private eyes in Hounslow to track down Rachel?'

Jon shook his head. 'Why would I? I thought she deserved a bit of time off work. And…well, until today, I had no idea she wasn't at home, though…well, yes, I can see that might be difficult. To be alone there. Sorry.'

Henry jumped when his mother exclaimed, quite gleefully, he thought, 'It's also a crime scene. A bloody attack took place there.'

Everyone looked at Althea, who was sitting primly and looking rather pleased with herself. McFli looked impressed.

Jon asked, 'What do you mean? What crime? Who's been hurt?'

Annie jumped in again. 'Our friend and colleague Christine Wilson-Smythe – yes, she's a professional investigator. She was attacked by an employee of the private detective agency you say you know nothing about.'

Jon looked…lost. 'I don't know what you're talking about. Christine Wilson-Smythe is a private investigator? But I…'

He stared, wide-eyed, across the room toward Rachel, who'd turned her back on him, and added, 'I haven't done this, Rachel.'

'You knew that Richard Edwards was allergic to mollusks, correct?' Carol was back to the direct questioning.

'Yes. I've already said I did. Everyone did. It wasn't a secret – in fact, it made sense that everyone knew – less likely to serve something to him that might be bad for him.'

'Did everyone also know about his epinephrine pen?'

'Yes, I believe so. Again, I don't think it was something he made a secret of. Though I…I can't say I was ever aware of where he kept it upon his person. The night he died he kept pointing at his jacket, holding his throat, and someone – I think it was Lila – thought to grab it off the chair, but there wasn't a pen in it. Yes – that's right – it was Lila. She was the one who found the pen on the floor later on when…when it was too late. She was terribly upset that she hadn't seen it earlier.'

Annie asked, 'An easy one for you, now, Jon. Is Lila's full name Delilah? And is her father's name Sam Stevenson?'

Jon shrugged, 'Yes, she's Delilah. Delilah Stevenson, though she insists upon Lila. But as for her father's first name? Sorry, no idea. We never reached that stage in our so-called relationship.'

Rachel's tone sounded harsh to Henry's ear when she sniped, 'You two have been in this "so-called relationship" for a couple of years, Jon. Haven't you met the parents, yet?'

'I've always thought our relationship to be essentially informal,' replied Jon, looking a bit pink around the gills. 'Not that it's anyone's business. Truth is, it's been a bit off and on again recently, though it is now most definitely off.'

Annie sidled up to Jon and asked, 'Has Lila given you any gifts recently?'

Jon reached into his pocket and pulled out a small silver tube. It was not unlike the lipsticks Stephanie kept on their dressing table, Henry thought.

'You mean this atomizer? Yes. She filled it with my favorite cologne, so I could freshen myself up when I'm out and about. She gave it to me a few days after Richard…passed. Said she'd wanted to give it to me at the celebration dinner, but felt it wasn't appropriate when…you know. So she gave it to me later on, and…well, things all got a bit intense after that.'

Annie and Carol both smiled. Henry had no idea what was going on. He waited with bated breath.

Annie said, 'Right-o, enough of this pussyfooting around. Here in this room, earlier on, you said to Lila that you hadn't meant to hurt her. Did you dump her when she gave you that gift?'

'No – though that was when she first mentioned…well, we had a bit of a row, to be truthful. She was talking about marriage again – and I'd thought that was just a passing phase. She'd been full of it before Richard had died, and even up until we found out about the fact that he hadn't written a will. Then? Well, she went a bit…odd. You see, the feeling, generally speaking, was that Rachel would make a sadly necessary, but excellent, replacement for Richard. Lila had quite a lot to say about that – and it wasn't at all flattering as far as you were concerned, Rachel, I'm sorry to say. And I'd made it clear that marriage wasn't on the cards, so I was in Lila's black books, too.'

Rachel said, 'I bet she had a few choice things to say about both of us then, eh, Jon?'

Jon nodded, then added, 'Indeed she did. But then, today, in the car, she revisited the matter of marriage quite forcibly. It wasn't until today that I felt the need to make it *absolutely clear* that there is no chance of us becoming man and wife. I mean – the way she was acting? She all but kidnapped me today. "A quick drive" was what she said, then I was stuck in her car with her for hours. When we finally arrived here, I was – as I am sure you'll understand – in need of the facilities, and it was as we were both coming out of the public toilets that I saw Rachel.'

Carol pounced, startling Henry. 'You had no idea that Rachel was here, at Chellingworth Hall?'

Jon looked flabbergasted. 'Why on earth would I? I didn't know that Richard's brother was the butler here…though I suppose he might have mentioned that at some point. But there she was – so I called out. Imagine my surprise when Rachel – who was coming down the stairs at the time – turned and ran up them again, screaming.'

Rachel snapped, 'Of course I screamed – you were the last person I wanted to see, and you started chasing me.'

'I didn't chase you – I followed you because I thought…well, I don't know what I thought, but it seemed the right thing to do. Lila followed me, of course, and then I was accosted by…well, Richard's brother, as it transpires, though I had no idea of that at the time.'

Annie was up next. 'Have you ever told Lila something like, "Of course I want us to be together, Lila, but I can't afford to get married right now"?' Annie's voice had a real edge to it, which made Henry feel uncomfortable.

Jon nodded, he looked quite embarrassed.

Annie sniped, 'Yeah, a lot of us girls who fall for the wrong bloke hear that sort of thing. If it's not one reason why you can't put a ring on our finger, it's another. And tell me, did you ever mention to Lila that thing about you and Richard writing those wills? Would she have been in a position to believe that, if he was dead, you'd cop the lot? That you'd finally be able to afford to make an honest woman of her?'

As Jon nodded, Henry could tell that the atmosphere in the room had shifted somehow, but he wasn't sure what it meant.

'Where'd you take Lila, Rachel?' Carol was heading for the door.

'The private bathroom connected to the bedroom I've been using.' Rachel stood and stamped her foot. 'What an idiot I've been. Lila! She's made a run for it, hasn't she?' Rachel joined Carol and the pair shot out of the room.

'Why would Lila have left?' Henry had to know.

His mother said, 'For heaven's sake, Henry, it's obvious. It wasn't Jon who poisoned poor Edward's brother, it was Lila. She thought Jon would marry her if he had the wherewithal, so decided to provide him with it by getting rid of his business partner, thereby – as she thought – allowing Jon to inherit the whole company.'

Henry could hardly believe his ears.

His mother looked as though she were enjoying herself. 'Then Lila found out that the company had gone to Rachel instead, so she hired the PIs in Hounslow to find her, then came here to…well, I dare say that if Jon hadn't well and truly broken things off with her in the car, she might have attempted to kill Rachel too.'

Henry gasped. 'I say. Really?'

His mother nodded, looking grim. 'An awful prospect, I agree Henry. Luckily for Rachel, Jon made sure that Lila understood that marriage wasn't on the cards, so she knew she'd killed Richard for no good reason – not that there could be a good reason to kill someone, of course – and she also realized there was no point in killing Rachel. Which is excellent. And now she's scarpered. And we let her go. And Carwen James will blame us for this. Though I hope he'll be able to understand why we all thought it was Jon who'd killed Richard. Annie – is the name Sam Stevenson important, by the way?'

Annie nodded. 'Carol just found out that Lila's father's a prominent allergist – got a place in Harley Street. He's even a mister, not a doctor, so a consultant, you know? Carol hadn't made the connection before, because she'd been checking for a Lila. I had to laugh about that. This is Carol we're talking about…and I know for a fact she's heard that song *Delilah* a million times, because it is one of Bertie's favorites. That, and *It's Not Unusual*, which – if you think about it – is what you could say about us sniffing out a killer.'

Mavis spoke up next. 'Do you think Lila gave you the atomizer – the murder weapon – so she'd have something to hold over you if you declined her advances, Jon?'

Henry was surprised at such a notion – and noticed that Jon Dacre seemed to be even more shocked. The man had lost most of his color.

'To be perfectly honest I'm having a terribly difficult time absorbing all of this,' said Jon. 'I can't imagine Lila *actually* killing someone. To get me to marry her? Dear Lord…that's…that's… She wanted me that much? That's…terrifying. *She's* terrifying. But if this so-called gift she gave me can help clear matters up, then please, have it.'

Henry turned his attention to his mother as she whined, 'Good heavens – what's going on outside?'

She bobbed about trying to see out through the window.

She bleated, 'I asked Chief Inspector James to tell his people they weren't to use sirens. What on earth is he playing at? Our visitors must think World War Three's broken out. There's something dreadful going on out there.'

Henry actually agreed with his mother for once, and everyone moved to the windows to try to see what was happening.

Henry was appalled by the sight that met his eyes. Members of the public were scattering in all directions. One car had smashed into the side of another, at right angles. Police officers were running about. It was absolute chaos. In the midst of it all, he spotted the frail figure of Lila Stevenson being helped out of the car that had done the crashing by a uniformed officer, just as Carol and Rachel appeared on the scene. He couldn't tell exactly what they were saying to the officer who was helping Lila, but it led to Chief Inspector Carwen James getting involved. Henry saw Lila being escorted back into the Hall, followed by Carol and Rachel, while the remaining police officers were – thankfully – giving their attention to the members of the public who'd had a nasty scare.

Henry turned, dumbfounded, and found that Edward was at his shoulder; thank heavens his nose had finally stopped bleeding.

'If Your Grace would permit, I'll work with our staff to make all the necessary arrangements to ensure that our day-guests are well looked after.'

Henry felt immediately calmed. 'Please do, Edward. We shall remain here.'

'Of course, Your Grace.'

Henry had a bright idea. 'Oh, and Edward?'

'Yes, your Grace?'

'Would you arrange for some tea to be brought in, please? And bring the chief inspector to join us here. The Lila person too.'

'Indeed, Your Grace.'

Henry felt quite warm when his mother patted his back and said, 'Good idea, Henry. Tea never hurts, does it?'

McFli yapped his approval at her feet.

CHAPTER THIRTY-TWO

Alexander stumbled into Christine's hospital room and found himself facing her father. He tried to peer at his fiancée as she lay in bed, but he was pushed out through the door.

'She's asleep,' hissed Aiden. 'Let her be.'

Alexander's heart was thumping. He was so close. 'But I need her to know that I'm here for her. Did you tell her that I'd texted? Did she know I was coming?'

Aiden nodded. 'That's why she's managing to sleep, now. So, let's talk. While we can. Your texts didn't explain anything. Where have you been? And why are you dressed like that?'

Alexander was only too well aware that he smelled rank. He'd faced disgusted looks and wrinkled noses for the past hour or so as he'd made his way pretty much right across London, diagonally, on public transport. When he'd finally emerged from the Tube system, he'd had to flash a twenty-pound note in a cab driver's face to encourage him to let him get into his vehicle. Given that the poor cabbie would probably have to use an entire bottle of air freshener after Alexander left him, and sanitize his whole vehicle, he felt the tip wasn't overly generous.

Although he was desperate to see Christine, Alexander knew he owed Aiden an explanation. He told him a little about the situation with Geordie – editing the truth as necessary, and not mentioning the involvement of anyone named Big Tony, nor the police. And he was finally able to put Aiden's mind at rest about the entire 'secret son' blackmail scam. He explained Sean's desire to make Alexander's life a misery because, in Sean's eyes, that was what Alexander had helped Geordie to do to *him*, by taking him to rehab. Twice. *Now three times.*

Finally convinced that Aiden understood that Alexander had no son, and that Sean had digitally manipulated old photos of Alexander – employing his knowledge and skills at computing – Alexander relaxed a little.

Aiden said he'd explain everything to Deirdre as soon as possible – but they agreed that the whole situation wasn't something Christine needed to be bothered with that day. The two men entered Christine's room shoulder to shoulder – but not before Aiden had forced Alexander to dump the hoodie he was wearing into a nearby bin, and replace it with a spare shirt that Aiden always kept in the boot of his car.

His fiancée was fast asleep, so Alexander greeted Deirdre, who he could see was looking exhausted. Aiden clutched his wife to his chest and suggested that, maybe, they could now take a break, and leave their daughter alone with Alexander.

Just a few moments after Christine's parents had left – moments Alexander spent gazing at the face he loved…no matter how much of it was covered with bandages – a doctor bustled in and introduced herself, quite loudly. She was new to Christine's case, she announced, and wanted to meet the patient herself.

Christine stirred, peeled open her good eye, and saw Alexander for the first time. His heart warmed when she grabbed his hand, and they held each other that way as Christine answered the doctor's many, many questions.

Alexander couldn't quite believe how relieved he was to see the love and emotion in that one, good eye as Christine gazed up at him. He felt the strain of the past few days hit him like a brick on the back of the head, and he flopped in the chair.

The doctor kept asking Christine for details about her pain level, what she could and couldn't see, and so forth, but Alexander didn't mind having to wait until she'd finished; he and Christine could talk for as long as they – or at least, as long as *she* – wanted, once they were alone.

He'd decided to tell her all about what had been happening as soon as she felt up to it, because he didn't want them to have even one secret standing between them.

Before she left them to themselves, the doctor threw some platitudes in Christine's direction, and urged her to not tire herself.

Standing at the door, she said, 'You really shouldn't notice any difference in your pregnancy – it's early days, and the fetus is well protected in there. But rest is important and, of course, we'll bear it in mind going forward, regarding medications, and possible surgeries. I'll drop by later on. Don't tire her out, please.'

Alexander felt his mouth fall open.

CHAPTER THIRTY-THREE

Carol had dropped Annie at the Lamb and Flag, where Tudor had been looking after Gertie, much later than Annie had hoped. She ran into the pub, where Aled was pulling a pint behind the bar.

'He's upstairs,' he said, 'I think war broke out between the dogs, so he went up to sort it out. They've gone quiet now, but I think he'll be glad to see you.'

Annie thanked Aled, then took the stairs as fast as she dared, and found Tudor flat on his back on the floor, having his face licked by both Rosie and Gertie. He was trying to push them both away, with good-natured shoves and feeble cries of, 'No, no…get off me now.'

Annie grabbed a couple of treats and called the pups to her. Suddenly, they didn't find Tudor's face as tasty anymore.

As Annie showered both dogs with petting and lots of, 'Good girls,' she saw Tudor manage to roll onto his front, then get to his knees, and finally his feet. He brushed himself off and straightened his shirt and waistcoat.

'Went down to pet them, then we got into a bit of a playful maul, and I went over. They wouldn't let me up, bless them,' he said, by way of explanation.

Annie was relieved. 'For a minute there I thought you'd taken a tumble. We can't cope with two of us being clumsy. Leave the falling and tripping to me, alright, Tude?'

The couple hugged. Tudor asked, 'Where've you been? I thought you were collecting Gertie half an hour ago. Aren't you supposed to be walking these two, then going to Iris Lewis's cottage for that meeting?'

'I was, and I am. If I march these two around the green sharpish, I can still make it. Gulliver's not due to arrive until teatime. Want to come with me for the walk, and I'll fill you in? It's been all go – we've wound up two cases today already.'

Annie's heart swelled when Tudor smiled at her. 'Sounds like you've had quite a day of it, and I can't think of anything I'd rather do than have you tell me all about it while we let these two have a bit of air. They got a bit stir crazy this afternoon. And they're both getting bigger. They need more room to play.'

Annie and Tudor put leads on the dogs and headed off around the village green. Annie recounted her time at the hospital in Brecon with Carol, and how the whole Dan Douglas thing had turned out, then she gabbled through the events at Chellingworth Hall, regarding the murder of Edward's brother.

'So this young woman, Lila, killed Richard because she wanted this Jon character to marry her? I mean…how did she think she'd get away with it?'

Annie paused, allowing Gertie and Rosie to give each other a good sniff. 'You know what? She had, Tude. She'd got away with it – until Edward got us lot involved. Now there's a thought…a killer could have walked around for the rest of their life knowing they'd managed to get rid of someone without anyone being any the wiser if we hadn't done some digging. Who knows – she might have done it again. That's a lovely idea – that we might have saved someone's life down the road, even though poor Edward's still lost his brother, and Rachel's a widow. I feel so sorry for her, Tude. From what she's said, her and Richard were happy together – making plans for their future. You know, like we are. Imagine someone coming and killing the person you love. Just terrible.'

Tudor spoke quietly. 'I'd never stop looking for who did it.'

Annie chuckled darkly. 'I'd rip them limb from limb. Well, you know, I'd certainly dump them in Carwen James's lap, in any case. Speaking of which – and off the point for a minute – Althea mentioned something about a bus trip when she was talking to him on the phone today, and she mentioned your name. What have you been up to that I know nothing about? Have you got a deep, dark secret, Tudor Evans?'

Tudor walked on. 'Nothing deep or dark, and it's not even a secret, really.'

'Glad to hear it,' said Annie with a chuckle. 'But there's something.'

Tudor nodded. 'Althea put an idea to the village social committee, and we're taking it forward. Everyone's going to get a note through their letterbox tomorrow, as it happens, and there'll be posters around the village, too.'

Annie nudged him. 'Aw, come on, Tude, spit it out. What's up?'

'No – no unfair advantages just because you're you, and I'm me. I don't want to spoil the surprise. And, in any case, aren't you due at Iris's now? I'll take the girls back to the pub, you go and see to Iris. You said she wanted you there for a bit of support, though why she wouldn't want Wendy with her – who's her granddaughter, after all – I don't know. Not that you won't do a good job, of course...but I'd have thought that family would be a better idea.'

'Yeah, I know, but Wendy's off at some music thing or other in Cardiff, and Walter Gulliver didn't want to wait until she got back. So, me it is. And I want to be there anyway. I'd ask you to come too, but I think Iris really did want just me. Besides, with her, and me, and Gulliver, *and* all those budgies in cages, it'll be a full sitting room as it is.'

Tudor laughed as he kissed Annie on the cheek. 'You mean I'm too big to fit?'

Annie kissed him back. 'Your body needs to be that big to fit your giant heart in there, Tude. Bye now, I'll come and collect Gert later, and we can have a bit of dinner together, alright?'

'I thought you had to finish weeding through those clothes of yours,' called Tudor as the dogs dragged him toward the pub entrance.

Annie tutted to herself – she'd been putting that off. 'I'll do it, Tude,' she called back, then tapped Iris Lewis's front door knocker with a rat-tat-tat; there wasn't a strange car parked anywhere, so she guessed she'd beaten Walter Gulliver to it.

Iris looked lovely: her snowy hair was gleaming, she was wearing a pretty floral dress that suggested to Annie that she kept it for best – better even than church, which was saying something – and her cornflower-blue eyes were sparkling.

She looked a little disappointed to see Annie, which Annie did her best to not take personally.

She smiled. 'Ah, Annie…he's not here yet. Come on in. Maybe he's been held up on the roads. The traffic can be horribly slow this time of year. Caravans, that's all I need to say.'

Annie chuckled as she stepped into Iris's living room – a mirror of her own, next door. 'Yeah, Car's always on about caravans. In Welsh, usually, which I know means she's swearing.'

'We don't really swear in Welsh, Annie. But we do have some lovely colorful ways of describing how something makes us feel.'

Annie knew this to not be the case for Carol, who'd been kind enough to directly translate some of her most choice exclamations, but Annie suspected that Iris wasn't the sort of person to use strong language under any circumstances.

'He's not really late yet, is he?' Annie knew she'd cut it fine, but wanted to reassure Iris.

'It's been all these years, I dare say a few minutes more won't matter.' Iris sat and invited Annie to do the same. Annie glanced around at the birds in cages; they all seemed to be quiet at the moment, for which she was grateful. Their tweeting, as a chorus, went right through her teeth.

The table was set – with spaces free for what Annie assumed would be a pot for the tea and a plate for cake – and the small room was spotless, with a waft of furniture polish in the air. Annie reckoned Iris had been keen to make sure everything looked its best for her visitor, as though royalty were about to walk through the door.

'I bet the old Queen went through her entire life thinking the whole world smelled of polish,' said Annie.

Iris looked sideways at Annie. 'There are worse things the world could smell of.'

'I dare say.'

Annie saw Iris jump when there was a knock at the door.

'That'll be him then,' said Iris. She took her time rising from her chair.

As sprightly as Iris was for her eighty-odd years, Annie had noticed the woman slowing down during the eighteen months or so that they'd been neighbors. And there'd been that little heart attack, of course.

Annie rose too, sticking out a helping hand.

Iris waved it away. 'I'll be fine, thanks.' She got to the door in a few steps, pulled it open, and Annie saw the silhouette of a short man with bowed legs, and a head with rather wild hair sticking out.

Iris stepped back, exclaiming, 'Wally! You haven't changed a bit.'

The man who entered the room was much as Mavis had described him, and the sticky-outy hairdo was because he'd pulled off a hat on the doorstep, it seemed. As he was ushered to a chair, he smoothed down his tufty, white horseshoe of hair, and beamed as he saw the birds.

'Oh, I love a budgie or two. You have a wonderful collection. You must tell me all their names…'

'I'll make a pot and get the cake – in the kitchen?' Annie thought it best to offer, and Iris gladly accepted.

Given that she was still only about five steps away, and through an arch, not behind a closed door, Annie could hear the aged couple exchanging gushing comments about how well the other looked, and how neither of them had changed a bit. That sort of thing always amused Annie in others, yet she knew it to be true; if ever she was in London and bumped into people she hadn't seen for decades, the person she'd once known was always visible there somewhere. Indeed, having seen photos of Tudor when he'd been a little boy, she knew that to be true of him too – yes, he was older, and much bigger, but the essence of him had never altered, at least, not as far as some slightly blurry pictures suggested.

With tea for everyone sorted, and cake on plates, Annie realized she was absolutely superfluous to requirements: any nervousness Iris might have felt at the thought of welcoming the famous Walter Gulliver into her home had vanished when her childhood chum Wally had arrived, instead. And as for their client's intentions? All good, reckoned Annie.

Walter was saying, 'I just wish you'd got in touch with me, Iris. It's not as though I've been hard to find this past thirty years or so. Couldn't keep my face out of the papers for most of that time. And I didn't even know your name.'

Iris poo-pooed the idea. 'Why on earth would I have done that? I was always happy to see how well you were doing for yourself, of course, but I didn't think you'd remember me. We were both just small children when you came to our farm, and then I went away with Mam, and that was that. I didn't think you'd have given me a second thought.'

'Oh but I did. I gave you, and David, and your mother and father so much thought, over so many years. Though not, I'll admit, while doing anything about it. It's only recently that I decided that I needed to track you all down. And I'm so pleased I did. Just sitting here, now, with you? I feel all the things I did back then. It was your family who made me, you know? Your father, showing me how things worked, how they grew, and how they were raised…all with care and patience. Your Mam taught me to read – and I'd have been nothing without that ability. David? Well, he and my brother didn't really want me to be doing things with them, I was too little, but at least you took me under your wing. Whenever I've thought of you, I've known you were the sister I lost…and now here you are. I understand you've had a career as a teacher and headmistress. I'm not surprised – you were incredibly good with me, you know.'

Annie felt the glow of friendship between the two, and she knew it was a sort of love. Familial love. Delightful. As an only child, Annie had never felt that, and hadn't missed it, as such – but she enjoyed seeing it, and feeling it, where it existed.

'So, tell me, where did you go, Iris? I remember you and your mother leaving the farm. She came back, but you didn't. What happened?'

Iris put down her cup and saucer carefully – Annie knew it was her best china.

'I didn't even know myself for years, Wally. Mam finally told me when I got married. I dare say she thought I wouldn't understand until then.'

She paused and smiled. 'Different times, they were. She was pregnant, you see, but not doing too well, so she and Dad agreed she should go to her sister so she could rest, and she took me with her because Dad said he had his hands full with the farm and you boys.'

Walter grinned. 'Oh yes, we were a handful alright.'

Iris winked at him, playfully. 'Anyway, when it came time, the baby died. She didn't rally for quite some time after that, and, when she decided she *was* up to going back to the farm, everyone agreed it would be better for me to stay with my auntie. I hadn't gone to school until then, and I was doing exceptionally well there, you see, and I had friends…one very special friend, truth be told. I didn't want to leave. I hate to say it, Wally, but having a girl for a best friend – someone I could do everything with – didn't really compare with having a little boy, and a load of animals, to look after.'

Walter smiled. 'I forgive you.' Annie noticed that he winked, and Iris blushed a little. 'And what of the rest of your family?'

Iris smiled, sadly. 'Dad went first. I think the war took it out of him. Even with three boys to help out, he worked himself into the ground. Literally. Had a heart attack. Dead before he hit the floor of the barn. David decided he'd give it a go, but it wasn't for him. Once Mam said she'd be alright with going back to her sister's place to live, he sold up. Killed in a car crash about seven years later. Mam died about twenty years ago. She got the rest she deserved,'

'And you say you got married?' Walter looked wistful.

Iris nodded. Annie knew about Iris's woeful marriage, and her secret, loving relationship thereafter. She wondered how Iris would respond.

'I did.' She sighed heavily. 'It was expected of me…and…I wanted a child of my own. I…felt the need to be a mother. He gave me one. My Siân. And her daughter, Wendy lives in this village, so she's a big part of my life, too. All of which is wonderful. But then…well, after my child was born, I was true to my nature.'

She paused, and looked at Annie with twinkling blue eyes that were beginning to look a bit watery, then returned her attention to Walter.

'Annie knows a bit about what I'm going to tell you – but no one else does. Annie's absolutely trustworthy, see? I met Helen, who was a nurse, and we managed to have a wonderful life together, with her as my "lodger". They were good years, despite…well, maybe you can't even imagine how difficult things would have been for us back then if the truth had come out, with me being a teacher in rural Wales.'

Walter sat back in his seat, glanced at Annie, then said, 'My partner was Harold. Everyone thought he was my personal assistant. We met in the 1970s. Active times for some who were open about their lives, but at a point where selling groceries was – apparently – the same as selling family values. Which our relationship didn't represent. I…I was never brave enough to speak up, in public, nor even in private. He died fifteen years ago, next month. I've been alone since then. We worked together and were happy partners, in every respect. When he died, I chose to redouble the effort I put into my business life, but it hasn't been the same without him. I can't deny that. I…I've had no one I can talk to about him since he's gone. We were incredibly secretive, you see. Felt we had to be, at first, and then…well, it's difficult to tell people you've been lying to them for years, isn't it?'

Annie could tell that Iris needed a tissue. She couldn't see any in the room, so began to fiddle about with her handbag, just in case she had some in there. She needn't have bothered, because Walter gallantly passed a pocket handkerchief to Iris, who took it, smiling, yet teary-eyed.

Walter spoke as Iris dabbed at her face. 'Your family was warm, and loving, and accepting, Iris. Mine wasn't. When I was sent to Lincolnshire to live with them there, it was a hard life. Your farm? Yes, there were always lots of jobs to do, but…well, maybe it was because I was younger then, and not much could be expected of me…but your father made it all seem like fun.'

He paused, and Annie saw something in his eyes change. 'My mother's cousin who we ended up with – we called him our uncle – never smiled. Not once, that I saw.'

He focused his eyes on Iris's table. 'To say that he taught me what hard work meant would be understating it. And yet he, as much as your family, made me the man I became – which is to say I was certainly hard-working, though in a different way. And, of course, I suppose you could say it all turned out alright. I became much more successful than I could ever have imagined.'

He paused, and looked up at Iris. 'I had that drive, you see? And yet I chose to focus on the fun parts of things…to always see the joy in doing a job. And that's what you Davieses gave me. Greatest gift of all, that is. And I'm so pleased to have the chance to tell you that. At our age, there aren't a lot of people we can talk to about years gone by, and our shared experiences. So now, Iris, *Blodyn Bach*, I'm going to ask you for another gift, please.'

Iris smiled through her tears. 'Ask anything, Wally. And if it's in my power to give it or do it, it's yours.'

Walter pulled out another handkerchief, this time for himself. 'Let's be friends again, Iris? Let's spend time talking about things like…oh, that lamb that had one black ear – remember that one?'

'You named it Ash, because its ear looked like it was covered in ash from the fire. And the one we hand-fed together…what was that one called?'

Walter stared at Annie, looking blank for a moment, then he smiled at her, and she couldn't help but smile back – he looked so completely happy.

He clapped his hands like a child. 'Arthur – we called him Arthur, after Arthur Askey, because he was so small.'

Iris giggled. 'TTFN!'

Walter gurgled. '*Aythangyow.*'

Annie felt her face ache, she was smiling so hard.

'Remember we went to see the film of *Band Waggon*…somewhere? Where was that, I wonder? I haven't seen it since. Oh, that was funny,' said Iris.

Walter reached across the tea table and touched Iris on the hand. 'We could watch it again, together. I'm sure I could rustle up a copy of it, somehow.'

Annie felt it was time to leave. She picked up her bag and said, 'I hope you don't mind, Iris, Walter, but my poor pup Gert's been without me all day. I'll go now, if that's alright with you two?' She was already beside the door.

Iris smiled at her. 'You go on. We'll be fine. Thanks, Annie – not just for being here now, but to you and the whole team for finding me for Wally. It means…a lot.'

Walter also grinned at Annie. 'You women have changed my life, you know. Well, what's left of it, anyway. With this lovely woman to help me feel young again, there'll be more joy and fun in it than there would have been without her. Thank you. You might be seeing a bit of me around this delightful village of yours in the future – we can't lose touch now.'

Annie opened the door. 'You'll be welcome. We all care about Iris, so – with her stamp of approval – every door will be open to you. Works with my Tudor on the village social committee, does Iris – meaning she's a woman of influence in these parts. So you'd better not tick her off, or you'll have a lot of irate Welsh people to deal with, not to mention one seriously dangerous Cockney.'

'I was going to ask if you were,' said Walter. 'You know I was from Woolwich, originally. You?'

'My parents were Windrush generation. East End. Moved about a bit, as you might imagine.'

Walter nodded sadly. 'Yes…the inability of folks to accept those who are different. I do what I can. Literacy and education programs for children and young people. Support for those who need it because of their…differences.'

Annie nodded. 'Trust me – I understand. I'll have to introduce you to Althea. She's the dowager up at Chellingworth Hall. You two together? Her with her title, and you with all that dosh? Now there's a pairing. Ta-ra for now, Iris. Take care, Walter.'

As she headed toward the pub Annie realized she'd now encountered her first multi-millionaire, and had liked him. Wonders would never cease.

5th AUGUST

CHAPTER THIRTY-FOUR

The Anwen-by-Wye social committee had ended up having to hire two coaches for the village trip to the National Eisteddfod of Wales, because – once the word was out – the demand for seats had been overwhelming. Most locals had jumped at the chance to not have to drive themselves to the event, while others had seen it as a wonderful opportunity to enjoy a community experience; to take a trip to a nationally significant event which they might not do, if left to their own devices, which was what all the letters in letterboxes, and posters, had emphasized.

Tudor and Annie had left Aled in charge at the Lamb and Flag: there weren't going to be many locals left to pop in for a pint, but there were always a few folks who dropped in on their way to or from visiting Chellingworth Hall – and their numbers were increasing, Tudor had noted, since the schools had broken up for the summer holidays. He also credited the revitalized Market Hall and the presence of an antiques shop, to give visitors something to actually do in the village, rather than just stop for a loo break, and hopefully order at least a half of mild and a packet of crisps.

'He'll cope. Aled will be fine,' said Annie as Tudor gazed at the pub disappearing behind them with worried eyes.

'I know he will, really. He's a good future publican, that one. Understands how the whole business works, not just how to pull a pint and slap a pasty on a plate. But he's still young.'

'I think it's interesting that Joan Pike is the person he asked to give him a hand,' noted Annie playfully.

She added more seriously, 'Carol trusts her with Bertie, so I think we can trust her with the Lamb, and the pups.'

She sighed. She'd miss Gertie. 'You were right – they'd get far too excited with all the people who'll be there, and we won't be tied to them all day. Besides, can you imagine how they'd be if they had to spend hours on this bus?' She chuckled. 'Mind you, I didn't even know that Joan and Aled knew each other. It must take some doing to get her to leave her mother on her own for hours. I understand why they didn't want to come – I know you said you could have arranged a bus with a lift to accommodate Joan's mum's wheelchair, but I don't think she really fancied it. I haven't been before – would it be difficult for her to get around there?'

Tudor finally settled into his seat. 'Well, it is all set up in fields, so there's grass underfoot in most places, but I know they put down those path things, too. And it's been dry for weeks. But, you know what? I think Joan and her mum are happy to stay in the village. And Joan won't be leaving her alone at all...I saw her push her mother into the pub while you were getting on the bus, fussing over Iris and Walter.'

Annie grinned. 'They're in the back seat, like a couple of kids. I think Iris packed sandwiches. Funny, isn't it, those two?'

Tudor agreed, 'When you told me he said he might be back here, I didn't think he'd start looking for a house in the area; he's only in Hereford now. That's not far.'

'Talking of sandwiches – well, I wasn't, but I was thinking of them – you did tell Aled about that block of cheese he needs to use up, didn't you? I can't believe we'll be in our new flat next week, Tude. I'm so...well, excited, of course, but it's a bit daunting too, innit?'

Tudor took hold of Annie's hand, which made her feel warm inside. 'It's all going to be fine. The kitchen is sorted, the pub is sorted. The deliveries are all in, and it's just us getting into the flat, now. And the most daunting thing about that is how you're going to fit in all your clothes.' He chuckled, and pecked her on the cheek.

Annie play-thumped his arm. 'Oi, I've got rid of a load of stuff, I have.'

She really had, and was beginning to wonder if she'd got rid of too much.

She sighed. 'And you're a fine one to talk. All those waistcoats and tweed jackets you have are really bulky. You could do with getting rid of a few of them, too. But don't get rid of all of them. I like your waistcoats. I like them when wear them like this – you know, just with a shirt and a bow tie, and I like them with your jackets, too. They give you a distinguished air.'

Tudor twirled his hand in the air like an ancient courtier. 'You're welcome, M'lady.'

Annie giggled. 'I talked to Chrissy on the video last night, just for five minutes. She's not looking too bad, considering. Her eye's going down quite well. Uncovered, now. She'd have enjoyed this – well, under normal circumstances. It's a shame she's still in London. I miss her. Still, she said she'd be back soon. No surgery. No permanent damage to her eye – she was lucky. Mind you, it looks like she's put on a few pounds. Sitting about being pampered, no doubt. I don't mean that unkindly, but she'd gone a bit hollow-looking in the face for a while, so she could do with a bit more meat on her.'

Tudor gave Annie the sort of smile that told her he was making a decision about what to say on the topic. He finally spoke. 'You're right, she was lucky. And it'll be good to have her back. Alexander's been a bit scarce, too, I've noticed. He was over at the antiques shop quite a bit when it first opened, but, there, I dare say Elizabeth Fernley's more than capable of running the place without him being around. Probably capable of running an entire country, that woman.'

'Speaking of being in charge,' whispered Annie, 'thanks for suggesting that Marjorie Pritchard should go on the other bus...to keep an eye on things. I think she'd have done my head in if I'd had to listen to her going on and on about what people should do when we get there. She wouldn't shut up at the meeting at the pub the other night, would she?'

'She was...thorough,' acknowledged Tudor.

Annie chuckled. 'Yeah, thorough. I get it – I think we all got it, in the end; there's a lot to choose from, so making a plan is important.'

Tudor mused, 'Yes, a plan. We're doing a lot of planning, these days.'

'Exactly. And in't the beauty of this sort of thing? That you just go with the flow. I want to have a wander and try out a bit of everything. You said there'd be Welsh gins I could try, and Welsh beers…and Welsh snacks. I don't want to have to follow a timetable.'

Annie noticed that Tudor had decided to look out at the passing countryside. 'Well, it might be worth having a squint at the schedule for the *Maes*, the main stage. I mean, we wouldn't want to miss a good competition, would we?'

Annie's neck started to tingle. 'What do you mean by a "good competition", Tude? Like what, for example? Everything's going to be in Welsh – I won't understand a word.'

Tudor looked…sheepish, that was it. 'They've got simultaneous translation at the *Maes*, so that's not a problem. And…well, truth be told, I'm looking forward to hearing a few good choirs. I don't get the chance, often, with the pub. It does something to my insides when I hear a good choir – I can't explain it. It just…well, it touches my soul. There. I've said it.'

Annie kissed Tudor's cheek. 'Far be it from me to stop the man I love from having his soul go all tingly. The choirs it is. At the *Maes*. See? I'm talking Welsh already.'

Carol and Albert were sitting comfortably across the aisle from David, who'd taken responsibility for the alarmingly large bag they needed for the day. Carol had wedged Albert's special seat beside the window, and was busy chatting to him about the main points of interest that were passing by. Albert seemed engaged, for the most part, and Carol hoped he'd remain that way for the rest of the journey, and while they were at the Eisteddfod itself.

She'd been to many an Eisteddfod over the years, some at school, some local to where she'd grown up, and some national, but this was Albert's first, and her first time as a parent, with a child to keep entertained.

'Face painting first?' David leaned across the aisle, so he didn't have to raise his voice.

Carol smiled. 'Why not? Then he can enjoy the whole day as a little…whatever he choses to be…and we can go from there. There's a big play area, and there'll be loads of kids there, I'm sure. And we can take it in turns if one or the other of us wants to go off and join in with, or watch, something specific. I wouldn't mind seeing the under sixteens' solo recitations. I used to do that, you know. I even won an Eisteddfod at school for it.'

David grinned. 'You've kept that a secret from me for long enough. Was it from memory?' Carol nodded. 'Remember it?'

Carol was tempted to give her husband an earful of all the pieces she'd recited over various competitions – of which she vividly recalled every word – but she laughed and said, 'One day, when I can stand to do it. I've never done it sitting down. It's a thing. Big difference.'

'How do you learn things like that? Lots of repetition? I've never done anything like it.'

Carol sighed. 'Mam. She used to test me. Goodness knows how many hours she listened to me going over and over a piece, until I had it perfect. She'd do it in the evenings. Looking back, I can only imagine she must have been tired to her bones, with the days they had on the farm. And yet she did it. Because I asked her to.'

'That's family, isn't it?'

Albert smacked Carol's shoulder to point out a blue car that had already disappeared before she spotted it. 'Good boy. Yes, blue.' As she ruffled his hair she hoped it had, in fact, been blue. He batted her hand away, which hurt her heart more than it should have done.

David hissed, 'So your lot are quite the local heroes again. Or should that be "sheroes"? That was a lovely piece they did about all of you in the paper, about reuniting Walter and Iris. Might get you some more clients. Shame you couldn't be in the photos.'

'No, no photos,' noted Carol.

'I get it, photos wouldn't be helpful if you need to pretend to be someone you're not at some point in the future. Not that I like the idea of you ever having to do that. Happy you're able to be at your desk, more often than not, though I know what you do is important – look at how you caught another killer.'

Carol smiled at the remembrance of how Lila Stevenson had reacted when confronted by the law at Chellingworth Hall. 'With Jon Dacre bleating, Rachel incandescent, and me, Annie, and Mavis recounting the situation as we saw it, she just capitulated. I know it'll take time for the case to come to court, but we'll all be there, when we're needed, to give our evidence. And Rachel's been able to go back to her home in Ealing knowing that she's going to get justice for her husband.'

David beamed. 'I'm so proud of you for doing all that. And you got that nasty piece of work Joseph whatever-he's-called put back in jail. But…yeah, stay at home more, Carol? I worry whenever you get in the car to go anywhere.'

'He's Joseph Douglas, and please don't worry, *cariad*. Like I keep telling you, I really never do anything dangerous.' Carol had chosen to edit a few details about her recent undertakings when she'd talked to David about them, and had made sure Annie would always follow her lead in such matters. Walking into Rose Cottage the way they had that day had been foolish. She kept telling herself that. And it could have been any of them at that house in Ealing.

'I tell you what,' said Carol, 'as long as you promise to not nag me about my work, I promise to not mention the fact that you've been spending a lot of time out at meetings recently.'

David leaned back in his seat and stretched his legs, as far as he could within the confined space.

'That's all over, now. Job done. Finally. And good riddance. I don't understand why clients who hire me to give them advice, choose to not take it. Then they end up whining their faces off when they have to pay me again to go in and sort out the mess they've got themselves into by not listening to me in the first place.'

Carol smiled. 'Sorry, *cariad*.'

David sighed. 'I know it's good for our bank balance, but the angst? I could do without that. And they really begrudge it, you know? As though them being too stubborn to do what I suggest is my fault, somehow or other.'

Carol couldn't help but grin. 'Talking of stubborn, did you see Henry getting onto the other bus?'

David smiled. 'Yeah, quite the performance.'

Carol shrugged. 'I mean, I think it's terrific that a duke and duchess have metaphorically taken off their ducal robes to join we common folks on a bus trip, but he didn't want to sit in the middle of the bus, did he? I saw poor old Stephanie having to make him move twice so they and Hugo could sit across from each other, like us.'

'Maybe he gets coach-sick?'

'How would he know? Do you think Henry's spent many hours on coaches in his life?'

David laughed. 'Can't imagine it, no. Well, I'm glad he's on the bus that's got Marjorie Pritchard on it, because I couldn't have coped with her all day, I know. If ever there was anyone who thought she knew better than anyone else, it's her.'

'When we all know it's me who's omniscient, right?'

'Correct.'

Mavis and Althea were in the back row of the second coach, and Mavis's bottom was already complaining. 'These seats back here bounce around more than any of the others, dear. Could we no' have sat a little farther forward?'

Althea was beaming, and began to bounce even more. 'It's fun, Mavis. Didn't you do this as a child? Run to the back row so you could hide, and be naughty? I know I did. Charabancs they were back then of course, nothing like this. This thing hardly bounces at all. And there's air conditioning. And a little TV on the ceiling so you can see the road ahead. There's even a loo, for heaven's sake. Who'd have thought it? A good idea to pay the extra for it, though. It might come in handy.'

Mavis hoped it wouldn't. Or that it would. She wasn't sure. 'Aye, well it's good of you to support this trip...well, to get it to happen, by funding it. I hope folks enjoy it. I've been to Highland Games gatherings before, but this will be my first Eisteddfod. What shall we do, dear?'

'Eat, drink, be merry, and watch a lot of people singing and reciting stuff,' replied Althea brightly.

'That sounds…excellent,' replied Mavis.

Althea whispered, 'I think we should avoid the folk dancing. Marjorie Pritchard will be making a beeline for that, so let's get away from her for at least part of the day. I'm glad that she and Sharon from the shop decided to sit next to each other at the front of the bus. It means we're as far away from her as possible.'

'You didnae want to sit close to Hugo? He is your grandson, after all.'

'Stephanie and Henry can deal with him. I'm delighted they've come, of course…it took a lot to persuade Henry that this would be a community event he shouldn't miss. But I admit it's a long time on a bus for an infant. There's likely to be at least one meltdown, I should imagine, and I really am too old to be bothered with all of that. I told Tudor to make sure that the coaches he hired had changing tables in the lavatories too, so at least that won't become a problem.'

'Henry seems quite settled, now that Edward's back to more of his usual self, I've noted,' said Mavis.

'I agree. Henry hates change. Always did as a child. I blame the nanny. Always on about routines, she was, and this is the result. Maybe their idea of having Hugo with them all the time is a better one? I can't say. And I'll be long gone before the child's old enough for us to be sure how he'll turn out.'

Mavis patted Althea's hand. 'You're healthy, for your age. You've a good few years left in you yet, I'm sure.'

'Well, however many I've got left, I'll make the most of them, you can be sure of that.'

'Oh, aye, of that I'm certain.'

'It's a shame Carwen James couldn't make it, after all,' observed Althea.

Mavis grinned. 'I think he's seen enough of us of late. And with more to come, I dare say.'

Althea nodded. 'I dare say.'

Mavis looked at all the tops and backs of heads in the bus, and smiled to herself.

Althea had wittered on about community, and shared memories, and shared culture, and she knew the wee woman was right. This was the sort of event that would be talked about in the months, and maybe even the years, to come in the bar at the Coach and Horses, or in the tearoom, which was what was to become of the Lamb and Flag. She recalled similar trips from years past – times she'd spent with her late husband and her two boys when they were bairns, off to the coast for the day, or even to a river in what passed for the heat of the summer in Scotland.

'What's got you smiling, dear?' Althea whispered in her ear.

'Happy memories,' replied Mavis.

'Good. Let's make sure we make some more today, like I hope everyone on these two buses does,' replied the dowager.

Christine looked across the private, gated garden to which her family's London home had access, and smiled as Alexander walked toward her, a pair of sandals in his hand.

He waggled them under her nose. 'Are these the ones?'

Christine took them from him. 'Yep, that's them. Thanks. I should have remembered that the ones I've got on dig in at the front. Not that it's a long walk back, but I don't want a blister, and there's one threatening already after all the strolling we've done here today.'

'No, you don't. In fact, you don't want any more injuries, of any sort, ever. Full stop. So if you could make that happen, that would be perfect. Thank you. Now – what about getting back to the house? Your mother said dinner at seven, because she wants an early night. And you'll want to shower beforehand, I know…now that you can do that without endangering your eye, and so forth.'

Christine bent down to change her shoes and stretched out her back. 'I think it's time for me to get back to Wales. Yes, I know, I know…desk duties only. But I need to tell them, Alexander. They all deserve to know. It could affect their livelihoods too. I wonder if Annie will dub it The Case of the Pregnant PI?'

Christine encouraged her fiancé to join her on the bench, where they sat holding each other's hands.

It was a warm afternoon, and she wasn't at all minding lazing about. In fact, she was relishing every moment.

'Do you want me to rub your feet?' Alexander looked unsure.

Christine chuckled. 'Well, you can if you want, but if that's one of those things you've read in a book – you know, something a pregnant woman wants – well, I might get to it in a few months, but my feet are just fine at the moment, thank you very much. Except for the almost-blister, which I would think is best left alone.'

Alexander grinned impishly. 'How do you know I've been reading up on pregnancy, and motherhood, and fatherhood?'

Christine kissed him on the cheek, and stood, smoothing down her summer frock. 'Because that's who you are, darling. Since the moment you found out, you've been like a dog with two tails, both wagging at once. I know I lost my cool when that doctor stupidly let it slip that I was pregnant, but…maybe it was for the best.'

They'd both done as much research as they could about how Christine's drinking, before she'd known she was pregnant, might have caused damage to their unborn child, and had agreed they'd cross that bridge when they came to it. They'd also agreed they'd concentrate on keeping her as healthy as possible for the next several months – and would get on with as normal a life as they could.

Christine continued, 'I can tell you're nervous about it all. We both are, we've acknowledged that. But we'll be grand.' She sighed. 'Mammy's being great, of course – all over me she is. Though some of the things she's been telling me are a bit scary…'

'Like?'

'Piles for one thing. But let's not go there. Yes, it's all the unknown…but we're on an adventure together, and we'll have a grand time…somehow or other.'

'You mean we'll wing it, and hope the kid turns out alright?'

Christine nodded. 'Mammy says that's basically what everyone does.'

Alexander let go of her hand to make sure the heavy iron gate closed properly behind them. 'I dare say they do, and Deirdre is, according to your father, always right.'

Waiting to cross the road, Christine said, 'By the way – I meant to tell you – when I talked to Annie on the video last night, she said to thank you for asking her mother about what equipment she'd recommend for that fancy-dancy new launderette you built down in Thornton Heath. Annie said Eustelle was delighted to feel involved, and glad to be able to put her years of experience managing a launderette to good use. And by the look on Winnie Singh's face when you let her walk into her new domain after unveiling the shop, she thought Eustelle had chosen well.' She kissed Alexander on the cheek.

'What did I do to deserve that? Or are we still able to show affection for each other without needing a reason?'

'That's for somehow managing to hide the fact from the lovely Mrs Singh that you were creating a new launderette for her to run, with a flat for her to live in upstairs, and a room out the back for all those people who spend so much time there. You're quite the man, Mr Bright. Something tells me you'll make an excellent father. Heart of gold, you've got. Though I will admit I'm glad to know you're not a father already. I couldn't believe it when you told me all about what Sean had tried to do. Blackmail, indeed. I'm only grateful that the...um...hang on...The Case of the Secret Son was something you were able to deal with relatively easily, though Mammy's still upset by it all.'

'I know she is. I can only hope she'll get over it one day, soon.'

Christine smiled. 'That she will, I'm sure. And, speaking of Sean – who I don't think I fancy meeting any time soon, by the way – has Geordie visited him at that place yet? Or is Sean still in the "no visitors" bit of his treatment? I saw that you and Geordie had your heads together at the unveiling party for the launderette yesterday. Now there's a case that, if only Annie knew about it – which she never will, don't panic – she'd be calling The Case of the Faithful Friend. Which is what you are. Especially given how Sean targeted you.'

She and Alexander had taken the time to have a heart to heart about Sean, the attempted blackmail, and Big Tony – who was now sitting in a cell awaiting trial – almost immediately following their heart to heart about her pregnancy.

'Geordie says Sean's allowed to see only him, so far, and that he's doing well. Better than he'd hoped, in fact. And I've offered to give Sean a job when he's ready. Though it could be a long time before that happens. He's even agreed to daily testing when he gets out, says Geordie. I think…I *hope*…the penny's finally dropped for Sean about what he got himself involved with, and that he might have been lucky for the last time. Even cats only have nine lives, and Sean's no cat. But it's an illness, we all get that – and there's temptation in so many places. It's a long road, without end, but we're hopeful.'

Christine stood on the front doorstep of her family's home, with her fiancé beside her, and gazed at the vibrant greens of the summer-leafed trees against the clear blue sky. She knew she was fortunate to be able to do that with both eyes, and took in the sharpness of the sight in front of her with the delight that only someone who has feared that the world will forever be a blur can do.

She had a new responsibility – she was creating another human being – and she knew that sharing that responsibility with Alexander was what she wanted to do. A wedding could wait. Pieces of paper didn't matter.

But what about the WISE women? How would they react? She believed they'd be pleased for her, of course, but…her being pregnant? Carol had managed to work through while she'd been carrying Albert, but…

'Penny for them?'

Christine smiled as Alexander opened the door.

'Just thinking about family, and friends. And dinner. I hope it's not too spicy, this curry that Daddy's decided to prepare for us all. I think Mammy might be regretting buying him that cookbook for Christmas – she's created a monster.'

'Here's to monsters,' said Alexander cheerfully.

As they entered the house, Christine recalled that her mother had told her to enjoy all the spicy foods she could now, because there might come a day when she couldn't face them. Christine didn't like that idea.

Henry sank into bed like a man who'd run a marathon. Or maybe someone who'd done one of those triathlons he'd heard about.

'How's your back, dear? Any better now?' Stephanie was at her dressing table, moisturizing her neck.

Henry's back was only slightly less painful than his feet. 'I'll survive, I dare say. I had no idea that carrying Hugo would do this to me. I should have left him in his pushchair.'

'It was good of you to do it, darling,' purred his wife as she got into bed beside him. He hoped she didn't wriggle about too much. 'He was getting quite upset with all that bouncing around on the tufty grass, and he loved his father carrying him.'

Henry knew Hugo had been gurgling happily for most of the day, though the thing he'd had to wear to swaddle his son on his belly hadn't been terribly becoming. That said, he'd been quite touched by the way that other fathers who were carrying their children in the same fashion had nodded and smiled at him whenever they'd encountered each other. He'd had no idea that such a camaraderie existed among fathers of infants. It had felt…odd, but quite pleasant. Unlike his back at that precise moment, which felt anything but good.

Stephanie kissed him gently on the cheek. 'Those painkillers will take effect quite soon, I'm sure, dear. Now let's try to get some sleep before he wakes us.'

'It was a wonderful day,' mused Henry as he tried to find a less painful position. 'That was the first time we've ever done anything where no one knew who we were. I rather liked it. It was like being…well, normal, I suppose.'

He finally managed to find an angle for his back where it didn't hurt quite so much.

Stephanie replied, 'At one point, I thought you came close to telling the man who refused to give you more ice cream on your cone that you're a duke. I'm so glad you didn't.'

'Heavens, no. Not the done thing. Not at all. But he was a bit mean, don't you think?'

'It was a medium cone, and you got a medium amount of ice cream, Henry. If you'd wanted more, you should have asked for a large cone.'

'As the man himself pointed out,' recalled Henry huffily.

'Go to sleep, Henry. Maybe you'd enjoy a trifle for dessert tomorrow?'

Henry's spirits lifted. 'Excellent suggestion, dear. I shall speak to Edward in the morning – then it would be ready by dinner time.'

'I've already spoken to him, dear, it'll be ready for luncheon, which will be much better.'

'Indeed.'

ACKNOWLEDGEMENTS

My thanks to my mum, sister, and husband, for their unwavering support, which allows me to continue with my writing. Writing might be a solitary pursuit, but it takes so many people to allow it to happen.

My thanks to Anna Harrisson, my editor, and Sue Vincent, my proofer; we've all tried to make this the best possible version of this story, and we've all done our very best to not let any errors slip through.

My thanks, as always, to every blogger, reviewer, librarian, bookseller, and social media user who might have helped – in any way – to allow this book to find its way into your hands.

Finally, thank *you* for choosing to spend time with the women of the WISE Enquiries Agency. I hope you enjoyed your time with them.

ABOUT THE AUTHOR

CATHY ACE was born and raised in Swansea, Wales, and migrated to British Columbia, Canada aged forty. She is the author of The WISE Enquiries Agency Mysteries, The Cait Morgan Mysteries, the standalone novel of psychological suspense, The Wrong Boy, and collections of short stories and novellas. As well as being passionate about writing crime fiction, she's also a keen gardener.

You can find out more about Cathy and all her works at her website: www.cathyace.com

Printed in Great Britain
by Amazon

39382283R00155